I0678871

PRIME OBSESSION

BOOK 1
THE PRIME CHRONICLES SERIES

MONETTE MICHAELS

Print Version, 2014.
ISBN: 978-0-9862730-0-1

E-Book, Published by Liquid Silver Books, imprint of Atlantic Bridge Publishing, 2009.

Editor: Terri Schaefer
Cover Artist: April Martinez

Copyright © 2009, 2014, Monette Michaels.

All rights reserved. No part of this publication may be reproduced, stored in a retrieval system, or transmitted in any form or by any means, electronic, mechanical, recording or otherwise, without the prior written permission of the author.

This is a work of fiction. The characters, incidents and dialogues in this book are of the author's imagination and are not to be construed as real. Any resemblance to actual events or persons, living or dead, is completely coincidental.

The Prime had witnessed her passage and rearmed the trap. Even if she'd missed slitting the Erian's throat properly, the trap would efficiently finish the lizard off. Her back trail was covered.

"Thanks," she said loudly, not sure where or how sensitive the microphones were in the tunnel.

"You're welcome, Mel."

She recognized that voice. It wasn't the male who had issued the distress call, but she had met the man on Tooh 2.

"Iolyn? Huw?" She smiled at the live camera to her right.

"It's Iolyn, Mel. Welcome on board the *Galanti*."

"Glad I could make it. What does it look like ahead?"

"Trouble," growled a low, unknown male voice.

Well, not exactly unknown. His was the voice on the distress call. And as it had on the jump station, the voice sent fingers of heat throughout her body. She forced back a low moan as she rubbed at her hip. Heat unlike any she'd ever experienced radiated from the marking she'd had for as far back as she could remember. Her birthmark, as her mother had always called it.

"Who's that?" She frowned, shaking off the unusual sensations caused by the unknown speaker. "What kind of trouble? Trap or pirate?" *Or you?*

"Me," rumbled the same male.

Mel gulped. That was what she'd been afraid of. Damn, her extra senses were really working spot-on this trip.

"Mel," Iolyn said, his voice practically drenched with suppressed amusement. "Meet my brother, Wulf. He is the captain of this ship."

"Iolyn, he doesn't sound very grateful that I'm here to help rid his ship of pirates."

"You should have sent one of your men," snarled Wulf. "This is no place for a woman."

REVIEWS FOR
PRIME OBSESSION

"*Prime Obsession* is a fast-paced space opera outfitted in shiny new gadgets and modern characters. … All in all, it's fun to be kept on the edge of your seat for the bulk of the ride."

—*Patrice of Joyfully Reviewed*

"Loved it."

—*Five Stars from Night Owl Romance*

"…Ms. Michaels kept throwing twists into the mix that kept you constantly on your toes wondering how things would be resolved."

—*Five Nymphs from Literary Nymphs Reviews Only*

ACKNOWLEDGEMENTS

This book could never have been written without the help of my critique buddy Sherry Crane and early critical advice from Bonnie Dee and Jayelle Drury. I would also like to thank my two beta-readers for their comments and encouragement: Laura Adlam and Holly Shelley. And, as always, thanks to my editor Terri Schaefer, who manages to find all my mistakes. Special thanks to Geoffrey Kidd, proofer extraordinaire, and his spot-on suggestions and to April Martinez, the best cover artist in the business.

Finally, I dedicate this book to my friend and fellow author, Linnea Sinclair, who writes the best damn science fiction romance in the universe.

CHAPTER ONE

A resort on Tooh 2, Mu Arae Solar System

"Captain! Captain! Mel! Dammit, wake up!"

Galactic Alliance Captain Melina Grace Dmitros roused from her light nap in the sun. The tenseness in her second-in-command's voice was vastly different than the relaxed, jovial mood from their earlier lunch with fellow officers. If she hadn't known better, she would've thought they were back on the command deck of their battle cruiser *Leonidas* and not lying by a pool in a seaside resort on the garden planet of Tooh 2.

Turning her head slightly to the right, she growled, "What is it, Nowicki?"

"We've got a problem!"

Commander Royce Nowicki angled his head toward the poolside café where only ninety minutes earlier they'd officially kicked off Gold Squadron's three-day leave. Prior to this well-deserved vacation, they, and Captain Garth Warten's Blue Squadron, had spent three standard months chasing pirates all over the Mu Arae Solar System.

Mel did not want to hear about a problem. Not one. But Nowicki's body language told her she needed to deal with whatever was bothering him. He did not raise false alarms.

Following Nowicki's gaze, she not only saw, but heard the problem.

Ensign Steve Parker of Blue Squadron was in the process of taunting and threatening three large men. From the look of their clothing, they were part of some diplomatic team. Great, just what she needed, a political powder keg.

Removing her dark sunshades, she squinted more closely at the objects of Parker's drunken rage. Depending on the race, the problem could be more or less serious.

It was more.

"Well, hell. Count on Parker to pick on the new Cejuru Prime ambassador to the Alliance. Is he suicidal or what?" She turned her head and glared at Nowicki. "And, dammit, how in the blazes did Parker get off Tooh 10? I thought he'd been confined to quarters for his last bout of insubordination."

"Insubordination?" sputtered Nowicki, his eyes fiery with remembered rage. "The cretin almost got you killed!"

Mel rubbed her side where the healing wound was now merely a faint scar. The regen bed had done wonders for the superficial healing, but the underlying muscles and nerves were still knitting back together. Nature could only be helped along so much.

"Warten convinced me he'd handle the matter. I gave him the benefit of the doubt. But, at the very least, Parker was to be confined to quarters while the Admiral and Warten decided what to do with him."

She scanned the pool area for Parker's commanding officer as she reached for her cover-up. Settling potential galactic incidents in a bikini was not protocol.

"Warten's not here," Nowicki stated what she had already determined for herself. "He left the café after lunch, said something about a date with a pillow."

"Sure. Fine," she muttered as she struggled into the sheer silken chemise which had looked just right for a day by the pool, but now seemed all wrong for the coming confrontation. And that there would be a confrontation she had no doubt. Parker was a hothead; he wouldn't back down. *Dammit.* "Garth is off tangling in the sheets with some tanned, voluptuous Tooh 2 cutie, and *I* get to clean up his mess."

Spying two other of her senior officers, she turned to Nowicki. "Get J'ar and A'tem. Call for military security. Then clear the area around Parker. I don't want any innocents hurt if the Prime decide to teach Parker a well-deserved lesson."

"Captain, what are *you* gonna do? Maybe we should just let the Prime pound him." Nowicki's pale blue eyes glinted at the possibility.

"You didn't wake me up so foreign dignitaries could beat up one of ours. You and I both know the Alliance does not need a galactic cluster fuck," she stated. "The Prime are joining us after centuries of isolationism. We *need* their knowledge and skills in fighting the Antarean raiders. I'm still not sure what *they* need from *us*, but I do know the Galactic Alliance Counsel is thrilled that they've chosen to fight alongside us. But it isn't a done deal."

"Great," snarled Nowicki. "So, you need to place yourself between Parker and danger—again—for the frigging peace of the galaxy. I should have just let you sleep and beat on the scum-sucking bastard myself."

"You did the right thing. Parker would never have listened to you. Then you would've been thrown in the brig for fighting or, worse, injured, and I really would've been annoyed." Raising one brow, she smiled. "Me? I outrank him. He hates my guts. And has always underestimated me. Plus, I owe him," she touched the healing scar again, "and am hoping to have to use *un*reasonable force. So, your job is to keep everyone out of harm's way. Understood?"

"Yeah, just be careful. He cheats."

"I know. Now go!"

Striding toward the café, she opened up all six of her senses and observed the three Prime males, testing their emotional response to Parker's insanity. The oldest one, the Ambassador—his name escaped her for the moment—spoke to Parker in what she could tell were low, calming tones. The Ambassador's emotional aura read as cool and calm, a true diplomat. Not so for his two much younger associates; they were all red-hot anger barely controlled.

Knowing Parker, the diplomatic route would just set him off even more.

Mel approached the four men. Cautiously. Quietly. Her heightened senses became even more so as adrenaline poured into her system. Her heart pounded. She licked suddenly dry lips and took a deep, cleansing breath. Her muscles twitched, readying themselves for whatever might come.

As she'd expected, anger roiled off Parker in waves, probably exacerbated by alcohol consumption. She could smell him; it was as if he'd bathed in potent Tooh 2 whiskey. Alcohol notwithstanding, Parker always ran hot; his temper could boil over in a flash. Definitely not officer material. Coolness in the heat of battle was always best. He'd only made it to the rank of Ensign because of political connections. If he survived this incident, she'd have to insist he be sent away from the Mu Arae system. There was too much tension in this sector of the Milky Way as it was without adding loose cannons.

"Ensign Parker!" She stopped about three feet from his right side, in his peripheral line of sight. He'd have to turn his head to see her fully. "*Stand down.*"

"Go away, you fucking bitch!" he spat out. She could always count on Parker to be disrespectful, mentally adding insubordination to the list of charges against him. "This is a private conversation."

"That's *Captain* Fucking Bitch, to you, soldier."

All three Prime turned their attention away from Parker. They eyed her bikini-suited body inadequately covered by the thin shift. Their pale amber gazes turned molten hot, darkening to the color of aged single malt scotch. She could smell, almost taste, the adrenaline levels shoot up in all three men. Their gazes projected a complex mix of emotions— concern for her, anger at Parker, and lust for her body.

Great. This could get ugly fast. A damn disaster in the making.

Historically, male Prime were described as overprotective of females and needed few reasons to fight. Right now, they had the perfect trifecta of excuses to hand Parker his head on an ancient Prime battle lance. Documented as the oldest humanoid race in the galaxy, the Prime hadn't survived this long without learning how to fight to win. They sure as heck didn't need her, a mere Terran female, to fight their battles. Yet, Parker would be dead meat if she left them to it. And a horrible diplomatic mess would then ensue, that most likely was the only thing holding the Prime back—for now.

If she handled the situation, Parker would be bruised, battered, and, hopefully, unconscious, and the new bond between the Prime and the Alliance could go forward. An additional plus, the new allies would see that Alliance female officers didn't need alpha male warriors to fight their battles.

Taking a deep breath, she said, "Ensign Parker, you are under arrest. I am not even sure what you're doing on Tooh 2. The last I heard Captain Warten had confined you to quarters."

Parker turned his attention from the Prime toward her. Exactly what she'd wanted.

Her gaze fixed on Parker as she watched for his move.

In a calm, authoritative tone, her eyes never leaving her opponent, she said, "Ambassador. Gentlemen. Please leave. I apologize on behalf of the Alliance if this man has insulted you or caused you any embarrassment. This is a military problem and I *will* handle it."

Around her, she heard—and felt—her men clearing the café. She let the noise and emotions of the curious crowd pass over her. Her focus was divided between Parker and the Prime. All angry alpha males. The situation was fluid, highly charged. Anything could change at any time.

The Prime didn't move away, but they didn't attack either. Maybe that was the best she could hope for, that the three warriors would stand and observe—at least until they thought she needed assistance.

Mel wouldn't let it come to that point. Despite her smaller size as compared to the large Prime males, she was of above-average height for a Terran woman and extremely well-trained. She was also well aware of Parker's weaknesses. Her strengths in battle were stamina, quickness, the ability to read her opponent, and, most often, her opponent's overconfidence.

She stood quietly, balancing her weight on the balls of her feet, ready to move.

Increasing anger and hatred flowed from Parker in invisible waves so hot they swept across her skin like a volcanic windstorm.

Nothing and no one moved. It was if the area surrounding the café was encased in a bubble, isolating it from the rest of the resort.

Then Parker's left eye twitched. His tell.

Her lips thinned into a grim smile. The three Prime males tensed as if to move.

She moved first, yelling at the Prime. "Stay out of it."

Mel dodged Parker's lurching move to grab her. Her fist drove into his stomach like a cannonball. Roaring in rage, he grabbed the strap of her cover up and ripped the garment away as she twisted and spun out of his reach. The silken fabric slid down her body to tangle at her feet. Leaping out of the puddle of silk, she sent a hard front kick to his gut, knocking him away from her. The percussion from the solid hit traveled up her leg into the healing laser wound across her obliques.

She grunted at the sharp, stabbing pain. Sublimating the ache, she turned it into responsive anger, anger that this shithead had ruined her first leave in half a standard year.

Like the bullheaded son of a bitch he was, Parker charged her. Anticipating his move, she stepped to the side, throwing a side kick to his groin. He turned just enough that she merely caught the edge of his hip.

"How's the side, bitch?" Parker taunted in a raspy voice as he circled her. He threw a booted kick at her healing wound as she spun away. His foot glanced off it.

Mel hissed, swearing under her breath. Moving fluidly, she delivered a reverse head kick. With the full power of her pelvic girdle, she caught him on the jaw. Hard. Really hard.

Holding his jaw, shock in his eyes, Parker staggered back. He bled from where he'd bitten his lip. He rubbed his jaw, shifting it from side-to-side.

Damn. Too bad, she hadn't broken it.

Spitting out blood and a tooth, he snarled as he circled, looking for an opportunity to hurt her. "They threw me out of the military because of you, bitch. You deserve whatever I dish out."

She stared at him, not answering. Why waste her breath? She needed it for the fight. Parker had always been an impatient fighter, always wasting energy. He'd be flagging, while she still had energy in reserve.

She'd have reserves, that is, if the pain from her reinjured side did not weaken her first. Pushing the throbbing agony to a place deep within her brain, she breathed slowly, deeply. Waiting.

"Captain?" Nowicki sounded scared. He knew her fighting ability, knew she could beat Parker. So, why all the concern?

Hell, she must look worse than she felt.

She sensed the three Prime moving closer, as if to render assistance. After all the trouble and pain she'd gone through to get Parker's attention away from the diplomatic team, she wasn't going to allow them to intervene, no matter how bad she looked.

"Stay out of this, Nowicki!" she snarled. "That's an order. Just keep everyone out of the way."

Parker was distracted by the exchange between her and Nowicki. His feral gaze looked beyond her to where Nowicki stood.

Using his momentary mental lapse, she went on the attack. Sweeping low with her dominant leg, she kicked Parker's legs out from under him. He recovered just enough to go only to his knees. As he struggled to get up, she kicked his jaw, the loud *whack* from her sandals echoing off the walls of the café patio.

This time the jaw broke. Her mouth twisted into a satisfied smile as she pictured him in prison, eating all his meals through a straw.

Continuing to use his off-balanced position to her advantage, she kicked him in the ribs and got off a shot at his nose before he managed to scramble backwards like a crab and use a low wall to struggle to his feet.

He charged her, all technique gone, acting only on his rage. Since Parker had a longer reach, both in his arms and legs, the only way she could beat him was to stay out of his way, keep him off-balance, and wear him down.

For the next two minutes, she did just that, coolly dancing around the enraged man, punishing him with hard, well-placed hits and kicks.

She took a few glancing punches and her side throbbed like a son-of-a-bitch. While there was no blood, indicating that the regen seal held on the surface, she knew something inside had given away. She was fading fast. She needed to end the fight.

After another well-placed kick that spun Parker into a table, Mel danced on her toes. She breathed deeply, blocking the pain, waiting to see what he would do next, watching for an opening to take him down once and for all.

Nowicki's "He's got a knife" sounded just as she caught a glint of light reflecting off something in Parker's hand.

Then he rushed her.

Surprising him, she moved into him with a twist of her body. She grabbed his knife-hand by the wrist and broke it, using a technique she'd learned from reading ancient Prime training manuals.

Bellowing with pain, he dropped the knife.

In a continuation move, she turned even more into him, then maneuvered him over her hip, flinging him away from her. He hit a retaining wall with his head and then slumped onto the ground, unconscious.

From the rush with the knife to Parker hitting the floor was a matter of mere seconds.

As military security ran over to the downed man, Nowicki reached her side and placed a supporting arm around her naked, sweaty middle. "You okay, Captain?"

"Sure, no problem." She lied through her teeth as she shrugged off his aid. Shoving her fingers through the hair which had escaped from her tightly woven French braid, she said in a harsh whisper, "Let go, Royce. I need to talk to the three Prime, make sure they know Parker is not representative of the Alliance."

"Fuck the Alliance and fuck the damn Prime," growled Nowicki.

Mel cast a cold, steely glare at her second-in-command. "Drop it, Commander. I'm fine."

If she let him know just how tired and in pain she really was, he'd natter at her like an old woman. She couldn't permit the high-ranking Prime to see her pain or exhaustion. She couldn't allow Nowicki to undermine her authority. They'd never countenance their military working in tandem with Alliance female officers if they perceived them as weak.

"No, you're not." Nowicki pulled her into his strength, angry stubbornness etched in every angle of his body. "You're bruised, bleeding, and pale."

The Prime observed the two of them carefully. Nowicki didn't understand what drove her to stand on her own two feet and now was not the time to take him aside and explain. He needed a diversion, a task that would dissipate some of his need to care for her.

She removed his arm from her waist. "Get a med kit from security. You can patch me up. I have the duty to smooth this over. I represent the Alliance," she lowered her voice even more so only he could hear. "We *can't* show weakness, Royce. Understand?"

Nowicki nodded, then mumbled under his breath, something that sounded like "damn fool woman."

Mel stopped her forward motion toward the Prime and the late-arriving Captain Warten. "What did you say?" Her left eyebrow raised.

"Nothing. Just sit down for chrissakes. I'll find something to cover you up. You're damn near naked!"

Mel choked back a laugh and the comment that he hadn't mentioned her near nakedness by the pool; she figured her second-in-command was riled enough. He never would've ordered her to do anything in front of civilians if he hadn't been so upset. She must look really wiped out. Unfortunately, she did feel a tad bit light in the head; she had to be bleeding internally again. That one kick Parker had gotten in had done more damage than she'd thought.

Pushing aside the urge to hold her right side, she straightened to her full five-foot-eight-inch height and approached the group of men watching her. Garth Warten, Blue Squadron's captain, had joined the Prime, and all four of them observed her approach with varying levels of concern.

Garth's gaze had guilt underlying it. As it should. Parker should never have been on Tooh 2.

"Gentlemen," she addressed the Prime.

Her hypersensitive ability to read emotional auras registered conflicting emotions from the Prime. Concern. Anger. Admiration. And, once again, lust.

The last reading bothered her the most. Just what she needed—three Prime males ogling her. "I would like to apologize again for Ensign Parker's rude and insubordinate behavior towards you. Please understand his attitudes are not representative of the Alliance."

The Prime said nothing. Damn, she hated diplomacy.

She waited, silently urging them to accept her apology soon so that she could go somewhere and collapse.

Their amber-gold gazes suddenly turned even hotter as they fixed on an area just above her right hip bone. Her birthmark, they were staring at her birthmark.

Instead of the lust she expected from them, she read surprise ... amazement ... joy in their reaction to her marking.

It was odd that she could read them so accurately. The extra sixth sense, or gut instinct as she liked to call it, she used to read people was working overtime. Or, maybe the Prime males' strong emotions stimulated her sixth sense. She'd never been able to read others this easily; in fact, during her fight with Parker, her senses had been more preternaturally sensitive than usual.

She shook her head, causing the room to spin around her. Damn, Parker had hit her harder than she'd thought. The puzzle of the Prime's reaction to her and their effect on her already unusual psychic gifts would have to be solved later. Right now, she needed to get the diplomacy handled so her men could take her to a hospital. Nowicki was right—she needed medical attention—and soon.

"Excuse my lack of dress, gentlemen, but I was on leave." And why she felt the need to explain herself, she'd never know. And why weren't they saying anything?

Capturing their gazes, she all but dared them to continue scoping out her body. To a man, they smiled and shifted their perusal to her face. Smug amusement was the emotion of the moment. Damn them. *Men!* She foresaw issues with the all-male Prime military fighting alongside Alliance female soldiers, and she made a mental note to send a memo to the Admiral about that.

"Here, Captain!" Nowicki thrust a shirt at her. "Put this around you while I check on your injuries."

"Never mind, Nowicki, I'll take care of her injuries." Captain Warten took her arm and sat her in chair.

Finally her fellow captain had decided to make his presence felt. Jerk. If she hadn't needed to sit down so badly, she'd have yelled at him for being the reason she was in this situation to begin with.

"Mel, are you okay?" Garth stared into her eyes. "Damn, your whole right side is one big bruise. What the fuck were you thinking, taking on Parker in your condition? Give me the kit, Nowicki."

He snagged the kit from her second-in-command and found an ice gun and applied it to her right side. She shuddered as the cold treatment numbed the throbbing bruise. "Parker is out of the service. He should never have been here."

"I totally agree," she said with a hiss as Warten swept the ice treatment over her bruise once more, jabbing a rib in the process. After which, he stuffed her into the shirt Nowicki had provided. "Where'd you learn your first aid? From the Marquis de Sade?"

"Sorry." Warten's lips tilted up at the edges, then thinned with concern as his gaze swept over her face. "Ensign J'ar, call over to the hospital and have them send a vehicle for your Captain. Stat."

Touching her colleague's arm, she said in a low tone, "Garth, I can find my own way to the hospital. I'm fine. Really."

Nowicki yelled over her shoulder, all irate alpha-male. "Dammit, Mel! Parker all but killed you on that last mission and now he's had another chance. Let us take care of you!"

"Captain Dmitros." The oldest of the three Prime approached her, a troubled smile on his strongly hewn face. "I believe your fellow officers are concerned because you are as pale as the sands on the Tooh 2 beaches. If we could be of assistance, our vehicle is outside. We can take you to the hospital so that you can be checked over, thus assuring all of us you are truly well."

"Thank you, Ambassador ... I'm sorry, I can't remember your name." She smiled at the man who reminded her a lot of her scholarly father, only a lot bigger and assuredly more deadly. His eyes—while smiling at her—hid a stronger will behind them. He would not desist until she agreed to go to the hospital. Again, reminding him of her father.

"Ambassador Tor Maren." He bowed his head to her, then gestured to the other two men with him. "Allow me to present Huw and Iolyn Caradoc, number two and three sons to the leader of the Prime, Ilar Caradoc."

The two dark-haired males bowed their heads in greeting.

Caradoc? Rifling through her memory, she finally placed the name. Caradoc was the most prominent family on Cejuru Prime from a royal line that went back to the beginning of Prime history. Her mother and father, space archaeologists and historians who specialized in ancient Prime sites, would be thrilled to hear she'd met them. The Caradocs were featured prominently in most of the historical documents her parents had found and catalogued on their digs. She'd grown up on the dig sites and practically learned Prime as she learned English and her parents' native Greek. She knew their planet's history as well as or even better than Earth's.

Mel tried to stand.

"No, Captain," Huw said. "Please do not rise. We no longer are treated as royalty. Now, our family is just part of the Prime leading council. We are mere politicians, here to help finalize the formal alignment of our planet with the Galactic Alliance."

"Why did you fight that man?" Iolyn asked, his brow creased in puzzlement. "You know we are warriors. We could have handled the situation."

"I meant no insult to your fighting prowess. But Parker is—was—an *Alliance* military problem. If you had defended yourselves and killed him, then there would've been a political disaster."

The three Prime nodded, acknowledging the truth of her conclusion.

Ambassador Maren said, "Ah, yes, a definite consideration. Thank you for aiding us in avoiding a diplomatic nightmare of universal proportions. We are in your debt. By the way, where did you learn your fighting techniques? You are quite effective for a female."

Mel gritted her teeth against a knee-jerk response to the man's unabashed male chauvinism. Instead, she said, "My military training encompassed all sorts of hand-to-hand and street fighting techniques. You will find *all* Alliance military personnel are proficient in some form of hand-to-hand combat."

"But you used other, shall we say, more unusual techniques," the Ambassador said.

"Oh, you mean the maneuver with the wrist? Caught that, did you?" She smiled, then grimaced as a wave of dizziness swept over her. Haltingly, she explained, "I found the technique on a very old data disk discovered in an underground Prime site on Obam IV."

"Obam IV?" Huw asked.

"It was where I spent most of my childhood and where my parents still live." She grasped the arm of the chair, but her surroundings continued to swirl. "Uh, they supervise a dig there. They are Prime site experts in the Alliance Space Archaeology Institute."

"We must meet your parents some day," the Ambassador said as he gently covered her hand with his. "They have raised a very strong and lovely daughter. May we escort you to the hospital? You are extremely white, and I sense your colleagues are very upset."

"Thank you. I do feel a little shaky." And sick to her stomach.

Nowicki snorted and mumbled, "About damn time."

Mel threw her second-in-command a nasty look, and regretted the quick movement almost as soon as she'd done it.

Using the chair arm and the Ambassador's strong hand, she levered herself into a standing position. As he assisted her toward the exit, the world began to reel. Hot and cold shivers raced over her body as white, yellow and red flashes and dots swept across her line of vision.

As she fainted into the arms of the Prime Ambassador, Nowicki swore colorfully in the background. She'd have to remember to cite him for language unbecoming an officer when she felt better.

———

MAREN STOOD OUTSIDE THE PRIVATE hospital room he'd insisted upon for Melina Dmitros. He couldn't call her by her military title, because she just didn't seem like a military officer—despite the fact she'd single-handedly taken out a large Terran male while recovering from what her fellow officers had assured him had been a life-threatening laser blast.

"She is a Prime female. How did she end up on Obam IV and then in the Alliance military?" Huw asked. "She should be on the home planet, safe and protected as all our women are."

"She is one of the Lost Ones," concluded Maren. "She has her *gemate* sign. All the female evacuees, even the infants, were exposed to potential mates prior to the exodus. You know most never returned when the planet's security was once again ensured. They were thought dead. Now, we know at least one survived."

A feeling of contentment, hope and sheer joy at her discovery swirled through Maren. Huw and Iolyn would be thinking and feeling the same as he. They had found a mate for one lucky Prime male. Melina Dmitros's discovery raised the possibility that there could be more *gemate* in the galaxy, cut off with no way to return to Cejuru Prime.

Why had they never considered such a possibility? But he knew why. It was a well-known fact that as long as a Prime breathed they would find a way to return home. But now, he realized, the youngest Lost Ones would not know who they were—or where they really belonged. It was obvious Melina had been raised as, and considered herself, Terran.

"There could be others out there," Iolyn stated Maren's thought out loud, a tinge of hope in his voice.

Iolyn and Huw, along with their eldest brother Wulf, were just a few of the Prime males with no mates. Their world had lost so many women from attacks by their mortal enemies the Antareans and a declining birth rate among the surviving females. The population growth on Cejuru Prime was less than zero. Without enough Prime females, there would be no future for their species.

This lack of fertile females had been the main reason the Prime Council agreed to end centuries of isolation from the rest of the galaxy.

Their race was on the verge of extinction. By joining the Alliance, the Prime could mingle and learn of the other humanoid races, many of which had Prime DNA from the millennia of space exploration by their ancestors. The mateless Prime males might be able to find compatible females and create a new generation of Prime.

Not the best solution, but the most viable. There were some on the home planet who would rather keep the bloodlines pure. But their leading geneticists warned of serious mutations if the current Prime bloodlines continued to intermingle, with the end result still being extinction. Even now, unmated females exposed to males were unable to generate the *gemate* sign, which was an indicator of an optimal match and the guarantee the children of such a match would be strong, intelligent, and healthy.

New blood—outside blood—was called for.

Maren smiled fondly at the two younger men. To them, Melina's appearance at this moment in time was a miracle. He hoped she would be one of the Caradoc's *gemate*. Huw, Iolyn and Wulf were like sons to him, his only family after he lost his wife, his sisters, and his mother in the Antarean sieges.

But the percentages were against them.

"Yes, Iolyn, there could be others, but that does not change the need for new blood," he reminded them. "One small woman will not save the Prime."

The brothers nodded.

The doctor treating Melina approached and smiled at them. "Captain Dmitros will be fine. A day or two on the regen bed and she'll be back to where she was before she tangled with the big brute in the emergency room. By the way, she did a lot of damage to him. Broken ribs, jaw and wrist to name a few of the worst."

Satisfaction and pride surged through Maren at Melina's accomplishments. A strong Prime female for a Prime male warrior. The Prime Leading Council would be ecstatic when he informed them of her existence.

"Thank you, Doctor. May we step in to see her?"

The doctor frowned. "She's asleep."

"We won't disturb her," Maren rushed to reassure the man. He could tell the doctor did not want to let three large unknown males, even though they wore their diplomatic emblems, enter her room. "Just to assure ourselves that she is recovering. She was very pale."

"Internal bleeding. But three units of blood took care of the problem."

Maren winced. *So much blood loss? How had she stayed upright and finished the* apayebo *off?* Huw and Iolyn all but growled at the doctor's words, muttering gutter Prime epithets.

The doctor scanned their faces and obviously saw what he needed to see. He nodded. "I heard she got hurt on your behalf. But please don't stay long."

The doctor's communicator trilled at him, and he strode away, taking an emergency call.

Interpreting his companions' anger correctly, Maren held out his hand. "No, you cannot kill the man Parker. Not after Melina risked her health to keep us from becoming involved in a serious diplomatic incident. It is far more important to read her *gemate* sign so that we can determine which Prime male has his mate back. Both of you must approach her, take in her scent, touch her hand—she might belong to one of you."

"Not mine," Huw said, the sadness in his eyes easy to read for those who knew him well. "I have no *gemat* marking. But Iolyn does—as does Wulf."

Iolyn smiled. "Even if she is not mine, she will be the perfect mate for some lucky Prime male."

Huw frowned. "We can't take her with us, Maren—the Alliance would come after her. She is an officer—an important one from what her men told us."

"No, but we can let nature and the power of the imprinting take its course. We just need to get her mate near her. Proximity, pheromones, and hormones will do the rest," Maren stated.

"Maybe she has another mate already," Huw said. "She has both Terrans and Volusians in her crew; both of those races have traces of our DNA in them and are compatible sexually."

Maren threw both young men a smile as he approached Melina's bed. "She isn't married as the Alliance calls mating. I asked. Her second-in-command was quick to tell me that she keeps all men at a distance. I think he was warning me off, because he wishes her for himself. Yet, she is his superior, so he settles, for now, in protecting her from others."

Iolyn grunted. "He is a stronger man than I. I could not be near my mate and not touch her. I would make her mine and warn all others off."

Huw nodded at his brother's statement. "As would I."

"Commander Nowicki is conflicted," Maren said. "Also, I did not get the impression Melina thinks of him in that way."

Iolyn smiled. "Nor did I. She treats him as a brother."

Huw gazed at the woman in the bed and uttered a low growl. "She is very beautiful. And her muscled body is very female. She fights just as Prime female warriors of old did, before our women had to stop fighting alongside their mates."

Maren nodded. "She is a beauty. Her dark hair and green eyes are very common among our women. My sisters had the same coloring." His brow creased as he studied her face. "She does remind me of someone, but I can't place it. I do know that the people who raised her are not Prime—I had them checked out while they brought her to the room. They are Terrans from a place called Greece."

Iolyn approached the bed. Leaning over, he inhaled deeply, then lightly stroked the back of her hand as it lay on top of the bedcovers. He shook his head. "She is not mine. My mark is not responding."

Huw touched his brother's shoulder in sympathy.

"Watch the door," Maren ordered. "I will check the *gemate* sign."

Lifting the sheet just enough to expose her hip and still protect her nudity, he found the intricate marking. He reverently traced the symbol that appeared on every Prime female when first exposed to the touch and scent of their perfect mate. Each imprinting created a unique set of markings—one on the female on her hip and one on the male on his chest near his heart. Exact matches in design.

Melina mumbled and twitched at his light touch, then settled back into a deep sleep.

Pulling his data pad from his pocket, he scanned the image into it and ordered a search of the Prime genetics database. All *gemate* symbols were stored at the time of imprinting and linked to their corresponding male match.

The data pad quickly beeped with a result.

Maren gasped, then rechecked the small screen. His eyes had not failed him. Melina Dmitros was truly the miracle he proclaimed her. Doubly so.

Happiness as he hadn't experienced in the longest time surged through every pore in his body, making him feel years younger.

Reverently, he pulled the blanket over her. Stroking the back of one finger across her pale cheek, he whispered, "Welcome back, little one."

He turned. "Huw. Iolyn. Meet your brother's mate. My precious niece, Olivia Maren-Wor *née* Melina Dmitros."

CHAPTER TWO

Two months later
Prime Starship Galanti

Anger sweeping through him like a molten wave, Kenric Wulf Caradoc glared at the body of the traitor Solar, who'd aided the space pirates in slipping past his ship's normally impenetrable security.

Turning to his brother Huw, he snarled, "Who helped him? This *apayebo* couldn't have done it alone."

"I don't know—and we won't be able to tell now." His brother eyed the dead traitor. "Once we went under Code Argenta, all personnel shut down their stations and reported here under standard emergency procedures. If Solar had help, that person, or persons, is either dead, with the pirates—or here, hiding in plain sight."

"Find Iolyn and Maren. Bring them to me," Wulf ordered. "Trust no one else. We need to plan, to watch. We are too far from Prime space. I have issued a call for Alliance assistance."

"What about any remaining traitors?" Huw's narrowed gaze swept the room.

Wulf smiled grimly. "Any traitors among us will show their true colors as time passes."

Code Argenta protocols would assure that. The Prime had a long-standing policy of not allowing any of its military equipment to fall into the hands of the enemy—or opportunistic pirates. The *Galanti's* destruction count-down clock had already started. Unless help arrived in time, it would continue to explosion. They had ninety-six standard hours.

Huw nodded and ran to find his brother and their friend Maren.

Settling his shoulders back against a bulkhead, Wulf's narrowed gaze swept the engine room several times. The cavernous room hummed with activity; the sound reflecting off the titanium walls raised goose bumps on his flesh.

Operating under reduced power, his highly trained crew went about their expected duties in the dimly lit room; their bodies cast ghost-like shadows on the pale titanium walls. All stations were manned continuously, the flashing lights and monitors adding to the surreal glow in the room. Each member of his crew could operate any piece of equipment on the ship. Those on duty monitored the security systems and watched live camera feed from inside the ship and without it. Others slept until it was their time to man the various stations.

Wulf noted with approval that the healthy aided the injured. They'd been fortunate to have lost so few lives. The surprise attack was responsible for the majority of his crew's injuries in the docking bay. Emergency protocols had kept their casualties down in the rest of the ship.

As expected, his men maintained the preternatural calm of Prime warriors preparing for battle, and possibly their deaths. Nothing seemed out of place, but an undercurrent of something "off" niggled at his subconscious. Somewhere in this room there was at least one traitor, maybe more, but even his highly attuned empathic senses couldn't single him or them out. There were just too many sets of strong emotions in the enclosed space. That fact, coupled with the interference of the computer and machine sounds, distorted his ability to test the emotional status of each man.

He turned to his left and switched the monitor on the master command console to an exterior view.

The pirate mother ship, a battle cruiser that had probably been salvaged, or liberated, from the Volusian military, lay off the starboard side, dead in space, operating on emergency power. They'd been lucky. The pirate ship's power source was of the type that his new beta-weapon could defang. If he and his crew survived, the Prime—and through the newly signed treaty, the Alliance—would have an effective new weapon to use against certain of their shared enemies.

Huw, Iolyn and Maren came to stand with him.

"What is our status, Wulf?" Maren asked in low tones.

"We control the *Galanti*. Engines have been shut back to emergency power. The pirates may be in possession of the command deck, but they have no power. Environmental is cut off on every level of the ship but this one. And the pirate ship is dead in space and has no working weapons."

Wulf motioned the three men closer as he scanned the immediate area to see if any one of the crew expressed more than a casual interest in what the four of them discussed. He saw no one in particular and the emotional levels in the room had not changed. If there were other saboteurs, they were not ready to make their move just yet. "Iolyn, what is the intruder count?"

"We are outnumbered by almost a three-to-one ratio," Iolyn responded. "We are trapped in engineering. The *apayebo* Solar corrupted the computer program controlling some of the maintenance tunnel traps leading to and from the engine room. Currently, I can't command them."

"So, we can't use them to leave and take the battle to the intruders." Wulf muttered several Prime epithets under his breath. "The good news is that they cannot use them to get to us, either."

"The self-destruct mechanism?" Maren asked.

"It is functioning as programmed, *and* I can still halt it at any time," said Wulf.

His brothers and Maren visibly relaxed at the news. No Prime wanted to die under a Code Argenta. They were warriors and would rather die in glorious battle. But they would go up with their ship as long as it kept the pirates from stealing the *Galanti* and its advanced technology.

"We need to monitor the crew in the engine room for signs of increased fear or stress as the countdown proceeds," Wulf said in a low voice that only carried to his companions. "I expect our other traitor or traitors will attempt to halt the countdown."

"What I don't understand is why any of our men would aid the pirates." Huw frowned. "This crew is the pick of the Prime military."

"I suspect the pirates were hired by the pure-blood faction and that some of our crew are sympathizers who have been persuaded that joining the Alliance is not the way to proceed," Maren offered. "Even though the treaty has been signed for months, the actual opening of a Prime embassy on foreign soil makes it more real. This is the rebels' way of sending a message."

"Capturing or killing the Prime leader's three sons and best friend would definitely be a message," Wulf concurred. "Unfortunately for them, it didn't work. Besides, father and the majority of the Council are committed to this course of action. This would not stop the alliance."

The others nodded.

"What are we going to do now?" Iolyn asked.

"We wait." Wulf stared unseeing at the monitor. "The pirates can't get away on the ship that brought them. With one precise hit, our beta-protean ray has damaged their engine's power source and shut down their weapons systems. They're helpless. They must take the *Galanti* to leave."

He switched the monitor's view to the ship's command deck, where several pirates stood arguing. "The Alliance will either arrive and help us liberate the ship and capture the pirates or we'll blow the *Galanti* and anything within fifty thousand kilometers into molecule-sized pieces."

"How many of the boarding party did we manage to kill, Iolyn?" Huw asked, leaning over Wulf's shoulder to get a look at the monitor. "The pirate leaders don't look too happy with the situation."

Wulf laughed grimly. "No, they aren't happy. Would you be? They now realize they can't leave on their ship—and can't control ours either."

"They lost about half their boarding team when we cut environmental to the other decks before they managed to put on breather-units, but as I said, they still outnumber us three-to-one," Iolyn said, consulting his data pad. "They lost at least five men in the maintenance tunnel traps in an attempt to get to the engine room."

Huw grinned at his brothers. "Bet they regret ever attempting to take a Prime ship."

Loud thudding noises at the engine room doorway attracted all of their attention. The pirates gathered outside were once again attempting to break through the door shields.

"What about the engine room's security? Did Solar manage to sabotage it?" Maren asked, concern in his eyes.

"No." Wulf's lips twisted into a smug smile. "I killed him before he got that far. The engine room shields are impenetrable."

The other men grunted in approval.

"Is there any chance we could retake the ship without external help?" Huw asked.

"Not without a great loss of life. They've concentrated their numbers on the engine room access ways." Wulf switched to the cameras in the hallways leading to the engine room. At least fifty heavily armed men from multiple races and species had hunkered down for the siege. "We'd be killed as soon as we let down the shields on the door."

"What about the maintenance tunnels?" Maren asked. "Can we control *any* of the traps so we can get out and take the battle to them?"

Wulf understood the old warrior's feelings. Sitting and waiting to be rescued was not the Prime way. But this time, it was the prudent choice. The treaty with the Alliance and their reasons for signing it were more important than a little glory in battle.

He shook his head. "Right now, we can't control the three crucial traps closest to the engine room. Anyone going in or out of here through those last three sections would be killed instantly."

"Can we repair the damage Solar did?" Huw asked.

Wulf shrugged. "We can try. It would take massive reprogramming—and might take longer than the time we have left."

"I'm willing to try, brother." Iolyn grinned. "It's not as if I have anything better to do."

Wulf nodded. His brother was the best programmer they had. If anyone could do it, he could. "Do your best. Start with the one immediately outside the engine room access to the tunnels. That would at least allow us into the hallway just outside the main engine room door—we might be able to take out some of the enemy from above and behind."

He switched the monitor view to the tunnel sections leading into the engine room. Two dead pirates, a Terran and some pseudo-reptilian species, possibly an Erian, lay in the tunnel at the second to last trap just outside of the engine room. The Erian still breathed, but could not retreat because the trap sensed motion and might finish the job it had started. "The pirates have already attempted to gain entrance. I don't think they'll try again."

Iolyn nodded and moved to another computer console to begin his work.

"I'll help, Iolyn." Huw joined his brother.

"Thus, for now, we have a stalemate," concluded Maren.

"Yes," Wulf said. "Until either the Alliance arrives, we help ourselves, or we self-destruct."

"Let's hope there is an Alliance ship close enough to respond," Maren said.

Wulf hoped so also. He more than anyone else on the ship, other than maybe Maren, had something to live for now. A woman with his *gemate* sign. Maren's niece. His *gemate*, his genetically ideal mate—Captain Melina Dmitros.

At the mere thought of her, his body throbbed with unspent passion. His heart ached at the thought of losing his chance to meet her. Since he'd first learned of her existence, all his thoughts, his dreams each night, had been of meeting the woman with whom he could share everything. His body. His mind. His soul.

When Maren and his brothers first told him of her existence, he'd wanted to drop everything and rush to the Alliance Military Command on Tooh 10 to steal her away. But his father and Maren had convinced him she needed to be approached cautiously, and then courted. After all, they'd reasoned, she'd been raised as a Terran woman. She held an important and vital military position. Despite the genetic advantage he had due to the *gemate* imprint, she still would not appreciate being swept away by a man claiming to be her mate.

Reluctantly, he'd agreed with their conclusions and thrown himself into researching Melina. He knew everything about her a data search, photo images, and his brothers' and Maren's words could tell him. But the important things—how she smelled, tasted, or felt in his arms as he made love to her—he could only discover once they met.

Wulf closed his eyes, the image of Melina fixed in his mind's eye, and prayed, something he had not done since his early childhood.

———

Jump Station Andromeda 2, Mu Arae solar system

MEL HUNG ONTO A COMPUTER console in the control center of the jump station, trying to keep from floating away. All around her red and yellow lights flashed and warning sirens blasted her eardrums, mixed in with the moans of the injured and screams of the frightened.

Papers, data pads, and anything not attached to a wall or floor drifted around her. What was more disconcerting was the number of blood globules hanging in the air. Some of it was hers, but most of it belonged to the two dead Antareans who now floated near the ceiling, or what now served as the ceiling.

Suddenly, the room rotated once more almost two hundred forty degrees.

Mel held on as everything suspended in the confined space bounced off solid surfaces like billiard balls.

"Nowicki," she shouted to be heard above the chaotic noise. "Find someone to shut those damn sirens off. And let's get the gravity fixed."

"Working on it, Captain," Nowicki shouted back just as all went silent.

The station slowly reoriented itself. The dead Antareans fell to the floor not two feet from her. Their scaly green skin covered in rust-colored blood. It had taken more than laser blasts to take the bastards down; lasers barely pierced through their tough hides. She'd finally resorted to her serrated battle blade. Severing their major blood supply had been their death knell. A messy one.

Was it any wonder the Alliance wanted to ally with the Prime? The Prime had fought against the Antareans' arrival in the Milky Way for eons and survived to tell about it. She wished she'd had some Prime inside information, or at the very least some of their specialized weapons, to stop the tough-skinned bastards. Might have saved her time and some of her own skin and blood. Combat by trial-and-error was no way to fight.

Feet solidly planted on the deck once more, she let out a breath. "Whoever fixed all that at once, please give them my heartfelt thanks."

"You're very welcome, Captain." Her chief engineer, Commander A'tem, sent her a snappy salute. "We have complete control of the facility once more, sir. The jump gate is back online and can accept space traffic once again. The Antareans hadn't gotten any farther than gravity control when we boarded."

The damn pseudo-reptiles didn't need gravity. They just used their little suckers and walked along any surface. She shuddered as she recalled how the one had dropped on her from above. But he was dead, she wasn't—and in the final analysis that was all that counted.

"Thank you for the report. Continue to render the jump station crew any assistance they might need." Turning to Ensign J'ar, she asked, "What is the status on the remainder of the Antarean boarding party?"

"Two-thirds are dead. The remaining third are contained in a cargo area and are under guard, awaiting Alliance military police to arrive and remove them to the penal holding cells on Tooh 10."

"Excellent work, Ensign."

The tall Volusian smiled. "Just doing our job, sir."

"Did we track the mother ship that carried the boarding party?" she asked Nowicki.

"Blue Squadron arrived right on our heels and picked them up. The Antarean ship engaged several of Captain Warten's battle cruisers and was destroyed in the ensuing battle."

Thank God for that.

"Convey my congratulations to Captain Warten and his men. Advise Alliance Military Command we are in control of the station and will finish cleaning up while waiting on the cruiser to take away the prisoners."

"Uh, Captain, ma'am." The communications officer of the jump station stood next to Mel, a nervous look on the woman's too-pale face.

"Yes? Ms. Baldwin, isn't it?" The young woman's nervousness melted away under Mel's use of her name and kindly smile. Being forcefully boarded by anyone was stressful, but being boarded by Antareans was especially scary. The new scourge of the galaxy was the stuff of nightmares. It was amazing the young woman wasn't on the floor in a fetal position. "What can I do for you?"

"There's an emergency call for any Alliance military ship within this region." The young woman swallowed. "It's from the *Galanti*. It's a Prime starship which passed through the jump about one galactic standard hour before we were attacked. They've been attacked also, ma'am."

"By Antareans?"

"No, ma'am," stuttered Ms. Baldwin. "Or, at least—"

"Replay the message for me, please." Mel strode over to the com-panel.

Ms. Baldwin keyed in the code. A deep, gravelly voice boomed from the speakers:

"This is the Prime ship Galanti, *carrying the ambassadorial delegation. We've been boarded by pirates. We are under a Code Argenta. Repeat, a Code Argenta. Any Alliance ship within*

ninety-six standard hours of this message, please respond as quickly as possible. Contact Prime Military Command for specifics on Argenta."

The message then repeated on an eternal loop.

Mel shivered. The voice of the unknown Prime male pierced her very soul. She knew she would do anything possible to reach him—them—in time. Especially since she knew very well what a Code Argenta was.

"Code Argenta?" Ensign A'tem muttered. "What does it mean?"

"It means," Mel said, "if we don't get to them within ninety-six standard hours of this message, they'll blow the ship."

"How do you know that, Captain?" Nowicki asked.

"I helped my father translate some ancient Prime military treatises. I thought that the self-destruct tactics were eliminated as wasteful and barbaric several centuries ago," she replied, frowning.

"I guess they brought them back." Nowicki grimaced.

Her second-in-command's distaste over the order of mass suicide by a military captain was obvious in his demeanor. The thought of having to make such a command decision made her sick to her stomach, but she understood the ancient Prime reasoning. It was a "scorched earth" philosophy: if we can't beat you, we won't leave you anything to help you kill our people. Maybe the Prime's ongoing battle against the Antareans had necessitated the re-institution of such a drastic measure.

"I guess," Mel finally replied.

Capturing Nowicki's gaze, she issued orders rapidly as she strode to the jump station control room exit. "Get ready to disembark. Leave one of our battle cruisers here to aid the jump station staff until the M.P.s get here. Send a message to Alliance Command that we will respond to the *Galanti*'s distress call. Then contact the rest of our squadron and

Warten's. Give them the *Galanti's* coordinates. Tell them to get there as soon as they can, then hold position well away from the *Galanti*. Figure safety distance for a total fission reaction and then add half again as much."

"Should I contact the *Galanti* and tell them help is on the way?" Ms. Baldwin called out.

Mel stopped and turned. "No. I don't want any other enemies in the area to know we are on the way. We'll contact the Prime only if we cannot make it to them in time."

They'd make it—or die trying. She wouldn't allow the Prime captain to sacrifice the Ambassador and his delegation or the ship's crew.

She led her men out the door and into the corridor leading to the docking spokes. "Tell Warten I want his ships to keep anyone other than Alliance ships from approaching the area. Plus, I don't want any pirates escaping the Prime ship. Only the *Leonidas's* teams will approach and dock. I'm not taking any chances on blowing up anyone else."

"So, we get to be the only lucky ones, huh?" Nowicki quipped.

"Yes. Isn't that why you signed on to this dog-and-pony show? For the thrills and chills?"

Nowicki just laughed and saluted as he waved her ahead of him into their shuttle.

CHAPTER THREE

Approaching the Galanti, fifty hours later

Getting past the pirate mother ship was anticlimactic; the enemy ship's weapons did not function.

The *Leonidas*'s sensors showed the old Volusian battle cruiser was dead in space.

Mel ordered one of her squadron's battle cruisers to lock onto the beleaguered ship and to tow it away from the *Galanti*—and the danger zone. Later, they'd board the pirate ship and place the crew under arrest for crimes against the Alliance. Right now, it was contained and out of the way.

She smiled. However they'd done it, the Prime had effectively trapped the pirate boarding party on the *Galanti*.

Unfortunately for the pirate boarding party, they were now sandwiched between two sets of predatory creatures—the Prime and the Alliance. This should be easy to finish—or at least it would be if they could contact the Prime and coordinate an attack on the pirates now on the *Galanti*. So far all attempts to hail the Prime on the ship had been fruitless. Something was blocking all signals in—and the only signal coming out was the emergency signal she'd already heard.

They'd have to contact the Prime face-to-face and that entailed boarding the ship.

Mel was pretty sure the Prime controlled most of the systems on the ship under the Code Argenta. Something drastic must have happened to keep them from overpowering the pirates.

She'd know soon enough.

Maneuvering her small transport for the final approach, she issued orders over her ear-com unit. "Prepare to board the Prime ship. Switch now to alternating com-code ZZY."

She wasn't taking any chances the pirates might be able to monitor her teams' communications. The codes would change every half-standard hour.

Each of the five small transports she led into the suspiciously wide-open docking bay of the *Galanti* checked in. All communications were now self-contained among their team. The rest of Gold Squadron and the approaching ships of Blue Squadron were not to communicate with her team until she gave an "all clear"—after the self-destruct mechanism was shut down.

"Okay, soldiers. Our first job is to secure the docking bay. No one else goes in and no pirates get off."

"That's clear, Captain," Commander A'tem said. She'd brought her chief engineer along in case the Prime needed assistance in stopping the self-destruct. Plus, the Volusians were noted for their fierceness in hand-to-hand battle. "How do you want to go about contacting the Prime once we are on board?"

"We'll seek out the one defensible position on the ship—which in all Prime military ships is the engine room."

"What if there are friendlies between us and the pirates? How will we tell the good guys from the bad?" Nowicki's calm tones came over the headset.

Mel had worried about that also, then she realized the Prime planned for such situations under Code Argenta. The ancient military plan was a drastic, harsh—and final—solution. Therefore, any Prime crew member who had not made it within the designated defense perimeter would be dead.

"We won't know until we get there, but I suspect the only live bodies we'll find on that ship other than the Prime in the secure location will be pirates."

And possibly the traitors who had allowed the pirates in. There had to have been traitors in the Prime crew. There was no other way to breach a Prime starship. The Prime weren't careless with security.

Mel added, "Prime history has shown that they will do whatever is necessary to eliminate the enemy."

"The Prime would've shut off the air to all decks once they had secured their defensive perimeter," Nowicki concluded in a flat, disapproving tone.

"That's my guess," Mel said. But it wasn't a guess. She knew that is what the Prime captain had done. She'd read of such situations in several Prime military histories in her father's private collection.

"But the pirates might have had breathing units," J'ar said.

"The pirates might not have suspected the Prime would cut off the environment as long as some of their crew might be outside the safety of the secured location," Mel said. "They would've only realized as their peers started to drop dead."

Only the hardiest, some of the pseudo-reptilian species or other humanoid hybrids who could go without air for a short period of time, would've survived to don breathing units.

"Man, what are we letting ourselves in for allying with the Prime?" one of her soldiers muttered. His shock came clearly over the com.

"The Galactic Alliance Council has valid reasons."

"Like what?" the same soldier asked.

"The Antareans," she said.

Those two words would evoke recent memories from the jump station for her team.

Mel took a breath, blocking out the too-vivid images from the jump station and more distant ones which still haunted her from childhood.

"The Prime have protected themselves and the rest of the Milky Way for eons from the Antareans. The Antareans kill, rape and mutilate with impunity. They do not surrender. They do not give up." Mel stopped and swallowed the lump forming in her throat, struggling to regain the control she was in danger of losing. "You have to beat them or die trying. Don't ever forget that. The Prime haven't, and they are still here to fight."

"Listen to the Captain," Nowicki said. "She's seen the results of Antarean land raids before in the Prater region."

Damn, she forgot Nowicki knew the story—one she'd only shared after one too many scotches one interminably long, sleepless night.

"What I'm trying to say is don't prejudge the Prime too harshly," she said. "They are now a part of the Alliance. Their methods, although draconian by our measures, work. Just be thankful we only have to fight pirates this go-round."

"I'm betting no other pirates will ever attack a Prime ship again—after this lesson," joked A'tem.

Laughter at the Volusian's conclusion came across the com. She sighed with relief. Her troops were wholly on board. They'd do their job and do it well for the pride of the Alliance and Gold Squadron.

"Let's go in. Shields on full. Take out anything moving in the docking bay."

A roaring war whoop from A'tem, J'ar and the other Volusians on the boarding team echoed across the ear-coms.

Prime Star Ship Galanti

MEL STOOD ON HER SECOND blood-covered deck within the last fifty-plus standard hours. The jump station hadn't been quite this bad, because they'd reached it soon after the initial SOS call. Here there was barely a surface which did not have blood, body parts, or bodies covering it. The Prime soldiers had put on a valiant effort, but they'd been surprised and most likely outnumbered.

Swallowing back the bile threatening to come up her throat, vomiting was not advisable when wearing a breathing unit, she stepped around one of the dead Prime crew, his weapon still clutched in his hand. She bent over and gently closed his eyes, murmuring a benediction for his warrior's soul.

As she made her way through the large bay toward the perimeter and the control consoles, Mel idly wondered whom the traitor or traitors had been who had shut down the ship's security against intruders and allowed the raiders to board. She guessed she'd find out later, once she made contact with the remaining Prime.

"Status, Nowicki?"

She moved to stand near her second-in-command as he re-entered the docking bay with his team. The control console monitors were all dark. All power to this level was cut off, and as suspected, environmental was dead. Emergency lighting provided an eerie glow in the cavernous bay.

"We checked the two contiguous levels, using the maintenance tunnels since the lifts are inoperable. All the bad guys we encountered are either dead or secured." He nodded toward the opposite wall to where the prisoners were being lined up by A'tem's team. The pirates wore leg and arm manacles. "All the Prime found are dead. No torture. Looks as if they died fighting after the initial invasion."

"Jesus," she muttered. "Why just the two levels?"

"One of the prisoners advised us that we were outnumbered, Captain." Nowicki angled his head. "As it was, we only subdued this bunch because of surprise. I decided not to risk the boarding party until we could assess status more completely."

Mel's narrowed gaze traveled the line of prisoners. A few of the pirates were Erians, a reptilian species which gloried in mutilating prisoners, very much like the Antareans. In fact, the Erians were rumored to be distant cousins of the Antarean race, separated by several centuries and a half of a galaxy.

"I would've done the same."

Nowicki nodded his acknowledgment.

"Any Prime women among the dead?" she asked, dreading the answer. The Prime diplomatic legation might have brought their wives, although she doubted it. The Prime hid their women away and protected them to the point of being excessive. The crew would always be one hundred percent male.

"No women."

Unconsciously, the tension which had stiffened her posture dissipated.

Nowicki shot her a look of understanding.

Her nightmares dated back to the Prater region and an Antarean raid. She'd survived—others hadn't. Since that time, she couldn't handle the evidence or even the thought of rape and mutilation. Her traumatic childhood experience was the reason she'd joined the military, to fight the dregs of the universe who felt the need to prey upon the helpless and unaware.

Nowicki had made sure she hadn't seen the bodies of the women raped and then killed by the Antareans back at the jump station. As fast as they'd responded, the lizard-bastards managed to mutilate two women. Guilt burned in her gut that they'd not been quick enough to save the women the horror.

Killing the two Antareans in the control room had helped somewhat.

So, no women on board the *Galanti* was a good thing as far as she was concerned. Space pirates, especially Erians, were almost as bad as Antareans in their treatment of captured women.

"Are we secure for now?"

"As far as we can be. The two levels we took had very few pirates." Nowicki frowned. "I'm betting the main thrust of the boarding party is on the level leading to the engine room and on the command deck."

"No bet there. It's certain," Mel said.

Ensign J'ar approached them. "One of the prisoners says he knows you, Captain. The guy's from Obam II. Has something to tell you. Won't talk to anyone but you."

"Bring him."

J'ar loped over to a man on the end of the row of prisoners, lifted him up, and all but dragged the prisoner over to where she and Nowicki stood. J'ar handed the Obam male a com unit set to the current code.

"Mistress Dmitros." The man bobbed his head in greeting. He was a typical male from the Obam region. Thin and tall to the point of being a walking skeleton with skin colored a pale orange. His sky blue gaze met hers briefly then shifted to the floor.

A brief memory of sharing a cool icy snack with him one very hot, dusty day flickered across her mind.

"Slate, isn't it? You dug for my parents on Obam IV."

"Yes, Mistress." His eyes looked everywhere but at her. Obam males culturally avoided looking foreign females in the eyes; it was considered rude.

"What are you doing with the pirates?"

"Thought we was in it for money and goods." That did not surprise her, it was why most of the Obam people helped with her father's dig—for the chance to find and steal treasure.

"But once on board found out differently. Then couldn't leave. So, exist." He shrugged.

Slate didn't act ashamed or even guilty. But she expected that. As far as he was concerned, he was not the same as the men he ran with.

She reached deep inside and used the extra sense no one knew about and which had saved her many times to read the Obam.

His energy was calm and his aura read as truthful as any of his race ever did. His voice presented the facts as they were—or as he perceived them to be. The Obam were like that, they took things as they came and adapted. The morality of it all was as fluid as their adaptive lifestyle. She'd bet he'd avoided the killing during raids. No Obam male she'd ever met had the balls to kill. They were even vegans. Stealing was okay, but killing was not in their genetic makeup.

"You know men like me, Mistress. We do not kill. Slate waited for escape."

"Do you believe him, Captain?" J'ar's Volusian pale blue skin tones had darkened to a deeper blue, almost as dark as a deep space void. J'ar was angry.

While Volusians were a warrior race, similar to the Prime, they abhorred anyone who fought without honor. Even more, they despised ambiguous morality such as Slate's. To J'ar, Slate was just as evil as a warrior without honor.

"Yes. Obam males are like that." She looked at Slate who smiled and good-naturedly nodded his agreement with her conclusion.

"Yes, Mistress. What happen to Slate now?"

"You will sit with the other prisoners. Later, once we control the ship, I'll make sure you are sent back to Obam for judgment."

"Thank you, thank you, Mistress Dmitros." Slate bowed his head, his chin almost touching his chest. Bringing his sly blue gaze to look past her right ear, he said, "You cannot make way to the Prime crew in the engine room. There are many, many pirates left." Obviously, Slate had been Nowicki's source for the pirate head count. "Most of them are lizard-people. Very, very bad, mistress. They not need air as much as human-types and tough to kill."

Lizard-people was Slate's name for the Erians.

With Slate's extra information, Nowicki's decision to stop at two levels was even more judicious. Erians were damn hard to fight. Their skin was thick and leathery. Lasers would merely sear them and they'd continue to fight, even more enraged. Just as the Antareans she'd killed on the jump station, a knife to their main blood supply was the best way to kill them quickly. Damn. Her men would have to fight hand-to-hand.

The risks had just increased. And the self-destruct clock still ticked in her mind.

"How many, Slate? An estimate is fine."

"Still living? One hundred, maybe?" He looked around the docking bay, his eyes reflecting his skepticism. "You have not enough men to take them. Why not bring more?"

"Later. I need to establish contact with the Prime." She turned to Nowicki. "Looks like the maintenance tunnels are the best bet to get to the engine room."

"No! No! Mistress do not do that. Slate could never face your sire Dmitros again here or in the afterlife. There is death in the tunnels. Five men went in and never came out. Please do not go."

"Thank you for the warning, Slate, but I know what I'm doing." She smiled at the Obam man.

Slate muttered dire warnings in a mixture of Obamian and Alliance Standard, his head shaking side-to-side with his agitation.

"Ensign J'ar take good care of Slate." She glanced at the line of prisoners, who eyed Slate with narrowed, angry glares. Many of the Erians would kill Slate if they could. "Might be a good idea to keep him away from the others. Have one of the guards get any other intel from him that they can. He is not lying."

"Thank you, Mistress." Slate bowed his head.

A still skeptical J'ar led Slate away.

Mel turned to A'tem and Nowicki. "We have, by my count, very few hours left on the countdown clock. I want you to take the away teams and the prisoners off the ship and dock with the *Leonidas* outside the blast perimeter and stay there until I give the all clear."

"What in the frigging hell are you planning, Mel?" Nowicki hissed under his breath. Her second only called her Mel when they were private or he was under the influence of a strong emotion. Since they were not private, he must be furious.

"I wasn't sure until Slate confirmed it."

"Wasn't sure of what?" A'tem asked.

"That we might not be able to get to the Prime crew's location and get the captain to turn off the self-destruct device. Slate just confirmed it."

"All we have to do is bring in ten more teams and take out the pirates," Nowicki growled.

"You know how the Erians fight. You had a hard time taking those few over there," Mel said, placing her hand on Nowicki's tense arm. "You heard Slate. The bulk of the remaining pirates are thick-skinned, hard-to-kill reptile-like men with enough cunning to know you'll have to engage them hand-to-hand. We'd eventually win, but it would take hours and a great risk of loss and injury to us. And then there is the self-destruct. I will not risk that many soldiers. I refuse."

She lifted her hand when Nowicki would've spoken. "Royce," she whispered. "Don't worry. I can make it through the traps. I read Prime dialect. I've read the military texts my parents unearthed and cataloged. I know the types of traps they use. They used them in their battle fortresses and I have encountered many of them on the digs. They'll use similar traps here."

When he tried to speak once more, she glared him into remaining silent. "Plus, the traps will be aimed at large male intruders. I am, if you haven't noticed, smaller than most men and female. I can get through."

"Dammit all, Mel. I don't like it." Nowicki ran a hand through his hair.

"I know. But there is no other choice. I'll be fine." She shot him a quick grin. "I'm betting they have cameras in the tunnel and maybe communications. I might be able to establish contact that way and get them to shut down the traps—and the countdown, and then I'll contact you and we can figure out how to flush the rest of the pirates out *with* the help of the Prime. We'll use the usual sequence of signals."

"Why not just have the Prime call us in when you get to a useable comm point?" Nowicki asked, still belligerent.

"No, no one comes back unless the order comes from me. I'm not willing to sacrifice the crew's safety when the pirates could contact you as easily as the Prime, and you'd never know the difference."

"Then let me go in," Nowicki begged.

Mel shook her head. "They're more likely to ignore a man and let him die. Me? They know the pirates don't allow women on their crews. I have to be an Alliance officer." She shook her head in warning as he opened his mouth once more. "I won't risk any of you."

A'tem looked from one to the other of them with a look of extreme concern in his navy blue eyes. "Commander Nowicki, the Captain is well within her authority to act in this manner. I do not think you have the authorization to say her nay."

"Thank you, A'tem." Mel smiled at the always proper Volusian. "I know I can always count on my Volusian officers to be the voice of reason."

"Dammit, Mel!"

She patted his arm. "I'll be fine, Royce. Now move it, mister. We don't have that much time. I'm counting on you to get these men away and to advise our ships and Captain Warten as to the plan."

"Yes, Captain." Nowicki saluted and stalked away, anger in every line of his body.

"I'll watch him, Captain. He'll be fine."

"Thanks, A'tem. He's the closest thing I have to a brother."

She'd always known her second-in-command felt more than brotherly love for her. His emotions right now were off the map of the proper relationship between a superior officer and her second. She'd striven never to give him any idea she might return that love. She couldn't return an emotion she didn't possess. She was pretty sure her whole squadron knew how Royce felt about her, but they also could never point to any action on her part that had welcomed or accepted anything more than close friendship.

A'tem's departing "Yes, ma'am" was a point in fact. His tone and manner stated he knew what she'd said was true; too bad Royce had never accepted her feelings as they were.

Galanti Engine room

"WULF, GET OVER HERE!"

Iolyn's voice roused him from a light nap. Wulf approached the station where his two brothers had been working on the tunnel trap overrides. Maren now stood with them.

Concern—and something akin to fear—etched all three men's faces.

"What's the problem? Another pirate in the tunnels?"

"No, your *gemate* is in the tunnels!" Iolyn said.

"What?" Wulf shoved his brothers out of the way and stared at the screens.

Muttering all the gutter Prime he knew, he glared at the monitor. A slender, raven-haired female clothed in a tattered Alliance Military Command flight suit with a breathing unit covering her face emerged from one of the deceptively milder traps. She approached a dead pirate, an Erian. She had a knife in one hand and a laser pistol in the other. An Erian's bile-colored blood dripped off the knife.

"What does she think she is doing?" he growled, slamming his fist on the desk. "And why is she carrying a bloody knife?"

She looked so small, so fragile—so easy to kill. This was not how he wanted his first look at her to be.

"She's doing her job," Maren said, cutting through Wulf's shock and anger. "And the cameras seem to be out in the earlier sections of the tunnel. We don't have surveillance on the docking bay and any of the tunnels leading into it. She must have entered there."

Wulf ignored Maren's calm tone. His focused senses could not get past Maren's earlier words. "Her job?"

The older man clarified his earlier comment for Wulf as if he were an infant learning his numbers. "Coming to the aid of a ship attacked by pirates. *Her job*."

"You think this is funny, Maren?" Wulf all but growled at his mentor, the man who was more a father to him than his own. "Your niece. My future wife. The mother-to-be of my heirs, who will in turn be future leaders of the Prime people, is crawling through a death trap and you are smiling?"

Maren's eyes glinted. "You need to see Melina this way. This is her job. She is a warrior just as you or your brothers. Watch and observe. It may give you insight into her character." Maren turned to leave, then hesitated. "You might think about how you will aid your warrior *gemate* in doing her duty."

"Why is she the one in the tunnel? Where are her men? And why in Balcon's balls don't we have communication with her? I am sure she must've tried to hail us once she reached the ship." Wulf beat on the blackened monitor that should've revealed the docking bay and its maintenance tunnels. The battle or the traitors had knocked out all eyes and ears in that strategic zone.

"She is sacrificing only herself," Huw stated. "It is what she would do. She wouldn't allow her men to fight the bastard Parker on Tooh 2—and he was your size, Wulf. The top of her head would only come to your mid-chest."

"That's supposed to make sense—or make me feel better about this situation? She is a woman," Wulf said, then muttered, "and my *gemate*."

"Brother, you are thinking as a Prime male with a traditional Prime female. Mel is not typical anything," Huw offered.

Easy for his brother to say, it wasn't his *gemate* in the deadly tunnels.

Muttering dire imprecations, Wulf shoved his brothers out of the way once again and shut down all the traps he could control between her current position and the engine room. The three most deadly, the last three in the final approaches to the engine room access, were still active and would be until Iolyn programmed around them.

"Huw, rearm the traps as she goes past them. We don't want anyone chancing into the tunnels behind her."

"What about shutting off the countdown?" Maren suggested.

"Yes. She is here. I will not risk her dying, not after she has come this far." Wulf's lips thinned. *She has to live so I can blister her ears for endangering herself.* "Iolyn, how far have you progressed in reprogramming the final three traps?"

"I almost have the one immediately outside the engine room back under control. But haven't even started on the other two," his brother admitted. Iolyn's face was pale with dread for Melina.

Wulf smothered his fiery fear and anger at the situation under a layer of icy control. He would not lose Melina. Not now. She was here on his ship. So close.

"Get communication back on in the section right before the first of the uncontrolled traps. She is small enough; she might be able to slither through those two traps with help."

Wulf knew all the traps on the ship were aimed at larger male bodies, probably short-sighted of his people, but they had never expected women warriors. The traps were a matter of timing and balance. He could talk her through them if he could contact her.

His brother followed his train of thoughts. "But what about the last one? No one could shimmy through it, not even Melina."

"I'll throw my body in front of the laser-array if I have to," Wulf growled. "She will not die."

"But you would," Maren stated.

Wulf stared at his mentor. "And she would live. That's all that is important."

———

MEL PAUSED TO CATCH HER breath. The first two levels had had no traps, but she'd killed an Erian pirate who'd heard her crawling through the tunnel over a hallway. The only thing that had made the kill easy was the fact the pirate had gotten stuck trying to crawl into the tunnel. She slit the main artery to his brain and left him bleeding to death, hanging half in and half out of the tunnel access.

She kept her knife close at hand after that. Her laser pistol was in her other hand for the non-Erian brand of pirates.

A hissing sound ahead slowed her approach. Eyeing the camera lenses which were spaced every fifty meters or so, she noticed the one just ahead of her indicated a live feed. Finally! She breathed a sigh of relief. Maybe now she could communicate with the Prime. She had a sneaking suspicion her luck on finding no trapping mechanisms would run out sooner rather than later.

"Can anyone hear me?" She repeated the message in Prime just in case the ears on the other end were not multilingual.

Some static came across the speakers in the tunnel. "... watch ... not..."

Well, that was damn-frigging-fabulous. They had internal communications issues, also.

Approaching the turn in the tunnel with a great deal of caution, she stopped right before the junction. The hissing noise now sounded as if a dozen snakes had made a home in the maintenance tunnel.

Peering around the corner, she spotted a large Erian. The hissing came from him. He'd been severely injured by the trap. Too bad he wasn't dead.

Damn, she really hated Erians! They reminded her too much of Antareans.

She eased around the corner and remained just out of his reach. And Erians had very long arms. Just another black mark against them in her book. How was she going to get past the bastard?

"What are you looking at, human bitch?" hissed the injured male.

"You, lizard-bastard," she stated in a calmly dismissive manner. "Looks as if you got caught in the trap."

"Yes-s-s," he slurred in a low, ugly sibilant tone. "They turned it off right before you approached."

"That was nice of them." She smiled at the camera and gave them a finger wave. "Guess I'll just have to put you out of your misery then."

"Try it." The Erian flicked his long forked tongue over the

seam serving as his mouth. "You look tasty. I could use some blood and protein—I heal faster that way."

Damn. Some of the pseudo-reptilian species, pseudo since they walked upright like humanoids, replicated injured body parts if they could stay alive long enough. She would have to make sure this one failed in the basic biological feat.

Mel examined the Erian, who stared at her with menace in his slitty yellow eyes. The trap had cut him in many places in a cross-hatch fashion. Timing and size would have gotten her through, but she was glad she didn't have to chance it. Now, she just had to get to the Erian and slit his throat before he touched her. Even bleeding and weak he could overpower her.

"What do you think, human bitch?" The Erian struggled to get up, but only made it to his hands and knees. He still presented a large obstacle. "You think you can get past me?"

She held up her dripping knife. The blood on it was yellow-green. "I just took care of one of your brethren. He's dead. So, yeah, I think I can."

The Erian smiled, which made his already ugly face look downright monstrous. He flicked his long tongue across his lipless mouth. "I've always wanted to taste me a human bitch. Too bad you won't live long enough to be my pet. I fuck really good." He thrust his pelvis forward, his spiked penis fully aroused.

"Watch what you let hang out, lizard," she snarled. "It'll get cut off."

To demonstrate, she aimed her laser at his sex organ and seared it off. He would not live long enough to regenerate it. Lasers might not work on their thick epidermis but soft tissue was fair game.

The Erian roared his anguish and fell back to the deck, cradling the area where his sex organ used to be.

Estimating the tunnel as ten feet high, she ran toward the downed Erian at full speed. Right before she reached him, she leapt into the air, tucked and rolled, reaching out with her knife hand to slit his throat as she passed over him. Landing on her feet, she sprinted down the next corridor. The satisfying sound of a dying gurgle followed her into the next turn, followed by the bang-and-crash of the trap.

The Prime had witnessed her passage and rearmed the trap. Even if she'd missed slitting the Erian's throat properly, the trap would efficiently finish the lizard off. Her back trail was covered.

"Thanks," she said loudly, not sure where or how sensitive the microphones were in the tunnel.

"You're welcome, Mel."

She recognized that voice. It wasn't the male who had issued the distress call, but she had met the man on Tooh 2.

"Iolyn? Huw?" She smiled at the live camera to her right.

"It's Iolyn, Mel. Welcome on board the *Galanti*."

"Glad I could make it. What does it look like ahead?"

"Trouble," growled a low, unknown male voice.

Well, not exactly unknown. His was the voice on the distress call. And as it had on the jump station, the voice sent fingers of heat throughout her body. She forced back a low moan as she rubbed at her hip. Heat unlike any she'd ever experienced radiated from the marking she'd had for as far back as she could remember. Her birthmark, as her mother had always called it.

"Who's that?" She frowned, shaking off the unusual sensations caused by the unknown speaker. "What kind of trouble? Trap or pirate?" *Or you?*

"Me," rumbled the same male.

Mel gulped. That was what she'd been afraid of. Damn, her extra senses were really working spot-on this trip.

"Mel," Iolyn said, his voice practically drenched with suppressed amusement. "Meet my brother, Wulf. He is the captain of this ship."

"Iolyn, he doesn't sound very grateful that I'm here to help rid his ship of pirates."

"You should have sent one of your men," snarled Wulf. "This is no place for a woman."

Mel sighed and bit back the harsh retort. Okay, sexy-to-die-for voice in the body of a male chauvinist. Well, no one ever promised allying with the Prime military would be easy. Alliance female soldiers would just have to prove themselves. Beginning with her.

"Sorry, Captain." *Not.* "But I'm the only one who speaks or reads Prime."

She started forward once more, found the Prime words for the engine room and followed the correct tunnel. "Besides, I couldn't risk my men. By the way, I do hope you've turned off the self-destruct. There are now two squadrons of Alliance battle-cruisers lying immediately outside the danger zone waiting for the all clear."

"Can you give it now?" Wulf's voice was calmer, not as snarly and filled with anger as before.

She wasn't sure why she could read this man's moods so easily, but she could. And why in the hell did it make her feel calm because he was calm? She'd never made it a practice to worry about any man's moods.

"There's something blocking external communications," she explained as she cautiously approached an access panel to a hallway labeled the weapons deck. "We tried to hail you before we boarded the ship."

Wulf's curses came across the speakers clearly. The growl was back in his voice.

Mel laughed. "Those are some new words for me. I learned your language from ancient texts. My contemporary colloquial knowledge of your language is lacking, I'm afraid. I caught *bhau*, balls or testicles, but what is *ansu*?"

"You don't need to know," growled Wulf. "It is not—"

Iolyn laughed and cut his brother's next, undoubtedly

sexist, remark off. "In your language, the closest translation is 'devil.'"

"*Ansu bhau*. Devil's balls." She grinned. "Can't wait to use it on an Antarean."

"You will never get near an Antarean, if I have anything to say about it," bellowed Wulf.

Staying alert to her surroundings, she wondered why Wulf sounded so possessive, because that was how she read his voice. And since when could she read voices? Her psi abilities usually only worked when she was in close proximity with the person she read. Maybe his emotions were stronger and traveled farther. She mentally shrugged.

"Well, it's a good thing I answer only to the Alliance Military Command, then, isn't it?" She stopped and opened her senses wide, seeking another presence in the tunnel ahead. "Besides, I killed two Antareans just over sixty hours ago—and wounded and left to die two Erians in this tunnel. They're dead. I'm not. 'Nuff said."

She raised a hand to the camera and signaled for silence just in case Wulf felt the need to holler at her again. Something wasn't right in the tunnel ahead. She hand-signaled asking for a recon report. Two clicks came over the speaker.

Thank God, the Prime still used their old hand signals. She'd remember to thank her father for letting her read all his Prime military finds. They were coming in very useful.

She raised two fingers to confirm.

The two clicks sounded again.

Two pirates dead ahead—and they weren't dead. She could feel their life signs. *Well, shit.*

Spotting a ladder to the right, she looked up. Ooh, goodie, handholds for zero gravity.

Holstering her pistol, she wiped the knife blade on her uniform pants leg and then gripped the handle between her teeth as she climbed silently up the ladder. Once she reached the handholds, she climbed like an upside-down-monkey along the tunnel's ceiling, halting just as the corner was reached.

Peeking around the corner, she spotted the two men. They'd obviously heard her talking, and now they awaited her. The good news was, they were merely humanoids. The bad thing was they looked meaner than shit. Oh well, the bigger and nastier they were, the harder they fell. A laser shot to the head of the big one would even the odds. She'd have to drop and fight the second one, since the initial advantage of surprise would be lost when she made her position known.

Taking her pistol out, she zeroed in on the forehead of the big blonde man.

———

"WHAT IS SHE DOING?" WULF lunged toward the access panel which led to the tunnels and would have ripped it off its hinges if his brothers hadn't held him back.

"You can't go in there. You'll get killed by the trap," Huw yelled, avoiding the elbow Wulf threw at his jaw. "Trust in Mel. She can take them."

He roared and tossed his brothers aside then reached for the door again.

"Stop it, Wulf," Maren ordered, placing his body between Wulf and the door. "Or I'll have you sedated. Do you want Melina to meet you the first time as you lie unconscious and in restraints?"

Wulf shuddered as he shook off his lava-hot rage. "I'd bet you'd do it, too."

Maren nodded. "Yes, I would. Melina would not thank you for getting yourself killed." He pointed to the screen. "See, one man is dead. The other soon will be. Watch and learn." The amused older man then added, "And I would lose the I-am-your-lord-and-master tone of voice with her. She will not appreciate it. She is a warrior and leader in her world."

"She is Prime and my mate," responded Wulf bluntly.

"Ah, that is a mere fact of biology," said Maren as he watched the screen with a slight smile on his face. "You need to add to those facts. She was raised by two Terrans who, to all accounts, loved her and gave her the best of everything. She was trained by the greatest military presence in the galaxy, besides the Prime, of course. And she commands more soldiers than you. She is *more* than a *gemate*, Wulf. You'll have to accept it so that she will accept the biology."

Wulf merely grunted as he watched his tiny Melina finish off the smaller man with an efficient slit to his throat and then calmly wiped the blood off on her already bloody uniform.

Taking a deep, shuddering breath, he shook off the lingering remnants of his rage—and fear. The connection between Melina and him, which had awakened upon her proximity and the sound of her voice, was strong. He felt her satisfaction at successfully eliminating two more of the enemy. He also sensed her caution—and her pain and exhaustion—and her determination to reach him and his crew.

Pride in her strength and courage threatened to choke him. She was a miracle. His miracle. And he would protect her whether she liked it or not.

He did not like being afraid.

Returning to the master computer panel to work on reprogramming the last trap, the deadliest trap, he snarled, "Someone find my mate some clean clothes. She'll need something to wear by the time she gets here." Then he muttered, "I'll be damned if she wears bloody clothes around me."

Someone laughed. Wulf looked around for the guilty party, but saw only blankly schooled faces.

———

MEL SALUTED THE CAMERA. "THANKS for the two clicks. It helped."

"No problem, Mel." Iolyn replied, not Wulf.

"Iolyn, what happened to your grouchy brother?"

She thought Iolyn might have choked back a laugh, but that could be static. The communications were still scratchy at times. "He's trying to reprogram the last trap."

"Reprogram? I don't like the sound of that," she said as she walked along the tunnel, trusting in Iolyn to warn her of any trouble ahead. "What's wrong?"

"Three of the traps were sabotaged," explained Iolyn. "We think so we couldn't use the tunnels to get out and make surgical strikes on the pirates. Wulf killed the traitor before he could shut down our other security measures on the engine room door."

"O-o-kay. So, you're telling me I have to work my way through three traps to get to you?"

"Yes." That was Wulf's voice. He was angry again. At her—or the situation?

"*Ansu bhau*," she swore. Seemed a fitting time for her first use of the Prime vulgarity. "Okay, tell me what is coming up, and how I can get through it in one fairly whole piece." She patted her fanny pack. "By the way, this pack has ear-com units programmed for a rotating communication frequency. You'll need them to bring my men in to help you—if something happens to me."

"Nothing. Is. Going. To. Happen. To. You. Not while I live."

Ooh, now the grouchy brother sounded pissed. And damn possessive.

"Thanks, Wulf, I think." She grinned at the camera. "That sort of sounded like a promise and a threat."

"You are correct, *gemate*. I promise you will survive so I might punish you for placing your life in danger."

"Wulf? Tone, son." A male voice admonished the very grouchy captain.

"Ambassador Maren? Is that you?" Mel asked as she

turned left and climbed down a ladder to the level just above the engine room.

"Yes, my dear. It is."

She smiled at the affectionate tone in his voice. "Am I nearing the first active trap?"

All of a sudden, dizziness assailed her. Her breathing grew uneven as she gasped to take in enough oxygen to stop the vertigo.

"Uh, guys?" She coughed, her throat burning. "My breathing unit is going stale. Can I take it off?"

"After this trap, *lubha*." Wulf's voice was now calm and all business.

His words, or his voice, steadied her. Her pulse rate slowed back to normal and her breathing eased. How weird. She hadn't even realized she'd tensed and exacerbated the situation.

Then the meaning of the last word sunk in. "I am not your *little love*, Captain," she snapped. "I am not little and have never been any man's love."

"I am happy to hear that, *gemate*. And you will be small next to me." Wulf chuckled.

Grouchy brother was laughing? Was this the same man who'd growled at her earlier? He changed moods so quickly she couldn't keep up with him.

"What's so funny?" she snarled.

"Nothing, Melina—and my name is Wulf," he admonished. Irritation definitely colored those last words, she noted. "Now, be calm," he continued. "You need the breathing unit to get you through the next trap. It is poison gas."

"Great. Does it poison on contact or just through breathing? Or both?" she asked, cautiously approaching a section of tunnel hazed with mist.

"Cursed independent woman, you must learn to trust me. I would never send you into danger unprepared," growled Wulf, then he sighed. "It is only through breathing, *lubha*— keep the mask on. The trap is only ten meters long."

"I don't know you well enough to trust you," Mel grumbled.

"Then trust me because I am an ally and fellow soldier," ordered Wulf.

Mel nodded and sent him a snappy salute. She entered the mist and walked quickly through it bracing her hand on the wall for support since she was still dizzy and now seeing double. Her breathing unit wouldn't keep her alive long in this stuff if she fell.

As she exited the mist, her knees gave way. She stumbled forward several more meters, then plopped onto the floor, catching herself on her hands and knees, before collapsing onto her stomach.

"Melina? What's wrong?"

Wulf's voice was filled with fear. It bothered her. He must never be scared—not a big strong Prime male. She would not allow it. As if she could do anything about it. She would've shrugged, but it took too much energy.

Suddenly, her pulse accelerated as adrenaline poured into her system. It was as if Wulf's fear had become—and exacerbated—hers, giving her the extra chemical boost needed to make it further away from the mist still trailing around her. That was crazy. She had no connection to him.

Damn, she must be more light-headed than she'd thought.

Using the new-found reserves, she belly-crawled along the tunnel floor, putting as much distance between her and the poison behind her.

The tunnel whirled around her as if she was in zero gravity space. Her empty stomach heaved. She snatched the breathing unit off her face, then choked and gagged. Only bile came up.

"Melina, *lubha*? Are you okay? Tell me!"

The command in Wulf's tone raised the hairs on the back of her neck. Why did this man affect her so? She shook her head and gulped in the relatively fresher air of the tunnel.

"I'm ... fine," she gasped, swallowing the bile still threatening to burn its way up her throat. "The air ... in the unit ... was bad—and I got ... dizzy. Not ... poison." She struggled to sit, her back against the cool tunnel walls. "Need to catch my breath a second—I'm fine."

She wiped her mouth on the back of her tattered uniform sleeve and reached for her water bottle, still attached to her pack. Taking a mouthful of water, she rinsed her mouth and spit, then took a couple of sips. Her stomach calmed down.

Closing her eyes, she reoriented. Taking slow deep breaths, she fully oxygenated her blood, which went a long way to solving her nausea and dizziness. After one particularly deep breath, she gasped and clutched her side.

The double-damned right side. Pirates, Parker and Antareans had all had their shots at that side in the last few months. She should buy regen table stock; she'd make a mint as much as she kept them in business.

The small human male in the tunnel had gotten in a good hit and sliced her there. She was bleeding. Damn, some of her dizziness might be due to blood loss. She surreptitiously looked at her right hand. Bright red blood covered her fingers and palm. Yep, she was actively bleeding.

"Melina! Talk to me, *gemate lubha.*" Wulf's not-so-dulcet tones echoed around the tunnel. Damn, the man could bring down a mountain with his roar.

"I'm just catching my breath, okay?" Mel stood up, sliding her back along the wall and using her strong and uninjured legs and glutes to push her to a standing position. "Can't a gal take a short break?"

"Take a break when you get to my side," ordered Wulf.
Bossy alpha-male.

"Yes, oh Obi Wan." She saluted the camera and strode forward taking a right turn at the sign pointing to the engine room. "What's up next in this Prime tunnel-of-horrors?"

Wulf muttered as if he consulted with someone. "Huw and I feel you will need to shimmy under the lasers on your stomach. Can you do that, Melina *lubha*?"

Concern in his voice now. Uh-oh, trouble ahead.

"Sure. But why are you afraid? I like your rude, conceited, angry tone of voice better, Wulf."

Huw spoke. "Mel, we are concerned because you are bleeding."

"Well, damn, I thought I'd hidden it fairly well. You must have very good cameras."

"This is not a joking matter." Wulf's words were clipped and stark. He was afraid again—for her. "Can you make it fifteen meters on a downward incline? You'll have less than a meter of clearance between the floor and the lower array of lasers."

Mel mentally did the math. Thank God, her ass was fit, round but tight. "Yes, I can. We trained to crawl under trip wires in booby-trapped forests. I was always the best at it since I was smaller than the men. But what will the last trap be?"

"Off—I hope," Wulf muttered.

Mel laughed. "I think that sounds like a deal. Next corner, I think. I hear the sizzle and burn of the lasers."

"One more thing, Mel," Huw said. "There is a dead human and a barely alive Erian in the way. You'll have to shimmy around them."

"*Ansu bhau*. Well, it couldn't be a piece of cake. No, never that," muttered Mel as she turned the corner and spotted the Erian, eyeing her, a leer on his lipless hole of a mouth. The dead human was not a problem. He was definitely dead. No human could be laser-burnt like that and live. She shuddered.

The human lay just inside the trap. She might be able to use him to run interference with the lasers and the Erian.

"Okay, here goes nothing." She pulled her knife out of its scabbard, just in case the Erian managed to reach her, and held it in her left hand, at ready. She needed her dominant right hand to help pull herself along the deck.

Getting on her stomach, she shimmied to the dead Terran. She shoved at him. Yep, she could move him. Alrighty then. Lifting the human up, she smelled his flesh burn even more and involuntarily flinched in reaction. Hell, he was dead and his thick body would protect her. Gritting her teeth against the smell and the slimy feel of the bodily gunk dripping off the dead man, she crawled under him and used his body as a shell. She'd once carried an injured Nowicki just this way through one of those booby-trapped forests she'd mentioned. Sort of on-the-job training, but the Prime need not know that. She got the impression they'd never reconcile women being placed into those kinds of dangerous situations.

"You think to escape me, human?" the Erian snarled.

Well, shit. She'd forgotten all about the lizard as she'd tried not to vomit from the grisly mess she held over her body. Peering out from under the dead human, she saw that she had almost traversed the trap halfway.

Something grabbed her ankle. She chanced a look back. Lizard-breath's frigging tongue had wrapped itself around her ankle. Damn, she hated pseudo-reptilian species.

Shifting even further under the dead, smelly and increasingly gooey human, she placed her knife on the ground and turned slightly to wiggle her laser out. It would be tricky, but she thought she could get a clean shot.

She aimed. One short burst of the laser and the tongue was decimated and her ankle merely scorched. Soft tissue had no chance against a laser.

The Erian's howl was garbled.

"Hey, be glad it wasn't your ugly dick," she muttered. "That's what I did to the last lizard I came across."

Replacing the laser, she picked up her knife, stuck it back into its sheath, then shimmied harder. Just as she was about to stop and rest, Wulf yelled, "Get that *apayebo* off you. You're safe now."

Sighing with relief, she heaved the dead weight to one side as she rolled the opposite way. She came to rest, her forehead against the cool, clean metal wall. She loved the smell of metal—it didn't stink like dead bodies—or her. She could just hug the floor and take a nap—she was that tired.

Nope, there was something she wanted more. She barely lifted her head. "Tell me there are showers and clean clothes in the engine room."

A deep masculine chuckle which she recognized as Wulf's echoed off the metal tunnel walls. "No shower, but water and clean clothes."

"That's good," she sighed as she lay still for just a little bit longer. "What next? The last trap off yet?"

"No," Wulf said, his tones almost soporific to her senses. It was as if a gentle tropical breeze caressed her inside and out. He was calm now—as in calm before the storm? The man had more mood swings than a hormonal teenage girl. "But it will be. I will not let you take any more risks."

There was that promise of possessive protection in his voice again. Oddly enough, she felt safe and secure instead of pissed off at the alpha-ness of it all. Captain Wulf Caradoc was on the job and things would be fine.

She shook her head. Yep, she must still be suffering from the lack of oxygen. She was the one to ensure other's safety above her own. No one had ever taken care of her before—other than her parents.

Shakily, she pushed her way to her feet, then glanced back at the Erian who glared at her with hatred burning in his dying yellow eyes. "You know, someone will need to clear the trash out of this tunnel."

"We'll handle it." Wulf's tones reverted quickly back to the don't-mess-with-me tone. "You've done enough."

"Hey, I'm not volunteering. The job is all yours." She headed in the direction of the engine room, using the walls to hold her up. "Tell me when to stop, okay?"

"Fifteen more meters. Then sit and rest. I'll come in to get you when it is safe."

Mel walked to just short of the trap. It was a solid laser wall. "Well, shit. I think I'll just follow that advice couched in the tone of an order. I'll be holding up the wall when you get here."

She was asleep by the time her head hit the floor.

CHAPTER FOUR

One large hand held her head as strong fingers gently shoved her face against the warmth of a firm male chest.

"Breathe, *gemate lubha*," a deep, raspy voice whispered against her ear. The tone of voice brooked no opposition.

"Wulf, is that you? Grouchy again, huh?" Mel sleepily snuggled closer and took in a deep breath. "Mmm, you smell good."

More than that, he smelled dangerous. Exotic. Perfect.

Wulf's aroma sent tendrils of an aching warmth throughout her body. Her heart thudded loudly in her ears, pacing itself to the heart beating beneath her head. Her breasts swelled and nipples puckered into tight achy buds as her womb wept in sympathy.

Some primal part of her brain blared: *Unknown danger ahead!*

She shifted and moaned. "What's happening to me?" she whispered as she tried to rouse from a fog of exhaustion and pain—and lust.

"You are hurt, *lubha*." Wulf's lips brushed her forehead with a kiss so gentle she wasn't even sure there'd been one. "Hold on, we're almost at the engine room. I'll attend to your injuries then."

"Why do you make me feel this way?" she grumbled, almost afraid to find out. No man had ever confused her this way, made her ache. Pain she understood and welcomed, since it meant she'd survived one more battle. But this aching was something unknown, something she feared she might not be able to dismiss.

Gathering her even more tightly to his chest, he murmured, "Put your arms around my neck. We have one more ladder and then we'll be to safety."

One-armed, Wulf held her to him as he descended the ladder. She wound both arms around his neck, noting the softness of the midnight dark hair at the nape. Absently, she played with the thick, smooth tendrils as she curled into his chest even further. She felt safe. No one else had ever made her feel this way. It scared her.

A low, very masculine chuckle swept over her skin, raising goose bumps. "You like my hair, *lubha*?"

She ignored him. Her answer would serve only to make him more conceited than he already was.

"I've looked forward to meeting you ever since my brothers told me about you."

While his words were superficially those of polite conversation, the emotion behind them poured off him in crashing waves. His feelings were so convoluted she couldn't separate them, but underlying them all, a strong, strident base note tied them all together. It was hunger, the primitive craving of a male for a female. A need she'd sensed between other couples, but not one she'd ever associated with herself. Not even Nowicki put off this much lust, and he'd wanted her for years.

Deciding she didn't want to go there, she brought the conversation back to business. The current-fricking-life-

or-death situation. "You *did* turn off the self-destruct, didn't you?"

"Yes, after we saw you in the tunnels." His face turned into her disheveled hair. He inhaled deeply and a low husky groan rumbled past her ear. Nuzzling her, he whispered, "We'll talk about your body's reaction to me—later—after we've regained my ship. I won't let you ignore this topic, *lubha*."

Mel stiffened. "I've no idea of what you're talking about, *Captain*." She stressed his title. She had to keep their interaction on a more formal level. They had a job to do.

"I know," he said, amusement in his tones. "But you will know all—later. And I am Wulf to you. Not Captain. Do not forget that—ever."

She shivered at his words. Somehow entering the tunnel had changed her life. And where the hell that thought had come from, she had no idea.

Wulf carried her through an open panel into the engine room. Ambassador Maren and Wulf's two brothers met them. Their shock and concern at her condition swamped her. Yeah, something had happened when she'd boarded this ship. No, it was after she'd entered the tunnels. Her empathic ability worked overtime now and on the highest level she'd ever experienced. Not even in the midst of battle with all the emotions of the dying and injured had she ever read emotions this accurately.

Mel smiled to reassure the three Prime males. "I'm fine."

Wulf's snort of disagreement rustled through her hair.

Maren walked alongside as Wulf carried her toward a sectioned-off area of the cavernous engine room. Huw and Iolyn fell in, one in front and one behind, as if they were protecting Wulf and her. The other crew members, maybe forty in all, all Prime males, stopped their duties as their procession passed.

Senses blaring, a red alert caused her already achy head to throb. The air smelled wrong—a foul stench caused her nose to wrinkle, overpowering Wulf's disturbingly sexy smell. Something wasn't right. Something in the atmosphere threatened her—threatened Wulf.

Dammit. She couldn't tell where, what, or who. Maybe, she was just exhausted, or, possibly, it was the lingering remnants of the fear she'd been sublimating since she entered the tunnels.

She sniffed the air. No, she wasn't imagining it. The malodor was strong, the strongest she'd ever smelled. Extreme hatred wafted on the subtle air currents in the large engine room. The objects of the rage were her—Wulf—and also Maren and the two other Caradocs.

Opening all six of her senses even further, she sought the source. She reveled in the strength and breadth of her newly attuned psi abilities.

Wulf's body stiffened against her as if startled. Did he sense the danger now? She knew Prime were reputed to be able to do so.

She captured his gaze with her own. His eyes blazed golden fire. The emotions pouring off him read as a combination of shock and awe. His body and senses were one hundred percent centered on her—not his surroundings.

He *couldn't* know what she could do. No way. He might read her emotions, but he shouldn't be able to read her ability to sense the same. No one knew about her psi ability. No one could; it was not in her records. She'd never admitted to her highly attuned senses around anyone. Not her parents. Not her crew. Instead, she called her insights, hunches or gut reactions which Nowicki and others believed in one hundred percent.

Searing hot anger cut through her mind like a sharp battle blade, tearing her away from her thoughts. The person, or maybe more than one since the energy was so malevolent, was in a rage.

Mel tore her gaze away from Wulf's blazing one and scanned the room slowly from side to side. Separating the mixture of emotions in the room, she found curiosity about her, exhaustion from the siege, anticipation for the final battle—and finally the hatred.

Ugly, dark, and red hot. Stinking so strongly it turned her stomach.

She must have made a noise because Wulf stopped walking. "What is it, Melina?"

"Hate," she whispered back. "I can't explain how I know this, but there is strong hatred in this room. For us—you, me, Maren, your brothers."

"Maren. Huw. Iolyn. Move in closer. Be ready," growled Wulf. His wrath now swamped her senses, overriding all other emotion in the room.

Funny, the smell of his wrath calmed her. A part of him which should scare her but didn't.

It was righteous. Strong. Honorable.

"You believe me? You sensed it too, didn't you?" she asked.

"Yes." His abrupt answer, his faith in her, for some reason, further soothed her excoriated senses. "Where is it coming from, little one?"

His arms tightened about her as if he could absorb her into his body to protect her. She flinched and he gentled his grip.

"I can't tell. You have to control your anger; it's overlaying the other's emotion."

Wulf grunted, then took several deep breaths. With each breath, his anger lessened until he was in control of it, ready to use it to fight and protect.

"I haven't seen this in many, many years," Maren whispered, awe-struck.

"What, Maren?" Mel asked as she swept the room with her senses even wider open.

"Battle symbiosis." The elderly diplomat whispered so his words carried no farther than the five of them. "You will not have heard of it, my dear. It has been lost to the Prime culture for many, many years."

She couldn't be bothered to figure out what Maren meant. Nor why Wulf and his brothers gasped at the older man's words. She'd just found the source of the enmity—and he was ready to explode into action.

"He's over by the computer array, next to the main entrance to the engine room."

Wulf turned. "Huw—"

Before he could finish his sentence, the man Mel had located moved forward, a laser pistol in his hand. Without thinking, Mel pulled her laser from the holster between her and Wulf's body, brought it up in one smooth movement, and shot the man, a full-powered blast into his weapon arm. The would-be assassin fell to the floor, screaming in pain, cursing her ancestors and her in gutter Prime.

The engine room was silent—the air so still it was as if the room held its breath, waiting to see what would happen next. All eyes of the crew were on her and the man holding her.

"Huw, secure the traitor," Wulf shouted so his men would realize Mel had saved their Captain and wasn't a threat to him. "We'll question him later."

Looking down at her, Wulf's lips thinned with some strong emotion.

Well, damn, the man was angry at her! Again! He was upset because she'd defended them!

Stupid male pride.

She sniffed, raised a brow, and dared him to say the words she knew he wanted to utter.

Growling under his breath, Wulf shook his head. "First, I'll see to Melina's wounds."

He strode once more toward the makeshift infirmary.

"My injuries are slight." She wiggled to be let down. He tightened his arms and squeezed her to stop her movement. "Really, I'm fine, *Captain*."

"Wulf." Shaking her, he whispered, anger making his

voice harsh. "Say my name." His words spit out like bullets from an ancient Terran gun.

She decided to humor the beast. After all, he was only a man.

"Wulf." She smiled at him, fluttering her lashes as she'd seen other women do when they wanted to enthrall a man.

He grunted.

"I'm fine. You can put me down." His look of incredulity cut off her next request for him to leave her alone. She tried a change in topic. "Always keep a man guessing," one of her few female friends had told her. "I need to contact the Alliance squadrons awaiting the all clear."

She peered at him, testing his reaction. Not much change.

A muscle clenched and unclenched in his jaw. His carotid pulsed so rapidly she was afraid his skin wouldn't hold it in. She had the strange urge to lick, then bite him right where the pulse called to her. Probably not a wise thing to do considering his anger simmered at just below a boil, scalding her senses. Outwardly, he controlled it, well, except for the tell-tale pulse. It was a cold rage. He'd look like that in battle.

She sensed it wouldn't take much for him to unleash his fury.

Yet, she persisted, secure in the knowledge he'd never loose his wrath at her. How she knew that she couldn't explain, she just did. "You do want to rid your ship of the pirates, don't you?"

"Yes," he spat out the word, "but your wounds are more severe than you realize. You are still bleeding. There is a blood trail from the tunnels. It is getting worse. I'm not even sure why you're still conscious to argue with me."

Maren, who'd followed them, interjected, "Wulf. It's the battle symbiosis. Please, be patient with Melina."

"I understand, Maren, but she's bleeding! *Diew*!" Wulf stroked her cheek gently as the muscle in his jaw fought the battle to keep his rage bottled up.

Contradictory man.

Wulf was a man of extreme emotions. A minefield Mel would have to negotiate carefully until she understood what this battle symbiosis was. She'd never heard or read of it. But whatever it was, Wulf both wanted and feared it.

Maren smiled at her. "We are concerned, my dear. Please let Wulf care for you."

Stretching to look around Wulf's broad shoulder to smile at the older man, she bit back a hiss of pain as her wound pulled from the motion.

"Wulf can tend to my injuries while I contact my ship. Deal?" She shot first Maren, then Wulf, a look daring them to disagree.

"If you must," Wulf said through clenched teeth.

He laid her on a bed in the sectioned-off area, then pulled a cart containing antiseptic wipes and surgical lasers to the gurney.

"What is the plan?" he asked.

Distracted by his shaky movements in pulling out what he would need to treat her wound, she warily eyed the medical array. "Do you have a medical degree—or something?"

"All Prime soldiers are trained in battlefield medical techniques. My triage treatment will hold until we can get you to a regen bed in our medical unit."

"A regen bed on the *Leonidas*," she automatically corrected. "Are you sure you're calm enough to wield a medi-laser?"

He shot her a narrow-eyed look. His anger level increased once more, to the point where she felt it bounce off her like sparks from a laser drill going through metal.

"Yes. And it will be a bed on my ship," he said, his tone sharp and so dismissive she wanted to slap him.

"I don't think so, big boy." She was glad to see his hands had stopped shaking. Nothing worse than ham-handed medical care.

Wulf removed the utility pack from her waist and threw it aside. His large hands ripped her uniform top off in one strong movement. Before she could protest that his whole damn crew could see into the cubicle, he reached for her tank-top undergarment.

She shrieked as she grabbed his hands and tried to pry them off her. "Wulf, stop it!"

"I can't clean the wound with the shredded cloth in the way," he explained, his words spoken slowly and with a patience she knew he didn't feel. His extreme anger had begun to fatigue her. "Do you want an infection?"

"No," she whispered, touching his tense arm with tentative fingers. She wasn't sure why she needed to assuage his anger. His smell, all hot, testy male, reached inside her and dragged an all-too-female placative reaction from her. "I'm fine. I've had worse. Please—don't be so angry."

"You shouldn't have *any* injuries." He gently removed her hands from his arm, then ripped the tank top away from her body as if it were a thin sheet of paper. "Now, be still, *gemate lubha,* so I can tend the wounds."

His thorough visual examination took in her full breasts and leanly muscled abs, then focused on her lower right side, several centimeters below the rib wound.

Wulf's nostrils flared with his sharp intake of breath. His golden eyes burned her like the Terran sun. Long, strong fingers reached for and then traced the tattoo on her right hip. He uttered in a low, hungry tone that tightened her womb. "*Diew.*"

She shuddered in reaction—an atavistic reaction ten times stronger than the one she'd felt when she first took in his scent in the tunnels. Warning buzzers and bells went off in her head. There was extreme peril here—one she'd never confronted before.

"What are you doing? I'm not injured there," she said, her voice unnaturally husky.

She glanced at the marking. It glowed, changed colors, and, then amazingly, swirled in a rhythmic kaleidoscope effect. Warmth permeated her whole body. Her womb wept and her sex pulsed. She bit back a guttural moan.

"Wulf?" She thrust out a hand, warding him off, warding off the feelings. "What's happening to me? What is it? An infection from the pirate's knife?"

"Wulf!" Maren's harsh tone startled her. "Now is not the time."

Mel tore her gaze away from the fiery glow of Wulf's amber-colored eyes as he swept them repeatedly over her naked upper torso, each time lingering longer on her marking. Maren's face was couched in lines of disapproval. His tone of voice held a warning.

"She is injured." In Prime, Maren added, "Remember our talk. She is unaware. Patience, my son."

The diplomat turned to her and handed her a large T-shirt. She could tell by the smell that it belonged to Wulf. She fought the urge to bury her face in the soft garment. "You can use this to cover yourself from the view of the other men."

As if he had just become aware of the audience viewing her naked body, Wulf turned toward the room at large and let out what Mel could only classify as a growl. "Get back to work. All of you."

The crew hurried to their stations. The mood in the room was one of awe and envy.

Mel didn't understand any of this. Instead of asking questions which she was sure would not be answered, she turned to Maren and said, "Thank you."

Time to get this show back on the road. She needed to get off this ship—away from the uncomfortable feelings Wulf aroused.

As he turned away, she stopped the older man. "Maren, don't forget. In my pack there are ear-com units for your primary personnel. They'll need them to coordinate the battle to regain the ship."

Maren nodded. "The outgoing communications will work now. Iolyn fixed the problem after you mentioned it. We were unaware the traitor had reached that area of the communications array." He snagged the pack from where Wulf had thrown it, removed one unit and tossed it to Wulf, then left.

Wulf stared at her, his eyes filled with lambent heat. His hands had stopped shaking and were warm, gentle and efficient as he cleansed the wounds front and back then laser sutured them closed. He then efficiently helped her into his shirt. "You need blood."

"It can wait until later." She tapped her ear-com with the prearranged signal. "Now, be quiet, I need to signal my men."

Wulf grunted and muttered something she recognized as gutter Prime.

She couldn't resist. "Language, Wulf. I may be a soldier, but I'm still a lady."

The look of shock at how well she understood his language was clear in his eyes. One abrupt nod was the only apology he gave as the etched lines of his face relaxed into an expressionless mask and his emotions stopped bombarding her.

For now, he was under control. She breathed a sigh of relief, just realizing how extremely wearing his feelings toward her were. No man had ever affected her this way—even the repellant Antareans had never pushed her to the limits of her emotional and physical control.

Shaking off her disturbing thoughts, she clicked the ear-com again and then sent the "all clear" signal. The answering code came instantly. Nowicki was on top of things as usual.

"They got the signal and are on their way. Fourteen transports from my and Captain Warten's squadrons. How do you want to proceed once they're on board and have re-secured the docking bay?"

She had a plan, but considering how overly alpha Wulf had proven to be she'd better get his input. After all, it was his ship.

"The man you shot?"

She nodded, but wasn't sure what the wounded traitor had to do with their plan to free the ship.

"He would have let the pirates into the engine room after he killed you."

"I figured as much," she replied. Did he think she was stupid? "But he aimed at you. Yet, he hated me, also. Why take the time to shoot us? He could've let the pirates in and possibly accomplished his goal. Why make it so personal?"

Wulf concentrated on tidying up the bloody cloths. Exasperated, she sighed. "What is going on?"

He swept one large hand through his hair and shook his head. "It's complicated."

"Has it anything to do with why the Prime have decided to join the Alliance after centuries of isolation?"

His startled glance said she had hit it on the head. Man, he *did* think she was stupid.

"Yes." He turned to dispose of the cloths. "Your Council knows the exact reasons why. I'm not sure you need to know— right now."

"Again with the *later* thing, Wulf?"

"Yes. You will find out all—later. After this," he swept a hand indicating the ship and the battle to regain it, "is over."

"Fine." Absently, she rubbed the marking on her hip; it had cooled somewhat since Wulf had touched it. "Did you give me an antibiotic?"

"Yes." He looked at the area she'd just covered. The look disturbed—and excited—her. It was possessive. "I did."

"Good, I wasn't too happy about getting a filthy pirate blade in my side. Who knows what he'd used it for—or on— last."

"Any injuries to you are unacceptable," Wulf stated in firm tones.

Oops, he was back to the lord-and-master pronouncements.

"Because I'm a woman?" She raised a brow, daring him to confess his male chauvinism.

He nodded. And his expression displayed no guilt over his antiquated attitude about women.

"Ah, you'll have to get over that, Wulf, if your soldiers are to work alongside the Alliance military. We have many women officers and soldiers. We expect equal treatment and respect."

"I'm not sure a Prime male is inherently able to accept such parameters, Melina."

"Like I said, you'll have to—that's just the way it is."

Feeling somewhat better now that she wasn't bleeding all over the place, she chanced reopening her senses to the room, taking the temperature of Wulf's crew as they prepared to battle the pirates to end the siege.

Treachery. Ugly, yellow, bilious waves of it sickened her.

She gasped.

Wulf started and moved closer to her, his body blocked her from the rest of the room.

"Move. Dammit. Wulf, move that big body of yours. There's another one."

Wulf stayed right where he was, forcing Mel to peer around him, first on one side, then the other.

"Well, well, the man I shot was not the last traitor. But, you knew that, didn't you?" She shot him an inquisitive glare.

It explained the reason why Wulf wasn't ready to make plans for the battle to regain the ship. He'd suspected there were other traitors inside the engine room. With no privacy, the turncoats could possibly overhear and spoil their plan.

His nod was curt. "Where is he?"

Again, he demonstrated his absolute faith in her ability to read danger. A warm feeling of what some might label contentment moved through her.

She placed a hand on his arm. His large body was tense, readying itself for battle. An almost too-calm look was on his face while underneath he boiled and the tell-tale muscle in his jaw worked incessantly.

"He's by the communications panel," she whispered, unconsciously stroking his muscled forearm. "Standing next to Iolyn. Be careful, he's watching us. I think he noted my scanning for him."

Wulf nodded, then moved, still blocking her body with his as he casually turned and located Iolyn. His posture stiffened and a low vibration tickled over her skin. The vibrations came from Wulf—he held back a berserker's rage. It simmered and popped just under his consciousness and somehow she'd tapped into it without even trying. His adrenaline rush became hers. Despite her wounds, her exhaustion, she felt as if she could take on the whole engine room—and win.

Shaking away her feelings as ephemeral, she hissed. "Stop protecting me with your body. Give me room to maneuver—and a weapon."

"Do you doubt I can protect you?" He all but snarled, his attention equally fixed on the man next to his brother—and on her.

The tone in his voice told her his question held more meaning than the mere words conveyed. Her answer was important, no, crucial, to him. And he would not move away until he had his answer.

"No. I know you can protect me," she said and realized that answer had come from deep within her core. This man would step between her and all danger. Always, even if it meant his death. It scared her to realize just how vested his emotions, feelings and actions had centered on her from the moment he took her into his arms. "But you need to understand I'm used to protecting myself and covering the men with whom I fight."

"*Ansu bhau!*" he swore. "Just sit there and let someone else protect you for a change."

Obviously, Wulf was in no mood to listen to reason.

"Fine. I'll stay here." *Unless I'm needed.* "Just leave me a weapon."

Turning, Wulf handed her the weapon from her pack. Sweeping a large hand over her tangled hair, he cupped her chin with the other large, very hot hand. Then he muttered in a soft, almost pleading tone, against her lips. "Be safe, *gemate lubha*. My brothers will cover my ass. Maren will remain with you."

Shocked into a total, stupefied silence, she watched him walk away.

CHAPTER FIVE

"Maren," Wulf called out softly as he approached the older man who'd been close enough to witness the whole exchange between him and Melina. The usually restrained diplomat had a grin on his face, indicating he'd been highly entertained.

Wulf frowned. "It's not funny, old man."

Maren chuckled. "I'd never thought I'd live to see the day when a woman would go toe-to-toe with you."

Ignoring his mentor's words, he said, "Please stay with her. Protect my *gemate*."

Melina's snort of disgust over his last words brought a reluctant smile to his lips. She was an obstinate, independent wench. He intended to make it clear from the beginning who was the male and who, the female. He didn't give a slime creature's hind end about her military training or position. She was a Prime female, and, thus, had a larger role in the galaxy than fighting. She was his mate—and would be, *Diew* willing, the mother of a future leader of Cejuru Prime.

"I'll watch her." Maren's eyes glinted with laughter, then he added *sotto voce*, "Until she is needed."

Wulf glared at the older man, not appreciating the man's misplaced sense of humor. Once Maren reached Melina, he moved to the middle of the room and joined Huw.

"What's going on?" his brother asked. "Is Mel truly a battle-mate? Maren said her senses fed on yours and yours on hers."

Wulf shrugged. "It seems so."

When Melina had sensed the first traitor, he'd only gotten a faint sense of her ability before he himself had felt the hatred. With this second traitor, he'd *felt* the hatred in the room *through* her, almost as if she filtered the room's myriad emotions and then amplified the one she had singled out. The legends had spoken of this symbiosis between certain mated pairs. As soon as Maren had voiced his conclusion, Wulf knew Melina was, in truth, a battle-mate. And that concerned him. He didn't want the mother of his yet-to-be-conceived children fighting, no matter how important a battle-mate would be to the current political climate on Cejuru Prime.

Tabling his thoughts of Melina's uniqueness, he turned to Huw. "She sensed another traitor. It is Ullyn. We must approach him carefully. He could harm many before we disarm him."

Huw nodded and matched Wulf's stride toward the computer array where Iolyn, unaware of the danger, stood talking to Ullyn.

As they approached the traitor, he turned and grabbed Iolyn around the neck, placing a laser pistol to his brother's head. "Stop, Wulf. Huw. I will kill him."

Both men stopped. The room went silent at the danger present.

"You can't escape, Ullyn," Wulf said in an even, emotionless tone. Underneath his emotions roiled. Then, a coolness passed through him like a breeze off his home planet's mountains. Whisper-soft words tickled his mind. *"Patience, Wulf. Patience. You are stronger. More clever. He is afraid. You have the upper hand."*

Melina. Battle-mate instincts and abilities long buried in her, awakened and stimulated by his scent and touch, aided him in battle. She probably wasn't even aware her thoughts flowed through his mind.

No denying it now. She was, in truth, his battle-mate.

"No, but I can open the door and let the pirates in," Ullyn snarled, bringing Wulf back to the present danger. Later he would deal with the reality of Melina's uniqueness.

"You will not win. The Alliance is even now on board and in control of the docking bay. They'll kill your allies sooner or later. No pirates will get off this ship to plague the galaxy. Letting in those outside this room will do you no good."

"You'll be dead." Ullyn nodded his head toward Iolyn. "He'll be dead. As will Huw and Maren. And your bitch of a *gemate*."

Wulf stiffened at the traitor's words.

Ullyn sneered. "Think we could not see the mark? It glowed against all that pale skin."

The menace toward Melina threatened to throw him into an uncontrolled rage. Again, the feathery cool touch stroked his senses. Her scent filled his nostrils. *"Patience, Wulf."*

"Why, Ullyn?" Wulf asked.

"To end the joining with the Alliance." Ullyn's lips curled into a sneer. "Not all Prime citizens desire to ally with the rest of the galaxy."

"But why use pirates?" Huw picked up the train of the conversation, helping Wulf stall until someone could move to disarm Ullyn.

Angry, Ullyn gestured with the laser. "Because they were a convenient tool. Stop stalling and asking stupid questions. Have every crew member throw their weapons into the center of the room."

No one complied. The room was still, but no ... Wulf sensed a movement along the wall, approaching Ullyn from behind.

Melina! Damn her battle-mate little hide.

A soft touch again stroked his neck, ruffling his hair as if to say "don't worry."

Their binding was so strong, so quickly, most likely due to the strong battle-mate genetics. Despite the situation, his loins ached to possess her to take their connection to the highest and most complete level of the *gemat-gemate* binding.

Huw's body language indicated he also had seen Melina. His brother moved to draw Ullyn's attention away from her movements.

"Stop right there, Huw," Ullyn yelled, his laser waving all over the place.

Huw stopped. "Taking on the pirates as allies is pretty stupid. They'll take your payment and then kill you. They are greedy, Ullyn, and they *don't* leave witnesses."

"You lie," Ullyn yelled. But his eyes narrowed in concentration.

Ullyn was a follower, not a leader. While Wulf wanted the mastermind behind the seizure of his ship, he wasn't going to let the small fish off the hook. The bastard had threatened Melina—and his family.

Someone among the crew gasped, betraying Melina's movement. Wulf wanted to kill the man who dared endanger his woman.

Ullyn whipped his gaze toward her. His weapon now fluctuated between her and Iolyn.

Wulf moved to draw Ullyn's attention, all instincts urging him to protect his woman.

Melina leapt at Ullyn as Wulf made his move. Their battle symbiosis was fully in sync; their brains worked together to find and defeat a common enemy. She latched onto Ullyn's weapon arm, shoving it up and away from Iolyn, away from her.

Iolyn broke free then turned to take over the disarming of the traitor.

"Stay out of the way, Iolyn. You, too, Wulf," Melina shouted as she torqued Ullyn's arm. The resulting snap resounded in the room.

Ullyn dropped his laser. Screaming from the pain, he stepped away and kicked at Melina, grazing her injured right side.

"Son of a bitch," she yelled and retaliated with another twist of the broken forearm she'd never released.

The agony in Ullyn's scream was evident.

Wulf approached the duo laterally.

Melina sent him a fiery emerald glare that burned to his soul.

"I said stop, Wulf." She snarled like an angry she-cat.

Huw and Iolyn also approached.

"All you Caradocs, just stay away. He's *mine.*" She turned back to the traitor and bit out the words, "Call me a *gemate* bitch, will you?"

Melina pushed Ullyn away from her and followed with a flying round kick, snapping his head back and shoving him into a computer panel.

Wulf waved his brothers away. He didn't want them to distract her, giving Ullyn an opening to harm her. He moved closer, just in case she needed him, but not so close so as to impede her decimation of one of his Prime warriors.

His connection with her told him she had this traitor under control. Despite his reluctance to see her as a battle-mate, he did.

Concentrating, he followed the instinctive path which had awakened upon holding and scenting her for the first time and fed her his strength as battle-mates of the Prime's glorious past had done for many millennia.

Ansu bhau, but she was magnificent, just as his brothers and Maren had advised him. Her supple strength, her ferocity, made him hot. It would take all his control not to throw her to the floor and take her in front of his men, claiming her in the most primitive of ways possible.

He snorted back a laugh. She'd emasculate him on the spot if he tried. *Later.* It would all happen later—in privacy. And he planned to take a long, long time learning all the secrets of her body. Of her fascinating mind. Of her woman's heart.

His crew crowded around, all respectfully giving her the room to fight. The mood in the room was one of awe. Pride. Envy. Many of his men had lost their mates because of the exodus. He thanked *Diew* his had been returned to him.

Narrowing his gaze, he observed Melina's movements. She was visibly tiring. He felt her exhaustion and pain as his. Even battle-mates had limits—plus she fought with injuries, blood loss. He'd give her a chance to finish it; he would not shame her in front of his men. But if she couldn't, he would. He could not allow her to harm herself, even to save face.

"Finish it, *gemate lubha*—or I will."

The crowd grunted their approval of his words. The whispers of "battle-mate" swept the room. They all knew of the legend, but had never thought to see one.

As Melina kicked and punched Ullyn in a rapid sequence of punishing hits, she panted out a response to his deliberately arrogant order. "I'm. Not. Little. Nor. Your. Love. And—Not a—*Gemate.* Either. Whatever in the *ansu bhau* that is!"

With her last words, Ullyn fell to the floor and didn't get up.

Wulf signaled two men to guard the downed man. He approached his tired little warrior who was bent over at the waist, taking deep breaths. She turned her head to look at him. "I couldn't let him kill Iolyn. You and Huw kept him talking long enough for me to get into position." Blowing out a deep breath and tossing her midnight dark hair out of her sweaty face, she sighed. "Plus, he had the audacity to announce he'd seen me naked."

She stood taller and arched her back as if eliminating a kink. Shaking her head wearily, she added, "Besides, you and your people need to see that female Alliance military members can be counted on in a fight. We're not *little* and we're not to be belittled with pet names such as *lubha* and *gemate lubha*."

Wulf smiled as he reached for her. "I can guarantee my men will never call you those pet names." *Or mention the fact all of them have seen you naked.*

He swept the men surrounding them with a glare. All bowed their heads in acquiescence.

Satisfied he'd gotten his point across, he swept Melina into his arms and up against his chest, inhaling her unique scent. He whispered against her hair, "You have no idea how special you are, *gemate lubha*. But all will be explained later."

"It's always *later* with you." She laid her head on his shoulder and took another deep breath, relaxing into his hold, and sighed. "Why do you smell so damn good?"

He didn't respond. She wouldn't have heard him anyway. Now that the battle was over, her previous injuries, blood loss, and exhaustion took hold and she slipped into semi-consciousness. The battle-mate connection which had aided her in the fight with Ullyn now subsided.

He smiled as she sleepily nuzzled his neck. The *gemate* imprinting was the strongest he'd ever seen. Not even his mother and father's bond was this close. The more Melina took in his pheromones, the more they touched, saw and heard one another, the more fully realized the *gemate* imprinting would become. Even now her brain regenerated genetic memory and connections to long-buried survival and mating instincts which had lain fallow while she'd been raised as a Terran.

At the rate she progressed, it wouldn't be long before he could take his courtship to the next level with her full compliance—total physical possession. He groaned as his cock hardened at the thought.

Rousing at the sound of his unrequited lust, she opened her eyes and yawned, fighting the sleep she needed. "What Ullyn said—is that why you are joining the alliance? Civil unrest?"

His mate had a mind like a trap. He smiled.

Maren closed in upon them. Wulf asked, "Shall I tell her?"

The most senior diplomat of their planet nodded. "She, of any, deserves to know."

Melina raised her head from his chest. "What does that mean? Me of any? Okay, I know, later."

He gently shoved her head back to his chest where it belonged. Just having her in his arms and her scent in his nostrils reinforced why it was important to rid his ship of the pirates. Then he could get her alone and make her fully his. The next level of his courtship couldn't come fast enough for him.

"So," she said, as she stroked the hair at his neck. "Tell me why you are joining the Alliance after centuries of ignoring us."

"Our race is dying."

"How?"

"Between the Antarean attacks over the centuries and the loss of almost sixty percent of our fertile females after a mass evacuation during the last major Antarean attack of the planet, we have a less than zero population growth."

"So, how does joining the Alliance solve the problem?" she asked, her forehead creased in concentration. He could almost see the wheels turning in her head as she reasoned through the possibilities. All the while she petted his neck as if she needed to comfort him.

A smile crossed her face as she lifted her head and looked him in the eyes. "You want to bring in new humanoid blood."

"Exactly." Maren confirmed.

Wulf could say nothing. He didn't want her to stop smiling at him. It took all his control not to seize her lush pink lips and kiss the sense right out of her.

"So, Ullyn is part of a neo-conservative, keep-our-blood-pure group?" She laid her head back down before he had the chance to do it himself.

"Yes." Wulf struggled to stay on topic when all he wanted to do was carry her off into a dark corner and love her until she screamed with pleasure. "We knew there was opposition, but didn't realize to what lengths they'd go to stop us."

"But the pirates?" Melina lifted her head again, this time to look around Wulf at the closely guarded traitors. "Are they stupid? Pirates are the murderous dregs of the universe. They have no honor. The rebels would be killed once the pirates got paid. They'd sell their own mothers to make a buck."

"They are fanatics, *lubha*, who can understand what goes on in their minds?"

He walked over to the gurney and placed her on it. "Let's see what you tore open while fighting. Then we can finish up the plans to retake my ship. I want you on a regen bed as soon as possible."

Melina nodded her agreement and tapped her ear-com. "Nowicki, where are you?"

Wulf heard Melina's second-in-command reply over his ear-com unit. "We've retaken all levels of the ship except for the area right outside the engine room. The pirates are dug in pretty tightly and I don't want to risk high casualties on our end. Most of them are Erians. Any help from your end would be appreciated."

"What are our casualties?" Melina asked as she winced at Wulf's probing fingers.

"What's wrong, Mel? Are you hurt?" Melina's second-in-command was awfully sensitive to the tones in her voice. Just how close was this man to his mate?

"Ow, Wulf. Can you be a tad bit gentler? I'm not a tough-skinned Prime, ya know?"

He gave a short, abrupt nod and swabbed more lightly at the knife wound which had reopened in her side. He was so jealous of whatever relationship Melina had with her second-in-command he didn't trust himself to speak without the anger coming through his voice.

Melina smiled and "mouthed thank you," then said, "I'm fine, Nowicki. Now report, mister."

This Nowicki could not keep his emotions for Melina out of even a cut-and-dried battle report. The thrice-damned Terran loved her. The only thing keeping Wulf from picking Melina up and hiding her away from the Alliance troops was the fact he could see and sense with all their *gemate*-connectedness that Melina did not return the Commander's feelings. Her voice and demeanor told Wulf she respected her second. This observation reaffirmed what his brothers had reported—she treated Commander Nowicki as a brother.

Even knowing and observing all that, Wulf was still jealous, envying the man all the years Wulf had lost with his *gemate*.

"We have no major injuries," Nowicki reported. "Just a few cuts and some laser burns. The pirates have lost about twenty men, most on the Command Deck. We have twenty other pirates in custody and on their way to join the others we'd already captured."

"Good. We've contained two traitors inside the engine room."

"Three traitors, Melina," Wulf corrected. "We killed one before you came in through the tunnels."

"Captain, who is that?"

Nowicki's voice was harsh with a strong emotion. Ah, the man was also jealous.

"I'm Kenric Wulf Caradoc, Captain of the *Galanti*. Thank you for all your efforts in regaining control of my ship. I do believe we can help from this end."

"How?" Melina asked, shoving Wulf's hand away from her hip where he stroked the *gemate* marking.

He laid two fingers across her lips and shook his head, asking for her silence—and trust.

She blinked at him furiously, but nodded.

"Commander Nowicki, go to the fourth level, weaponry and weapons control. You'll find stun grenades. I believe there are enough to disable the pirates who are left."

"That should work. We throw the stun grenades. You'll open your doors and take out the ones trying to escape your way and we can get the ones coming our way," Nowicki concluded.

"Exactly. We couldn't do it before, because they had a highly strategic position and outnumbered us."

"What about the maintenance tunnels?" Nowicki asked. "Can the pirates use them to escape?"

"No, the traps are deadly and still active," Melina said, taking back control of the conversation.

Wulf grinned. His *lubha* did not like being out of the loop at all.

"Okay, we'll signal right before we throw the grenades," Nowicki said.

"See you soon, Nowicki."

———

MEL SAT ON THE GURNEY in the makeshift medical unit and let the Prime crew assist her soldiers in regaining control of the final pirate-occupied area of the ship. She easily monitored all the activity over her ear-com and the visual monitor Iolyn had set up for her. Ostensibly, she was coordinating the action. Mostly she was staying put so Wulf's carotid artery would not explode from his neck. He hadn't wanted her to jeopardize her little *bhau*, ass, one more time on his or his ship's behalf.

Truth be told, she wanted to sleep on a nice regen bed for about twenty-four standard hours. She was tired and even she realized she'd used the last of her reserves in the fight with Ullyn. She wasn't even sure where she'd obtained the reserves she'd used to fight him.

Plus, she didn't want to endanger any of her men—or Wulf's.

The two traitors sat, manacled at the arms, wrists, legs and ankles, then to each other and to a support beam. They weren't going anywhere.

She, apparently, guarded them. Ha!

"You don't know what you are, do you, bitch?" spat Ullyn.

"Ullyn. I am getting a bit tired of you calling me a bitch." She glared at him, then turned away to study the action on the screen. "I'm an Alliance Battle Squadron Captain. You may call me Captain Dmitros."

She hoped her feigned disinterest would open him up. She *wanted* him to tell her what was going on. He'd tell her more if he thought she didn't care.

What was odd, and getting spookier as the hours went by, was she could read the Prime crews' emotions—well, that is, if they did not guard them. Only Wulf, Huw, Iolyn and Maren seemed to know to control their feelings around her, but the rest of the men were like a frigging emotional download into her brain. What even surprised her more was that she was able to single them out and read individual feelings.

Her senses, always highly attuned, had become more so since she had met Wulf. Why was a question she hoped these two would answer.

Wulf and Maren were withholding information from her—and it had to do with the names Wulf called her. *Gemate. Gemate lubha.* And the terms Maren mentioned, battle symbiosis and battle-mate. She particularly didn't like the sound of that last word. There was also the increasing sense of belonging she'd felt since she met Wulf. A belonging to him—and to the Prime as a whole. If she hadn't known her parents were Greeks born on planet Earth, she would think she was Prime.

"You're Wulf's *gemate*."

Well, that was blunt. But she had sort of figured that was what Wulf thought. He'd called her that enough.

She shrugged, focusing her attention on the final leg of the battle outside of the engine room doors. From the corner of her eye, she watched Ullyn. He waited for a reaction. She wouldn't give him one.

"You, stupid bitch." Ullyn glared at her. "You're his mate. His woman. His wife, if you want to think of it in Terran terms."

"Now, how could I be his mate? I only just met him a few hours ago."

"You're one of the Lost Ones. You have to be. You have his *gemate* imprint on your hip. The whole crew saw it," said the traitor she'd wounded, a man named Prolow.

Everyone had seen her naked torso? She'd thought only Ullyn had. Hadn't Wulf's big-ass body blocked most of the view? She frowned, then recalled Wulf growling and ordering the crew back to work. Damn, she'd kick his butt for exposing her in such a way.

"I think you're making all this up."

She turned her attention back to the monitor, continuing to pretend she didn't care. Underneath she seethed. Something was going on and she was the only party who didn't know the score.

The more information she could pry out of these two, the better she could deal with whatever lay ahead. Somehow, even without new information, she'd sensed Wulf would not let her leave this ship—at least not without him by her side. Plus, he'd already stated he wanted her in a regen bed in *his* medical unit.

"Listen, you stupid cow. You are Prime. Your *gemate* mark glowed when Wulf touched it. That only happens in imprinted pairs," explained Ullyn. "All the female evacuees before the last Antarean battle for Cejuru Prime were imprinted with their genetically optimal mates' pheromones before they left. Most of the females never returned, depriving a whole generation of Prime males the chance at breeding more females for the next."

Her mind reeled with the possibility that her whole life had been one big lie. How could that be?

She turned and gave them her full attention.

"Okay, for the sake of argument, let's say I'm a Prime and one of the so-called Lost Ones," she said. "Then what you tried to do here doesn't make sense. By joining the Alliance, Wulf found me. Mightn't this open up your planet to receive Alliance aid in finding other survivors? This would further your cause for genetic purity."

Prolow shook his head. His lips twisted into a sneer. "You don't understand. Our birth rate is so low that even if we found all the lost females alive we could not raise the birthrate for several generations. The Prime leaders would still permit interbreeding with other humanoids. We can't allow that to happen. Prime blood must remain pure."

"But that means your race as a whole will die out. Correct me if I'm wrong, but inbreeding would reinforce genetic defects and hasten the end of your race. Don't you see that?"

Prolow's jaw grew hard. "You do not understand, woman. We must remain pure. If *Diew* chooses our race to die out, then it must die with pure blood intact."

Mel shook her head. Fanatics. The Prime leaders were correct: New blood would strengthen and allow for more selective mutations. This had been proven within the Alliance as more races joined and commingled. The Prime would have a chance of survival with potentially even a stronger set of bloodlines. All humanoids fought to survive; it was the natural order of things.

While Prolow and Ullyn surely believed the line of propaganda they fed her, it still rang false. Allowing a whole species to die out was just plain stupid. The rebel leaders might have another agenda—one not told to the rank and file minions such as Prolow and Ullyn. She wondered what it was.

Well, whatever it was would be the Galactic Alliance and the Prime Council's problem. Not hers. She was just a soldier.

"What's battle symbiosis?" she asked. She might as well pump these two stooges for all they were worth. She didn't want to place her faith in Wulf's continued promise of explaining all *later*. She didn't plan on being here later.

"You believe you are a Prime and Wulf's mate?" Prolow asked.

"No, I'm humoring you." She noted the battle outside the engine room was nearly over. She wanted all her answers before she left the *Galanti*. She wanted to know what questions to ask her parents, the people who raised her for as long as she could remember.

"Battle symbiosis has not been seen since several centuries ago, before the Berean Wars." Ullyn paused, his brow creased in concentration. "The stories say some mated Prime fought alongside one another and worked as one unit."

"Battle-mates?" she whispered.

"Yes. In a perfect *gemat-gemate* match, the mated couple's hearts beat at the same rhythm. What one sensed so did the other. One's adrenaline aided the other's. Legends even say they could communicate with their mind during times of strong emotions—during battle and making love." Prolow leered at her.

Ullyn added, "The mind-connection allows them to anticipate each other's moves so as to become the perfect fighting machine."

"So, Prime females used to be warriors?"

"Yes. Some," Prolow qualified, "not all mated pairs had this battle symbiosis, you understand. But those who did were the leaders of their time."

Mel turned toward them. "I'm not sure about anything you've told me, but let me clue you in about partnering with pirates. You should be happy we caught you, stopped you, because the pirates would've turned on you, killed you and then where would your cause be?"

"You know nothing, bitch." Ullyn glared at her in defiance.

"I may know nothing." Shakily, she rose and turned the monitor off. "But your mercenary allies just got their asses handed to them."

———

"MEL, WHAT'S GOING ON?" NOWICKI said through gritted teeth. "Captain Caradoc looks at you as if he wants to eat you for breakfast, lunch, dinner, and his night-time snack. He almost cut me in two with a glare when I held you up so you wouldn't fall flat on your face."

"I'll explain later," she hissed under her breath. "Let's get this wound up. Garth can take charge of the prisoners and escorting the *Galanti* to Tooh 2. We need to get me out of here and back to Tooh 10."

"What we need to do is get you to the *Leonidas* and onto a regen bed. You're a mess, Mel." Nowicki growled. "Is there gonna be a problem getting you off this ship?"

"Maybe." She sighed and rubbed her forehead. "I'm tired. I hurt. I can't explain it all now. And we don't need the resulting diplomatic incident if the Prime try to keep me on the *Galanti*. We need to sneak out."

"Shit, Mel. Caradoc is heading this way." He rubbed his mouth, whispering through his fingers. "Can you faint on cue?"

"Yeah, but Wulf will just sweep me into his arms again. And whatever you do, don't call me Mel in front of him. It would be like waving a red flag in front of a bull."

Nowicki's face reddened with anger. "Why in the fuck was he carrying—?"

Cutting off his question, she lifted a finger and pointed it at him. "Just stop. I've had it up to my neck with alpha-male chest-thumping." She let out a huff, keeping an eye on Wulf's progress across the now overly crowded engine room. "I needed to be carried when he did it, so do not go there. Men! You all try to protect me—and I resent it."

"Mel, I never ... he can't keep—"

"Oh, yeah, you do—and he could. If he wants to keep me here, every man on his crew will back him. You just don't understand what you're dealing with here."

"And you do?"

"Unfortunately, yes. Except Wulf doesn't know I know."

"Know what?"

"I'm Prime," she hissed.

Nowicki's jaw dropped open.

"See, I said it was complicated. Just follow my lead." She pulled his arm and spoke loudly. "Nowicki, let's go check with J'ar on the computer problem you had on your approach."

Wulf stopped a few feet from them. "A problem, *lubha*?"

Mel smiled and waved one hand airily. "One of the transports had a small computer glitch in its approach schematics. Ensign J'ar needs my input. I designed the system."

"Really?" Wulf looked impressed. "Can one of my computer specialists assist in any way? I really think you should be lying down in my medical unit on a regen bed. You are very pale, *gemate lubha*."

"I'm fine right now, Wulf." What a lie. She wanted to lie down so badly she'd kiss an Erian's slitty mouth to achieve it. "I'll check into the medical unit for a diagnostic scan after we fix the problem."

"Just in case, I'll send Iolyn down. He has some experience with guidance systems. I'd go myself, but Maren and I need to interrogate the traitors. We want to find out how extensive their rebel faction is."

"Sounds like a good idea. You surely don't need a civil war on your hands," Mel agreed. "We'll meet your brother down there."

She turned and walked away. She didn't have to turn around to know he watched her. She could feel his possessive gaze burn down every inch of her back. Unfortunately, her traitorous body shuddered in achy anticipation of his touch. Her mind told her this was biology—the imprinting the traitors told her about—but her body wept at leaving him.

Dammit, she needed distance—and time—to assess what was happening to her.

Nowicki walked at her side. "Now what? And what's that about a civil war on the Prime planet? And what the fuck is a *gemate lubha*?"

Holding onto her second-in-command's arm for support, she angled him in the direction of the door. "Forget the civil war. Forget what he called me. We need to move. Now."

She would not panic. And, she sure as hell would not turn back to look at him one last time. She also built all the mental walls she could so Wulf would not pick up on her thoughts or emotions. Prolow and Ullyn had said battle-mates could read minds during times of stress. She wasn't sure if it was true, but she'd sensed what Wulf would do before he did it near the end of the Ullyn confrontation. She wouldn't take the chance he could read her decision to escape now. God knew, she was stressed as hell.

"Why?" Nowicki looked over his shoulder. "What's the hurry? It will take him a while to interrogate the prisoners."

"Because those two traitors will be happy to inform Wulf that they revealed to me that I am a Prime female." They made it out of the engine room. "If Wulf knows, he'll know I'm escaping him. He won't like it."

No need to tell Nowicki about the mind-body connection—he would freak and go all alpha on her again. She could not—refused—to deal with any more alpha-ness today.

They took the lift to the docking bay where their transports were located. "Switch your ear-com to alternating sequence Code EEGT. I had J'ar go over to it when you liberated the engine room. He's waiting for us on our transport. A'tem is on the *Leonidas* and has our squadron ready to go to jump. We'll be the last of our teams off this ship."

Nowicki smiled wickedly. "You had this planned from the minute we opened that engine room door, didn't you?"

"Yes. It will take the *Galanti* at least twelve standard hours to get back on line. Plus, Garth will run interference."

"I like the way you think, boss." Nowicki signaled J'ar on his ear-com. "As for you being Prime, are you sure?" At her brusque nod, he asked, "What are you planning?"

"I'm taking leave and going home to Obam IV. I owe it to the people who raised me to find out the truth from them."

"He'll follow, won't he?" Nowicki frowned. "That word '*gemate*' is very close to our 'mate.'"

Yes, it was.

Mel allowed a small sigh to escape her lips. It was too late to reverse her genetic reaction to Wulf. It had been too late when she first heard his voice back at jump station Andromeda 2. Hearing it in the tunnel just reinforced it—and inhaling his scent, being in his arms, cemented the bond.

And she'd admit—she was attracted.

She liked the way her battle senses heightened because of him, the way he made her even stronger. She liked the way his strong arms felt around her. She loved his scent, all male musk, cinnamon, vanilla, and something spicy that was all Wulf. She wanted to lick him all over and see what he tasted like. She liked it when his jaw clenched and his carotid pulsed as he battled not to yell at her. Heck, she even liked it when he growled at her in that bossy, commanding tone. And most of all, she liked the fact he made her hot, achy and wet. She'd even wondered what the act of sex would be like with their heightened senses.

Hell, she was more than attracted; leaving now was like losing a piece of her body and mind.

But she was *not* a subservient Prime female, one to be hidden away and protected. She was a warrior—the battle-mate of Prime legend—and that was how he had to see her. Accept her.

Since the attraction went both ways, she'd made the decision in the engine room he had to woo her. She was not a gift to be dropped in his lap. He had to earn her.

"Yes." She finally answered Nowicki's concerned look and question. "I expect he'll follow, but he'll be meeting me on my turf. He'll have to deal with me—the me who was not raised to be some Prime's breeding machine."

CHAPTER SIX

One standard week later
Galactic Alliance Military Command on Tooh 10

"Wulf, sit," ordered his father, Cejuru Prime Premier Ilar Banan Caradoc. "You are wearing a hole in the rug."

Wulf turned and glared at his father. "I can't sit. Melina is gone. And these military bureaucrats are hiding her whereabouts." He ran his fingers through his hair. "I read her medical report. She required three units of blood and three standard days on a regen bed. I need to see for myself that she is healed. I need to touch her. I ... I—"

What he wanted was to tear apart the military base at Tooh 10 until he either found Melina or forced someone to tell him where she was. The not knowing how she fared threatened his much vaunted Prime control. He'd never felt this out of control in his thirty standard years.

His father stood and approached. He laid a calming hand on Wulf's shoulder. "I understand, son. Your mother and I couldn't be apart for even an hour after the imprinting was awakened early in our courtship. Melina has to be suffering also. We will demand that they reveal where she is. They don't understand the dynamics of the biological coupling."

Wulf nodded. He was glad to have his parent's support. On his own, he hadn't made much headway in locating Melina.

Immediately after the freeing of the *Galanti* from pirates, Maren had notified Wulf's father and the Prime Council that Melina was a definite match, a battle-mate of legend—and missing. His father had dropped everything to speed to the new Prime embassy on Tooh 2. With his arrival, the Galactic Alliance Council put pressure on its military to divulge Melina's location.

The military finally agreed to provide the information. In a few minutes, Wulf would have his answer. His personal star cruiser was ready to depart once he had the coordinates.

The door to the meeting room opened. Maren entered, followed by Melina's superior, Admiral Nelson, the leader of the Alliance military in the Mu Arae system, and Commander Nowicki, Melina's first officer.

Wulf surged to his feet and crossed the room in a single bound. Taking Nowicki by the collar of his dress uniform, he lifted the man up, his feet dangling and kicking a foot or so off the floor.

"Where is she, you devil-blessed bastard?" Wulf shook him and tightened his hold until the Terran's face turned blue. "You took her off my ship."

"Put him down, son."

Wulf's father pried his fingers from Nowicki's throat. The Terran dropped to the floor, gasping for breath.

"She doesn't want to see you, Caradoc." Nowicki managed to spit out between gasps for oxygen.

Wulf growled and started for the downed man. His deepest desire was to wipe the smirk off Nowicki's face permanently.

His father held him back. "Let me handle this, son."

Nowicki had struggled to his feet; his hand absently massaged his throat. Good, he had hurt the bastard.

"Commander," Wulf's father said, "By now, your Captain will be suffering, both physically and emotionally. Melina and Wulf cannot be separated for any great length of time, not until after they fully consummate the *gemate* bond."

Nowicki glared at them. The man opened his mouth to say something when the Admiral cut him off. "Sit down, Commander Nowicki. Let Premier Caradoc explain about this bond."

Wulf's father inclined his head toward the Admiral. "The bond between my son and Melina was created over twenty-seven standard years ago during a mass evacuation of our planet. My son was three standard years old and Melina, the daughter of Ambassador Maren's sister, was six standard months old. It was unusual to do so at their very young ages, but we felt it was needed. The process protects the Prime females from mating with males too close in blood-ties."

The Admiral's forehead creased as if he pondered what Wulf's father had just conveyed. Nowicki just snarled, his whole demeanor one of repudiation of anything Wulf or his father had to impart.

Wulf stood up. "Father, they don't understand. We're wasting time. Melina could be in danger of harming herself; she doesn't understand the bond. She could be in pain." His hands fisted at his sides. He'd never felt so helpless in his life.

Concern flared in Nowicki's eyes. The commander didn't want Melina to hurt. That was the only thing they would ever agree on—Melina's safety and health.

His father nodded. "Sit down, Wulf. Let me explain further." He dropped back into his chair. "In each generation there is one genetically optimal match for each Prime female. This does not preclude other potential matches, but biologically, over the centuries, we have found that the match which is optimal is best. The *gemat-gemate* markings only appear on optimal matches."

"How does this matching occur?" the Admiral asked. "They were practically—and literally—in diapers."

"Normally, we do wait until puberty, but ... let's just say the circumstances were exigent at the time of the exodus." Wulf's father sighed. "The match is more sensory than hormonal. There is a part of the Prime brain that processes all the sensory and extra-sensory emanations as each male is passed by an unmated female. If the match is genetically optimal, the female develops the *gemate* marking. The male develops a similar marking called a *gemat*. Melina was the optimal match to my son. Her symbol lay dormant until she met him on the *Galanti*."

"But what does this bond have to do with Mel's well-being?" demanded Nowicki, his fists bunched on the table in front of him.

Wulf, spacing his words deliberately for maximum effect, responded, "Melina and I have begun the first stage of Prime courtship—the linkage through hearing, scent, and touch. She needs to see, hear, touch and smell me to feel safe, calm— and to remain physically well."

"Physically well? Is this separation life-threatening?" asked the Admiral.

"Possibly," Wulf's father stated. "Already her mental state might be such that she'd take reckless actions, endangering herself. Gentlemen, we can't allow that to happen. Besides being Wulf's mate, she is a battle-mate. The Prime have not had a battle-mate in several centuries."

His father paused, then heaved a great sigh. "She is vitally important to the future of our planet. My son will lead after me—and, if he and Melina are blessed, their son after them. We need the strong battle-mate line to give our people a proud link to their past as we forge ahead and intermarry with other humanoid species to save our future."

The Admiral nodded. "She went home to Obam IV. She told me that she needed to talk to her parents ... uh, the people who raised her."

"Admiral!" Nowicki turned toward his superior, anger in every line of his body. "She doesn't want to see him."

"That's not true, Commander," the Admiral said. "She confided all to me before she left. She knew you would come after her, Wulf. She pretty much described the feelings you've just attributed to her."

"What was her mental state? Was she depressed?" Wulf closed his eyes and groaned. She needed him and still she'd left. His eyes flashed open as a further, even more horrifying thought entered his mind. "Is she afraid of me?"

"Melina Dmitros has never been afraid of anything our training or Alliance enemies have ever thrown at her, including you," the Admiral said with an amused grin. "By the way, she said to tell you that you'll have to court her. There would be no shortcuts because of some genetic code she had no control over." The Admiral paused, his eyes glinting with suppressed laughter. "She also said you had to *earn* her. She is *not* a gift. *Her* words, not mine."

Wulf's lips twisted into the first smile he'd had since he realized Melina had left the safety of the *Galanti*. He turned toward his father and Maren. "I told you she was a fighter."

"Yes, you did, son." His father slapped Maren on the back. "Maren told me the bloodlines through his mother's side had many battle-mates in the past. We are a very lucky family."

Hugging Wulf, his father added, "Go, woo your battle-mate. And then bring her to Cejuru Prime. I wish to meet my new daughter." He turned and skewered the Admiral with a piercing gaze. "I assume Melina has enough leave so she can visit her home planet and be introduced to her people?"

The Admiral nodded. "She expected that would happen. She has taken an open-ended leave of absence."

Nowicki gasped at the news. The man's gaze turned bleak.

Melina's superior hesitated. "Will she be coming back to

the Alliance military? We need her, Premier Caradoc. She is one of our most effective squadron leaders."

Wulf's father turned his head. "Son?"

"I expect so, father." Wulf frowned. He'd rather she didn't, but he knew asking her to give up her career would not be the way to woo her into accepting him as her mate.

"I've seen her fight. I've felt the battle symbiosis. It is … unbelievable." Wulf rubbed his hands over his face. "She'll want to come back. But, we would have to serve on the same ship because of the bond."

"That can be arranged, Wulf," Admiral Nelson said. "I'll put together a proposal and send it to you as you travel to Obam IV."

"That would be fine, but," Wulf shrugged, "I can't speak for Melina as much as I would like. As Maren has so pointedly told me time and time again, she is not a typical Prime mate. She and I will discuss how the military partnership will work alongside her other duties."

"And what would those other duties be, Caradoc?" Nowicki asked with a snarl.

"Why being my mate, or wife as you Terrans call it," he smiled, "and bearing my children, of course."

"I almost pity you, Caradoc," growled Nowicki. "Mel is one hundred percent a soldier. Babies have no place on a battle-cruiser."

"I quite agree, Commander. My children will not be raised on a battle-cruiser."

Let the jealous bastard chew on that one.

Nowicki lied. The man did not pity him; he envied what Wulf would possess. The Terran had never possessed Melina; Wulf had sensed no intimate connection when she was around Nowicki. All proprietary feelings were on the Terran's side. He would ensure that the Commander would never get a chance to act on his feelings for his mate. Melina would *know* only him in the future—no other.

"She was a soldier before the bond awakened," Wulf added. "Once we fully consummate the bond, she'll be forced to make choices."

"Will they be her choices, Caradoc?" Nowicki asked.

"That is none of your business, Commander."

Wulf had only shared what he had because Maren and his father had felt the Alliance Military needed to know the genetically imperative nature of the bond. There would be compromises on both sides, and he and Melina would deal with those as they arose. That would be their private business, and no one else's, especially a jealous wannabe lover such as the Commander.

"But no matter what path she chooses, Commander," Wulf stated, a warning in his eyes and voice for the Terran who loved his woman. "We will be side-by-side, a unit. No *gemate* bond has ever been broken while the mated pair both lived. She is mine—forever."

Nowicki cursed, shot Wulf one last killing glare, and stormed out of the room.

Obam IV dig, one standard week later

"WHERE THE HELL *IS* THE man?" Mel viciously wielded a small brush to dust off an artifact so that she could classify it. If she'd known how strong the bond already was between her and Wulf, she'd have stayed on Tooh 10 with the protective might of the military between them and duked this out sooner.

"Did you say something, Mellie?" Irina Dmitros, the only mother she'd ever known, sat next to her, occupied with a larger piece of the same artifact. An early Prime weapon.

"Nothing, Mama." Mel threw the brush onto the table and gently placed the artifact in the correct specimen box. No use taking her erratic emotions out on an innocent artifact.

"Mellie, your father and I told you Wulf will come to claim you. If all you told us is true, one of your female ancestors could've worn that breast plate over there," her mother pointed to a beautifully worked piece of metal and with inlaid semi-precious stones lying on a table, "in battle on this very planet. No Prime male in the history of Cejuru Prime has ever abandoned a *gemate*, especially a battle-mate."

Her parents had quickly clarified Mel's position *vis á vis* Wulf. She was his by genetics. Neither of them could fight it. Her parents had also told her the current status of Prime females as protected possessions had not been the norm. They'd concluded that the low birth rate and the loss of females had driven the Prime males to turn their back on their battle-mate heritage. Losing fertile women to war was not an option where the survival of a species was concerned.

It would be up to Mel, they said, to kick some Prime male butt and convince Wulf she could still be a Captain in the Alliance Military and meet his needs as a mate. After all, battle-mates had fought alongside their mates during the Berean wars and had managed to bear children. Her father had copied several battle-mate diaries to her personal computer for her to read and use to bolster her argument about continuing her military career.

Logically, it sounded like a great argument, but her parents had not met Wulf. He was an *über*-alpha-male. She was pretty sure the word "compromise" was not in his vocabulary.

Her mother put down her part of the ancient weapon she'd cleaned and reached for Mel's hands. "Have you truly forgiven your father and me for not telling you how we found you?"

"Yes, Mama." Mel pulled her mother into her arms and hugged her tightly. The familiar scents of dust and her mother's favorite jasmine perfume comforted her. "I couldn't have asked for better parents."

She'd been rescued from the wreckage of a Prime ship. The only survivor. Her Prime mother had sheltered her infant's body with her own and saved Mel's life.

Mel held her mother away from her. "Besides you and Papa taught me everything I know about the Prime. You gave me my heritage." She grinned. "Now, I'll be able to help you with your work. You'll have an inside source to all their libraries and museums."

Her mother laughed. "Your papa is already making a list of questions for your Wulf. And an even longer list of treatises he wants to find to supplement the ones he has found on the Prime digs."

Her Wulf.

Just the thought sent a shiver down her spine. He was hers as much as she was his. Somehow it seemed only fair. If he were as half as uncomfortable as she'd been in the two standard weeks since she'd left the *Galanti*, he was in deep pain. She felt as if someone had ripped out half her heart and had set fire to her womb.

"Mellie." Her mother touched her cheek. "When you first arrived here, well ... you were angry with the whole situation. With Wulf. Now, you seem more resigned to his mating with you."

"It's the bond, *agape mou*." Mel's father stood in the doorway, smiling fondly at his two women as he always called them. "She is missing him, eh, my little Mellie?"

"Yes, Papa." Tears filled her eyes and she never cried—ever. She blamed the hormones rioting through her blood. Emotionally, she'd been a frigging mess. "I just want him here so we can have this out and do whatever we need to do to move on."

"That means physically mating, Melina. Did you read the manuscripts I gave you on this bond?"

"Yes, Papa." She sighed and shifted in her seat. Just the thought of making love with Wulf had her wet and aching. "I'm restless. I think I'll go into the catacombs and dig some. Work off some of this energy."

Work off the sexual frustration, was more like it.

Her father nodded. "Good idea, Melina *mou*. I'll send one of the Obam workers to call you for dinner."

"Thanks, Papa."

The last sight Mel had of her parents was them embracing. The love they shared glowed like a halo around them in the late afternoon sun. She smiled and wondered if she and Wulf would ever look that way at each other.

From the smaller dome where the dig had offices and cleaned and stored artifacts, she entered the main dome where the living quarters were located. Obam IV had a thin, dry, dusty atmosphere, thus necessitating the domes for a clean, breathable environment. The planet was dying, and the Alliance Space Archaeology Division wanted to record and preserve as much of the early Prime history as explorers in the Milky Way as possible. The theory was that Prime DNA could be found on every planet where humanoid life was found, or had existed in the past. So far, it had proven true. The Obamian population, now living on a more habitable planet in the same solar system, had a trace amount of Prime DNA. Obam IV had proven to be a major way station for the Prime's past exploration of the Milky Way.

Nodding to several of the dig members, she made her way to her room, where she picked up her personal breathing unit, her digging tools, and a laser pistol just in case any of the legendarily large Obam IV rodents, called ROUS for some obscure reason, still inhabited the catacombs. Rodents survived hardily even on dying planets.

"Hey, Mel," called out one of the students. "Need any help?"

"No. Just going to work off some energy on the burial chamber."

The student laughed and waved. "Good luck. It's a bitch of hard rock down there."

Mel smiled. Just what she needed to work up a sweat and sublimate all the hormones battling for supremacy in her body. If Wulf didn't get there soon, she'd be using the self-pleasuring device the military issued to all female officers. She'd never used it before, but she sure as heck was tempted now.

———

Obam IV, later the same day

THE GROUND SHOOK. DUST DRIFTED over her from the catacomb's packed dirt and rock ceiling.

Startled, Mel looked up from the carving she traced.

Earthquake? There'd never been any tectonic activity here.

Another shaking. The metallic support beams and wall liners in the burial chamber moaned as if in sympathy with the vibrating earth. Rocks tumbled off the trash pile to land close to her seated position.

"Better go topside and see what's going on," she muttered. She stood up, picked up her breathing unit, and put it back on. The normally clean, cool underground air was now thick with dust, making it hard to breathe. Besides she'd need it topside. It was an oddity on Obam IV that the underground usually had a more breathable mix of oxygen and nitrogen than the surface. The Prime had somehow set up a natural filtration system, the secret of which was still just that—a secret.

Another shaking. The tremors were too evenly spaced and of equal force for a natural occurrence.

Obam IV was under attack.

But who? And why? This was a dying hunk of rock. The archaeological dig was the only activity on it, and the finds were more of galactic historical value than monetary.

Mel raced her way through the maze of catacombs she knew so well and ran out into the dying light of the day.

Against the orange and purple glow of the setting sun, a large Antarean battleship hovered in the sky. Its weapons aimed at the domes on the planet's surface, decimating them.

"Mama! Papa!" She wound her way among the inadequate cover of rocks and debris toward the two main domes.

There was nothing here for an Antarean raider, not even enough humans to make it worth their while to rape and pillage.

Shocked realization halted her frantic forward motion for a split second. They'd come for *her*. A full-blooded Prime female. Wulf's battle-mate. An Alliance officer. She knew it as surely as she knew that she had to get the people in the domes underground and send out a distress signal for the Alliance to come and rescue them.

Shoving through the broken door of the main dome, she stopped and choked back a cry of horror.

Bodies lay everywhere like broken pieces of artifacts. The Antareans had hit the main dome first—and hit it hard. Keeping an eye on the ship in her peripheral vision, she went from person to person to see if she could find anyone alive.

The ship fired once more, hitting the rock wall behind the dome. Mel dove under a heavy support column, covering her head until the debris shower ended. Cautiously, she crawled out from under the sturdy protection. No moaning. No rustling. No sound but the wind whistling through the holes in the dome and the whining sound of the laser cannon as the Antareans bombarded the area surrounding the domes.

She checked everybody in the dome. No sign of her parents. They must still be in the secondary dome.

Anger, grief, along with desperate hope swept through her mind. The other dome had not been hit as hard. It was protected by a mountain of rock on two sides; her parents could still be alive.

Running from the death and massive destruction in the main dome, dodging and climbing over obstructions, she entered the smaller shelter. Dust devils fueled by the erratic winds of Obam IV whipped through the massive destruction.

Where were they? Moving forward, she tossed debris aside.

Groans came from the rubble. Near the back where the structure had the most natural protection. Hope beat back her despair.

Climbing over mangled support beams, she searched for the source of the sounds of life.

She found her parents under a large metal beam. A sharp cry left her throat. Her mother was dead. No neck had ever meant to be at that angle.

"No-o-o-!" she screamed. Grief coupled with rage almost drove her to her knees. Her heart bled at the loss of her mother. She struggled to calm herself, to shove the debilitating emotion to a place deep in her mind. Later, she would pull out the emotions and succumb to them. If she did so now, she'd be dead also—and wouldn't be able to seek justice on behalf of those murdered.

Another groan told her that her father still lived. His body curled around her mother's. His arms caressed her. His tears drew streaks on her mother's pale, dirt-covered, still face.

Mel knelt by his side. "Papa!" She touched the bloody gash on his head. It was not bad, but the piece of metal lodged in his chest just right of his sternum concerned her. "Let me get you out of there."

Tears welled in her eyes, obscuring her vision. She dashed them away. *Don't be weak, now, Mel.* Later, she could grieve later. Right now, she had to get her father out of here and into the catacombs, a much more defensible position. The cannon no longer fired. The Antareans would land and send out search parties for survivors.

"Go, Melina *mou*." He coughed, frothy blood covered his lips and chin. "I'm dying—and I will not leave your mama."

"Papa, no!" Her tears came back with a vengeance, streaming down her dirty cheeks. "I need you. Come with me." With a strength she hadn't known she possessed, she pulled a large piece of the dome superstructure off him.

His bloody hand reached for her and brushed at her tears. "No crying, Melina *mou*. You can't let them find you. You can't let them ... win." Amazingly, he smiled. "Be strong, Melina. Live well. Mama and I ... will watch over you ... from beyond."

He closed his eyes then turned his bloody face into her mother's hair. With his last breath, he sighed, "Irina."

Screaming her anguish, she threw herself onto her parent's bodies. Seconds passed. Possibly minutes. Seconds or minutes she did not have. She didn't want to leave them, but she had to. All her instincts and training told her to move.

Touching their dear faces, breathing in their familiar scent one last time, a calming warmth stole over her. Their souls had gone to be with their God now. They were safe—no one could hurt them any longer.

Shoving away, she covered them as best she could. She didn't want the Antareans to desecrate their bodies. She would come back and give them a proper burial.

Saying a silent prayer, she left them to check for any other survivors in the secondary dome. She found none.

After leaving the smaller structure, she hurried back through the main room. She packed some fresh food and water—there were other supplies hidden in the catacombs for just such an emergency. She could hide and survive until Wulf came for her, or the Alliance responded to the distress call.

Entering the communications room, which had somehow survived the blasts, she coded the distress call, put it on a permanent loop, and then fixed the equipment so the enemy couldn't turn it off. She hid the machine inside a compartment built into the rock floor of the main dome. Then she set the booby trap. Any lizard-bastard who tried to open it would get an unwelcome, and fatal, surprise.

The Antarean ship was making its landing approach. Because of the size of the ship, they would have to land on the dry lake about fifty kilometers away. Depending on the land vehicles they carried, they could be here in less than thirty minutes. She wanted to be underground well before then; she had traps to arm.

They'd look for her body. Not finding it—they'd search for her. She looked forward to it. They would pay for killing her parents and the innocent scientists.

Someone had told them about her. But who? The rebels wanting to punish Wulf and his family for the treaty with the Alliance? Possibly. But why would the rebels deal with Antareans? No, it had to be someone else. Maybe someone who had it in for her? Hell, she had to have enemies after seven years in the military, who didn't? But she couldn't think of anyone in particular.

Whoever it was had access to her file, or to Wulf's family— or to Alliance and Prime confidential communications.

Another traitor. She only hoped she'd live long enough to tell Wulf. He'd be furious. She smiled grimly—it was nice to know that if she died, he'd avenge her.

Hefting a damaged door aside, she rushed into her room and picked up her military duffle, which she hadn't totally unpacked. Shoving the precious data disks her parents had given her from the Prime ship that crashed with her all those years ago into the pack, she ran into the main dome.

Her last stop before entering a secret way into the catacombs was the dig's cache of weapons and explosives, including the latest in Prime technology: a dart gun which pierced reptilian-species hides. It delivered a lethal poison, killing the bastards instantly. She hadn't asked her father how he had come by it; she was just glad he had.

She holstered the dart gun and loaded ammunition for it, along with some of the explosives into another pack. Slipping out of the dome, she used the natural cover for as long as she could, then sprinted across the open area and entered the catacombs.

She knew the maze of tunnels well, having played hide-and-seek in them as a child with some of the other scientists' children. She'd survive and take out as many of the enemy as she could. She had a feeling the Antarean ship had orders not to leave either without her or proof of her death.

She didn't plan to oblige them either way.

Wulf's personal star cruiser, same day

"GALACTIC ALLIANCE MILITARY COMMAND HAI...LING *Galanti II.*"

"Caradoc, here." Wulf wondered what the Alliance wanted with him. The only radio communications he'd had in the time he'd left Tooh 10 were from his family or Maren and the Admiral with his proposal on shared command for Wulf and Melina.

"Wulf, this is Admiral Nelson. We just got a coded distress call from Obam IV. Captain Dmitros sent it." The Admiral paused and Wulf's stomach clenched in fear. "Uh, Wulf, the scientific expedition has been attacked. By Antareans. We're sending the closest Alliance battle-cruiser, it's about two standard days away. You're closer by more than a day. We thought you should know what you're heading into."

"She's alive—you're sure?" Wulf asked, his throat so constricted he could barely get the words out.

"She was as of a half standard hour ago. She is the only survivor. She gave no indication of her condition. All other attempts to raise her have failed." The Admiral sighed. "She's been trained by the best. She'll go to ground and take out as many of them as she can. Trust in her, Wulf."

"I'll get Melina out of there. I'll update status in ten standard hours. My crew will coordinate with the responding Alliance ship."

"That would be the *Leonidas*. Commander Nowicki will shave every second he can off the trip. He's pushing at full warp speed now."

"I'm sure he is. I hope to have Melina on my ship and en route to Cejuru Prime well before he reaches Obam IV. He and the *Galanti* can handle the aftermath and cover our tail."

"Good luck, Wulf." Admiral Nelson signed off.

Wulf shoved his burning rage into the deepest part of him. Right now, he needed a cool head. He had to get to Melina as quickly as possible. Later, he'd tap into his wrath and kill every blessed Antarean who'd dared to threaten his mate. Not one of the devil's bastards would leave the planet.

CHAPTER SEVEN

Obam IV, twenty-plus standard hours post-attack

The rock wall at her back was cold and damp, the ground beneath her equally so. Hardness aside, it still felt like the softest couch to her tired, aching body. This was the first time Mel had rested since the Antareans had landed and begun their search for survivors. For her.

Taking a drink from a bottle of water, she closed her eyes. With a shaky hand, she massaged her dirty, aching forehead. The rhythmic pounding behind her eyes would not end soon. All her senses were wide open, and had been since the attack on the planet. Until she had either killed all the Antareans, they left, or rescue arrived, she'd have to bear the pain. As long as she was open to the emotions of an approaching enemy, she could outrun and hide from them.

The pseudo-reptilians' emotions were primitive, but pronounced. Hatred was always the easiest emotion to read in most species. It also caused a bitch of a headache.

For now, no one was near. She could afford to take a short rest.

Mel mentally took stock of her efforts over the last twenty standard hours. She'd left the relative safety of the catacombs on several seek-and-destroy missions. Figuring that the Antarean ship had a full complement of crew at one hundred, she'd already managed to take out twenty percent of the scaly, slit-eyed bastards.

Satisfaction temporarily muffled her aches and pain like a warm woolen blanket. At this rate, she might be able to take out half before help arrived.

So far, the enemy hadn't caught sight of her. Odds were her luck would eventually run out. She'd canted the percentages toward her side of the graph by varying the catacomb accesses she used to launch her attacks. Right now, the raiders probably thought there was more than one survivor. It was all a matter of time before her keep-them-defensive strategy failed and they decided to hit the catacombs in an all-out-assault.

She laughed silently. That would be a mistake on their part. In the catacombs, many of them would find death. She'd activated all the ancient Prime traps which still worked, which were the majority. The Prime had built their fortifications to last.

What the Prime claimed, they kept.

A telling point and one which turned her thoughts to the imprinting between Wulf and her. His body, more correctly, his neuro-sensory functions, had claimed her as a child. In his mind, she was his. She knew he wouldn't rest until he had her in his sight and under his protection once more.

Now, whether she'd remain there or not depended upon his approach. She'd been serious when she'd left the message with Admiral Nelson about wooing.

Ansu bhau! Who was she kidding? She could never be apart from him again. Her mind, body and soul reached for him even now. Oh, man, she hurt! Inside and out. The cuts, bruises and muscle pulls would go away with time and rest, but the fiery ache in her gut and loins, the emptiness in her mind and heart, would only be salved when Wulf arrived.

The imprinting was strong. She couldn't deny it existed, no matter how much the rational part of her brain tried. The *gemate* connection reminded her of its needs and wants every single second—and had done so since she'd stepped off the *Galanti* and left Wulf behind.

A low, guttural moan came from deep within her throat. She rubbed an impatient hand across her aching breasts and perked nipples and then pulled the damp crotch of her pants away from her overly sensitized folds. Never having been one to cater to her sexuality, she now had a new respect for her female Prime ancestors. One had to hope that once she and Wulf had come to terms about their future partnership and actually consummated the physical relationship, the drive toward sexual completion would die down to manageable levels.

Forcing thoughts of naked limbs tangled on cool, clean sheets to the primitive part of her brain where it belonged, Mel concentrated on surviving. She reexamined her current situation. The next major offensive? Taking out the Antarean ship. The scaly-skinned bastards would not leave this planet. She'd die before she let them escape justice. If she didn't kill them all, she wanted them stranded on this planet so the Alliance could come in and finish the process.

A loud crash echoed down the tunnel followed by foul shouts. Then a wave of vile-smelling hatred blasted her senses like a photon torpedo.

With a shudder, she ratcheted back her senses. She swallowed the bile that threatened to erupt every time she smelled an Antarean and took a swig of water to erase the taste. After several calming breaths, she widened her sensory probe in small increments so as not to overwhelm her already throbbing head.

The projected energy of the enemy's feelings was strong, almost overpowering. At least two ... no, four, Antareans were near. And they weren't happy. They were furious. Two of them were weakening.

Must have hit a trap. Her lips twisted in a fierce smile.

"Let's party, lizards," she muttered.

Standing, she climbed the rock wall using hidden hand holds disguised as decorative symbols carved into the granite. At the top, she reached a passageway shielded from the lower tunnel by a waist-high curtain wall. On all fours, she crawled in the direction she'd felt the Antareans' presence, near a pretty nasty trap approximately one hundred meters away from her former resting place.

As she crawled, she once again marveled at the ingenuity of the ancient Prime warrior-explorers and the fortifications they'd left on every planet they visited. Every Prime site she'd ever worked on or visited with her parents had similar curtain walls, traps, hidden tunnels, and rooms. The construction was superficially crude, but the underlying technology—air filtration and water purification systems, lights, and other improvements—was evidence of their brilliance. Better yet, the installations still functioned after many, many centuries.

Through her hands-on familiarity with her parents' research, Mel had the advantage over the Antareans. She knew the turf, they didn't.

Thanks, Mama. Papa.

The Antareans entering the catacombs were under a death warrant, whether by a Prime trap or her hand.

A carved marking on the curtain wall indicated she was above the trap. The noises from approximately six meters down confirmed it. A painful hissing reached her ears. The smell of Antarean blood, metallic and fetid, wafted on the gentle currents of the subterranean ventilation system. Once again she mastered her innate revulsion at the smell; it was so thick she could taste it. She wiped her mouth with the back of her hand as if she could erase the nauseating flavor. She couldn't. Only time and distance would banish the foul sensations.

A keening wail and more hisses pulled her back into the moment. She sensed anger. Apprehension. Fear. Resignation.

Mel put her eye to a slit in the wall. Trapped under a fall of sharp, jagged metal bars were two Antareans. Several of the bars had skewered the large pseudo-lizards in multiple places on their thick-skinned bodies. Pulling the bars out was not an option. The bars contained viciously sharp barbs angled such that they would rip out organs if removed. Eventually, the victims would either bleed to death or die of thirst. And what was better yet—they knew it.

Two other Antareans stared at their dying comrades. They couldn't leave; they were caught between the triggered trap and a wall that had sprung into place behind them when their buddies had fallen into the snare.

Without knowledge of the catacomb's secrets, they'd never find their way out.

She imagined them envisioning a slow and lingering death from thirst and hunger. Fortunately for them, she was in the mood to kill Antarean butchers today. Yep, it would be just like shooting rats in a box.

She pulled the Prime-designed dart pistol to do the job. For all intents and purposes, her laser hand weapon was useless against Antareans. Their skin was just like the Erians, their distant cousins in lizard-ness, thick and leathery. It took a much stronger laser blast, such as one from a laser cannon, to penetrate the Antarean derma. And even when a laser managed to penetrate the less thick areas of their bodies, such as a tongue, the reptile-like races could eventually regenerate damaged body parts.

The super-charged dart gun sent titanium-tipped poison darts deep into the lizard-races' dense bodies. It was the perfect weapon. Thank God, her parents had managed to get one for the dig. Their past experiences with the Antarean raids in this sector would save her from fighting hand-to-hand.

She stood up and shot both Antareans, one in the throat and one in the torso. The quick-acting poison released immediately as the darts burrowed into the bodies. The two had just enough time to look up and see her before they fell on top of their more slowly dying comrades.

Her kill tally was up to twenty-four—and counting.

Dropping behind the belly-high wall, she set off in the direction from which the four had come. The safest way to play this game was to keep moving, force the enemy to fall into the traps, and take out any survivors.

Her biggest obstacles?

She had a finite number of the poison darts, considerably less than the remaining number of Antareans. Every shot would have to count.

Also, she'd need to sleep soon. Cat naps wouldn't hold her for long. She'd eventually need REM sleep. At this point, she'd been up for about thirty standard hours. The longest she'd ever gone without true sleep was seventy-two standard hours during survival training. Wulf or the Alliance would be here long before she collapsed—she hoped.

Finding another observation slit in the curtain wall at the junction of two tunnels, both of which were equipped with death traps, she sat down, her back to the cool rock wall. As earlier, she allowed her senses to roam, alert for the enemy's approach. She pulled the water bottle from her pack along with a dehydrated fruit-and-nut bar. She took a drink and forced herself to eat, even though she had no appetite. It was important to keep her metabolism revved; she needed to be fully fueled so she could fight at a moment's notice.

Closing her eyes, she prepared for a short nap.

Pain shot through her body, jerking her away from the wall.

She grasped her right hip and massaged a nagging, burning pain. Had she been shot? No, she'd had no close calls. Did she hit the hip on a sharp rock? Much more likely.

Dammit, she couldn't afford any injuries if she wished to stay ahead of the Antareans.

She looked down. No obvious tears or blood. Must be a bruise.

The pain flared once more, causing her to gasp. This time the sharp ache echoed in her heart and then her head.

The sensation was a strong, rhythmic pulse. Her body heated. Her gut churned with nausea. Shivers of awareness tripped up her spine and triggered a latent memory.

"*At last!*" her body seemed to say.

Working through the multitude of sensations, Mel peeled down the two layers of material that covered her right hip to confirm what everything primal in her already acknowledged.

Her *gemate* marking glowed. Swirled. Sparked with incandescence. Just as it had when Wulf first touched it on the *Galanti*. Just as his rage reached out to her as she'd sped away from him on the *Leonidas*.

He was close. He was angry. *Very* angry. The roiling rage she'd sensed he could produce had erupted with a vengeance. Her mind's eye viewed the Antareans fleeing him and his weapons. He'd seen the domes; he thought she was dead. How she knew this she wasn't sure, but she did.

Now that she realized the pain she felt was his, she worked on getting it under control. Her body and senses had been wide open and searching for him ever since she'd left the *Galanti;* by narrowing the part of her which was connected to Wulf she was able to lessen the impact of his emotions while still monitoring them.

Could he read her just as she read him? Possibly. More than likely—if his own strong feelings didn't override the ability.

She had to try to reach him. The manuscripts her papa had given her had said something about battle-mates having some level of telepathy. She hoped they were correct and not some fantastical legend.

Wulf, I live.

Nothing.

Wulf, I—am—alive. Safe. Calm down. Your emotions are causing me pain.

She concentrated so hard on her message she felt she might burst a blood vessel.

His angry heat turned to icy shock and just as quickly was replaced with a blinding happiness. Reining in his widely vacillating emotions, he sent her what she needed—soothing, almost sensual, warmth. It was as if he'd reached out and enveloped her within protective arms.

She sank against the rock wall. He'd gotten her message. She smiled the first real smile she'd had in days.

Gemate lubha. I'm coming. Stay safe.

Then a surge of energy infused each and every cell in her body. Her heart sped up. Steely resolve steadied her nerves—and Wulf's.

Her Prime warrior readied himself to kill Antareans. To find her.

Re-energized by Wulf's nearness, this would be an excellent opportunity for her to set the explosives on the Antarean ship while he distracted and harried the enemy on the ground.

Yeah, he'd told her to sit tight, but staying safe while others fought was not her style. Besides, the Antareans were far too busy running for their lives from the mighty Prime warrior and his ship to worry about one little planet survivor.

Mel stood up and headed for the hiding place where she'd stashed the explosives. After that, she'd make one Antarean ship into a heap of scrap metal—if Wulf hadn't already done so by the time she reached the surface.

———

MELINA'S MENTAL TOUCH SOOTHED HIM. Against all odds, she was alive. The rusty prayers from his youth had been answered.

Better yet, she seemed relieved that he'd come. The separation had been just as hard for her as it had for him. The fact she could feel his emotions so far away and then communicate with him proved how strong the imprinting was. If it was this strong after only the initial awakening, he could only imagine how closely they'd be connected once they merged physically and were in constant contact.

Primitive instincts told him to get to her, pull her to him and never again let her out of his sight. With only her at his side could he be complete.

But to get to her, he had to go through an unknown number of Antareans.

The molten-hot rage that had been Wulf's constant companion for the last twenty hours subsided. Like an icy armor, his nerves now steeled themselves for battle.

He'd caused Melina pain with his fury. Protective instincts he'd never used before sought his mate, then sent what she needed from him—soothing warmth, stroking and holding her in ephemeral arms until he could do so in person.

Without the potent mix of anger and grief he'd experienced after seeing the destruction on the planet—after he'd thought she'd died—he could now sense his *gemat* sign as it pulsed and swirled in reaction to her nearness. His loins ached with the need to claim her.

Soon. After.

Melina was still in danger. His message of staying safe was instinctive and one she would ignore as beneath her notice. He knew her now. His battle-mate would continue to fight until either the last Antarean *apayebo* was dead or he took her away from this unholy rock.

Guess he'd better even the odds in their favor. Then, he could land and begin his search for his runaway mate.

Eyeing the area around the scientific expedition's domes, he swore. No one could have survived the barrage. Melina must have been elsewhere when the attack occurred. Admiral

Nelson had mentioned Melina's distress call confirmed she was the only survivor. His *gemate* had lost her parents—her friends. She'd been alone, yet she had survived. His pride in her strength and courage increased triple-fold.

But now, she no longer had to fight alone.

Narrowing in on a large group of Antareans attempting to get back to their ship, he swept the ground with a laser cannon barrage, forcing them to run back from where they'd started. The domes.

"Uh-unh, no you don't." His words uttered as a low rasping growl, echoed within the small command area.

Smiling grimly, he swept the domes with a fusillade of laser streams. The living left the collapsing structures and headed for the catacombs.

Now that was absolutely unacceptable. He sensed Melina was in the ancient Prime underground fortification.

He lay down a stream of laser fire across the path of the Antareans, successfully halting their progress. Then he precision-blasted them into subatomic size particles.

"Let's see them regenerate now," he snarled.

His ship swooped over the hills that protected the catacombs before circling back around to take another pass over the valley. He passed over the Antarean ship, sitting on a dry lakebed. Time to take out the *apayebote's* only way to escape.

Just as on his initial approach to the planet, his sensors did not indicate any life forms on board. The Antareans must have been awfully sure of themselves to leave the warship empty. But why wouldn't they be? The only person on Obam IV who would be dangerous to them was Melina—and they'd discount her as a threat. All reptile-like species considered females as biological conveniences and nothing more.

As he prepared to take a strafing run, movement at the back of the ship caught his eye. He made another low, slow pass and spied a small figure. Melina! She placed something inside one of the weapon slots. He sought her mind. She was going to blow up the ship.

"That's my battle-mate," he whispered, torn between admiration for her guts and the desire to spank her for placing herself in danger.

His assumption that she wouldn't stay put had been correct. He shook his head. They'd have a small talk about obeying one's *gemat* in dangerous situations. She should have trusted that he would take out the Antarean ship.

An angry snort flickered through his head. *"You could have said you were going to do it."*

He'd forgotten she was also tuned into him. This telepathic connection would take time to get used to.

She looked up, hands on her hips. *"I'm not helpless. If I were a man you would've expected me to share the load."*

He choked back a laugh.

She waved, then pointed to a large spot made for landing a ship on the top of the hill overlooking the lake bed. *"Land there. I'll make my way and meet you at the catacomb entrance to the plateau."*

"I see it."

He swooped over the landing spot marked with Prime symbols. He'd be able to find the entrance to the catacombs from the markings. The high ground was eminently defensible and would keep his ship safer from attack by any remnants of the Antareans. The catacombs would be deadly to anyone not Prime, or to one like Melina who had studied it. No Antareans would make it to the top without falling into a trap.

It seemed almost appropriate that they'd come together for the first time—and they *would* come together, he was not taking a chance that she'd get away from him again without the final awakening—in a Prime site his ancestors had abandoned over a millennium ago. This site was built in a time when battle-mates were plentiful and the Prime race had been at its most powerful.

After he made love to Melina and tucked her safely away on his ship, then he'd root out the remainder of the devil-blessed *apayebote* who dared to come after what was his.

———

SMILING AT THE COCKY WAY Wulf handled his star cruiser, Mel placed the final set of charges.

Wulf had gotten as many of the Antareans as he could from the air. Those remaining had gone to ground. The next phase would be going after the stranded remnants of the raiding party—stranded, that is, after she blew up their damn ship.

Mel grinned with anticipation. After a short rest, Wulf and she could team up and go hunting. She was certain Wulf wouldn't want to leave any of the Antareans alive. She was just as certain he'd try to cut her out of the fun. But that wasn't going to happen. After all, even he acknowledged she was his battle-mate.

All was quiet now that Wulf had stopped strafing the ground with laser cannon. No Antareans were anywhere near their ship. Wulf had scared them away.

She scanned the sky. Wulf's ship headed for the Prime landing area on the plateau above the catacombs. He should be able to read the signs to the entrance, since she knew the Prime military still used the symbology of their ancestors. Her sojourn through the maintenance tunnels on the *Galanti* confirmed that fact. Many of the traps were similar in nature. He would be fine, plus he could always touch her mind and ask if he needed help. Like that would happen, she snorted with amusement. But he'd learn—eventually. Compromise was a two-way path.

Mel turned back and connected the last firing device. She'd blow the ship by remote once she got to adequate cover.

She needed to get a move on. Surviving Antareans would soon crawl out of their holes and head to the supposed safety of their ship now that Wulf was not pursuing them from the sky.

Shrugging on her backpack, she tightened the straps across her chest. At a quick trot, she headed toward the lakeside tunnel entrance hidden behind a rock wall.

Feelings of hatred swept over her just as a laser shot sent dirt and bits of rock flying around her feet. Without hesitating she broke into a run, zigging and zagging, making herself as small a target as possible. Fifty meters would see her behind the rock wall. She could then reset the entrance trap and be safe from any pursuers.

A shot seared her thigh. She stumbled and fell. Rolling over and up onto her knees, she pulled out the dart gun and prepared to shoot the Antarean who pursued her.

A laser blast knocked the weapon from her hand.

Turning her head, she squinted against the glare of the sun. A dark shadow emerged from behind a pile of rocks. Shock caused her jaw to drop open.

The person shooting at her was not Antarean.

"Parker!"

"Yeah, Parker," said the man with a sneer. He moved to stand over her. "How do you like my new friends?"

"You dickless traitor." Keeping her eyes on his face, Mel scooted away, her injured leg slowing her movement.

His eye twitched.

She rolled to the side just as he shot, aiming for her other leg. He missed, but not by much.

She managed to scramble to her feet, then placed most of her weight on her good leg.

"Damn, I missed." A supercilious smirk twisting his lips, her former nemesis holstered his pistol and stalked her as she limped backwards, toward the rock wall hiding the catacomb entrance.

"I don't need a gun to take you down, now do I?" A heated, ominous glance swept over her body from top to bottom. "Leg hurt much?" He laughed, then licked his thick lips. "You know? I've always wanted to do you over good." His hands went to the zipper on his flight suit. "This is as good a time as any. Killing always makes me horny."

The look on his face was one she'd seen many times as she helped police the galaxy. Sexual depravity etched every line of his face. He would hurt her—rape her—then slowly kill her.

"You come near me, I'll kill you."

"You can try, bitch. Take off your clothes." Parker stopped two meters from her, just out of her kicking range.

"No," she snarled.

"Then I guess I'll have to do it myself."

His smile told her she wouldn't like the way he'd accomplish the maneuver.

His ugly gaze never left her as he pulled a knife from a scabbard attached to his belt.

Consciously, Mel had erected mental walls as soon as she'd sensed danger. Now, she reinforced them. She had to cut off her connection to Wulf and hoped this mental exercise would do the job. She didn't need any lectures or distractions from her alpha-male. All her concentration had to be on winning this fight. Even worse, she didn't need Wulf roaring down the side of the mountain in a berserker rage to save her. She could save herself by using Parker's biggest weakness ... his sense of superiority. And in doing so, she'd prove to Wulf, once and for all, that she was his equal on the battlefield.

Mel backed away until she sensed the rock wall just behind her. This should be far enough away from the Antarean ship. Slowly, she pulled a knife from her belt with her damaged hand.

Parker eyed her move like a cobra watching its prey. "Oooh, a knife fight. This should be fun." He laughed, the sound as sick and evil as his soul.

Predictable Parker. Always so easily distracted, dirtbag.

As he kept an eye on her knife hand, she reached behind her into an outside pocket on the pack and flipped open the detonator for the charges. She pushed the button as she lunged for Parker's knife arm.

Multiple explosions rent the air. The ground trembled. Rocks tumbled all around them. Prepared for the blast and its resulting concussion, Mel managed to keep her balance and forward momentum.

Parker lurched and stumbled as if he'd been on a week-long bender, dropping his guard. "What the fuck?" he shouted.

The dumbass never learned.

Mel slashed his wrist, causing him to drop his knife. Pivoting on her good leg, she swept around and slashed the knife across his throat before he'd even finished screaming at the pain from her first strike.

Blood spurted from the severed carotid and the major vein in his wrist. Parker fell to the ground.

He didn't get back up.

Mel wiped her knife on his pants leg and resheathed it. Checking his breathing, she found none. The knife had sliced clean through his carotid. The traitorous bastard had died too easily. At least she now knew who'd sold her out to the Antareans and led the enemy to kill her parents.

New scents of evil preceded shouts of rage. The enemy had seen her—and they weren't too happy with her over the loss of their only means of leaving the planet.

"Time to go." She retrieved the dart gun then hobbled behind the rock wall and into the tunnel. She stopped only long enough to rearm the death trap.

Weak from her own blood loss and pain, she used the tunnel walls to hold her up as she traveled the path which led to the plateau entrance. To Wulf and safety.

She smiled at the irony of her thoughts. For all her independence, knowing she had a Prime warrior to back her up was comforting. She had no doubt that, even now, if she had to she could defend herself. But why waste the energy and risk further injury when she had a Prime male jonesing to take care of her? Maybe this "mating" deal was a win-win situation.

Of course, she'd never tell Wulf that. His male ego and bossiness needed no supplementing from her. A battle-mate had to have some secrets from her man.

After slowly traversing two levels of tunnels, she realized she wasn't going to make it. She had to sit down. Rest. Wulf would have to come to her.

Looking around she realized she was near the conjunction of two of the main catacomb corridors. She couldn't stop here. It wasn't safe. So far she'd lucked out and hadn't met any Antareans.

But they were near. She could sense them.

Now, how to get to a safe place so she could take down her mental barriers and let her mate know she needed him? To this point, she'd been successful in blocking her close call, the resulting injury, and her exhaustion from Wulf. She'd been fairly sure he'd cut corners, become careless in an attempt to get to her, and she didn't want his death or injury on her conscience.

She'd have to find a place to hole up and then send him a "little help" call. With her hidden and safe, he could methodically make his way to her.

Mel wondered if all battle-mates had had to cater to their mates' over-protective tendencies. She sighed. Just like most male-female relationships, the woman had the harder job in the Prime imprinting. And damn, Mel hated compromise.

Turning a corner, she spotted the markings for an access to another higher path shielded by one of the waist-high curtain walls.

Gritting her teeth, she reached for and found the first handhold with her uninjured hand and began the laborious, approximately six-meter climb. About half way up, her injured hand gave way, pushed beyond its limited capabilities. Only her strong hand and tenacity kept her from falling. She breathed heavily as she hugged the cold stone wall. She was so close to the top, but wasn't sure she could make it the last few feet.

Echoing down the tunnel were the unmistakable sounds of the enemy.

Her senses flew open. Four Antareans heading her way. Fast.

Dammit. She was stuck like a fly in a web on this damn rock wall.

Her strength diminished, she gave in and reached for Wulf. Compromise was better than dead.

"Wulf? Uh, a little help here." She sent him a mental image of her predicament.

"Lubha?" His angry growl reverberated through her mind. *"You're injured!"*

"It's fine. Just tired."

His mental muttering in Prime didn't come across their link as clearly as his growl had, but she got the message. She could almost feel the spanking he promised. She choked back a totally inappropriate laugh. She thought she might just like a spanking—from him. And his growl made her womb ache with need. She must be perverted.

"Ansu bhau, lubha. Get up the wall, woman."

A phantom hand planted on her ass practically shoved her up the rock face. As she struggled over the curtain wall with her last bit of energy and the aid from the mind-body connection, ghostly fingers caressed her bottom as they released her.

Safe, she lay on the rock ledge, gasping for breath as the cavern spun around her. *"Thanks, Wulf."*

A warm caress swept over her back, imparting warmth and strength. *"I'm on my way."*

After several long minutes, Mel dragged herself along the upper path in a belly crawl, away from the sounds of the approaching Antareans. She ignored her injured thigh as it scraped along the rough floor, leaving a bloody trail. She used her forearms to pull her along.

There was a hidden room just ahead. A safe room, her father had called it. It had water and light and warmth. She'd played in it as a child, the perfect, secret hideaway for a young, adventurous girl.

Finding the unique rock glyphs indicating the entrance, she triggered the door mechanism. The sliding panel opened as silently as the day it had been built. She crawled inside and pulled herself upright. Touching a pressure pad, she closed the door and then hit another sensor and turned on ambient lighting.

She limped to a chaise her father had placed in the room and sat down. She shrugged off her pack and let it fall. Pulling it to her side with her good hand, she snagged her water bottle and drank the rest of its contents. Placing her pack and the bottle on the floor next to the day bed, she lay down, carefully arranging her wounded leg, cradling her wounded hand against her chest. The bleeding had stopped on her hand, but her thigh had been traumatized during her crawl. It needed tending. She couldn't find the strength to do it. Wulf would be here soon—he could tend her, he'd like that.

Before lapsing into unconsciousness, she pictured the cross-tunnels, the doorway, and the symbols to access the room.

Wulf's acknowledgment tickled her mind. It was sort of nice to have this telepathic connection. She slipped into a deep sleep knowing he would find her. All was well.

CHAPTER EIGHT

After four frantic hours, ten more dead Antareans, and one minor laser laceration of his own, Wulf finally found the doorway behind which Melina hid. He'd followed her mental directions and then a trail of her blood. The blood scared him. Frequent mental touches told him she was unconscious but alive. It was the longest four hours of his life.

Tapping in the door code that one of his ancestors had programmed almost a millennia ago, he entered the dimly lit room.

"Melina? *Gemate lubha*?"

His worried gaze searched the shadows and found her on a sleeping couch, curled into a ball. He hurried to her.

Clenching his fists at his side, he resisted the urge to gather her into his arms. Instead, he knelt and assessed her injuries. Blood pooled under her from a wound in her thigh; the blood had congealed and there were no signs of continued active bleeding. One small, dirty, bloody hand hung over the edge of the sleeping couch as her other supported her head. She shivered in her sleep. Touching her forehead, he found it cool and dry to the touch. No fever, just chilled. That he could do something about. Glancing around the room, he spotted the room's control panel. He moved to it and uttered a command in Prime. A low hum indicated the ancient heating mechanism in the safe room still operated. The room began to warm almost immediately.

After raising the lighting in the room, he returned to Melina's side. Sitting on the edge of the chaise, he inhaled her scent. No aural evidence of infection. His connection to her measured a steady pulse and normal respirations.

He heaved a sigh of relief. Her injuries were not life threatening. Her sleep was one of exhaustion.

Wulf stroked a lock of silky dark hair from her forehead; her normally neat braid had long since unraveled. She murmured at his touch, then quieted. He edged further onto the couch, needing to touch her. As he massaged the nape of her neck, he wondered how she'd blocked her pain and weakness from him. He'd never heard of such a thing between imprinted mates. It hadn't been until he'd received her call for assistance that he'd realized she was hurt—and even then she'd hidden the extent of it. He would have to have a serious talk with his little warrior about hiding these types of things from him. Her welfare was of great import and not something to be concealed at any time.

A slight gasp and a creasing of her forehead drew him from his thoughts. Touching her mind lightly, he found pain disrupting her healing rest. This was unacceptable.

Spying her pack on the floor under the sleeping couch, he rooted through it and found a field med kit. He emptied it and located a pain medication patch. He placed it behind her ear.

With her pain under control, he set about seeing to her injuries. After injecting a local anesthetic with a pressure syringe, he ripped open some antiseptic wipes and cleaned her leg and hand injuries. The hand wound was minor. He treated it with the healing cold laser she had in her kit, then wrapped it. The leg wound was deeper and would need regeneration so as not to scar permanently. He sealed the wound so it would not start bleeding again then wrapped it in a light pressure bandage. Finally, he gave her a therapeutic dose of antibiotics.

He'd done the best he could with the materials at hand. The sooner he could get her on board the *Galanti*, the better.

Despite her injuries, he had an overwhelming need to hold her close. The skin-to-skin touch of *gemat* to *gemate* had healing abilities. Stripping down to his underwear, he cut off her already shredded pants. He couldn't remove her t-shirt without rousing her, so he left it. The skin he'd exposed would have to suffice.

Carefully, he moved her to the far edge of the couch and then laid next to her, pulling her into his arms, her head lying on his chest, her lips touching the edge of his *gemat* symbol. Her legs tangled with his, her injured hand lay across his waist, holding onto him with a strength belying her injuries. Once settled against him, Melina emitted a sigh of what he could only classify as relief. Her warm breath feathered across his skin. The panic and emptiness he'd felt since she'd left him on the *Galanti* disappeared as he inhaled her scent, absorbed the feel of her. He brushed fervent, light kisses across her forehead. She made him whole.

Melina murmured in her sleep, then nuzzled his neck, inhaling deeply. A shudder went through him. His heart pounded. The primordial need to connect, to conquer and claim his mate in the most basic of ways coursed through him, heating his blood. A low growl reverberated throughout the room. He fought to control his more primitive urges. Melina was in no shape for the type of sex his body desired, no, demanded. His mouth brushed her forehead with the lightest of kisses. He'd waited this long; he could wait for a better time and more conducive surroundings.

"You always smell so good." She murmured against the pulse throbbing at the base of his throat. She peeked up at him through incredibly long black lashes, her green eyes dull with exhaustion and pain. "I hurt."

"I know, *lubha*. The pain medication should take the edge off soon." He brushed away some hair caught in her lashes. "How did this happen?" He lightly touched her bandaged leg. "When I headed for the plateau, you were fine. I saw no Antareans anywhere near the ship." *I would have landed and killed them if I had.*

"It was Parker."

"Parker?" He searched his memory for a split second. "The man you fought at the Tooh 2 resort?" After his brothers' recitation of the incident and his viewing of the resort's security feed, he'd made a mental note to look the *apayebo* up some day. Now, he wished he'd acted on the thought sooner.

"Yeah." She shuddered, then took a couple of deep breaths. "He must've heard about me being Prime from one of his old buddies in Blue Squadron. That kind of news would have swept through the Alliance base. He turned traitor—led the Antareans to me and—to my parents."

Her last words ended on a sob. Her extreme sorrow pierced his heart.

"Where is he?" He forced a calm into his voice he did not feel.

"I killed him," she whispered, her voice filled with the evidence of her tears and so much sadness and regret that Wulf wanted to find Parker and kill him all over again.

He brushed another kiss across her temple and wiped away the moisture on her pale cheeks. He had a feeling his woman did not cry often.

"I'm sorry about your parents, *gemate lubha*." He massaged the back of her neck, feathering her hair through his fingers. The motion soothed him as much as it did her. "I promise none of the raiders will escape me. I just wish—"

"Shhh." Shaky fingers touched his lips. He kissed the abraded tips, evidence of her struggle to survive. "You came as soon as you knew. It's my fault ... I ... I, uh, should never have run from you." She caressed his jaw. Even in her sorrow and pain, she tried to soothe him. He wasn't sure she even realized she did so. Her breath hitched and a slight grimace of pain crossed her face. "I should've stayed, faced you ... faced this bond we have, then gone to my parents to find out the truth."

"I would've come with you. I never would've kept you from the people who raised you. I wanted to meet and thank them for caring for you as if you were their own. They would have been honored on Cejuru Prime."

Her eyes filled with even more tears. She acknowledged his words, his feelings with one small nod. Tracing his lips with one finger, she asked, "Will you help me take them there? To bury?"

Shuddering at her touch, he took her hand in his, gently nibbling her fingers then pressing a kiss into her palm before enfolding her smaller hand within his. "Yes. Their ashes shall be kept in the Caradoc tomb. They are your family, so they are mine."

Melina smiled mistily. "They would've loved that—to be entombed with the most important family in Prime history." She nestled her wet cheek against his chest, her hand idly stroking around his *gemat* marking. She exhaled softly as if the weight of the galaxy had been lifted from her shoulders. Blinking up at him, she whispered, "Thanks for the shove up the wall."

"That is what mates do, little warrior." He kissed the tip of her nose then frowned. "Don't put it off so long the next time."

She chuckled then winced. "Don't make me laugh. It hurts."

"I'm serious, Melina *lubha.*" Moving her hand to cover his *gemat* sign, he tilted her chin up so he could capture her tourmaline-colored gaze with his. He stroked her straight little nose with his index finger then tapped the tip. "You are vitally important to me. We are a team. What hurts you, hurts me."

"That's why I blocked it. I didn't want you distracted." She placed her fingers over his mouth. "No, listen to me. I sensed your emotions as you approached the planet. You were ... well, out of control. When you finally sensed me, you calmed down. I didn't want you to lose the battle-calm because of me. This connection we have is a good one, but it can also be a detriment ... a distraction in the heat of battle. If I need help, I'll ask for it. And I did."

He understood her reasoning. And in a way, he admired it—for any other soldier, but not for her.

"I'm sorry, Melina. We need to touch one another's mind in some form or another at all times, and the need will only grow stronger. I *need* to know you live and are well—or I'll become dangerous to any who cross my path—friend or foe." He shook his head. "I don't understand how you can hide your feelings, thoughts, from me. It must be the battle-mate genes. No other *gemate* can hide her pain or danger from a mate, especially after the initial awakening."

"I've always opened and closed my mind to read sensory impressions." She shrugged. "I just used what I've learned through trial-and-error over the years. Maybe I've built up walls no other Prime female has needed to build." She paused and nuzzled his chest as if she needed to connect with him, even more evidence of the increasing need for them to touch, to bond physically. "I'm used to my privacy, Wulf. I'll probably throw those walls up without even realizing it."

He tucked her head against his chest; her lips rested a mere inch from the *gemat* marking. It pulsed in response, seeking her touch. "We'll have all the time in the universe to figure out how our minds—and bodies—mesh after we get off this planet."

She shivered. He wasn't sure it was because of his words or her physical condition. Touching her mind, he found her shields firmly in place. Damn, she was hiding from him again. He wasn't sure he liked that at all.

"Melina..."

"Is the Alliance sending anyone?"

"Changing the subject? Little coward." He tipped her face up and took her lips in a gentle, nibbling kiss. Her lips remained tightly closed as he sought entrance to the warmth and taste of her. Licking and nipping at her lush lower lip, he muttered, "Open your mouth, Melina. Kiss me as you would a lover."

"I've never had a lover," she whispered, her eyes closed and her cheeks blushing a warm peach color that reminded him of sunsets on his home planet.

Surprise, shock, and wonder swept through him. "Open your eyes, *lubha*." Searching her face, he saw only truth. Her mind was still blocked, but he didn't need the confirmation of her actual thoughts. She didn't know how to kiss a lover. Therefore, she was innocent, a virgin still.

"How can this be so?" He eyed her. "You are twenty-seven standard years old. You've worked and trained alongside mostly men. Are they blind?"

"No, they aren't blind," she hissed, punching him lightly on the chest, just missing his pulsing *gemat*. "I wasn't interested until—"

"Until?" queried Wulf, trying hard not to grin, to roar his satisfaction.

"You *know* when." Her green eyes blazed at him.

Yes, he did know. At the first touch of her in the tunnel on the *Galanti*, something broke open in both of them and had been building ever since—and would continue to do so until their minds, bodies and souls were so tightly interwoven that one could not exist without the other.

He smiled. "Then it is my happy duty to teach you how lovers kiss."

Shyly, Melina buried her face in his chest; this time her

lips brushed over the *gemat* marking. His body hardened as his sex pulsed and throbbed. Everything territorial in him coalesced, urging him to conquer and claim in the most elemental way.

He stifled a groan. He'd tell her about the direct connection between the *gemat* and *gemate* markings and a sexual response once they'd graduated to full lovemaking. He, definitely, no matter how hot the urge to make love to her became, would not take his *gemate*'s innocence in a survival room in an ancient Prime site.

"Wulf, I don't think—"

"Just a kissing lesson, love." He peppered light kisses across her forehead and down to her cheeks. "This is not the time for intercourse. Even Prime warriors have some sense of romance."

"Really?" She grinned. "No clubbing me across the head and dragging me off to your cave for some rousing sex by the fire?"

He laughed. "That would be the Terrans' cavemen, *lubha*. We Prime warriors are much more refined in our approach to mating."

"That I'll have to see." She licked her lips.

He groaned. "Don't tease me."

"What?" Her eyes widened, her confusion evident.

"Licking your lips excites me."

"Really?" She licked them again and waited.

"Really," he muttered as he swept his tongue along the seam of her mouth, tasting her. She was sweet, spicy, succulent—and pure temptation. "Open for me."

She parted her lips on a sigh. He lowered his head and captured the remnants of the soft breath with his mouth. He swept his tongue inside, claiming her as his. No other man had ever had her this way—and no other ever would. She was his. Somewhere deep within his psyche a beast roared.

Mel had never really been interested in kissing any man. The couple of soldiers who had tried had quickly been dissuaded. After several such instances, she'd gotten the reputation as an "ice queen," an appellation she'd encouraged. Thus, no man had ever touched her as Wulf now did.

Instinctively, she realized the imprinting probably had something to do with her lack of romantic interest in other men—and her current, almost urgent, need for Wulf. Without touching his mind, she still registered his overweening pride and joy in the fact of her inexperience. His teasing assurances—and who would've thought the big alpha-male had a sense of humor?—that he would not attack her now, in this cold, sterile cavern, relieved her. She'd only have one first time. She wanted to be free of the nagging pain which currently touched the edges of her consciousness—and be strong enough to meet her mate as an equal partner.

Wulf's firm male lips nibbled at hers. His terse whisper to open up reached something deep inside her mind. He wanted more than her mouth, but was willing to settle for her tongue and lips—for now.

Parting her lips, Wulf's tongue surged inside and immediately claimed every square millimeter. Never one to be acquiescent, Mel mirrored his movements and tangled her tongue with his until he allowed her into his mouth. He tasted exotic. All spice. All male. All Wulf. Her womb clenched, sending moisture to her vaginal lips, preparing her for sex. Inhaling deeply, she took in his unique scent.

The invisible ties connecting them tightened another notch.

Moaning in the back of her throat, her body sought to get as close to his as possible. Her hand rubbed the hot spot calling to her from just above his heart. His answering groan and a not-so-subtle hardening of his body, of his cock, told her the markings which indicated their imprinting played an even more intimate role in their lives.

Wulf's hand stilled hers. With another low groan, he muttered harshly, "I was going to wait to explain but ... *lubha*, if you keep touching me, my mark ... I will not be able to keep my promise about waiting to make you fully mine."

Mel laid her head back on the crook of his supporting arm. "What do you mean?"

In answer, Wulf massaged the area above her right hip—her *gemate* marking. She gasped as pure aching need burned in her loins. Involuntarily, she arched toward him, her hips seeking completion.

"The markings are—" She moaned with need as his calloused fingers gently stroked over her marking with a circular motion.

"My mark. Your mark. They are erogenous zones." Her eyes were drawn to the marking on his chest. It glowed and pulsed with varying shades of yellow, red and orange. "Just another way mates have to pleasure one another."

Mel felt her cheeks redden. "Oh—"

"Yes, oh." He smiled as he caressed her burning cheeks. "Normally, I'd want you touching me that way ... but I promised and—"

"My touching would make it more difficult, and uncomfortable, to keep your promise?"

"Yes." He touched his forehead to hers. Taking her lips with his, he gently and thoroughly kissed her. Breaking off, his voice harsh with arousal, he muttered, "Maybe we'd better wait until later to continue this lesson, little warrior. I find that I want no barriers at all to the completion of our lovemaking."

Mel thought for a second or so. "Does this mean I can't touch you? Kiss you?"

"No, no," he hurriedly responded. "We both need to touch—and to touch frequently. It just means we have to be careful how. Right now, I'm so hard that any more kissing or touching would make it impossible for me to hold back."

"I understand," she whispered against his lips. "I'm wet—and aching. It's as if a part of me is missing. I can't imagine how your, um, penis must feel."

"About the same. It seeks to find its place within you." He traced the seam of her lips with his tongue before pulling his mouth away. Shoving her head gently to his chest, he gathered her hand in his, rubbing her fingers.

Taking a deep breath, he said, "Changing the subject." She smiled. It was nice to have a strong man taking care of her for a change, especially when she could feel the extreme need pulsing from every pore of his body and soul. "You asked earlier if the Alliance was on its way. It is. Both your crew and my crew are headed here. We'll stay hidden in the catacombs until they orbit the planet. I'll pop out to my ship while you rest and send out a coded message as to our position and give them my com unit frequency so they can signal when they land."

"What about the remaining Antarean raiders?" She snuggled back against the arm holding her as they lay face-to-face on their sides. His sudden, sharp intake of air sounded like an angry snake warning prey. One of her legs had inadvertently nudged his fully aroused cock.

"Sorry," she mumbled, blushing with embarrassment. He hadn't been kidding. He was thoroughly aroused, so much so that she could almost feel his penis throbbing within her mind. *Oh, good gods, how will that ... that ever fit?* Her loins pulsed in sympathy, aching for him. "Maybe you had better let me have the chaise to myself?"

"That might be a good idea," Wulf rasped. "Your lush body is far too tempting."

Damn, he noticed how round my ass is. She'd always hated her round bottom; it had attracted far too much attention from male soldiers.

Wulf carefully untwined his body from hers. Lifting her, he placed her on her back then covered her near nakedness with a blanket. No small feat since she was not really that small, even though he kept labeling her so, and she was well-muscled.

"And, *lubha,* don't worry about my size. You will be able to handle my size—you were created for me by the One." He paused. "I love your bottom."

"There will be times you shouldn't be in my head, Wulf," she admonished sourly, not realizing she had dropped her mental shields.

"As I told you, mates need to be in each other's minds so we can anticipate and meet our mate's needs." He stroked her arm, taking her bandaged hand gently between his. "As battle-mates it will be even more imperative that we are in each other's minds so that we can coordinate our fighting."

"Will I be fighting?" Mel asked. She was curious because from what she'd sensed from Wulf back on the *Galanti* and from what she knew of the current Prime culture, she'd thought she'd probably have a battle on her hands to keep her Alliance command.

"Yes." Wulf captured her gaze with his amber one. "Maren—and my brothers—convinced me that as you are a battle-mate and my equal in training and more than my equal in the size of the troops you command that I—and Cejuru Prime—would be foolish not to reestablish the legends of battle-mates' fighting superiority."

"How will this work?" She yawned, fighting the lethargy that suddenly swept over her. Damn, she was tired.

"Lie back and rest." Sitting at her side, he stroked her face. "Admiral Nelson sent the Alliance Military Command's decision on my request that we serve on the same star ship. My ship will be commissioned as an Alliance ship. We will lead Gold Squadron under our joint command as battle-mates on the *Galanti.* Nowicki will captain the *Leonidas.*"

Smiling, she could barely keep her eyes open. "A promotion for Royce? He'll like that, and he deserves one."

Wulf traced the line of her brows, causing her to gasp. "The Prime warships previously under my command will join the Gold Squadron, almost doubling its size. After a period of adjustment, and after we see how the merger into Gold proceeds, the rest of the Prime fleet will be divided between the Alliance and a Cejuru solar system fleet for local security."

"Sounds good." Frowning, she slitted her eyes open. "You don't mind sharing the leadership of Gold?"

"Melina," he touched her lips with his, "because of our mind-body connection, we will automatically share strategies and act as one. What the military chooses to call our reality should make no difference as to how we'll react to situations. Together we will lead the strongest fighting machine in the galaxy. The dregs and refuse that prey on the innocent will run in fear of Captain Melina Dmitros-Caradoc and her battle-mate husband. Our legend will be the basis for song."

From her limited experience and knowledge of Wulf, and Prime males in general, she hadn't expected this open acceptance of sharing power. Was this his compromise? And would it work? Only time would tell.

Yawning widely, Mel muttered, "That's nice," and fell asleep with her mate's lips gently tasting hers.

Wrapping his little warrior in a solar blanket he found among her pack contents, he laid her back against the chaise and tucked her pack under her head—after removing some leftover explosives. He appropriated the Prime-designed dart gun and extra ammo. It always helped to have the proper weapon when hunting pseudo-reptiles.

He leaned over and placed a gentle kiss on her soft mouth. She muttered something unintelligible and wrinkled her nose before slipping even more deeply into a healing sleep. A smile crossed his lips. To think he would wake up to her beautiful face each morning for the rest of their lives made him happy.

"I'm going out to send the message to our ships and reconnoiter. Stay here and sleep, little one," he whispered against her ear. He reinforced his message with a mental touch—her senses were wide open as she slept. She'd be aware of him—and more importantly aware of any danger that might attempt to intrude into the safe room.

With any luck, he and either his crew or hers would eliminate the rest of the Antareans and recover the bodies of her parents and their dig team before she awakened. His mate had more than done her duty since the attack on the planet. She could let him—and others—take care of the cleanup for a change. While what he had told her was true, they would fight side-by-side and be a team of which legends were made, he still intended to protect her as much as possible. She'd have to learn to live with his protectiveness. It was all about compromise.

CHAPTER NINE

Mel awoke and stretched before she recalled the wound on her leg. She groaned, then bit her lip. Damn, that hurt. Rubbing lightly at the burning stiffness, she gingerly swung her legs over the edge of the sleeping couch. She had no idea how long she'd slept, nor how long it had been since Wulf had left to check in with their two ships. A fairly lengthy amount must have passed since she was more rested than she'd been since the attack.

If Wulf had left soon after she had fallen asleep, he should have been back by now. Alarmed that he hadn't come immediately back to her side—which was something she was fairly sure he would've done—she opened up the doorway she'd created in her mind to their mental connection and reached for him.

Fiery red rage blasted her mind. She filtered out Wulf's anger then scanned for information as to his well-being and whereabouts. Dull, throbbing pain. Adrenaline-pumping, pounding pulse. Wulf was cornered, injured and fighting for his life. Through his mind's eye, she recognized the spot. She could be by his side in less than three minutes.

Jerking to her feet, she gasped, then pushed aside the pain. Already her body drew upon her own supply of adrenaline, preparing her for the battle ahead. A battle to save her mate's ass.

Mel grabbed her pack, stuffed the survival gear and the all-important med-kit back into it. Seeking her weapons, she noted the dart gun was gone. Only her laser pistol, her battle knife, and a few of the explosives she'd used on the Antarean ship remained. She shoved the explosives and detonators into the pack and holstered the pistol. She slipped the knife into the scabbard on her uninjured thigh.

Seeking Wulf's status once more, she touched his mind lightly so as not to distract him from his battle with the Antareans.

"I am fine, lubha. *Stay in the safe room."*

Wulf's order was so ridiculous it didn't deserve a response. As if she could stay put while he was in danger.

Mel left the safe room, then dropped to her hands and knees to crawl toward the intersection of three corridors where Wulf made his stand. One of the hallways had a trap which could be triggered, thus cutting off at least one set of the enemy. The other two hallways could also be defended from above.

Over their mind link, she constantly monitored his body's reactions. His pain was bearable; his strength, enduring. He fought intelligently and fiercely, but he had no chance to defeat the Antarean forces from his current position. His back was—literally—up against a wall. He needed her help, even if it were just for a distraction to give him a strategic edge.

She worked her way around to the path with the trap; she wanted to approach it from behind the enemy. It took longer to get there, but her ability to take the enemy by surprise would be greater.

"Wulf. Be prepared for panic from the enemy. I'll be triggering the death trap in the corridor to your far left."

A low rumble sounded in her head. Wulf wasn't pleased she'd disobeyed his order to remain hidden, but wasn't shocked she had.

"We'll be discussing this habit you have of not staying put... Be careful, little warrior. You are my life."

"As you are mine—isn't that what you've told me?" she replied pushing her own anger through their connection. *"I have just as much right to protect you as you do me."*

An amused chuckle ticked her conscious. *"Yes. Thank you for reminding me."*

Satisfied she'd gotten her point across—although she was sure Wulf would still lecture her on staying put later—she grabbed a handy, loose rock, a nice solid chunk of granite from the looks of it, then crawled to the slit in the waist-high curtain wall. Time to take out some Antareans and remove some of the pressure from her Prime warrior.

The filthy lizards had him cornered at the three-way intersection. He was behind a blind of rocks and had all he could do to keep the Antareans from rushing him. So far, he'd managed, but the pseudo-reptiles would soon either get reinforcements or make a suicide run to kill him.

Rising to sit back on her calves, she peered over the wall. The Antareans were fully engaged in their attack on Wulf. Their rears were not covered. She grinned. Major mistake on their parts.

Standing, she dropped the rock on the pressure plate the enemy had somehow managed not to trip. A noise must have given her position away since the enemy laser fire hit just about head level, missing her left ear by mere millimeters and hitting the cave wall. Shards of rock from the near miss struck her cheek as she dropped behind the rock wall before their aim could become more accurate. She swiped at the blood on her face, then smiled. Her rock had done the trick. A groaning, grinding of rock over metal plates indicated that the ancient trap had been engaged. The subsequent cries of horror from the two Antareans in the endangered hallway were music to her ears. Two of the enemy were now lizard-shish-kebobs.

Silence fell over the battle zone. The other four Antareans must have stopped firing in shock—or horror—at what had happened to their comrades.

"*Wulf! Go!*"

"*I'm on it*, lubha."

The dart pistol twanged loudly in the preternatural silence after the trap's triggering. The sounds of return laser fire told Mel that Wulf had not gotten all of them.

"*Dammit.*" She peered through the slit. Wulf had killed only one of the remaining four.

"*Language*, lubha. *I can handle them. You stay hidden.*"

"*Just shut up, Wulf. Be ready for my move.*" An answering angry growl rumbled through her mind. "*Stop growling—and wait for my signal. Be mad at me later.*"

An exasperated male snort had her smiling. Shuffling back the way she'd come, she took another side hallway which would bring her in behind two of the remaining enemy.

If she had another dart gun, it would be easy to take them out from above, but she didn't. Timing would be everything. It would have to be explosives—or her jumping them and slitting their throats.

"*No jumping from six meters and slitting throats. Try the explosives.*"

"*You could be hurt from the resulting explosion.*"

"*Don't worry about me.*"

As if that would happen. She'd assess Wulf's chances of surviving an explosion versus her taking out the enemy with a knife when she got into position.

The echoing sounds of laser fire pinged off the solid rock ceiling of the catacombs. Dust rained down, making the air hazy and hard to breathe. She coughed. Damn, she wished she'd thought to grab a rebreather. Too late now.

She coughed again, then choked as she tried to keep from coughing. The sound would give her away, spoiling her surprise. She halted and took a sip from the water bottle in her pack, then rinsed and spit the grittiness from her mouth. The moisture helped enough to stop the cough reflex—temporarily. She needed to get in position and get this over with, so she could cough all she wanted.

Monitoring Wulf's physical welfare constantly, she reviewed the layout and the relative positions of the enemy and her man. While he had a great defensive position, any move he made to escape the results of an explosion in the close quarters would either kill or wound him seriously.

Neither was an acceptable option.

Jump and knife, it was.

She'd only have one chance at each of the two Antareans in the one tunnel. Surprise only went so far with Antareans. After their initial shock at having a woman drop on them, they would follow their instinct to kill. And they had it all over on her as to size and strength. She could not beat them two-on-one.

Wulf would have to take out the third guy. She would have her hands full.

"Wulf?"

A low angry grumbling was her answer. She laughed silently. He'd read her mind and did not like the plan. At least he was predictable. She must be perverse that his angry, grouchy, mad-at-her-risking-her-life growls made her hot.

"Hot, eh? I'll remember that."

"You do that."

Even though he didn't like her plan since it involved a high degree of risk for her, he was experienced enough in close-quarters battle to know that she had the better chance of taking out the two as he handled the other—with the least risk to both of them.

"Let me know when you're ready, battle-mate. I'll back you up with the two as soon as I dispatch mine."

———

WULF LAY DOWN A BARRAGE of laser fire with one hand as he waited for the closest of the enemy to give him a target for the poison dart from the gun in his other. His *gemate* was due for a lecture—and a spanking. Then he would growl and make her hot. He snorted with amusement. So, she liked his growls. Well, she was in for a lot of them since she seemed to tick him off at regular intervals.

By Balcon's balls, she made him happy. She was the perfect mate for him. Feisty. Intelligent. Fearless. He decided he wouldn't want her any other way. He couldn't even remember why he'd thought he needed a meek, stay-in-her-place gentle woman like most of the women on Cejuru Prime. Not that he still wouldn't worry and lecture, he would; it was in his nature to be protective of his mate. It was a good thing she seemed to thrive on the arguments—and he knew he would love the making up.

Mind on the job, Wulf. I'm in position.

I'm ready whenever you are.

He felt the moment she went over the barrier wall. As she leapt onto the back of one of the Antareans, screaming a blood-curdling battle yell she must've learned from one of her Volusian officers, Wulf leaned around the protective rock wall and shot the throat of the Antarean who had him pinned down. He was on the run as his mark dropped, writhing on the ground in his final death throes. Passing the downed enemy, Wulf held onto the dart gun and dropped his laser. With his free hand, he grabbed his knife and slit the dying *apayebo's* throat for good measure.

Now, to Melina.

Her shout of pain froze the very marrow of his bones. Horror swept through him as blinding pain hit his mate and communicated to him before she shut him out with her infernal mental walls.

In the few seconds it took him to dispatch his Antarean, Melina had managed to slit the throat of the raider whom she'd jumped. But, as he went down, bleeding out from the severed artery, he'd flung her into the rock wall behind them. She'd hit hard and was now on the ground, shaken, injured.

Wulf sensed nothing from Melina. He let loose with a Prime battle cry. The last Antarean had almost reached her when Wulf shot him with the dart gun. The fast-acting poison dropped the filthy lizard instantly, a look of agony in his acid yellow eyes.

Holstering the dart gun, he wiped the bloody knife on the last Antarean he'd killed and then sheathed it in the scabbard on his belt. He knelt over Melina, gently checking her for broken bones. She groaned and muttered something. He let out the breath he hadn't realized he'd held. Now he sensed a low level of mental connection seeping through her mental shields. She was conscious enough to keep the majority of her pain and thoughts from him. No brain damage, then. If there had been, she wouldn't have been able to keep him out. She was protecting him again.

"Melina, love. Open up. I need to assess your health through our connection. I can handle the pain, *lubha*. Let me in, please."

"Well, I'm glad one of us can handle the pain."

She dropped her shields. Her anguish throbbed through him, making him gasp.

"Happy now?"

He didn't know whether to laugh, cry or growl. She might be injured, but her indomitable spirit was still healthy.

"Growl, please. Maybe the endorphins from the resulting lust will make me feel better."

"Melina, what am I going to do with you?" Carefully, he lifted her into his arms, cradling her against his chest.

"Find me a soft regen bed?"

Wulf chuckled and kissed her forehead, breathing in her unique scent. "That's the plan."

Walking back to where he'd tossed his laser pistol, he held her against him with one arm as he dipped to pick up the weapon and reholster it. Then he followed the tunnel leading to the plateau. He wanted Melina within the safety of his star cruiser. With any luck the landing parties from the *Leonidas* and *Galanti* were already on the ground. He'd been making his way back to let Melina know help had arrived and was in orbit when the Antareans cornered him.

"Wulf?" Melina touched his jaw with a stroke of a finger. *"Antarean just around the corner. Just one."*

Wulf drew the dart gun as he carefully lowered her to the ground, leaning her against the wall. He didn't doubt she was correct. Female battle-mates were reputed to taste, smell and feel the enemy well before their men. Peering around the corner, he spotted the back of one Antarean as he peered down another hallway. Wulf took the shot. The Antarean fell, his gasp of shock trailing off into a death rattle.

He reloaded the dart gun and kept it at hand as he went back for Melina. His mate safely cuddled against his chest once more, he approached the plateau entrance to the catacombs. The sound of rock fall, then feet thudding on the packed dirt floor alerted him that they were not alone. He brought the dart gun up, ready for whoever entered the catacombs.

"Wulf, no!" Melina's eyes slitted open as she weakly touched his hand, staying his action. *"It's Nowicki and Huw. We're safe now. I'm really tired. I'm going to sleep now. Don't worry, I'm fine."*

Wulf's eyes teared up, realizing his woman had stayed conscious enough to protect him. Nuzzling some strands of her hair aside, he placed a light kiss on her forehead and murmured, "Melina, you are a gift from the One. I am humbled he chose you as my mate."

A faint amused and very feminine snort sounded in his head. *"Tell me that the next time I don't stay where you put me."*

He laughed.

"What do you have to laugh about, Caradoc?" Nowicki's harsh angry tones sobered Wulf quickly. Melina's former first officer still had a large chip on his shoulder over losing a chance at Melina. Tough.

He sent the jealous man a slitted glare. "My mate said something funny."

"I didn't hear anything." The good captain had a perplexed look on his face.

Huw shouted with laughter. "So, it is true? Battle-mates can really communicate telepathically?"

Wulf nodded and moved past the two men, into the sunlight and thin fresh air of the high plateau.

Huw handed him a breathing unit and placed one on Melina. Her relieved sigh whispered through their link. The rich air lessened her discomfort. But he was still placing her in a regen bed and having the doctor on the *Galanti* check her out. She'd been through a lot the past few days and was a mass of bruises, laser burns and bumps.

"What's he talking about, Caradoc? Melina isn't telepathic," Nowicki said, pulling Wulf's thoughts away from his mate's health.

"But she is." Wulf glanced at his brother. Huw's eyes were alight with excitement and joy for his good fortune. It would have been so easy for his brothers to resent him for finding his *gemate*, but they didn't. "Most Prime have empathic abilities and can read emotions from most other species. We use those abilities to help in battle and even business negotiations."

"Yeah, I knew that," Nowicki admitted, "and Mel always had hunches. She read a battlefield better than anybody. But talking to you with her mind, come on, Caradoc. That's fantasy."

"It's not. Melina is a battle-mate."

"You said that before, back on Tooh 10. Just what the fuck is that?" Nowicki asked, skepticism coloring his every word.

Huw let out an exasperated sigh, telling Wulf his brother was just about fed up with the Terran male's attitude. "A battle-mate is one of the rare *gemates* who can telepathically connect with her *gemat* during times of strong emotions. All *gemat-gemate* couples have some empathy and heightened connections to their mates, but battle-mates go beyond that. In battle, the couple is connected symbiotically. It is said that battle-mates such as Melina also have more heightened awareness in all of their senses."

"It's true, Huw," said Wulf. "Melina could sense Antareans approaching even in her semi-conscious state. She warned me well in advance so that I could defend us."

Huw's mouth dropped open in shocked awe. "You are truly blessed, brother."

"I hope that you will someday find the happiness I have." Both knew it would take another miracle for Huw and Iolyn to find their imprinted mates in the vastness of the universe. He still couldn't believe he'd found Melina.

The two men paced him as he hurried to his star cruiser. "I'm taking Melina to the *Galanti* so the doctor can check her over and put her in the regen bed. Then I will return to help you in rooting out the remaining Antareans. We will also need to recover the bodies of Melina's Terran parents and the other scientists. I have promised Melina her parents will be entombed on Cejuru Prime in the Caradoc family tomb."

Huw nodded. "I'm sure father and mother will approve. Mel wouldn't be alive if the Terran couple had not taken care of her."

"Hold just one damn minute." Nowicki reached for Melina. "I can take her back to her ship, the *Leonidas*. I still have yet to hear from her that she wants to be with you."

Wulf's growl started low in his diaphragm. Huw backed up, his hand over his laser pistol, ready to defend Melina and him.

The atmosphere was so rife with strong emotions—his rage, Huw's concern and shock, and the *apayebo* Terran's jealous hatred—that Melina roused from her unconscious state. Her emerald-colored eyes were dull with pain and exhaustion as her weary gaze swept the scene. Wulf could feel her assessing the other two's emotions and touching his mind to determine where the threat was.

Sighing, her trembling hand stroked Wulf's jaw. "Back off, big guy. Nowicki doesn't understand." She struggled to sit up within his cradling hold.

"Stay still, little warrior." His voice held a mixture of love, amusement, and concern. "You are hurt. Weak as a she-kitten."

"This she-kitten has claws." Melina shot him a look filled with amusement. Turning her head toward the stubborn Terran, she said, "Royce, I go where Wulf takes me." Soothing the throbbing muscle in Wulf's jaw with a stroking finger, she smiled. "Although I find I have a hard time staying put."

Wulf laughed, throwing back his head. His joy at his mate's sauciness filled him, chasing away his anger. He engulfed her stroking hand within his and brought it to his lips for a kiss. "We'll work on that, eh?"

"Sure." Melina attempted one last smile before she slipped back into unconsciousness.

"Melina? *Lubha*?" He growled in a low continuous rumble as he hurried into his ship. This was not a healing, restful sleep. Her mind was filled with pain, exhaustion, grief, hunger, and images of bloody scenes from her recent battles. She needed the blissful, untroubled sleep a regen bed would provide in order to recover her strength.

Over his shoulder, he shouted. "Huw, take over for me. Find the rest of those *apayebote*. I'll be back just as soon as I get Melina settled and am assured of her health."

Huw's response, if any, was cut off by the closing of the hatch.

Wulf settled Melina into the co-pilot's chair, buckling her in. His worried glance flicked toward her as he went through the procedures for a planet-takeoff. She was too still.

Touching her mind, he found no walls. She was not conscious enough to keep him out. That worried him deeply. Yet, her life signs were strong. She would be fine once she spent some time in a regen bed, he told himself.

"*Galanti*, this is Wulf. Have the doctor meet me in the shuttle dock with a regen bed. My *gemate* is injured." He didn't want any delays in getting Melina the medical attention she so desperately needed.

"The doctor has been advised and will meet you, Captain," Lt. Commander Dakkin, the ship's chief communications officer replied. "Safe trip up, sir."

"See you in a quarter hour." Wulf took off, plotting the shortest intercept course for the *Galanti*.

CHAPTER TEN

Same day, on board the Galanti

Mel awoke with a suddenness that had her gasping for breath.

"Mel? Are you all right?" Iolyn's concerned voice drew her attention to the side of what she realized was a portable regen bed. Wulf's brother sat beside the medical unit, in a black leather chair with a data pad on his lap.

"I'm fine. Something woke me." She lifted her head and swept the room. First impressions were of austere pale gray walls, subdued lighting, and a huge bed on a dais, covered with a black spread made of some subtly shiny fabric and canopied with black and silver-gray drapery. It wasn't any place she'd ever been before. "Where am I?"

"Wulf's quarters on the *Galanti*." Iolyn placed the data pad on the floor, then stood and approached the regen bed. He fiddled with some dials, then raised the clear dome allowing her to sit up. "He didn't want you in the medical unit. He wanted you to have complete quiet and privacy while you healed and rested."

"He wants me in his bed, Iolyn," she said drily. "This is the closest he could get to that goal until I was healed."

Iolyn chuckled. "Yes, you've figured him out." He tapped the com badge on his chest. "Let me call one of the doctors in to check on your progress."

She reached out and stilled his hand before he could tap it again and send a message. "No. Don't. Something is wrong. Something woke me from the deepest sleep a regen bed can generate, Iolyn. What does that tell you?"

A frown crossed his brow and he reached for his laser pistol. "*That* tells me that Wulf's battle-mate senses danger."

"Exactly."

"Let me call for security."

"No. We don't know who we can trust."

Iolyn emitted a low, grumbling growl. Unlike Wulf's growls, the sound did nothing for her. "The crew is loyal to Wulf and all the Caradocs, hand-picked from the oldest family lines on Cejuru Prime. As of now you are one of us, you are safe here—or should be. But I can't dispute your senses. You've been right too many times."

"I know this is hard for you, but at this moment, I only trust you, Huw, Wulf, and Maren."

"With Maren on Tooh 2 and Huw and Wulf are on the planet—" Iolyn replied.

"—I only trust you and me. I'll trust no one on this ship until I've had the chance to meet and scan them." She kicked off the covers, then realized she was naked under the sheet. "Damn, don't look."

"Too late." Iolyn turned his back. "And we won't tell my brother that I saw anything."

"He'll know anyway. He'll see it in my head." She sighed. "Find me something to put on, please? I can fight nude, but would rather not."

"Right." He picked up a shirt from the back of the chair where he'd been sitting and thrust it at her behind his back. "Here's one of Wulf's shirts. He ordered clothes from the fabricator for you, but they haven't been brought up yet."

Mel held the soft, woven t-shirt to her face and inhaled. Wulf's scent was all over it. Like the shirt he'd given her the last time she'd been on the *Galanti*, the smell calmed her. Smiling, she shrugged the shirt over her head.

There was no residual pain with her movements. She glanced at her hand. Totally healed. Raising the shirt, which reached her knees, she examined the leg wound Parker had inflicted. It was starting to scar over. She flexed her leg and was happy to feel no weakness or pain. She'd do.

"You can turn around now."

"All in working order?" His concern washed over her in waves.

"I'm fine. As good as I was when I fought Parker on Tooh 2." She smiled to underline her words.

"That should be more than good enough." Iolyn returned her smile, then frowned. "I feel the danger now. It's close—but I can't tell how many are coming."

"Two. And they're trying to get through the outer door's security right now." Low rhythmic beeps could be heard through the closed bedroom door as the two attempting to gain entry cycled through various code overrides.

Mel glanced around the very masculine and sterile room. There were three doorways, one was to the main room of the suite. "Where do the other two doors lead?"

"Closet and bathroom." Iolyn angled his head to the third door. "That's the only way in and out of the bedroom. Wulf felt this was more defensible than the medical unit, also."

Had Wulf anticipated a problem when he'd left her on the ship? Or, was he just cautious? She'd bet on the latter.

"Okay, this is what we'll do." Mel moved to the large bed and pulled the raw silk coverlet back. Piling up some pillows as if she slept in the middle, she then pulled the silken spread back over them. "They're here to kill me—and whoever is guarding me. I'll go into the bathroom and you can hide in the closet. We let them get into the bedroom and then we take them out. Stun or wipe?"

"I want to say wipe." Iolyn snarled. "But my brother will want to question them."

"Stun it is, then." Mel held out a hand. "Got an extra gun?"

"Take mine. I can get one from Wulf's closet." He headed for the door leading to the closet. "I can't read your mind, Mel as Wulf can. What's the signal to take them out?"

"Why when they shoot at the lumps in the bed, Iolyn, what else?" Her lips twisted into a grim smile. "That should make any action on our part justifiable."

"Works for me." He entered the closet. "Oh, and just to make it clear, no one was supposed to approach this area of the ship without Wulf's explicit permission, so any action we take will be valid." He shut the door, leaving it open just a crack.

Mel entered the luxuriously appointed bathroom and looked longingly at the large marble tub. Damn, she'd love to soak in bubbles for a whole day. Maybe later. She vocally ordered the lights off and cracked the door so she could see the doorway into the room. The assassins were close. She could almost feel the change in air pressure as they opened the door from the outer corridor into Wulf's quarters.

It seemed like forever, but finally the door into the bedroom opened with a low whoosh as it slid into the recess in the wall.

Two men entered and approached the bed.

Dumbasses. They should've shot from the doorway. Obviously, amateurs. A professional assassin would have shot first.

The lead man aimed at the bed and let forth a full, what would have been, killing blast.

Simultaneously, Iolyn and she hit the two men in the room with stunning blasts to their torsos. One fell onto the smoldering bed, smothering the danger of fire with his body; the other toppled to the floor.

"Check the outer corridors to see if anyone else is lingering around," Mel ordered as she left the safety of the bathroom and approached the downed men.

"On it." Iolyn paused and checked to make sure the men were truly unconscious before he left the room.

She heard the outer door open, then close and lock. She kept her weapon on stun and aimed at the two downed Prime soldiers. They were harmless for now, but the stun would eventually wear off. They needed to be restrained. Since the bedding was ruined, it could be used to bind the men.

Placing the laser pistol down, Mel searched and found a knife in Wulf's bedside top drawer. What a coincidence. That was where she always kept her extra knives. She grinned and made a mental note to let Wulf know that great tactical—or paranoid—minds thought alike.

After cutting several long strips from the strong silken fabric, she bound both men, hand and foot, and then gagged them after making sure they were breathing easily. Wulf couldn't interrogate dead men.

The attacks by the rebel faction from Cejuru Prime worried her. She didn't think the Caradocs and Maren were taking them seriously enough. Now that she had a vested interest in the survival of Wulf and his family, she'd investigate the group herself. New eyes and a more objective viewpoint might shed more light on the rebels' true motivations. She just didn't buy the keeping-the-blood-pure argument that the traitors Ullyn and Prolow had fed her in the engine room on her last visit to the *Galanti*.

The sound of footsteps had her snagging the laser pistol from the bedside table and aiming it toward the bedroom door.

"Mel?" Iolyn's voice called out. "I'm coming in."

She relaxed and laid the gun back down. "It's okay, Iolyn."

He peered around the doorway. "I see you have everything under control." His amber gaze—so like Wulf's—

swept the shredded bedding. "I never did like the all black-and-gray theme my brother had for this room. You'll want to redecorate, I'm sure." He winked at her.

"I'm not much for decorating. It wasn't something we were taught at the academy." She laughed. "Did you see anyone lurking out there?"

"No one. It seems the crew is following the directive Wulf issued before he went to the planet."

"So, how many more rebels do you think there are on board?"

"No clue. There shouldn't be *any*." Iolyn dragged his fingers through his short black hair, his lips thinned in anger and frustration. "As I mentioned before, this is a hand-picked crew. After the last time, Wulf wasn't taking any chances with your life, since he hoped this would become your Squadron's flagship." He grimaced and looked away, guilt and anger pouring off of him. "I wasn't supposed to mention about the ship..."

"It's okay, Iolyn," she reassured him. "You didn't let the cat out of the bag. I know what the Admiral and Wulf planned. I don't have a problem sharing command with Wulf on this ship. It's better than him hiding me on Cejuru Prime to turn out babies every year. It's Wulf's compromise—and for a Prime male, I am sure it is a major concession on his part—and I'm willing to meet him on it."

"That's a relief. Huw, Maren and I had tried to prepare him before he met you the first time, but he had a very narrow view of a *gemate's* place in his life."

"I know." She laughed. "I think the battle-mate thing convinced him I'd be of more use next to him than on the home planet getting into trouble."

Iolyn smiled. "Yes, alone you could get into all sorts of trouble. Look at the situation we're in now. He was pretty sure you'd be safe here with me looking after you and everyone else forbidden to enter the room until he returned."

"So, no doctor looked me over?" She was curious as to how far Wulf would go to protect her.

He shook his head. "No, the doctor *did* attend you. Wulf wouldn't have let you go untreated. But he only allowed the medical team to examine you while he was still on board. I was under orders not to let the doctor back in unless you were in severe distress. He planned to be back before you came out of the regen bed."

Sounded as if her overly possessive alpha-male Prime warrior was still a tad bit over-protective. "Um, who stripped and cleaned me up? The medical team?"

Iolyn let out a bark of laughter. "Uh-uh. No one touched you any more than necessary to examine you. Wulf took you into the bathroom and carried you into the shower and cleaned you up himself. Your old uniform is history in the recycler. He personally uncovered only the lacerations, wounds and bruises he wished the medical team to treat."

"Are all Prime males so possessive?"

"Wulf is. Most Prime males allow their women to be examined for medical reasons without being present." Iolyn shrugged. "Give Wulf time. He just found you." He paused then added soberly, "He's afraid to lose you."

She smiled at the earnestness in Iolyn's voice. He wanted his brother to be happy and her to be happy with his brother. "Don't worry so, Iolyn. I'm not going anywhere. And Wulf likes to growl, and I like it when he growls. Think of it as ongoing foreplay."

He choked back a laugh. "I'd rather not think about that at all."

Movement from the floor halted her next comment.

"One of our friends is rousing. Think they'll tell us anything?" she asked.

"No. They won't." Iolyn kicked at the one on the floor. "This one is a second cousin of ours. The one on the bed is a cousin by marriage. As of now, they are traitors. They swore oaths to fight the enemy of the Prime and, now, the Galactic Alliance. They have violated both oaths. They know under Prime law they'll be executed for their treachery, so why would they tell us anything?"

"For leniency, perhaps?" She stared at Iolyn, willing him to work with her on this.

"Leniency? Maybe the Alliance would allow such—and if Wulf asked, perhaps the Prime Council would also." Iolyn paused. "But Wulf won't be lenient. Ever. Don't ask him, Mel. Not even for you would he spare the men who would've shot you as you slept. They have not only dishonored the Prime as a whole, but the Caradoc family in particular."

Okay, so he wasn't going to work with her on this. Damn. Too bad her telepathy only worked with Wulf.

"You know what this means, don't you?" she asked.

"No."

"It means we don't know how many more there are on board. You and I can't go around the ship, questioning each and every crew member without opening ourselves up for attack. If there are others, they'll come to find these two—so I have to hide somewhere the enemy won't find me—just until Wulf returns. Then he and I can go over the ship and root out the other traitors, with you and Huw covering our asses."

"I agree. So, where do we hide you?"

Mel waved him into the main room of Wulf's quarters. Better not to have this conversation around the enemy just in case they got loose before Wulf returned and all this was brought into the open. She followed him out and closed the door into the bedroom.

Speaking in low tones, she said, "I'll hide in the maintenance tunnels. Preferably between the laser trap and the poison gas trap near the engine room entrance. Those are the two deadliest traps on board. No one would attempt to get to me through them. Wulf can come get me when he returns."

"I can call Wulf back now," Iolyn offered.

"No, if you use open communications, someone could monitor. We want any other rebels to think I am still locked in this room." Mel pinned him with a stern look. "*And* you have to go about your business as usual."

"Won't they wonder why I'm not guarding you?"

"Did anyone know about that order other than Wulf and you?"

"No, only Huw, and he's with Wulf."

"Then the crew will think nothing of seeing you out and about doing whatever you normally do. The door will be locked, and the area around Wulf's quarters will be off-limits per his previous orders." Mel frowned. "You'll need to watch your back, too. Ullyn and Prolow would've killed all of you that first time I boarded the *Galanti.*"

"I'm going into the tunnels with you." He held up a hand as she opened her mouth to protest. "No, Wulf would kill me if I left you alone. And any other traitors will just ... well, they'll just have to wonder where we and their two murderous friends are."

"That'll drive them nuts." She looked longingly at the closed door and thought of the now destroyed, comfortable-looking bed. "Can we find something comfortable to sit on? That tunnel is cold and hard. Plus, some food and drink would be nice. I'm starved."

Iolyn smiled. "I can arrange that. We can enter the tunnel from Wulf's closet. It is his emergency exit. Wait here, I'll be back as quickly as I can."

"Be careful. I'll contact Wulf—light a fire under him. Maybe we won't have to be in the tunnels any longer than it takes for him to get from the planet's surface to the ship."

"How are you contacting him?"

"How do you think?" She smiled and raised a brow at him.

He stared at her with open-mouthed awe. "Does the battle-mate connection work so far apart?"

"It does. I sensed him as he approached Obam IV. I suspect that as long as we're in the same star system..." She shrugged. "Of course, he was in a rage and just pouring emotion into the atmosphere. But since I'm stressed and really, really want him here, I think I can manage it."

Iolyn was speechless. His mouth moved and his eyes were moist with the strength of his emotion.

"It's okay, Iolyn. I know that I'm something out of the current Prime milieu. You'll get used to me."

He came to her and pulled her into his body and hugged her. "You are a miracle, dear sister. Thank you for staying safe so my brother could find you."

Embarrassed by his emotional response, she shoved at his chest. "Go. Find me some food and something to drink. I'd kill for a soft drink. I'll hold down the fort."

He nodded, then left, locking the door to the outer hall behind him.

As she sought to touch Wulf's mind, she prowled the outer room of his quarters. Like the bedroom, its decor was uninspired. It had basic, utilitarian furniture: one couch, two chairs and a low table. Everything was black fabric-covered with silver metal trims and accents. A dark wood—or maybe it was an ebony stone of some sort—bar with various liquors on a mirrored shelf was featured in the corner of the room. In the other corner of the room stood a shelving unit with some books and trophies from various sports she knew were Prime in origin but had never seen played.

Maybe she could do better in decorating than Wulf; how hard could it be? Gods, was she thinking about getting all domestic and nesting? She shook her head. Her crew would never believe it. She was so undomestic she had to hire a professional shopper to buy her off-duty clothing. And cooking? Forget it. She used to help her mother make Greek food, but she mostly chopped and blended. Wulf wasn't getting much of a mate.

Skirting the bar, which, she found, was made of an ebony-colored, striated stone which gave the impression of wood grain, she found a small cold unit and opened it. *Eureka.* Juice. She pulled out a bottle of something that looked like orange juice and opened it. Taking a whiff, she found it to be exactly what it looked like. She drank it down in three gulps.

The sugar surge raced through her body almost as soon as the juice hit her stomach. A cold, masculine-tinged rage hitting her in the center of the same organ followed quickly on the heels of the sugar high. She'd gotten through to her *gemat.* To say he wasn't happy was more than an understatement.

"Wulf? What's wrong?"

"Melina? You should be asleep."

"Don't equivocate. I'm awake, and feel your rage. What's going on?"

"We found the bodies of the scientists."

"They were dead, Wulf. I checked. I would never have..."

"No, lubha, *you wouldn't have left anyone alive to be butchered. The animals desecrated the bodies, that's all. It made me furious. I am sorry my rage awakened you from your healing."*

"You didn't."

"I didn't what, love?"

"You didn't awaken me. The rebels coming to kill me awakened me."

Wulf's roar of rage swept through her mind like the shock wave of an ionic blast. Maybe she should have worked her way into the explanation instead of just dumping it on him. He wasn't taking it well at all.

"Wulf. Darling." Darling? Wow, that had slipped out so easily. She blamed the snarling rage on her behalf. It demonstrated his love for her and made her hot. No one had ever loved her—or cared about her well-being—as completely as Wulf. *"I'm fine. Iolyn and I took them out. Calm down,* gemat. *You're giving me a headache."*

She repeated her words and endearments until the roaring in her head settled to a low, rumbly growl. Damn, but she liked his growls.

Iolyn entered the room with two packs. He raised an eyebrow, questioning if she was ready. She held up one finger. He nodded and entered the bedroom, presumably to open the secret entrance into the tunnels.

"Melina, you are truly fine?"

"You can tell. Touch my mind, and through it, my body."

Soft strokes feathered over her. She shivered at the gentle, loving touches. She could've sworn his relieved sigh rustled her hair.

"I'm coming back to the ship. Stay safe."

She caressed his jaw in her mind and knew he felt her when his low, sexy groan tickled her consciousness. *"Iolyn and I will camp out in the maintenance tunnels near the engine room where you first met me. We'll set the traps."* She sent him images of her and Iolyn resting on camp bedding and pigging out on junk food.

Wulf's laughter tickled her mind. *"I love you,* gemate lubha. *I'll be there soon, and we will seek out any others who might harm you."*

"That's the plan, my love."

Iolyn entered the outer room. "You done yet?"

"Yes. Wulf is coming. He knows where to find us."

They entered the bedroom. Iolyn held a finger up to his lips, signaling her to be quiet. Mel noted that he had moved both the rebels to the bed, covering them with the remnants of the bedspread. He'd also blindfolded them.

Entering the closet, they shut the door. "You can set the traps after we get between them, can't you?" she whispered.

Iolyn held up a small computer pad. "This will do the job. And I'm using a one-time set of codes. Only Wulf's override codes can shut the traps off."

"Good. Let's go picnic. I'd like to catch a quick nap before

Wulf walks me all over this ship, seeking out any other traitors."

Iolyn laughed. "I'm betting he has other plans before you do that."

"What could be more important than finding any other traitors?"

Iolyn just winked and said, "Think about it."

Mel's burning cheeks were her only answer as Iolyn boosted her up and into the tunnel access.

CHAPTER ELEVEN

Wulf, along with Huw, entered his quarters immediately after making sure the landing party secured the bodies of Melina's parents and the scientists in an empty shuttle bay. The few Antarean prisoners taken were escorted by ship security to the containment cells on the lowest deck. He would interrogate them personally later, much later. Let the apayebote stew for a while.

Eventually, the Prime would turn the Antarean prisoners over to the Alliance for justice, since that was the way things were to be done under the new treaty. The captured Antareans would never see the light of day again—they had attacked and killed innocent Alliance civilians. Even the more liberal Alliance didn't allow murderous raiders to escape justice. It was one thing the Prime could truly admire about the Alliance: Justice was swift and met the crime.

Wulf stalked through the outer room to his bedroom. Even though he knew Melina had gone to ground with his brother in the tunnels, a sudden stabbing of fear pierced his subconscious, causing him to reach out to her, to check on her safety. He touched her mind gently. She was safe. He drew in one calming breath and let it go.

He'd be with her soon, but first he had to deal with the two who would have hurt her. He glared at the two lumps lying on his disheveled bed; they moved like two she-cats in a bag.

"Want me to see who they are?" Huw asked, a fierce frown on his face.

Wulf nodded, his jaw clenched from a combination of anger and disgust. No matter who they turned out to be, they were related to some of the most prominent families on Cejuru Prime. Disappointment tasted bitter in his mouth. This time the emotion was aimed at himself. He'd hand-picked this crew, wanting only a safe, secure crew surrounding his *gemate* warrior. He'd failed her.

Huw pulled the shredded coverlet off the two men and then turned them over. Pulling off the blindfolds, his brother left the gags. Time for talk would come later. Right now, he just wanted to see who'd betrayed him, betrayed his mate. Huw's gasp of shock echoed his own. Ensign Donte Caradoc, the son of his father's cousin Darga, and Engineer's Mate Regin Twiller, the husband of his cousin Mara, lay blinking against the brightness. Stun burns on their torsos bore witness as to how Iolyn and Melina had subdued them.

A flash of murderous rage burned away his bitter disappointment.

Turning to Huw, he found his brother was as angry as he. "Throw them in the containment unit."

"With the Antarean prisoners?"

The bodies on the bed moved more erratically at Huw's words, muffled cries escaped around the confines of the gags.

"Yes." Wulf turned away from the obviously terrified traitors. "I'm going to retrieve my *gemate*. I want them out of here, away from her." He walked toward his closet and the hidden escape tunnel. "Destroy the bedding and have the bed made up freshly. I don't want anything that touched those two touching Melina."

"Wulf," Huw called out.

He paused at the closet entrance and turned. "What? Weren't my instructions clear, brother?"

"Putting them in with the Antareans might not leave them in a condition to tell us anything about who sent them—and about any others who might be on the ship." Huw paused. "I suggest moving them across the corridor to my quarters, then Iolyn can help me guard them until you are ready to interrogate them."

Wulf muttered every Prime swear word he knew. He'd let his anger and guilt color his order. Huw was correct. There could be other rebels on board. As much as he would like to kill these two—and putting them in with the Antareans would be a death sentence—he needed to know more about what they'd intended. Melina's future safety—and that of his family—might turn on the knowledge he could gain from these two. He couldn't let his emotional response to their perfidy rule his actions now.

He nodded. "You are correct, Huw. Thank you. I let anger rule my tongue. I'll send Iolyn to you as soon as I have Melina in my arms."

Huw smiled. "I felt your rage, and share it, but knew you would regret it later. Go, get Mel. I'll remove all traces of these two from the room."

Wulf's smile grew shark-like. "As for these two, let them think about the fact that if they don't answer my questions, and fully, they *will* be put in with the Antareans."

He entered the tunnel through the hidden entrance. He could have entered through the engine room, but the fewer who knew where Melina had hidden, the better. Who knew when she might have to resort to the hiding place again?

Quickly covering the six levels between his quarters and the engine room maintenance tunnel, he stopped just before the first engaged trap. He pulled out his data link and connected to the ship's main computer, then entered his override codes. Scrolling to the screen containing the engine room tunnel traps, he shut them down.

Wulf skirted the corner and hurried through the ten-foot-long trap. Iolyn and his *gemate* were another ten feet past the trap. His brother sat on the floor with a blanket-wrapped Melina on his lap. Her head nestled on Iolyn's shoulder. She was asleep, lines of exhaustion and lingering pain creased her forehead even in her rest.

He fought the possessive jealousy that threatened to overtake him. This was Iolyn—and he trusted him.

Spotting him, Iolyn held a finger to his lips. His gold eyes glimmered with relief at Wulf's appearance. "She just fell asleep. One moment she was telling me stories of a pirate raid on Centauri Sigma that she and her squadron had cut short and then she was out." His brother smiled down at Melina. "She was worried about you. She couldn't touch your mind once we were in the tunnels."

"I've taken a page out of her book and learned how to shield." He bent down and lifted her from Iolyn's arms. All the tension that had built since she'd told him of the danger vanished at the feel of her within his arms. He inhaled deeply, calming himself with her unique scent now underlain with his from his shirt and his shower gel. "I didn't want her to touch my mind and see her parent's bodies. The bastards ... well, you know what Antareans do."

Grimacing, Iolyn stood up and stretched. "So does she, brother. She's seen it firsthand. You can't protect her from everything."

"I can try." He rubbed his cheek against Melina's silky black hair. She'd left it down; the silken tresses lay in waves over his arm. She mumbled in her sleep then turned her face into his chest and nuzzled him. A sigh followed by a slight upturn to her lush pink lips pleased Wulf. Even in her sleep, she recognized him.

"I'll head back to my quarters through the tunnels. Huw has moved the two rebels to his quarters. You and he will stand guard until I can question them."

The two paced side-by-side through the tunnel.

"They won't talk, Wulf. They know they are dead men." Iolyn's glance swept over Melina. "She'll want to help question them. You know she has abilities which will help determine if they lie or not."

"I don't want her near them." His mouth tightened.

"She'll insist. After what Huw and I have told you—and now that you've seen her in action first hand—you should realize that she can handle it. She isn't afraid of Donte and Regin. She knew before they even broke in that danger approached. She put together the plan to stop them. She'd not thank you for cosseting her."

Wulf sighed and rubbed his cheek against the top of her head. "You're right... I know you are. I seem to be letting my fears for her rule my thoughts."

"She won't thank you for that, either," Iolyn said with a chuckle. "In fact, she'd probably hand you your ass if you suggested she needed protection from the likes of those two."

Wulf snorted back a laugh. "Yes, I'm sure she would try." He brushed a kiss across her forehead and smiled when she wrinkled her delicately upturned nose in response. "She *will* be an asset in the questioning of Donte and Regin. I will ask her if she wishes to help."

Iolyn led the way up the ladder leading to the next level. "By the way, she thought you might want to parade her by the whole crew to seek out any other traitors."

"That's not how I wanted her to meet her new crew, but it can't be avoided now, not after Donte's and Regin's betrayal." He handed Melina up to Iolyn then climbed the ladder and immediately took her back into his arms. "I want to bring some hand-picked members of her squadron onto the *Galanti*. She'll feel better having people she knows around her—and it will make it truly an Alliance command ship."

It would also make him more comfortable, knowing she had loyal allies he could trust with her safety when he could not be at her side.

"That's a good idea, brother. Mel told me the only Prime she trusts are you, me, Huw and Maren."

Wulf's mouth tightened. He was angry that his mate should feel unsafe among his, and her, people. "She is correct, but for two—she can trust Mother and Father. As for the rest of the family and the rest of the population of the home planet, I'm afraid we must approach it on a case-by-case basis."

"Father will be devastated at this treachery."

"No, Iolyn. He will be coldly furious—as I am."

———

WULF LAY NAKED IN HIS bed, curved around an equally naked—and sleeping—Melina. Once he'd reached his quarters, he'd sent Iolyn to Huw and programmed the highest level of security on his door. Anyone attempting to get in would be killed by a large surge of electricity. Besides him, only Huw and Iolyn knew how to bypass it. They'd only bother him if the ship came under attack.

For the next few hours, he planned on making love to his *gemate*. It was long past due, the final step to their unique bond.

Tightening his hold on Melina, he pulled her hips back against him. His hand massaged her flat stomach and over her womb where one day their child would grow. His rock-hard cock throbbed against the seam of her perfectly shaped bottom. It wouldn't take much movement to slide into her feminine warmth from behind, but he wanted her fully sensate and participating the first time he joined her body to his. The first time for a *gemat* and his *gemate* not only entailed a physical joining, but also a further and more complete joining of their minds and souls.

Or, at least, that was what his mother had drilled into his head for nearly two standard hours after she'd first learned of Melina's existence.

His father, on the other hand, had covered the same material in one compound sentence: "Ensure your *gemate's* pleasure first and the rest will follow, son."

Wulf figured his father's advice was sound or his mother wouldn't have found the mind-soul joining about which she'd lectured. And, the One knew, his parents had a strong, loving binding. They still acted as if they were just mated.

He smiled and brushed a kiss across Melina's pale satin-skinned shoulder. Now, he, too, would have the kind of intimate partnership his parents had shared for many, many years.

Brushing silky hair from her neck, he nuzzled the exposed nape, tasting her with his tongue. She tasted like clean, warm skin with a tang of the citrus shower gel he'd used on her when he'd first brought her up from the planet. Soon, his scent would be all over her. He smiled at the thought. *Mine.* She was his and his alone.

Melina murmured in her sleep, yet she didn't pull away from his ministrations. In fact, with one sighing exhale, she cuddled his throbbing member even more firmly against her bottom.

Emboldened by the delightful response his actions had elicited, he kissed his way from the back of her neck to her ear. Taking the lobe between his lips, he sucked on it as his hand continued to massage her stomach and then traveled down to her curl-covered mound. Her lips parted on a breathy moan as she tilted her head back against his shoulder. He now had easy access to her lips.

Never one to miss an opportunity, he curved over her and took her lips with gentle, nibbling kisses as he manipulated her labia and spread her feminine moisture over her sex. Another low moan had him taking advantage; he swept his tongue inside to taste and claim her mouth completely. The kisses shared in the catacombs had been too long ago and not nearly enough to assuage his hunger for her flavor. This time he'd fully learn the feel and taste of her.

As he savored her, he stroked his index finger through the curls and gently entered her vaginal opening. Massaging her clitoris with his thumb, he stretched her opening, preparing her for intercourse. She was very tight, but the more he stroked and massaged, the wetter she became until he could add another finger.

"What are you doing to me?"

"Loving you."

"Wouldn't it help if I were awake?"

Her amusement tickled his mind with silent laughter. He smiled against her lips as he continued to sip gusty moans from her mouth.

"Yes, love. You being awake would be a big plus in this endeavor."

"All right."

Melina opened her eyes to an intense, bordering on orgasmic, pleasure. The last time she'd awakened in this room, men were on their way to kill her. This time, all she felt were the passionate emotions from the man lying behind her, his heavy arm anchoring her to the bed. The hand on that arm was more than half way to fingering her to what would be the first orgasm she'd ever had that was not self-induced. Damn right, she wanted to be awake for that.

Easily breaking away from Wulf's ravenous lips, she whispered huskily against their firm, moist warmth, "Hungry, my Wulf?"

Her soon-to-be lover chuckled, nipping her lower lip with his teeth, then licking away the slight pain. In reaction, her womb spasmed and sent even more moisture to the opening between her thighs where one long finger massaged her vaginal walls. A very hard, large and pulsing penis poked between her thighs, seeking entry to the space Wulf's finger now possessed.

She shuddered at the thought of him taking her this way; he could very easily slip between her soaking wet labia from behind. She should be afraid of his length and breadth, but she wasn't. She was excited, so aroused that all she wanted to do was pull him into her now so the building pressure could be released.

But she couldn't, his arm held her hips immobile. Her lover obviously had a plan, and he wasn't ready to take her yet.

"I am *very* hungry, *gemate lubha*," he muttered against her lips before taking another nip, followed by a lick, "for you."

And he was, she could tell. Feelings poured off him in tsunami-like waves. Desire. Need. Want. Lust. Pride. Possessiveness. And love.

The last was the clincher. Her heart melted at the strength of the love Wulf felt for her. No one had ever aimed all those emotions at her before, but especially no one had ever loved her in the way Wulf did. It was an all-inclusive kind of love. He loved her for her good points and bad. For her strengths and weaknesses. For her mind, body and soul. He saw her for who and what she really was—a lonely woman doing the best job she could in what was, even in the twenty-fourth century, a man's universe.

Angling her head, she met his fiery golden gaze, the color of Gliesian honey. "And what will it take to satisfy that hunger, *gemat*?"

Wulf scattered light kisses over her face and then finally her lips before pausing to answer. "Your pleasure. I want to give you so much pleasure that the galaxy will feel your release.

Then and only then will I be able to claim my own." He licked the line of her lips, thrusting his tongue inside to tangle briefly with hers as his talented finger kept up a similar rhythm in her achy opening and his thumb massaged her throbbing clit.

Mel closed her eyes and moaned as the buildup to orgasm tightened within her like a coil. When the potential energy was allowed to release, she'd lose her mind to the pleasure. Insanity never sounded so good.

Turning her head into the pillow, she whispered, "The pleasure is already too much. I've never—"

"I know, love. I know." He peppered soothing kisses across her forehead as his hand continued to incite the buildup to a fiery explosion.

"Wulf, I need ... touch me." Mel lifted a heavy hand and touched her breast. "Touch me, please."

Wulf swept his lips back to her ear and sucked on the lobe. Removing his hand from her sex, he shoved the blanket from their bodies. Lifting her slightly, he pulled out the arm which had been under her and turned her over onto her back. Blanketing her with his body, he braced himself on one sinewy forearm; his pelvis nestled snugly between her thighs, his penis pulsing against her mound—so close, but not quite where she wanted him. She wiggled, attempting to move her aching sex closer to what it needed to ease the pressure.

"*Ne, ne, lubha.*" Wulf, muttering in Prime, lay more heavily against her hips, halting her heat-seeking motion. "Your pleasure first—before mine. If I entered you now, you wouldn't enjoy it."

"Wulf, I—" His mouth swallowed her protests.

Groaning, he broke away. "Trust me on this, *lubha.*"

Whispering against his lips, she said, "I trust you—but—please—please make it quick. We can go slowly later." Then she sucked his lower lip into her mouth and gently nipped it. "I need you *now.*" She bucked up against him to emphasize her point.

"My hungry little battle-mate. Have some patience."

"Patience is highly overrated in this context."

His laughter filtered through their mental connection as he took control of the kiss, thrusting his tongue into her mouth in the rhythm, she knew, he would soon use to make her his own.

After releasing her lips, Wulf braced himself once again on a forearm as his free hand massaged her achy breasts. His torrid gaze swept over her face as he plumped and massaged the generous curves in an erotically reverent manner. What Wulf did to them had to be illegal in most solar systems.

"Do you like this?" Wulf paused to taste a nipple as his free hand massaged the other.

"Oh, yeah." She sighed and arched her back as he nibble-kissed his way to the other nipple and took it between his lips for a good suckling. "I always hated them—they were too big—and men ogled—"

"Any man caught ogling these beauties will die by my hand," he growled just before he turned his oral attention to the other nipple. "I love your breasts. I love your sexy, fit body. I love your tight, round ass, especially when it cuddles my cock, tempting me."

Mel arched off the bed, thrusting her pelvis up and against Wulf's. "Wulf, I ache. I need to ... hell, I need to come. I don't need slow ... I don't *want* slow. I want *you* ... need you in me!" She grabbed at his lean hips with both hands and pulled him against her as she again thrust upwards. "Now!"

"A demanding little battle-mate, too." He chuckled, a nipple held loosely between his lips. The vibrations across the moist and sensitive tissue sent shivers down her spine and triggered a mini-climax. "I am a lucky man."

"Wulf! Oh my God ... now!" She arched once more, nearly unseating him. "Now. Trust me."

"No, *lubha*..."

"Now, dammit." She released his hips and grabbed his head and brought his face up to hers. "I need that big, hard cock in me and some movement ... now."

Mel could see the worry on his face. And she understood it, she really did. He didn't want to hurt her. But he was hurting her more by prolonging the tension. At that moment, her body was so tense, she was in pain.

Touching his mind, she gathered his father had told him some crap about ensuring her pleasure first. Well, she'd just see about that. How about they ensure it together? She'd use the information she'd gleaned from him in the catacombs. Angling her head, she sought his *gemat* marking and then traced it with her tongue—licking, nipping and mouthing it.

"*Lubha, ansu bhau.*" Wulf threw his head back and groaned, one long, low guttural sound that vibrated through her and set her insides to quivering. His penis expanded at each lick of her tongue. Throbbed with each nip of her teeth. His precum moistened the skin above her mound.

Nibbling and kissing the glowing hot mark over his heart, she sensed that her own *gemate* marking glowed warmly in reaction, pulsing in time with his cock. And the sexual tension—hers and his—built ever higher; through their mental link their levels of excitement and arousal fed one another's. Something had to give—and soon.

"Now, Wulf," she whispered against his bonding mark. "Make me fully yours, my warrior *gemat.*"

Wulf lifted her chin until her gaze met his. His blazing golden eyes firmly fixed on hers. He moved the head of his cock to her opening, gently seating it. The throbbing of his member set her pulse pounding in a parallel rhythm. "I love you."

As the last word sighed from his lips, he captured her mouth with his and he entered her body with one firm thrust. Her single gasp of pain was captured by Wulf's mouth. Strong, but gentle hands stroked her trembling sides from her breasts to her hips. Soothing her. Inciting her.

She was so full of hard, warm cock—and she loved it.

She massaged his chest, his marking now a deep dark red. The marking's color undulated in time with her pulsating womb. Touching his mind, she shared her pleasure in his possession. *"Move, my Prime warrior. I am fine."*

"You are so strong, my beautiful battle-mate. All silken supple strength. I love you."

Then he moved. One slow pull out, then one long gentle thrust in. Then again—and again. The slow thrust-and-pull movement gently abraded her vaginal walls and rebuilt the sexual tension the pain had chased away. His mind touched hers, feeding her his pleasure in the tightness of her sheath. She shared her pleasure with each push-pull.

His hands stroked, concentrating on her breasts and her *gemate* marking. And all the while he kissed her as if his next breath depended upon her lips.

As the build-up continued, Wulf's pace increased until they reached the point of no return.

With his mind fully open to hers, he shared all that he was. *"Open to me, Melina mine. Share my mind, body and soul from now until death and beyond."*

Mel placed her hand over his marking and stroked it. *"Until death and beyond, I am yours."*

Wulf's hips thrust harder now, feeding the friction that took her even higher. With each deep thrust he rotated his hips, grinding against her clitoris until the aching pressure exploded into release sending her mind and soul spinning. Wulf's shout of pleasure preceded his following her onto a plane of existence that was theirs alone.

As their climaxes continued to feed upon one another's, Mel couldn't tell where her pleasure ended and Wulf's began. Through their shared minds, stars imploded, galaxies were created and destroyed until their pleasure coalesced into one infinite point of bright light, blinding their minds' eyes to anything but the joy they shared. At the height of their shared peak, when Mel was sure she couldn't handle any more, the bright light fractured, and everything that was past and everything that might be swept over them on a tidal wave of ecstasy, finally ending in the gentle warm darkness of exhausted sleep.

CHAPTER TWELVE

For the first time in his life, Wulf woke up with a woman lying nestled against him. He liked the feeling.

The memories of the hours of shared pleasure made him smile. Sex had never been so good. Making love to the woman Prime biology had chosen for him, and the One had kept safe, was far different from experiencing the act with the sex surrogates on Cejuru Prime.

A drowsy and disgruntled voice muttered, "What sex surrogates?"

He peered down at the woman who'd rocked his universe. "It's not important."

Melina braced one small hand against his chest and pushed herself up against the pillows, resting her head next to his. Now at eye level, she glared at him through narrowed eyes, her green eyes flashing golden sparks. "You were thinking about it—and comparing me to whatever in the hell they are—so I'd say it's important."

"You're jealous!" he said, sure his shock was reflected in his voice.

"Damn right, big guy. So spill it."

Her roiling emotions buffeted him. Anger. Hurt. Worry. Sadness.

Damn, she was a bit more than upset. He hurried to allay her basic worry first.

"There is no comparison between the surrogates and what we experienced making love. You were in my mind as I was in yours." He stroked a finger down her elegant nose. "Sex with you is infinitely better than sex with the surrogates. With you, I shared all that I am. The sex surrogates never touched on the real me. It was just a physical act."

"Okay, fine." She nipped his finger as it traced her lips. "But what are they? They're not mentioned in any ancient Prime tomes that I ever read. Am I going to have to share you? 'Cause I have to tell you, I don't share well." She wrinkled her nose as if the idea stank like a ripe Erian.

Wulf chuckled, then leaned over and took her lips, giving her the deep and thorough wake-up kiss he'd been waiting to deliver as he'd watched her sleep. Reluctantly, he pulled away. "No need for jealousy," he breathed against her moist, luscious rosy lips. "I have no need for the surrogates now. I have you."

Melina pursed her lips. "Okay. Fine. Sheesh, getting a straight answer out of you is like, well, I don't know what it's like, but it's damn hard."

Stroking his jaw, she said, "Wulf, I don't need the long version here. I trust the bond between us is true, but I'm not up on contemporary Prime society and mores. After all, the Prime have been isolationists since before I was born. So, educate me. What are these surrogates? Will I meet them in public? Do Huw and Iolyn visit these surrogates? Will our soldiers, meaning the non-Prime ones, be able to visit them on leave to, um, purchase sex? I don't want to say something politically incorrect and cause a galactic incident."

"Last question first. No. Our non-Prime soldiers will not be allowed to visit them. They are not prostitutes as the

Alliance defines such. The sex surrogates have a specific role within Prime society—and you will meet them at social functions and in public. They are not a dirty secret. Greet them as you would any new acquaintance."

"That's good to know. Maren will need to provide some social guidelines to our diplomats—and we'll need to make sure the Alliance Military Command knows this also. Go on, keep explaining."

She snuggled into his side and began stroking her hand down his body. His cock hardened at her touch. Wake-up sex sounded even better than a kiss. The sooner he satisfied her curiosity, the sooner he could make love to her.

Wulf leaned back on his pillow, pulling her head onto his shoulder. He brought her trailing and teasing hand up to cover his *gemat* marking, then placed his hand over hers, anchoring it there. The marking radiated a gentle heat. He could smell her arousal. He smiled. She'd be as ready for him as he was for her.

"Yes, I want you, too. Now, answer my questions so we can play." She wiggled her fingers against his chest.

"Yes, ma'am." He grinned. Damn, she made him happy. "Iolyn and Huw might occasionally visit the sex surrogates just as I had in the past. I don't ask. And they won't tell you about it, so don't ask. The Prime are driven by their hormones just as all other humanoid males are."

She let out a delicate snort. "No need to tell me. I command several hundred of them. Keep going—sex surrogates?"

He kissed the top of her head. "Just as some men don't have their *gemates*, there are women who have lost their *gemats*, either before they bonded or through death after bonding. These women move into houses furnished by the Prime Council and provide sexual favors and, in some cases, instructions to unmated Prime males. As a young man, my father took me to one of these sexual surrogates so I would know how to make love to my *gemate*—or any other woman I chose."

"So," Melina stroked his marking with a very talented finger, "your father always had a plan to open up your mating system, for lack of better terminology, to the galaxy at large."

"Yes." Wulf groaned as she delicately licked the marking she had so adroitly aroused. "Melina, love... I know you are sore, little one. I can feel your stiffness and pain. Are you very sure you can handle me again? I can wait—"

She delivered several nibbling kisses along the pulsing vein in his neck. The sinking of her teeth into the place where his neck joined his shoulder gave him her answer. His penis jerked at the thought of entering her tight, warm, moist opening once more.

"I'm not fragile, Wulf. I smell your need. It's what woke me up. It awakened my own needs."

His mate wanted him, and she wanted him—now.

After their first time, when his little warrior had incited him so quickly to action, he hadn't held back his passions. He'd taken her three times during the night. Each time had been as explosive as the first. By all reasoning, she should be exhausted and bruised from the excesses of their time together. Yet, she wanted him to take her again, dominate her, and he was happy to oblige.

Shoving her gently from him, he rolled her over onto her stomach, then supported her hips with a firm pillow. "Is that comfortable, *lubha?*"

"Yes," she whispered. "Take me—take me hard."

With a low, harsh growl, he came over her back, kneeing her thighs apart. Nibbling the back of her neck, he stroked her buttocks with both hands, marveling at the soft skin and the firm roundness. Holding her where he wanted her with one hand, he tested her readiness with first one, then two fingers. His fingers came away sopping wet.

"Wulf! Stop teasing." She arched her back, thrusting her perfect ass against him.

Licking her essence from his fingers, he muttered against her ear. "So, you like this position?" Before she could answer, he thrust his cock into her vaginal opening, then remained still as she adjusted to the fullness.

"Oh, yeah. Now, Wulf. Move. I'm so close."

"My pleasure, *gemate lubha*." Holding her hips with both hands, he set the punishing rhythm which would take them both to the plane of existence that only the two of them could share.

———

Snuggled against his side, Mel sighed. "I could begin and end every day this way. It just works out all the tension. My muscles are like soggy noodles." She lifted one arm and let it flop onto the bed, then giggled. "Damn, I think you're the cure for tight muscles."

"I'm glad to be of service." Wulf stroked her hair, then placed a nuzzling kiss on the top of her head. "And I'm willing to provide such—any time."

She grinned and tweaked a convenient male nipple. "Yeah, I bet." She massaged away the little sting she'd given him. "Who knew I'd like sex so much? All the guys who hit on me on Dad's digs and later in the military just made me feel, well, icky. The thought of having sex with them made me physically ill."

"That's the way it's supposed to work." Wulf pulled her more closely along his body. "It's a biological fail-safe to keep the Prime female from mating with the wrong male."

Mel thought about that for a moment. "So, when you had sex with the surrogate, it didn't make you sick?"

"No, it only makes the female ill if she has sex with the wrong male. We've theorized that biology has selected out that the male shouldn't go to his woman inexperienced, but that the female must remain untouched for the sake of procreation." Wulf shrugged. "Doesn't seem fair, does it?"

"Nope." Mel frowned. "So, do the sex surrogates feel sick when they, uh, service men who are not their *gemats*?"

"They take hormones to counteract the side effects. This also prevents conception." Wulf stroked her hair.

The vibes coming off Wulf bothered her. After the orgasmic release they had just shared, he should be as relaxed as she. Mel touched his mind lightly.

He was worried about the traitors.

"Everything is fine, Wulf," she reassured him. "I've opened the empathic part of my mind periodically to read the general emotional temperature of the crew. Things are cool. We have time for a bath and food before we go talk to the two idiots who tried to harm me."

Wulf tensed, then growled. "I want to kill the cretins."

"Well, you won't." She stroked his jaw, massaging the tenseness away. "You'll turn them over to the Alliance Military Command on Tooh 10 along with the Antarean prisoners before we head on to Cejuru Prime to meet your father—and bury my parents."

A sharp pain pierced her heart. She'd been so entranced with the furthering of her relationship with Wulf, she had forgotten all about them.

Wulf pulled her even closer and rubbed his jaw against her hair. *"I'm so sorry about your parents, little one."*

His sympathy and love came across their mental connection strongly. It was as if he had wrapped her in an emotional security blanket as well as his arms. This *gemat-gemate* bond was pretty darn nice at times.

Wulf grumbled. "And why won't I turn these rebels over to the Elder Council on my home planet for Prime justice?"

Mel turned and braced her arms on his chest, touching her forehead to his. "Because your planet is a signatory to the Galactic Alliance now and those two rebels first have to be tried for the attempted murder of two Alliance military officers—Iolyn and me. Then Cejuru Prime's Elder Council can have them after the Alliance is done with them. *If* they manage to survive fifty standard years in the penal colony in the Umbraxi solar system."

"I'd still like to kill them," he mumbled. "But, as a substitute, fifty standard years freezing their balls off on that hunk of ice sounds like a pretty good punishment."

She placed a quick kiss on his oh-so-cute pouty lips. "Yep, the Alliance Military Command is nothing if not mean." She pushed away from him before he could grab her for a fuller kiss, then rolled off the bed. "By the way, did I forget to mention that they send convicted serial killers and rapists to the same prison?"

Wulf's grim smile told her he got the mental image. Back in the days when she was a lowly transport captain, she'd made a delivery of prisoners to the penal colony. Her memories of the prison and the prisoners' living conditions were stark and horrific.

"Bath? Or shower?" she asked as she entered the luxurious bathroom attached to their quarters.

"Bath, love." Wulf came to her and caressed her arms. "You are sore. You need to soak. Plus, I have this fantasy of washing you."

"Is that a hint that I can wash you, also?" she teased.

Wulf raised one arrogant eyebrow and his lips quirked. "That's another fantasy of mine. How did you guess?" He winked, a teasing glint in his eyes.

His little-boy grin sent a thrill through her. Her Wulf enjoyed the playfulness as much as she did.

"I can read minds, you know?" she whispered then winked back.

"How lucky for me." He leaned down and sucked her lower lip into his mouth then released it. "What am I thinking now?"

Eyes open wide, she peered up at him. "Again?" Then she risked looking down. "I guess so."

"Only if you are not too sore, love." He brushed his cheek against hers.

"Guess we have to break in the tub some time," she said. "Now is as good a time as any. But I will need food after this. I think I can feel my ribs poking out through my skin."

"Bath-sex. Bath. Then food. I promise on my honor as a Prime warrior." Wulf held out a hand and led her to the tub.

———

IT WAS AMAZING WHAT BUOYANCY DID for the sex act, Mel thought. Freefall sex might be fun, too, although they'd probably need some equipment to keep their bodies together.

"We can try that in one of the simulation rooms in my father's home on Cejuru Prime, if you'd like," Wulf offered. "It is similar to making love in water, but drier." He winked. "And yes, an elastic band *is* a requirement."

Mel stuck her tongue out at him. "Funny man."

In front of the full-length mirror mounted in the closet, she turned this way and that in an attempt to see how the uniform Wulf had made for her fit. It seemed too tight to her.

"Does this make my butt look big?"

An exasperated masculine growl was her only answer.

"Wulf, I'm serious—and hungry. So don't mess with me. Is this uniform too tight over my rear? I don't want our crew distracted looking at my ass—or breasts—while we're chasing down Antarean raiders or pirates."

"First off, the Prime males on this ship and any others under our command in the Gold Squadron will not stare at your feminine attributes or they will have to deal with me personally. If I sense any man here or in the Gold Squadron as a whole making what I would call sexual remarks or overtures to you, they will end up on the deck hurting very badly." Wulf glared at her. "So, the answer to your question is: The uniform fits perfectly. It is exactly as I ordered it. Your ass is perfect as are your breasts—and they are all mine."

"O-o-kay, then." She'd never solicit his opinion on clothing again. It made him grouchy. Or, maybe he was just hungry. Like her. "Feed me, Wulf."

Her still-ruffled mate took her elbow and led her from their quarters.

"Where do we eat?" she asked as they walked to the elevator at the end of the officer quarters corridor.

"As in your military, we have one large dining area that is open around the clock. If you and I wish privacy, we can have food delivered to our quarters."

"I'm fine eating with the men," Mel said, happy to hear that the Prime's military protocols weren't all that different from the Alliance's.

"Good, after you." He waved her into the open elevator.

Mel nodded at the two Prime standing to the back of the lift. They wore what she had come to recognize as engineering patches on their sleeves. The two men saluted. Their auras were respectful—and envious. She imagined she'd sense a lot of envy on board. Too many Prime males would never see their true *gemates*. But with any luck they might find a mate and some happiness among the other humanoid species in the galaxy. She wondered about the biological issues in having children with someone outside of their particular hominid branch.

"Maren has already asked the Galactic Alliance Council to advertise for the best and brightest biologists, genetic specialists and doctors in the galaxy to join our researchers on this exact topic."

"Bet that went over well with the Prime fundamentalists."

"As you might expect, it created a furor. I read the communiqué on the issue while you finished your bath." Wulf's hand caressed her lower back gently, slipping down to massage her ass. The movement blocked from the other men's view by his body. *"Are you okay? Was I too rough?"*

"I loved it. With our minds this open, you know how I feel."

"You're so small. I'm afraid of hurting you."

She had never considered herself small, but could see how he would think that considering his much larger body.

"I've fought huge Antarean, Erian, Terran, Volusian, and Prime males—you can't hurt me by loving me."

The door opened onto the dining level. The noisy room quieted as the men saw who entered the room. Wulf gently urged her forward, his hand once again at her waist. The light kiss he brushed on the top of her head had her blushing, but gave her the courage to face what had to be at least thirty large Prime males. They could be very intimidating *en masse*.

"Wulf, no kissing in front of the crew," she hissed as she nodded and smiled to the men they passed on their way to a table.

"The devil with the crew," he whispered against her ear. "They'll get used to it."

She glared at him. He grinned at her.

"That is *so* not military protocol." She stalked to an empty booth at the side of the large room and scooted into the banquette. "You need to save the love-stuff for our quarters and in private, *gemat*." Her words were clipped as she glared at him.

Wulf sat next to her. "And you, my little battle-mate, need to lighten up. Sex between bonded mates is not a dirty secret in Prime society. Terrans are too puritanical."

"You didn't think so when I had your cock in my mouth," she retorted.

"But you aren't Terran, just raised as one."

The room once so quiet now buzzed. The word "battle-mate" was passed from one Prime to another just like the antiquated Terran game of telephone. The room rumbled with the word and emotions it conjured. Every male eye in the room was on their table.

"Wulf?" She sought his reassurance. Not normally shy, being the center of awe and adulation was disconcerting. "They act as if we are gods or something."

"To them, battle-mates are the stuff of legends," he explained. "The last battle-mate came from the Maren line before the Berean Wars."

"Yeah, the traitor, Ullyn, told me that back when we first met. How long ago were the Berean Wars? I should know, but have forgotten." She picked up the menu for the day. It was written in Prime. She could read it easily, but things would have to change once they started merging the crews. Maybe they could have it in Standard Galactic and Prime; she would mention that to the Admiral.

"Several centuries," Wulf answered her question as he signaled the steward. "The Antarean attacks and sieges plus other environmental factors had already cut into our birth rates. The Elders of the time determined that women, already in short supply, needed to be kept out of battle situations for the future of our race. Plus, not all Prime women had the genes to become a battle-mate. Those inborn abilities only ran in certain lines."

"Such as my and Maren's family line?"

Wulf nodded and smiled. "Such as yours." Despite her warning of no public displays of affection, he pulled her closer against his side and kissed her lips, stroking a finger down her cheek. The air around them grew warmer. The man put off heat like a fire. "I am so very fortunate. And, this ship is blessed with good fortune to have you. The Gold Squadron will set the standard in the Alliance Military for excellence with our battle symbiosis."

Embarrassed by his high praise and uncomfortable with all the baggage that came with being a battle-mate, Mel looked away from the fires blazing in his golden eyes. The waiter stood at the side of the table, a grin on his face, waiting patiently for Wulf and her attention.

"Wulf," she placed a finger on his lips as he leaned in to kiss her again, "order. The poor man is waiting."

He grinned and mouthed the word "later."

"My apologies, Darog."

"No problem, Captain." The steward bowed to Mel. "Welcome, Captain Dmitros-Caradoc. What would you like to order?"

She looked at the menu again and ordered in Prime what she knew to be the traditional Prime morning meal—a sort of hot grained cereal with a side of fresh fruit and a sticky sweet topping that was very much like honey and a cup of a coffee-like drink.

Darog beamed at her, then thanked her in his language. "Captain Wulf?"

Wulf ordered what she had plus a smoked meat then dismissed the man. After the man had left, he turned toward her. "I informed my crew once I knew that I'd be bringing you home with me that I should be called Captain Wulf and you, Captain Caradoc. Does that bother you?"

"Yes, it does."

Wulf frowned. She waved off anything he might say, then stood. In both Prime and then Standard Galactic she asked the men in the room to please call her Captain Melina and to spread the word to the others.

Sitting back down to cheers, she smiled at her warrior. "If they can call you Captain Wulf, then Captain Melina is just fine with me."

"I love you, Captain Melina."

"Back at you, Captain Wulf."

———

MEL WASN'T SURE WHAT TO expect when she and Wulf entered Huw's quarters to question the two rebels. She sure didn't expect to see them still trussed up like game birds about to be roasted on a spit. The only difference from when she'd tied them up to now was the blindfolds; from somewhere, Huw or Iolyn had obtained black leather ones like she'd seen in some of the shops on Tooh 2 that catered to certain more risqué sexual acts.

The men's emotional auras had also remained unchanged; both were still defiant and tinged with a killing hate. Their base emotions filled the atmosphere immediately around them with an oily, black and bitter-tasting sheen. It nauseated her, making her wish she'd avoided the overly sweet Prime topping on her breakfast fruit.

Wulf rubbed her lower back as he placed his lips next to her ear. "You are unwell, *lubha*. You don't need to question them. My brothers and I have enough empathic ability to tell if they lie or not."

The back rub calmed her nausea. Or, maybe it was just the warmth of Wulf's love and concern which soothed her.

"I'm fine." At his skeptical snort, she touched his chest. "Really, I'm fine. Plus, we're stronger together. We need to determine if there are *other* rebels aboard. I refuse to feel threatened on my—our—ship," she whispered. "Although I feel that we can pretty much eliminate the men we just left in the dining area. I sensed nothing from any of them that was threatening to us."

"I agree. I read the room through you. The sensory readings were amazingly clear through our connection," he murmured.

"That is why I need to remain," she said, making her point. "We'll talk to these two, first—and then the rest of the crew, if needed."

Wulf nodded and turned toward his brothers, who'd silently observed the whispered consultation. "Sit them up, Huw. Iolyn. Remove the blindfolds and gags."

Wulf's brothers jerked the two rebels into sitting positions on Huw's bed and removed the bindings from their faces. Two sets of gold-brown glares fixed first on her, then on Wulf.

It was all Mel could do not to step back from the force of their hatred. Fanatics, Maren had called the rebels. He was correct. If the rebellion was widespread, the Prime Elder Council would have a major problem on its hands. Hell, even a small rabid group of fanatics could do a lot of damage. History on Earth, Volusia, and on at least a dozen other planets in the galaxy was proof of that.

"Too bad the Antareans didn't finish you off, Wulf," spat the one Iolyn had told her was Ensign Donte Caradoc, a second cousin to the Caradoc brothers.

"I am not easy to kill, Donte," Wulf replied, his tone acidly lethal. Mel prayed Wulf never aimed that deadly tone at her. "And, what do you have to say for yourself, Regin? Does my cousin Mara know you are a traitor to our people, to her family?"

"It's you who are the traitor, Wulf." Regin attempted to stare Wulf down, but failed. After a minute of uncomfortable silence, he then muttered, "My mate knows nothing of this. Leave her out of it."

"He's telling the truth about your cousin Mara, Wulf," Mel said quietly. "Regin does believe you are the traitor to the Prime and not him. Donte's comments also rang with truth. Ask them your questions." She sighed. "They are easy to read."

Donte and Regin stared at her, fear now coloring their aura in varying shades of darkness.

"What are you? A Terran witch?" Regin asked, his voice strained.

"She's Prime—and a battle-mate," Huw said. "Fully bonded to Wulf. Remember the legends of fully bonded battle-mates, Regin? Don't bother lying. They'll know."

The prisoners looked at one another. "We will answer no questions," Donte replied, his mouth firmed in a stubborn line.

Donte would be surprised at how easy he was to read. His shielding was non-existent. His emotions were an open book.

It was obvious that male Prime didn't use their empathic abilities much, except during times of stronger emotions such as a battle or a siege. She'd have to work with her Prime crews now that they would be a part of Gold Squadron. There were other species in the universe who read emotions besides the Prime. While they would never have her ability to detect nuances, they could do better on both interpretation and shielding with proper training exercises.

"An excellent idea, Melina. Now that the Prime have joined the Alliance, we will meet more and more of these empaths."

She smiled at him. She really liked that he could follow her reasoning. Small changes in an opponent's reactions could reveal vital information under the right circumstances.

"Ask them your questions, Wulf. I will chime in as needed."

He nodded. She noticed both prisoners watched them closely. She thought that they just might be a tad more frightened now than before. The battle-mate legends must be really something; she'd have to get some of them to read.

"I really don't care if you answer or not, Donte," Wulf said, "but I will ask my questions anyway." He paced from one side of the bed to the other, pausing to look first at Donte, then Regin. "Besides you, are there any other men on board this ship who wish to harm my *gemate*, myself, or my brothers?"

Both men looked away from Wulf and down at their laps, remaining silent.

Mel concentrated on their emotions. The fear and hatred were still there, but now there was an element of triumph as if they knew something the rest of them did not know.

Playing the odds, she voiced her opinion. "There is someone—or something—on this ship that could harm us, but I can't tell exactly what. Yet."

Both men's heads jerked upwards. Their widened gazes now fixed on her.

She moved to stand alongside Wulf, who placed his arm around her back and pulled her into his side. Absently, he massaged her waist.

She stretched the odds even further and said, "I would check all the ship's emergency systems as soon as possible."

The prisoners' emotional levels escalated through the ceiling. Wulf jerked next to her as if he'd been shot.

"Good work, my gemate. *We now know they have sabotaged something on this ship. That means we can probably expect another attack upon the ship before we reach Tooh 10. With damaged systems, we'd be sitting ducks."*

"What if we had decided to go to Cejuru Prime?"

"Donte or Regin would have just radioed their comrades and given them the intel. Either way, the attack would have to occur somewhere in the more unpopulated areas of the galaxy, away from the heavily trafficked space lanes where help would be more easily accessed."

Mel nodded. *"Makes sense."*

For the benefit of Huw and Iolyn, she said, "Wulf and I believe these two have sabotaged something on this ship." She spoke with more calm than she felt. "I don't get the impression it would destroy the *Galanti*. More than likely, they mean to incapacitate a system needed for our defense."

Again the prisoners' emotional levels shot up. Their heated reactions confirmed her speculations. Playing the odds had paid off. With a thorough testing of the systems, they should easily find what the traitors had done to the ship. She prayed to all the gods she knew that they would find and fix the problem before the traitors' cohorts attacked the ship.

Pushing her luck and intuition to its limits, she added, "I would check weapons, security on docking bays, and possibly the beta-weapon you are testing. The rebels plan to attack the ship before we get to Tooh 10."

"How can you know this?" Regin sputtered, ignoring the glare and harshly uttered "Shut up, fool" from Donte. "The legends say nothing of a battle-mate reading minds of any other than her warrior-*gemat*."

"The legends don't know everything," Wulf growled. "Iolyn, Huw, throw these two into solitary confinement after you check them thoroughly for any implanted communications devices or locators. Then have a ship-wide systems check run, comparing it against the last maintenance done on Cejuru Prime. If anything has been altered since we left the home planet, I want it checked over manually. Crews of three, just in case we have any lingering traitors on board."

Donte and Regin's reaction to Wulf's last words had Mel breathing a sigh of relief.

"There are no more traitors," Mel said, smiling. "They just confirmed that, don't you agree, my *gemat*?"

Wulf swept a warm hand down her back, hugging her to his side. "I agree, *gemate lubha*."

Iolyn and Huw hauled the two rebels to their feet, untying their legs so they could walk, then marched them to the doorway.

Dragging at Huw, Donte turned his head, shouting over his shoulder. "If they don't kill you before you get to Tooh 10, our comrades will manage it eventually no matter where you go. Enjoy fucking your slut battle-mate while you can. She won't live to procreate," he snarled.

"Get him out of my sight before I kill him." Wulf roared, his fists clenched.

Mel grabbed his arm as he attempted to move toward Donte.

"He's out of here, brother." Huw dragged Donte from the room. The door closed behind them.

Mel picked up one of Wulf's clenched fists and rubbed it against her cheek, then kissed the whitened knuckles. "Just words, Wulf. Spoken from fear. You had to feel it. He said what he said because of his own doubts about his comrades succeeding. We scared them out of the absolute sense of complacency the rebellion leaders instilled in them."

"I know, Melina mine." His large body still shuddered from the effects of his anger. "But I can't handle the thought of you being harmed. I just found you, if I—"

Wulf's words trailed off, but the emotions behind them were clear. Her big Prime warrior was afraid. That was not acceptable. She stepped into his full embrace and placed her arms around his waist. With her head nestled on his chest, she absorbed his vitality, his strength as she decided how to assure him that she would live a long, long time.

"My darling warrior, I love the fact you love me so much. Even more, I love the fact you want to protect me. I've never had anyone in my life that has cared as much as you."

She brushed a kiss across his marking and even through a couple layers of fabric, she could feel the answering heat. "I plan on being with you for the rest of our lives. And, whenever this fear of losing me hits you, just remember, I am an Alliance officer. I've been in danger every day since I joined the military. This is nothing new. And, now, with my increased empathic abilities and our ability to connect to each other's minds, it will be much harder for the enemy to take either of us by surprise."

Mel held her breath, then smiled. He had taken her words to heart—but with their partnership so new, she imagined she would have to remind him of her strength—and love—from time to time. She'd been snatched from his life twenty-seven years ago; she understood his fears of having her taken from him again.

"Our connection is pretty amazing, isn't it?" He nuzzled her hair from her ear, then kissed the tip. "And I value your experience and training—never think that I don't, but—"

And there was always a "but."

"—we still we must be very careful," he finished, brushing a kiss across her forehead as if in apology for his over-protective alpha-ways.

"Hey, ask my old crew." She reached up and traced the pulsing muscle along his jaw with her lips. "My middle name is 'cautious.'"

CHAPTER THIRTEEN

"*Ansu bhau!*" Mel swore.

As she crawled out of the narrow confines of the shield array maintenance tunnel, she added a few more pithy invectives learned in her many years in the military. Cursing wouldn't fix the problems, but it did allow her to let off some of the anger roiling in her gut.

Huw following her out snorted back a laugh. "Very creative, but crude. I think I'll start a list for future use now that I am part of the Alliance."

Mel shot him a wry grin. "I'll send one to your com-box."

She swept some hair off her face. Damn all men and their fondness for long hair on women. She'd like to see how they'd like hair in their faces all the time. That morning, between deep, luscious, panty-dampening kisses, Wulf had begged her not to braid her hair, but to let it flow, and like a sappy idiot, she had. Okay, so she was easy, but the man could kiss.

She let out a disgusted sigh. Hair styles and Wulf were the least of her problems. Defective, loose, or missing couplings on the exterior connections to the shields were.

"Good news is—the power sources still work," she said, dusting off her uniform, making a mental note to have maintenance clean the shield array tunnels more often. "We just can't get the power to the exterior shields. Bad news is— we need a space dock or a stable orbit around a planet out of the path of meteor showers to make repairs. Both of which are harder to find in this part of the galaxy than an Erian's teeth. It's an easy fix once we get outside the ship."

His good-humored grin of a moment ago gone, Huw nodded. "I agree. Closest space dock in this part of the galaxy that can handle a ship our size would be the Alliance Military Dock orbiting Tooh 10. Wulf might know of another one, but I don't."

Something, a specific place she'd heard of from a trawler captain with whom she'd shared a bar table many years ago, niggled at the back of her mind. She'd have to check the charts for this part of the galaxy to see if she could jog her memory.

If Tooh 10 was the closest, that wasn't saying much. Their current position placed them in a vastly under populated area of the Cygnus-Orion spiral. Tooh 10, in the Mu Arae system, was located more centrally in the spiral. Right now, they were in the middle of frigging nowhere. Well, nowhere if you didn't count the asteroid belts and other detritus of former solar systems floating around, threatening to make big holes in space vehicles without shields.

"Dammit all to hell! We need those shields. We might be able to handle small hunks of rock with the auxiliary shields, but I wouldn't put good money on that bet. All it takes is one leftover hunk of a former planet running into our shield-less hull and we are fodder for a salvage yard."

The deep creases on Huw's forehead indicated his thoughts paralleled hers.

Mel blew a lock of hair from her mouth, then glared at her brother-in-law as if her bad hair day was his fault. It wasn't—it was Wulf's.

"And, how in the hell did they bollocks up the exterior shield structure after leaving Cejuru Prime? Did anyone on board request an extra-vehicular inspection?" she asked.

"No. And only Wulf can authorize an EVI," Huw said. "And, now, you, of course."

She nodded. "So, they did it in Cejuru Space Dock." She stated the obvious conclusion. "Do you think they just loosened the couplings? The vibration of jump flight would eventually knock them completely loose."

"Maybe, but unlikely. We made several jumps and used the shields multiple times on the way to Obam IV to get to you and Wulf," stated Huw. "I'm betting the saboteurs installed defective couplings which failed under stress of repeated uses or, better yet, put something corrosive on them to cause them to break at a future time."

"Whatever they did to them—bottom line, we don't have our primary shields, just the auxiliary." Mel turned and headed for the nearest elevator. Huw matched his longer-legged stride to hers. "The rebels figured that eventually we'd have to use the shields in an emergency of their or some other unknown's making in the middle of nowhere. End result? A Grade-A cluster fuck."

"Yeah, couldn't have said it better myself," agreed Huw.

Thinking back to the two men who'd tried to kill her and Iolyn, she frowned. Something about this scenario didn't ring true. An EVI took specific knowledge and training in zero G. Any monkey could mess up the couplings. A good knock with a hammer, some acid dripped on them, or leaving them loose would produce the current result. But a spacewalk required someone with skills.

"Do either Donte or Regin even have the experience and knowledge to do the EVI?" she asked. She'd done hundreds of them in her early years in the military. All transport captains knew enough basic engineering to fix their ships since they often made deliveries to the most far-flung areas of the galaxy under some of the worst conditions, which almost always necessitated a zero-g space walk. She had even more of an advantage. The military had paid for her engineering degree and she had first-hand experience making repairs under zero-g conditions.

"*Ansu bhau.* Why didn't I think of that?" Huw glanced at her, an angry scowl creasing his forehead, and said, "No, they don't have that kind of experience. That would mean that someone in Cejuru Space Dock is part of the rebellion."

The elevator opened at their approach. "Yes." Mel led the way inside and ordered "bridge." They rode to the command deck in silence as if the far-flung perfidy of the rebels had temporarily rendered them speechless.

Wulf's head jerked up as the elevator opened onto the bridge. He turned his head and smiled at her, but then frowned.

She checked her mental filters to see if she had inadvertently left them open. No, she hadn't. He was reading her emotions, not her mind.

"What's wrong, Melina? Huw?"

She stepped to Wulf's side aware all the eyes of the bridge crew were fixed upon her. Self-consciously, she smoothed her hair back behind her ears.

Wulf's amber-colored gaze followed the movement then heated, turning his eyes into the color of molten gold. His aura glowed red-hot. She didn't have to touch his mind to know that he recalled how they'd spent their off-duty time. He wanted her again. Now.

An answering warmth swept through her, making her wet.

"Behave, Wulf. Now is not the time to get all amorous on me."

"I was just admiring my gemate's *beautiful hair."*

"You are so in trouble. As soon as we get a handle on what we're going to do about this mess we're in, I'm going back to our quarters to take a shower and braid this damn hair."

"Not damn hair. Beautiful hair. I like it down."

"Wulf!"

"Melina ... later, my love. Make your report. The crew is wondering what we are discussing."

Taking a deep, calming breath, she made a report of her and Huw's findings.

Anger stole the light from his fiery gold eyes. "This, added to the fact that three out of five of our main weapon systems have had their energy source partially or fully discharged, places the ship in a dire situation."

"Well, shit," she swore. "How long to recharge?"

"Twenty standard hours—maybe more. As long as we find nothing else damaged," Wulf replied. "Anticipating that we might have other, more serious damage as yet undetected, I ordered Gold Squadron to change course and to head back to meet us at top speed. We'll need their escort to Tooh 10. Once we reach Tooh 10, I feel we should have the *Galanti* totally overhauled and given a clean bill of health before we head to Cejuru Prime."

The potential for an ambush before they made the Alliance Military space dock was left unmentioned by Wulf, but was in the forefront of everyone's mind.

Mel sensed the mood on the ship was still one of disbelief and outrage that their own people had turned on them and sabotaged their ship, endangering the entire crew. And for what? Fear of change? That reason, the reason that Donte, Regin and the other rebels she'd encountered had espoused, didn't work for her. In the long history of the Prime, they'd made many changes and adaptations in order to survive, including mating with other humanoids on planets they discovered and/or colonized. Why this lust for purity of bloodlines now? No, there was something else going on behind this "rebellion," and Mel would find out what. But first they had to make it to Tooh 10.

Shoving aside her concerns over the rebels' motivation, Mel nodded. "Agreed. It would be irresponsible to put off a complete maintenance. Hell, besides the rebel threat, there are Antareans out there gunning for any Alliance ship. Not to mention, killer hunks of rock that could put a hole into us in a split second. A damaged ship equals a dead crew."

"Good. We are of the same mind." Wulf's lips thinned into a grim smile. "I also notified Alliance Military Command of our situation. They've notified any and all Alliance ships in the area to stand ready to assist."

While she'd been crawling around in the tunnels, her *gemat* had been busy, doing exactly everything she would've done. They made a good team.

"Well, they can notify any or all Alliance patrols in the area they like, but it won't do much good. This is not a part of the galaxy that sees regular patrols. Other than the Obam system, there are no other stars with habitable zone planets out here."

This part of the Cygnus-Orion spiral was literally almost empty as compared to the rest of the spiral. Not much need to patrol empty space.

Wulf nodded. "I know, *gemate,* but I wanted to cover all bases, especially since Captain Nowicki was ordered back to Tooh 10 ahead of us."

"Good move. You're already in the CYA-mode of Alliance military ops." She grinned at him. "That was a lesson I learned early on, even when I was only a first officer on troop and supply transports."

Mel moved closer to Wulf and placed a hand on his fisted one. His anger and fear, for her, for his crew, but not for himself, was palpable. The need to touch him, to soothe him, was far stronger than her distaste for public displays of affection in front of their crew. He was hurting, and she *needed* to make him feel better. Plus, touching him comforted her, also.

Inhaling his heady male scent, feeling the gentle heat generated by her stroking of his hand, her anger over the current dire situation dissipated. As some semblance of calm settled over her—and in turn, over Wulf, she realized that together they were not just a good team, but they were also stronger as individuals. Together, they could handle whatever came their way. "Things aren't that bad, Wulf. We still have maneuverability," she said as she let go of his hand and ticked the positives off on her fingers. "We also have secondary weapons systems and auxiliary shields, not to mention fifteen space fighters armed with torpedoes. We could defend ourselves until the *Leonidas* and the rest of the squadron reach us."

Murmurs of approval at her words came from many of the crew on the bridge. The word *battle-mate* whispered around the bridge as if on a gentle breeze through a tall meadow of grass. The crew's faith in her abilities humbled her. She hadn't even proven herself in battle yet and they trusted that she, no, that she and Wulf, could bring them through.

Wulf smiled. "And, as my crew has so rightly pointed out, we have the advantage of superior tactical leaders, battle-mate. We are stronger together. That is a plus the rebels and our enemies have not counted on."

"You were reading my thoughts."

"Yes. When you leave it open, I touch your mind constantly. It is a prime imperative."

"I'll keep that in mind." A slight smile twisted her lips. She'd thought her filters were impervious. Wulf was becoming more proficient in touching her thoughts, as she did his. She'd have to work on strengthening her filters. A girl had to have *some* secrets.

A sudden, horrible thought wiped the smile from her lips. "Long-range sensors. What's the status?"

Wulf replied, "Working optimally and increased to maximum range of five light-years." He pulled the long-range scanner onto his command screen. "Very little activity except for ... are those Alliance military transponder codes?" His head turned toward hers. "I thought you said there was little or no military presence in this area."

"There isn't—normally." She took a closer look at the blips on the screen. "They look like our codes, but not any I recognize in particular."

Mel's senses went on red alert.

"Mr. Dakkin, please relay these codes to Alliance Military Operations on Tooh 10 and ask for identification," Mel requested of the communications officer.

The silence on the bridge became oppressive; it, combined with the emotional bombardment of the crew, overwhelmed Mel's psi abilities. She threw up her empathic filters, leaving only her personal connection to Wulf open, and that, more narrowly than before.

"Got them, Captain Melina," Dakkin announced, his voice so loud in the silence that Mel jumped, startled. "Captain Sinclair is standing by."

"On screen, please," Mel requested.

On the large forward monitor, a small, attractive blonde sat at a large console, dressed in the royal blue Alliance uniform worn by Command Ops personnel. Her face was preternaturally calm, but her sky blue eyes held a hint of worry.

"Hi, Linnea."

"Hey, Mel," Linnea said, a slight smile on her lips. "I was going to congratulate you on your marriage, but it might be out of place at the moment. I got the word just a bit ago from both Captain Nowicki," her eyes shifted toward Wulf, "and the other Captain Caradoc that you're heading back this way for repairs. I've already placed Space Dock 14 on standby."

Linnea and Mel had gone to flight school together, piloted transports in the same unit. Mel had always admired her friend for her A-type attention to details. It made her one of the best Operations officers in the fleet.

"Thanks, Linnea. But something else has come up," Mel said. "Our long-range sensors show Alliance military activity within three light-years of our current position near the Ursa solar system. Last I heard, we didn't send patrols into this area of the galaxy unless requested. Is something going on in Ursa space that we need to know about?"

Linnea frowned and pursed her cupid's bow of a mouth as she clicked keys. "Mel, I've got you on the screen. Yeah, I see those transponder codes you're talking about." She hummed under her breath as she rapidly keyed in data. Her lips turned down in a frown. "Good eye. They look like ours, but they aren't."

She paused to talk to someone behind her, off screen. "We're scrambling Blue Squadron to investigate. Gold will be ordered to increase to maximum emergency speed to intercept you and provide protection."

Some more mumbled words to someone off-screen. "Confirmed once more. These bogies are definitely heading your way, Mel, but their top speed does not match anything we have. So, whoever was clever enough to mimic our codes has more antiquated vessels. Hold a sec, we have more intel on the unknowns."

Linnea clicked some more keys, her lips pursed in concentration. "Ensign Jo-tah tells me that our sensors are showing that the five bogies are C-Class light battle cruisers. Probably decommissioned Alliance equipment used by one of our smaller allies and sold for salvage."

Her blue eyes darkened with concern, Linnea asked, "What's the *Galanti's* final damage assessment?"

"Bad enough that we'll have a hard time defending ourselves against even antiquated C-class cruisers," Wulf interjected. "I'm sending you the full damage report now."

He keyed in the details and transmitted.

More background mumbling from, presumably, Jo-tah, then Linnea said, "It'll be close. On your current trajectory and speed, Gold will intercept the *Galanti* in about one to two standard hours *after* the bogies catch up with you. The good news is Garth and Blue Squadron will be so close behind them that they'll be in danger of riding up the bogies' as—... um, hind ends."

"Thank you. That's what we calculated, Captain Sinclair," Wulf said.

"Just tell Royce and Garth to hurry up," Mel added. "As it is, we'll have to do some fancy maneuvering to keep the enemy on their toes until the rest of the good guys come to play."

Linnea nodded. "Keep us apprised, Mel. We've already notified Admiral Nelson about the situation. He has ordered us to provide anything we can to help you." None of which, Mel knew, would get to them in time. "Good luck, *Galanti*. Tooh 10 Ops out."

"Thanks, Linnea. *Galanti* out"

Wulf exchanged a long look with Mel. She didn't need to read his mind to know what he asked. She nodded. "It's your call."

"Go to yellow alert," Wulf ordered the command deck crew. "When the unknowns are within a quarter of a light-year, go to battle stations."

The once-silent bridge erupted into controlled and smoothly executed activity. She sensed no panic.

While the bridge crew went about their duties, she watched over Wulf's shoulder as he quickly scrolled though the star charts in their immediate vicinity. He was looking for something, something specific. She wanted to know what it was.

And, there it was. She felt the small whirl of excitement, then satisfaction, as it crossed his mind, then was gone. Darn it. He'd shuttered his mind. And pretty damn effectively for someone not used to doing so.

But he had done so too late. Mel knew what he'd seen. The point on the chart was that niggling memory she couldn't recall earlier. And she knew what he intended to do since it was what she would've done. The plan would work. It would be the difference between surviving the upcoming confrontation with the unknown ships heading toward them and sure death. And, she was the one to execute the plan. While Wulf knew that, she sensed, he had instantly rejected it. He would have to learn to stop his knee-jerk reaction of protecting her sooner or later.

She was drawn from her thoughts as Wulf asked her a question. "So, Melina mine, do you think these unknowns are part of the rebel plan?"

Good question. "Maybe. I'm keeping my options open."

The bogies could be mercenaries hired by the rebels on Cejuru Prime. But the bogies' presence was too coincidental, coming right after she and Wulf had destroyed the Antarean raiding party on Obam IV.

She continued, "It could be the Antareans. They don't like their ships being blown up and their plans spoiled. Before we nailed their asses, the attackers of Obam IV could have put out a call to one of their allies. Most likely the Erians, who've have been known to scavenge, or pirate, old Alliance military equipment. The Erians also have the knowledge of how to fake Alliance military codes—they use fake IDs when they are hijacking ships in the space lanes."

"The codes didn't fool you," Wulf said softly, pride glowing in his eyes. "Why?"

"Just a gut feeling," she said, "along with the knowledge that the Ursa solar system likes to police its own space—and only calls for help in extraordinary circumstances. Being on the edge of the Cygnus-Orion spiral has taught them to become more self-reliant than the solar systems in the more densely populated parts of the spiral."

"So, it was an *educated* gut feeling?"

"Yeah. Wulf—Donte and Regin," she frowned, "didn't—couldn't—sabotage the shield array. So—if the unknown ships are part of a rebel plot—then their rebel bosses sent them on a suicide mission, don't you agree?"

"Yes." Wulf smiled, grimly. "In the rebel leaders' minds, Regin and Donte would be martyrs to the cause."

"Exactly," Mel said. "I'm betting they didn't sign on for that. Think they might answer some questions now?"

Wulf showed his teeth in a fearsome smile. "We can only try, *gemate lubha.*"

———

QUESTIONING THE TWO REBELS GOT them nothing but the sense the two were surprised at hearing the shields were sabotaged. It also became clear they were more afraid of the rebel leaders than of their own deaths.

Now more than ever, Mel wanted to get to the bottom of the real reason behind the rebel movement. Donte and Regin might be purist fanatics, and even that was doubtful since neither of them were as adamant about their cause as Prolow and Ullyn had been, but the leaders of the rebellion need not be. They could have far more base reasons; she was betting on power or money—or both.

Leaning against the wall outside of the containment unit, Mel sighed. "Well, that was useless."

"It was a good idea," Wulf leaned forward to brush some hair off her face, then gently cupped her jaw. "You look tired. Go, grab something to eat, then rest."

Mel covered his hand and brought it to her mouth and kissed his palm. "What about you? Huw and Iolyn can handle things until we go to red alert. This might be the last quality time we have alone until we get to Tooh 10."

His eyes smiled at her. "You believe we'll make it through this, Melina mine?"

"Absolutely," she grinned. "After all, we are the first battle-mate pair in hundreds of years, right? Who would want to mess with us?"

Wulf chuckled. "Are you beginning to believe the legends also?"

"No. It's just that we both know how to kick ass."

Wulf threw back his head and laughed. She smiled.

"So," she whispered as she cradled his hand against her jaw, "would my *gemat* like to come back to our quarters, take an, um, shower, eat and then rest on the bed with his *gemate*?"

Wulf leaned in more closely and brushed kisses over her forehead, cheeks, nose and then lips. "He would."

CHAPTER FOURTEEN

Ten standard hours later

Wulf woke with a smile on his lips; memories of the best sex he'd ever experienced had him reaching for Melina in the hopes of revisiting the sexual bliss. He turned and found her gone. The depression where she'd lain was cool to the touch. He sought to touch her mind and found it closed off with thick and impenetrable shields. Sitting up, he checked the time. He'd been asleep for ten standard hours. He'd never slept so deeply or long—ever—while on board ship. Especially not under a yellow alert. He shook his head. The combination of the warm shower, the sex, the food, and then even more sex was better than any medication ever prescribed for sleeplessness.

He was vexed Melina had blocked her mind again. He thought after all they had shared she would have learned not to cut him off. Obviously, she had yet to realize how important it was to remain open to her bonded mate. The mental walls were unacceptable, especially now that they'd bonded fully. He needed to know where—and how—she was at all times, or he wouldn't take responsibility for his resulting unstable disposition.

Yes, that's the way to present it to her. She needed to let him in for the safety of the crew and all others. That is something she would understand—the duty to do whatever it took to protect others. Now, all he had to do was find her and explain her responsibilities to her mate. One or the other of his brothers would know where she was.

Hitting the com unit by his bed, he spoke, "Bridge, this is Wulf. Status and whereabouts of Captain Melina."

"Wulf," Iolyn spoke over the link. His brother's voice seemed strained. Any remaining lethargy from just waking disappeared at the disquiet in Iolyn's voice. "We expected you to sleep longer. Mel said you were particularly tired."

"Where is she, brother?" Wulf growled. He would have to explain to his brothers that they were not to cover for Melina. It was their duty as well as his to protect her.

"Um, well, you see—"

"Where. Is. She?" Wulf asked, forcing an icy calm he didn't feel into his words.

"She's outside the ship with Huw," Iolyn breathed out in a rush, then added, "—fixing the shields."

"What?" So many emotions hit Wulf at once that he'd be hard pressed to single out any particular one. But of them all, anger, fear and hurt churned his gut the most. He took a deep calming breath in an attempt to control the emotions before they controlled him.

"Why didn't Melina speak to me about this?" Wulf asked his brother.

"You'd have to ask her that, brother."

"I will—as soon as I pull her back into the ship." He had a sneaking suspicion the answer to that question would be very important to the future of their relationship.

He surged to his feet and headed for the door before he realized he was naked. Changing direction, he went into his closet and grabbed some clothes, which he pulled on as he left the bedroom, barely remembering to pick up his personal com-unit. "What's the *Galanti*'s current position?"

He was afraid he knew.

As he hit the door leading from his quarters to the corridor, he had his pants on, only partially closed, and was pulling on his shirt.

"An abandoned Volusian space dock orbiting the fourth planet of the star RC888."

Damn her. She'd snuck into his head, figured out his plans, then distracted him with shower-sex, food and more sex. He'd underestimated her. He thought he'd mentally blocked his plans from her. For her own protection, of course—not that she would view it in that light.

He stopped suddenly, swearing viciously. That was the crux of the matter and the answer to the question he'd posed to Iolyn. Melina had been afraid he wouldn't listen to her, that he'd say "no" to her doing the space walk to make repairs. And, to be honest, she would've been correct. His reasons for wanting to do the job himself were excellent and might have convinced her, but she hadn't trusted him enough to confront him and argue the matter.

"*Ansu bhau*," he swore once more, angry at her for her lack of trust and at himself for causing her to feel that way. He signaled Iolyn. "I'm on my way to the Extra-Vehicular Inspection staging area. Connect me to the EVI team's com-units so I can monitor their communications."

He all but ran into the opening elevator, then snarled the word "engineering."

"They aren't talking much, Wulf," Iolyn said. "But I'm patching you through."

"How long have they been out there?" he asked.

"Two standard hours and counting."

Wulf growled. "You should have awakened me."

"Mel asked me not to," Iolyn replied, "she thought she would be done before you woke up."

"*Ansu bhau*, Iolyn," Wulf snarled, "don't ever cover up for

Melina again."

"She outranks me. Should I have disobeyed an order?"

Wulf mulled that over. "No, she is your superior officer ... but—"

"That's what I thought. You're connected."

Iolyn must have told Melina and Huw he was awake and now connected, because the first words he heard were Huw addressing him.

"Wulf, your *gemate* is amazing. She repaired all the defective couplings in less time than I ever could and now she's making sure the others are sound." Huw paused, taking a deep breath. "We've accomplished so much, so fast that she decided to do a quick external scan of the weapon systems arrays to make sure nothing more was done to them than draining power. We should be done here soon, if nothing comes up."

"Are you spotting her?" His voice was shakier than he would've liked. *Diew*! All the things that could go wrong skittered across his mind like leaves in the wind. The space dock was long-abandoned. The super-structure consisted of rickety metal girders and other pieces of equipment that could fall apart from a lack of maintenance. With no active shields on the dock, anyone working outside could be hit by an errant meteor or showers of space dust and rocks, especially in this region.

The main, and only, reason he'd selected this particular dock was because it was close and the best option, not because it was in the best shape. And, of course, he'd expected to be the one outside the ship with his brother—not Melina.

Wulf ran shaking fingers through his hair. Roiling emotions still churned his gut. He was close to losing all semblance of calm. He wasn't proud of it, but couldn't help it. No matter how upset he was that she'd felt the need to sneak behind his back, his primary concern was for her safety. She was out there, in danger, and he could do nothing about it. He felt helpless—and that was a feeling he had never experienced before.

"Yes, he's spotting me," Melina answering his question to Huw. Her voice was calm, but breathy from her exertions. Zero-G work was exhausting for a large, well-rested male—and she wasn't large or male and couldn't have had much rest. "Wulf, don't be mad at Huw, Iolyn or the crew. I ordered them. I was the most qualified to do this—and you know it."

He left the elevator and ran down the main corridor dividing the engineering level into halves. Reaching the staging area door, he strode into the control room, his eyes fixed on the large monitor displaying the exterior view of the ship as the robotic cameras followed the EVI team.

"I know you're qualified, *lubha*, but this space dock creates more risk than most EVIs," he said. The words came out more calmly than he felt; his voice was only slightly husky from the tension trapped in his throat. "I want you to come in now. I'll come out and help Huw with the rest of the external examination." He wanted her frail body inside, away from any stray meteor that might hit her.

The two figures floated along the surface of the ship, tethered only by one cable to the ship. The falling apart and pockmarked docking bay was worse than he remembered. Streams of meteors streaked past the space dock, visible through the many holes made in the superstructure of the docking bay by previous hits.

Fear speared his heart, causing him to gasp.

"Don't bother suiting up. We're almost through." Melina's voice held a hint of exasperation and, damn her, amusement. There was no evidence she was even aware of the large rocks whizzing all around her. Although she had to be.

"You'll be happy to know, Captain Wulf," Melina said as her suited figure turned to follow the ship's surface back toward the air lock, "that the weapons look untouched. All the main shields are now fully functional. We'll have a much better chance of surviving to make it to Tooh 10 now."

"Captain Wulf?" He growled. "You shouldn't poke a stick at a Prime warrior when he is justly concerned over his *gemate's* safety."

"*That's* the Wulf I love so much," Melina said with a laugh. "Those growls of yours kept me going that time in the tunnels."

Melina took a deep and shaky breath. She missed a handhold but quickly recovered the slow, painstaking motion which would bring her back into the ship.

"Get in here now, Melina." She was weakening. "Or, do I have to come out and bring you in?"

He turned to order an EVI suit prepared for him when she spoke. "Calm down, *gemat*. We're coming in. Just one short leap and we'll be in the air lock."

The two figures shoved off the ship to make the short journey toward the exterior access and safety. Two suited crew members stood in the open hatch, monitoring the winch that retracted the two's tethers and making ready to assist the EVI team inside once they were close enough.

Wulf let go of the gut-wrenching fear that had completely engulfed him since he'd learned Melina was outside the ship. She would be inside soon. She was safe, or she would be only until he delivered some blistering home truths about closing her mind and her not trusting him enough to discuss her plans *before* she executed them.

Several large thuds resounded through the ship.

He'd relaxed too soon. The view screen showed multiple large rocks, bigger than a full-grown Prime male, and definitely bigger than Melina, streak across the view provided by the robotic cameras paralleling the two into the ship.

"Sensor reports on the meteor shower." His horrified gaze locked onto the screen. He winced as one rock whizzed through the space just vacated by Huw. "Winches on top speed," he ordered.

"Already are, sir," responded the technician monitoring the two space-walkers' suits and connections to the ship.

"Shower is two kilometers in width. No way is the space dock going to avoid getting hit. No end in sight. A large number are getting through the dock's superstructure. So far the hits on the ship are minor. No breaches reported." Another tech reported then turned from his monitor. "Sir, we need to raise our shields. Potential hull damage is a high probability."

"We'll wait. As soon as the EVI team is on board, raise the shields."

"Yes, sir."

Wulf, along with every other man in the EVI staging area control room, held their breath and watched the progress of the two fragile figures making their way back to the ship. The silence was fraught with tension.

Finally, Huw entered the air lock then held out a hand to help the others pull Melina inside. At the last minute, she kicked away and floated toward the aft of the ship as far as her tether would allow.

Gasping sounds of shock escaped each man in the room.

A large space rock hit where she would have been if she hadn't moved. Now, a small hail of rocks and dust bombarded the area where the air lock opened into the space dock bay. Through the dust, nothing could be seen. Nothing was heard but static and the rat-a-tat-tat and thuds of rocks and dust hitting the body of the ship.

"Melina!" His cry echoed in the once-again still room. He turned to enter the staging room air lock. Two crewmen grabbed him and held him back. "Let me go."

"Sir. It is still depressurized. You have to wait."

Wulf took several deep breaths. Shrugging off the hands of the men, he let out a shaky breath. "You're correct. Thank you." He turned to the crewman monitoring the two spacewalker's com devices. "Any communications?"

"Communications are disrupted, sir. Electromagnetic disturbance from the dust."

"Life signs?" Wulf didn't even recognize the strained voice as his own.

"Still online, sir. They are both steady," replied the technician monitoring the suit operations. "Balcon's balls, sir, neither one of their pulses has even elevated. It's as if they were taking a walk on a beach on the home planet."

He let out the breath which had stuck in his throat.

"Status at the door?" His tone was sharp, but calmer now that he knew her heart still beat.

"Ensign Roh has reported both are inside and safe. Dirty, but safe."

"Dirty?"

"Roh reports the suits shredded somewhat, sir, but the damage was nothing the resealing fabric couldn't patch."

"Get the room pressurized, now." He paced the area in front of the door leading to the hatch. As he paced, he commed the bridge. "Navigator, get us out of this tin can. Full shields. Plot an intercept course for the rest of our squadron at top speed."

Iolyn entered the EVI staging control room and joined him as he paced. Wulf shot him a narrow-eyed look. "I'm going to spank her and tie her to the bed." After he made sure she wasn't hurt—and he kissed her senseless.

Iolyn choked back a laugh. "She said that would be your reaction."

"She knew I'd be mad, and she did it anyway?"

"Uh huh." Iolyn laughed at his look of disconcertion. "She said, and I quote, 'I'm not going to waste my breath arguing with the stubborn man. If he thinks he is going to try to go around me and endanger himself doing a job I am far more qualified to do, he can think again.'"

Wulf stared at his brother. "She didn't trust me, Iolyn. I had good reasons why I should have been the one to do the

EVI with Huw. The condition of the space dock alone should have convinced her that sometimes size is more important than experience." His voice quavered. "I've never been so scared in my life." He could've lost her.

"And she had good reasons for doing the EVI. She read your mind, you know. You had already made the decision to do it—and you didn't discuss it with her, either. You keep forgetting, as she pointed out to Huw and me, that she is your *equal* on this ship." Iolyn heaved a disgusted sigh. "And, why was this any scarier than her crawling through booby-trapped, pirate-infested tunnels or fighting off a whole ship of Antareans on Obam IV? Brother, you are going to have to trust her judgment. She has made it this far in the military and managed to stay alive. Something that her enemies cannot say."

His gaze fixed on the air lock's pressure readings, Wulf ran his fingers through his disheveled hair. "I know. I know. But I just found her—and I'm afraid ... well, I'm just afraid. She is so brave and fearless it terrifies—and pleases—me. She is a perfect mate for me and my way of life, but the thought of losing her paralyzes me. It would be like losing a part of myself that I never knew I'd even missed before meeting her."

"I don't *know* these feelings you have, Wulf," Iolyn said, a look of commiseration on his face, "but I *understand* them. The poets of our planet have often written of the feeling of oneness with our bonded mates. I only hope to experience it one day."

Wulf laughed a short, rusty sound. "And I can't wait to see how you'll cope with the fear of losing your woman. I'd rather face down an entire platoon of Antareans than risk losing her."

The air pressurization readings finally reached one hundred percent.

"About damn time." He ran into the air lock. All activity within stopped. It was like being in the eye of a cyclonic dust storm. Nothing moved. All eyes fixed on him.

Then Melina moved. With a muttered curse that had the crewman closest to her laughing, she shrugged off the last of the shredded EVI suit.

Wulf's gaze frantically swept over her body, noting the cuts. The blood. The dirt. More blood. The jagged tears in her uniform. And even more blood.

The knowledge that under her clothing there would be even more cuts, abrasions and bruises had him growling, a low, constant tone that built in crescendo as he stalked toward her. He couldn't help it. She was hurt—and open to him now. He felt her pain—her exhaustion—and some other emotion he couldn't quite place.

He stopped one foot shy, then walked around her, marking once more, in even more detail, everywhere she'd been hit. Only her face was unscathed and only because of the extra protection of the titanium-shelled hood. He wouldn't look at the helmet she wore. Any serious dents in it would push him over the edge of the erratic fear/anger combination he struggled to control.

Coming around to her front, he stopped, his hands fisted at his sides. He wanted to pull her into his arms, but was afraid he'd hurt her even more.

"Where's the damn medical team?" he gritted out, his jaw so tight he could barely open it to talk. His gaze never left her; he was afraid that if he looked away, she'd disappear.

"On their way," someone said.

Her eyes, her jewel green eyes that had mere hours ago been drenched in the pleasure they'd shared stared back at him, dulled with pain, exhaustion, and the emotion that he now could clearly read as fear.

Agony threatened to drive him to his knees. "Melina mine," he rasped, uncaring that they had an interested audience. "Please ... please, don't be afraid of me." His eyes moistened with tears of regret that he'd caused her to fear him. He unclenched the fists at his side and held out his arms. "Come to me, little one."

Tears streaked down her face as she walked into his embrace. Her head lay on his chest, her cheek resting against his heart and the symbol that bound them. Her arms wound around his waist and held onto him as tightly as he held onto her.

"You are so angry at me," she mumbled into his shirt, rubbing her cheek over his heart, which pounded in time with hers. "I'm sorry. I didn't know. I didn't realize how much my going outside would affect you." She leaned her head back and looked into his eyes. "This is stuff I did—do—all the time in the military. I just ... well, I just wanted to prove to you and the crew that I can pull my weight."

"I know, *gemate lubha.*"

He pulled her closer to his body, wanting to absorb the shudders rippling over her slight frame, to smother her with love and protection so that she never hurt again. The fact he was the cause of her distress tore him apart inside. Other than the time she'd cried for the death of her parents, he had never seen her cry. He never wanted to be the cause of her tears again.

He brushed a kiss across her forehead, soothing away the worry lines he'd placed there. "I know. Please have patience with me. Most of my anger is at myself. Iolyn and Huw keep telling me I need to cut you some slack and trust you to do your job."

He pushed her head gently back to his chest and rubbed his cheek across the top of her head. "In the future, please come to me. Trust me to discuss things with you. Argue with me. Call me an alpha-male throwback. But, please, don't go behind my back." He let out a heavy sigh and whispered for her ears alone. "I woke up and you weren't there. Not physically. Not mentally. Not even empathically. I was so afraid. I thought I'd lost you—again."

"I'm sorry." She rubbed her cheek against his chest, taking a deep breath. "I didn't mean to frighten you."

Sighing, she nestled against him, the shudders which had racked her body gone now.

"I know." He kissed her hair, inhaling her fragrance and found a deep well of calm into which his residual anger and fear dissipated. They stood there for a few seconds, sharing in the calm that being fully open to each other always brought a bonded pair.

"Wulf?"

She shifted within his arms, but he refused to let her go. "What, Melina mine?" he mumbled against the silk of her hair, one hand caressing the nape of her neck.

"I hurt. I'm dirty. And I'm tired." She let go of his waist and placed her hands on his chest, pushing until he gave her enough space to look him in the eyes again. "Take me to our quarters. I need you—and a shower and some sleep."

"I want the doctor to check you over," he said. "To calm my nerves."

She leaned back within the circle of his arms and studied his face. "Only for you."

"Thank you, *lubha*." He kissed her forehead.

Wulf turned her within his arms, then lifted her against his chest. "Send the doctor to my quarters, Iolyn. Huw, you are off-duty until we go to red alert." As he reached the door to the corridor, he added, "Iolyn, you are in command. I'll get Melina settled and then come to relieve you."

Both brothers nodded, grins wide on their faces, their thoughts as clear as his own. He'd have to talk to them about keeping their minds off what he and Melina might be up to in the privacy of their quarters.

"Wulf?" Melina's hand stroked his still-tense jaw. "Don't you have something to say to our EVI team? Huw and I could not have done the job without their support. When the meteor shower hit, they grabbed and pulled us in, endangering themselves in the process."

Renewed fear pierced the relief at having her in his arms. *Diew!* He shuddered. He really had almost lost her.

"You didn't. I'm here. Safe."

"Next time you think about going into danger. I want to be the one at your side. It was the not knowing what was happening, the not being there to help you that scared me the most."

"I understand."

"Remember, we're stronger together."

"But we can't discount our individual strengths either."

"I understand what you are saying—and I'll promise to try to be more reasonable and less overprotective."

"You are kind of cute when you get all growly, though."

She flashed a mischievous grin and then spoiled it by yawning.

He kissed her. Abruptly, he realized everyone in the room stood staring at them with silly smiles on their faces. These same men were the only reason she and his brother were alive.

"Wulf," she urged. "Don't you have something to say?"

He swept a gentle finger over her cheek and rasped out, "I will want to know what happened, all of it, later. Once you are rested."

She nodded and turned to kiss the hand caressing her. He kissed her once more, whispering against her lips. "Don't ever scare me like that again. My heart can't take it."

She returned the kiss. "I'll try not to—I promise."

Satisfied that he'd gotten his point across, Wulf turned his attention to the men who'd gone back to work cleaning up after the EVI. "Good job all. I'll be recommending you, both individually and as a unit, for commendations. Huw, make a note of that."

"That's a good captain," Melina mumbled into his chest as her eyes closed and she drifted off into sleep.

CHAPTER FIFTEEN

Eight Standard Hours later

Well-rested after a solid seven hours of sleep, Mel entered the Captain's conference room in search of Wulf.

He sat alone. Beyond him the expansive port window framed a fiery red, blue, white and peach display of a star cluster in a nebula thousands of light-years behind the *Galanti*.

How many times had he sat in the observation area, watching as the galaxy whizzed by? How many times had he sat in that chair, attempting to figure a way out of a tight corner? How many times had he questioned his place in the grand scheme of things, wondering when his number might come up and if he would live to see another mission?

"Too many times to count, *gemate*. Too many damn times."

He turned and smiled at her. What had put that smile on his face? With a light mental touch, she read his emotions. Happiness. Love. Both emotions were tied to her—only her.

A sense of well-being swept over her. This was right; *they* were right.

He held out a hand, beckoning her to join him. "I now have more to fight for. To live for. I have you and our future together. So, I expect that I will find myself in this chair, watching the galaxy whiz by many more times."

Mel walked over and kissed him lightly on the lips. "But no longer alone."

"Yes," he whispered against her mouth. "No longer alone. Forgive me for my loss of control earlier?"

She pulled away from the luscious warmth of his mouth then leaned against the arm of his chair. "Nothing to forgive. We still have much to learn of each other. We are both used to being in control, to acting as we see fit. It's a learning curve, this battle-mate relationship."

She stroked the back of his sinewy hand with one finger. "More like a learning cliff. The biological connection is there and has been ever since that moment we first met in the maintenance tunnel. For me, the emotional connection has been there also, almost from the beginning—though I tried to deny it." She shook her head, laughing at herself. "I didn't trust it, at first. It's the psychological connection, the learned trust, I have the most trouble dealing with. Sharing command decisions goes against all my training and experience. But, I know that it, too, will come."

Wulf reversed the grip she had on his hand and brought hers to his lips. "Thank you. I'm not sure I deserve your understanding, but I'm grateful for it." He rubbed his cheek against her hand. "For me, it is the emotional connection that is overwhelming. Intellectually, I *know* you are strong and capable, but my fears for your safety override my brain and I react emotionally. I've never had that happen before. I will try to overcome the issue, but it might take time. Prime males have deeply rooted protective instincts when it comes to their mates, even strong battle-mates. Have patience with me?"

"Always. You're worth the trouble," she teased. Pulling her hand away, she cupped his jaw and stole another kiss.

His eyes glowed with love as he reached for her face and took control of the kiss. His tongue swept into her mouth and claimed every single millimeter like the conquering warrior he was. It was a kiss that promised hot nights on cool sheets. And even hotter, sultry afternoons of tangled sweaty limbs.

Mel moaned, returning the kiss, trying to get closer to the promise of passion.

The quarter-hour reminder of yellow alert status sounded, startling them both.

Groaning, Wulf pulled away and whispered, "Later, *gemate*."

Sitting back in his chair, his molten gaze traveled over her, setting her nerves ablaze. One look from Wulf was worth more than all the foreplay any other male of her acquaintance had ever attempted.

"You are rested?" His voice was husky with restrained heat.

Taking a calming breath, Mel walked to his other side and sat down. "Yes." Answering his unspoken question, she added, "My cuts and bruises were minor. I'm fine."

Another of his heated searching glances and, then, a light mental touch had her pulling up the maintenance report on the status of the weapons systems to distract him from his intimate examination of her wellbeing. "I'm fine, Wulf. How's the weapons' recharge going?"

A disbelieving grunt was his only response.

Obviously, she hadn't masked the lingering pain from the injuries she'd obtained during her EVI walk. If she could have, she would've denied all injury. But he'd seen the evidence in the EVI staging area and, later, after he'd escorted her back to their quarters. Once there, the doctor quickly examined her, efficiently wielding the ice gun on her bruises and lasering her lacerations and abrasions.

Wulf had stood over them both, alternately cursing each hurt as it was revealed, then lecturing her on the prime importance of her safety for his mental health and the ultimate well-being of every single crew member—for every living being in the galaxy. Then he'd dismissed the doctor and tucked her in bed. As he kissed her, he had pressure-injected her with a sleeping agent which had put her under for over six and a half standard hours.

The sneaky bastard.

She would've done the same for him. They really did think alike. She grinned.

Still working on shifting Wulf's attention back to work and away from her physical status, she commented, "Looks as if we're still at least five standard hours away from full power on the two forward weapons and two standard hours on the aft."

"They are making progress." Wulf caressed her left hand as it hovered over the keypad. "When we get to Tooh 10, let's take some time, visit Maren at the embassy on Tooh 2. Maybe stay at the resort for some rest and relaxation, and what the Terrans call a honeymoon."

She smiled and turned her hand up to clasp his. "That sounds like a plan."

Wulf smiled. "Good." He pulled his hand from hers and swept an errant lock of hair from her cheek, tucking it behind her ear. "Why don't you pull up the nav screen? Let's see where the unknown ships are currently."

Wulf's affectionate touch was distracting, but Mel sensed his need to handle her. And, if the truth be told, she needed the contact. Something about their bond demanded that they reach out to each other often. If not mentally, then physically. Damn, this would never work on an Alliance vessel. Military protocol required decorum at all times while on duty. Married personnel were required to keep their affection under control and save it for the privacy of their quarters.

"Then, I will touch you mind-to-mind in front of the non-Prime crew. Our Prime crew members understand the need to

touch—and what we do here, in private, is not against protocol. We are mated."

"I can work with that. But if I snap at you from time to time, be patient. I'm not used to being touched all the time."

"I will be as patient with you as you are with me."

"Well, that *could make life interesting."*

Wulf chuckled, stroking a finger down her cheek. "Life with you is all that I want."

"You're an awfully smooth talker for not dating much. Did the sex surrogates teach you that?" Waving her hand, she said, "No, never mind. They are in the past."

"Yes. In the past. They have nothing to do with us." In a low, husky voice, he added, "They meant nothing to me, Melina."

"That's good to know."

A quick touch of his mind and she found that he told the truth—in his mind the sex surrogates had been a means to an end, nothing else. If they had meant more, she might have had to hunt them up and bitch-slap them. Any of them approaching him on Cejuru Prime in the future would find out quickly that this battle-mate did not share. God, this was so not like her. Jealousy over a man. Of course, she'd never cared for anyone before. So maybe it was just a female thing.

Mel turned her attention back to the nav screen.

"Uh, the bogies are about a light-year away," she said as she keyed in another set of numbers. "Gold Squadron has closed the gap and is now only about one and a half light-years away from intercepting the *Galanti*. It'll be close. But, figuring the Gold's better speed, Royce might get here around the same time as the bad guys."

She keyed in a few more variables to confirm her conclusion. "The enemy has to know Gold is on its way. Do you think that will scare them off?"

"What do you think?" Wulf turned his chair at an angle to face her.

"No. They'll attack us," she said. "Because, if the rebels hired them, they don't get paid unless they do the job. And, if, as I think, the bogies are allies of the Antareans, they'll attack or the Antareans will make them wish they were dead."

Wulf smiled. "My thoughts exactly."

"So, what's the plan? Make them chase us all over the place until Gold gets in position?"

"Is that what you would do?" Wulf asked, one dark brow raised in query.

"Depends." She pursed her lips and thought for a bit. "We have shields. We have outstanding maneuverability. We have fighters that can harry the enemy and deliver some knock-out blows to their weapons and shields. We have two aft weapon systems fully on-line."

She looked at him. "I'd shift course and see if they followed. If they did, then I would plot a course for them, hailing them to ask their purpose in this sector. See how they react. If they prepare to fire upon us without responding, then I'd go on the offensive and take out as many of them as I could. If they're smart, they'd retreat and then we send some of Gold's light battle-cruisers after them and force them to yield. Then, I'd drag their asses back to Tooh 10."

"Sounds very similar to what I would do," Wulf said. "Another advantage we have that you are not as familiar with is the beta-weapon we used on the pirate's ship."

"What does it do exactly? When we came upon the pirate's mother ship, they were dead in space. No power to the engines and no weapons, but the ship itself looked as if it had not sustained any battle damage."

Wulf swiveled his chair back so he once again stared into streaming space. "The beta-weapon disrupts the ship's energy source. Thus, if the beta-weapon is aimed at and manages to hit the correct spot in the ship's reactor, it interrupts the production of energy. No energy—no weapons, no power.

The ship is relegated to using emergency back-ups to maintain even the most minimal of life support."

Mel frowned. "But the types of power sources are different from ship-to-ship, and even among the same type of ships within different militaries. If it is the wrong kind of power source, and you manage to hit exactly the right spot—which in and of itself is no mean feat—you could destroy everything within the vicinity."

"Exactly. We were lucky to have the specs for the particular type of Volusian battle-cruiser that the pirates had stolen. The weapon will not work with every type of power source. And, as you mentioned, some ships are harder to target with precision. But for the ones that it will work upon, it is an effective weapon that can take out an enemy without killing everyone on board," Wulf said. "For our current situation, I have Huw seeking the specs for the light battle-cruisers that are speeding toward us. If the C-Class battle cruisers are as old as Commander Sinclair says, they might be a simple fusion reactor, easily disrupted by changing the nature of the core material."

"We can only hope. So, what we do now?" Mel asked.

"We wait." Wulf stood and held out his hand. "Dinner with the crew?"

"Yes. I'd like that. I want them to become comfortable with a female around, since I have in mind several female soldiers from the *Leonidas* to bring over." She took his hand. "Plus, I've always found the crew appreciates their captain acting as if death wasn't waiting around the next corner."

"A definite morale booster," agreed Wulf as he guided them from the conference room.

Red Alert—Battle Stations

AFTER NO RESPONSE TO THEIR hail and after a slight change of course, which the bogies mirrored, Wulf ordered the *Galanti* to red alert. The hunted was now the hunter. Just the way Wulf liked it.

"Commander Nowicki has communicated they are less than one standard hour away," Huw relayed.

"Tell them we plan to proceed with the attack on the ships operating under false Alliance Military identity codes," Wulf said. "Relay this information to Alliance Military Command: *The five unknown battle cruisers have refused to identify themselves and have acted in a threatening manner. We now consider them to be a threat to this ship.* Galanti *will attack and subdue the unknowns.*"

"They've been informed, Captain." Dakkin, the communications officer said.

"Mel is in Weapons Control," Huw reported from his position at engineering control, "in case you didn't know."

Wulf turned and smiled at his brother. "I know. She told me—her mind is totally open. We made a pact to keep the line of communications accessible during battle."

"That's a relief," Huw said, a smile on his lips. "Iolyn and I didn't want to continue in the roles of interpreters and mediators for each of your actions."

"Don't worry about it, Huw. I've always known that Melina was strong and smart and quite capable of running this ship without me. And she now knows that my emotional responses to her being in danger are just that—emotional—and not based on a lack of trust in her abilities. I've promised to have patience with her when she acts precipitously—but with the mental link open, I will not be as apt to overreact."

"I'll pass that along to Iolyn," Huw said. "He'll be relieved. And Mel? What did she promise to do?"

"She has promised to trust me."

"Didn't she trust you before?" Shock was evident in Huw's facial expression.

"She didn't come to me with her plan to go outside the ship on the EVI because she felt I would have forbidden her." Wulf shrugged. "She was probably correct. To that point, I had acted the overprotective male and she feared that I wouldn't listen to reason. Now, she knows I might huff-and-puff but I'll listen to her with an open mind."

"It will be hard for you, won't it?" Huw said, a deep crease of worry drawing a line between his brows.

"If you mean, letting her walk into *known* danger? Yes— but I will always try to be by her side during those times— to lessen her exposure." He laughed. "And she'll cover my ass, too. We are very much alike in that way. Both of us are protectors as well as warriors."

"Captain!" Commander Ard, the Science Officer broke in. "The five unknown ships are on screen and within firing range. They are powering up their weapons."

"Battle stations," Wulf ordered. "Full shields. Prepare the beta-weapon. Put all fighters on standby."

Each station reported in affirming battle readiness.

"Melina. The bogies are preparing to fire upon us."

"Hold the fort, Wulf. We may have a way to get you full weapons fairly soon."

"We'll manage."

"Of course we will. I'll be up as soon as we get things straightened out down here."

Wulf turned back toward the large monitor on the command deck. The forward view showed the bogies approaching the *Galanti* in a V-wing formation, definitely an attack formation.

Turning to Huw, he asked, "The lead ship is a first-generation Volusian C-class light battle cruiser. How about the others? They look different."

Huw frowned over his monitor. "They are all C-class in specs. The modifications seem to be in the superstructure. Power sources on all five seem to be upgraded from first-generation. But they are still using nuclear fission in their reactors. The beta-weapon might work if we can target around the mods on the superstructure."

"Weapons, prepare the beta-weapon to fire."

"Aye, sir," the Weapons Officer responded. "Beta-weapon firing solution is programmed. Will record for study later."

"Take out the lead ship and then target the others. First, the ships on either side of the leader, then the last two. Make them count, Ensign. This fight could be over before it even begins."

"Yes, sir."

"Fire," ordered Wulf.

The sound of the beta-weapon reverberated throughout the command deck due to its proximity to the upper levels of the ship.

The enemy ships returned fire with the exception of the lead ship and the one to its immediate right. The beta-weapon had done its job on two of the five ships.

"How are the shields holding?" Wulf gripped the arms of his command chair as the ship rocked from a hit.

"Holding," Huw replied.

"Weapons, fire the beta-weapon again. Helmsman, use Delta-A evasive maneuvers."

"Firing, sir."

"Delta-A evasive maneuvers engaged, sir."

The command deck crew seemed to hold its breath as the beta-weapon fired and hit each of the three remaining ships. Two still had maneuverability.

"One of the ships is breaking away, sir. They are making an attempt to come in behind us."

"Use the active aft weapons and take them out if you can, Ensign."

"Aye, sir." A slight pause. "Direct hit, sir. They are crippled and heading away from us."

"Sir, three of the five enemy ships are now dead in space," Ard reported. "My readings show environmental is cut in half on each. Life signs have congregated amidships. All shields down, no weapons, no power to the engines."

"The fifth ship is also retreating, Wulf," Huw said. "We are losing two of the five."

"Contact Gold, let them know what heading the remaining two bogies are following. Ask them to pursue and subdue."

"They have been so informed, sir," Dakkin replied. "Gold is plotting an intercept course for the remaining two bogies. Commander Nowicki asks our status."

"Advise him that we are fine and will remain with the three dead ships until either he or Blue arrives."

"Acknowledged, sir." Dakkin said.

The doors to the elevator swished open. Wulf scented Melina before he felt her touch his mind to tell him she was here. Without turning around, he asked, "I take it we have all weapons online?"

"That is so freaky," whispered Huw. "That you know when she is near you without looking."

"It is wonderful, Huw, not weird." Wulf smiled as Melina sat in the chair next to his.

She shook her head, her long, dark hair settling about her shoulders like a glossy silk cloak. "Yes, all weapons are online. The weapons engineer and I found a way to replenish the power to them faster."

"Good work, Melina." Wulf smiled at her.

"Looks like we didn't need them after all." She smiled back. "Well done, Wulf."

"We have an excellent crew," Wulf replied.

"Yes, we do. The weapons engineer was willing to accept my outside-the-box solution to rerouting power to the damaged weapons. Of course, what we did isn't something I'd recommend doing every day, but it worked." She added under her breath, "Just don't plan on using any of the recreation decks any time soon."

Wulf snorted back a laugh. "Borrowed some power from the simulators, huh?"

"Took *all* the power from the simulators. The time on Tooh 10 for inspection and maintenance is now an absolute necessity. I don't want to be present when they try to unravel our creative jury-rigging. The head of Alliance Military Command maintenance might shoot me." Hesitating a moment, she said. "And, damn, don't you men ever clean your maintenance tunnels? They are filthy. I had to stop and change again."

"I take it that we will be doing so in the future?"

"Count on it," Melina added. She angled her head toward the three dead ships, sitting dark and motionless. "So, what's the plan? Wait until their auxiliary power starts to fade, then board them?"

"We won't have to wait that long. Blue should be here soon and we can send in fully armed boarding parties to take control of the prisoners for transport to Tooh 10."

Wulf turned to face his Science Officer. "Mr. Ard, can you give me any idea of exactly what we are dealing with on these three vessels?"

"As I mentioned earlier, life signs are congregated amidships on all three vessels. They are oxygen-breathing, carbon life forms. Seem to be a mixture of species. None are Antarean, although some are close and are probably Erian. Ships are at full complement for a C-Class light cruiser. Thirty crew each, for a total of ninety."

"Definitely too many for us to handle alone," Melina agreed. "Sounds like pirates. So my guess was wrong. They aren't Antarean allies, but mercenaries hired by the rebels."

"It looks like it," agreed Wulf. "I'm sure they were

unpleasantly surprised to find we were not helpless, as they were probably promised by their employers."

"Yeah, I bet that whatever they were paid, it wasn't enough to serve the rest of their natural lives, freezing their asses off on Umbraxi 9," Melina said, smiling wickedly. "So? Who leads the three boarding teams?"

Wulf sought the mood behind the question. Her aura stated she'd be fine with whatever he decided. Obviously she'd touched his mind and read the normal Prime protocol in cases such as this: Prime military never risked their captains on potentially hazardous boardings of unknown enemies. That's what they made First Officers and Security Chiefs for.

"After Blue arrives, Iolyn will lead the team from our ship. Garth has signaled he'll be here within one half a standard hour and has two boarding teams ready to go."

"Good." Melina smoothed her hand down Wulf's forearm. "Just tell me how I can help." She pulled up the current data on the ships. "I'll study their environmental systems. We might need medical teams to follow the armed boarding parties. Also, the mods made on the superstructures on two of the three are very odd. Want to make sure there are no surprises waiting for our guys."

"I'm a very lucky man." Wulf gently shoved a lock of her hair behind her ear, his hand lingering on the curve of her cheek. He'd never realized how lonely command had been prior to meeting Melina. All he knew was that he never wanted to be that alone again.

"Damn right, you are." She shot him a cheeky grin as she turned to her data link. "You got a *gemate*, a co-captain and an engineer to boot. Now let's figure out what our boys will be facing when they board those ships."

CHAPTER SIXTEEN

Five standard days later, Tooh 2 Resort

Naked, Mel lay on her stomach on the suite's bed, still warm from a mid-morning lovemaking session. Through pleasure-heavy eyes, she watched Wulf pull on a sport shirt.

Such a shame to cover up those muscled abs, but it was a necessity. If he didn't, she would most likely commit wholesale murder. And that wasn't frivolous conjecture on her part. Earlier that morning when she and Wulf had finally emerged after spending three straight days in their resort suite, she'd glared at all the women who ogled him as he'd dried off after a swim. Maybe a traditional Terran wedding band would help stave off the unwanted female attention? Or, perhaps a prominently placed tattoo reading "Mine"? Better yet, and her personal favorite hands-off notice, a laser stun to one of the leering female's gut?

Grinning, she shook her head. She never thought the day would come when she'd get possessive over a man.

Tearing her mind away from thoughts of murder and mayhem, she turned toward thoughts of ripping his shirt off, dragging him back to bed, then tracing his solar plexus with her tongue. No, she'd done that already. Besides, it wouldn't be fair. He was so excited and looking forward to the challenge of the upcoming fishing expedition he and his brothers had arranged.

Rolling onto her back, she stretched like a cat. The sun filtering through the sheer drapes covering the ceiling to floor windows warmed her nude body. She couldn't recall ever feeling so relaxed and happy in her entire life. Her movement had captured Wulf's attention. All of a sudden it wasn't just the sun that heated her body.

"So? Just what kind of sports fish are you and your brothers out to catch?" she asked, in a attempt to divert his thoughts from joining her on the bed for yet another round of sweaty, mind-numbing pleasure. She really was trying to be good; he was excited as a kid about going fishing.

Wulf's eyes heated as his gaze swept over her nudity. "Tobruk. Very similar to Terran shark."

Then he smiled. She loved it when he smiled. His happiness was important to her. They could always make love after he returned. She sat up and pulled on the silk robe Wulf had bought her, covering the temptation of her nudity.

His gaze followed her movements. "Later, *lubha*." His voice was husky and full of sensual promises.

"Definitely, later." She smiled. "Tobruk, huh?"

Frowning, she recalled seeing a picture of a tobruk once. They had lots of teeth. Very long sharp teeth. And a large, sharp bony prominence called a horn. And were big, very big. Well, she knew this wouldn't be a tame fishing trip, but tobruk?

"You eat them?" She scrunched her nose as she braided her hair.

"No. We catch them, get our picture taken next to them, and then toss them back into the Tooh Sea for the next lucky fisherman."

"Sounds like, uh, fun to me," she said, sarcasm liberally lacing her tone. She'd have to remember always to be busy when fishing was mentioned. While she liked sports, catching creatures large enough to eat a person was not her idea of fun or relaxing—or a sport. Must be a male thing.

Wulf slipped his bare feet into deck shoes. His long, muscled and deeply tanned legs looked as lickable as his stomach. In fact, his whole sun-kissed body was lickable, as she'd proven after their early morning foray to the pool. After the women at the pool had literally salivated over him, she'd felt an urgent need to reclaim and mark every square millimeter of his body. You'd think the brazen hussies had never seen a nearly naked Prime male warrior before.

"Probably most of them hadn't," teased Wulf, reading her mind. A wicked grin curved his mobile lips, lips which had reclaimed every bit of her as well. "I think I like you jealous. The results are *sinful*." The last word uttered in the low growling tone she loved so well.

"Only for you am I sinful." She winked.

Mel rose from the bed and walked toward him, the silken robe showing more of her body than it hid. His golden gaze burned as it stroked over her.

"Kiss me goodbye?" Raising her arms, she twined them around his neck and licked his lips until he opened them for her. She stroked his tongue with hers as her fingers played with the dark, silky hair at the nape of his neck. His large body shuddered against her. His aura heated. His arousal was as strong as hers.

Breaking the kiss, she whispered, "All those nasty women can find their own Prime warrior. This one is taken."

"Most assuredly, *lubha*." He nibbled at her mouth. "I want no other."

She trailed her hands down his body, finally wrapping her arms around his lean waist. Her head resting on his chest, she listened to the heart beating rapidly just for her. He stroked her, his large hands claiming every inch from her nape to just above her ass. Then his large hands each cupped a butt cheek, massaging them. Her womb clenched and liquid warmth coated her folds. The sexual heat that should have been quenched after their three-day lovemaking marathon flared into full flames once again.

"Wulf, if you keep doing that," she husked. "You won't make it to your little fishing trip with the boys."

"They can go without me," he whispered, his voice harsh with his own arousal. "Later has just arrived. I can't leave you unsatisfied, *gemate lubha*. It would be remiss of me. And, it *is* our honeymoon."

Guilt reared its ugly head once more, threatening to stomp on the pleasure her lover's hands aroused. Wulf had really been looking forward to the outing.

Maybe they could manage both?

"When were you meeting them? Maybe we can get a quickie in." She unbuttoned the top of his shorts and slid her hand inside to massage his hard, throbbing cock as it strained to meet her touch.

"They can wait." He leaned back to peer down at her fingers fondling him. "It seems something's come up."

Laughing, she stepped back, letting go of his penis, then took his hand to lead him back to the rumpled bed. "Something definitely has—and I know just how to take care of the matter. We Alliance officers are trained for all sorts of emergencies."

"How forward thinking of the Alliance," he growled.

When she reached the bed, she released Wulf's and turned to face him. She sought his fiery gaze, then slipped the sheer robe off first one, then the other shoulder. The little nothing of a garment fell to the floor in a silken puddle.

"While I love the negligee, *lubha*, I much prefer you this way."

He stepped within arm's reach and picked her up. Laying her on the bed, he followed her down, covering her body with his. Happiness flowed from his mind to hers, filling her with such joy she thought she would burst.

"Tell me what you want, Melina."

Mel's arms reached for him. Placing her lips against his, she whispered, "You. I want you."

"You have me." A low groan escaped his lips as his cock entered her body, filling the aching emptiness. "As I have you, thank *Diew*."

———

MELINA PULLED ON A SUN dress. She needed no bra. Her firm breasts, ones he knew intimately and completely, were full, firm, and luscious. They filled the low-cut bodice perfectly. Her only underclothing was a lacy thong that he'd chosen from the resort's computerized shopping arcade. He smiled in satisfaction. In fact, all of her underwear was now of his choosing. He'd quite happily gotten rid of all the boring, military-issue undergarments. Only *he* would know that under her uniforms she wore the finest, briefest silk and lace garments.

His eyes gleamed at the thought of the little number she would wear later this evening under the evening dress he also had chosen for her. It was a sheer, flesh-colored teddy that could be removed with the untying of two little bows. He planned to remove it with his teeth.

Groaning at the mental image, he rearranged his cock in his shorts. It amazed him at how his body was always primed and ready for hers. His past life had been a cold, sexual wasteland compared to the life he now shared with Melina.

At first, his *gemate* had protested about his choosing her clothing, especially her undergarments, but he'd prevailed. It had taken hours of lovemaking, but by the end of the second day on Tooh 2, he had persuaded her. He visualized many years of overcoming all her stubborn, independent ways using that all-too-satisfactory method. His winning argument had been that while she might have to wear a uniform, what she wore under it was not dictated by military rules. It was all about compromise.

"What did your brothers say about you missing the outing?" She looked at him in the reflection of the mirror in the luxuriously appointed bathroom.

"They laughed. A lot." He winked at her. "They just rescheduled the fishing trip for after lunch. They'll be by to pick me up soon."

He stepped close behind her and pulled her body into his, nestling her ass against his crotch. "I'm already hard for you again." He kissed the top of her head, capturing her shining green gaze with his golden one. "I think it was a wise decision that we chose not to stay in the suite Maren prepared for us in the embassy. Too many ears and empathic abilities would have, um, hampered our honeymoon celebration."

"I try to forget the Prime are empathic." Melina blushed rosily. "But I'm Prime, and I know that I've always sensed strong emotions."

Sex evoked pretty damn strong emotions, he thought.

She continued, "It didn't bother me on the *Galanti* as much as it would've at the embassy." She shrugged, causing her body to rub against his.

He groaned. "Careful, *lubha*. My brothers would never let me live it down if I miss this trip again."

She frowned at his reflection, jabbing an elbow into his ribs. "Don't even joke about it. How am I going to face your brothers ever again? They know what we've been, um, doing here for the last three days."

He chuckled as he nuzzled the side of her neck. "Don't worry about what they sense. I will warn them to be polite. And if they don't heed my brotherly warnings, I give you full permission to kick their impudent asses if they ever say anything to you about our sex life."

Melina turned within his arms. "I'd tell you—and let *you* kick their sorry butts as I cheered you on."

"Ahh, teamwork," he whispered against her lips. "I like it."

"Exactly," she whispered back and kissed him lightly.

Putting the temptation of her from him, he stepped back, holding her shoulders, his thumbs stroking the soft, sun-kissed skin. "What are you planning to do while we're fishing?"

"I'm going to the spa and getting my body scrubbed with sea salt and herbs, then lightly oiled and massaged. Followed by a shampoo and trim and then a manicure and pedicure. I want to look my best for the reception Uncle Tor is giving us this evening."

"If I weren't promised to my brothers, I'd come and watch." He wiggled his brows.

"No, you wouldn't. It is women only in that portion of the resort." She laughed and wiggled out from under his hands. "But you can examine the results, more intimately, later tonight after the reception is over." She winked at him.

"It's a date. I have plans for the teddy I bought you." Wulf wiggled his brows again, making her laugh, then reached for her to grab one last kiss. The door chimes interrupted him mid-swoop. "Save that kiss for later. My brothers are here."

"I'll save you more than a kiss."

"I am so blessed."

———

Mid-afternoon, Tooh 2 Resort Spa

MEL SIGHED. LIFE WAS PERFECT. She was loved by a wonderful man who accepted her and her career. She'd just spent the last three days celebrating that love with non-stop sex which had reached heights she could never have imagined. And now, she sat in a luxurious spa, being catered to right and left. Life could never get any better than this.

Spas were her new guilty pleasure. She'd never been to one before, but would make it a point to visit this one whenever they were in port and had some downtime. Maybe they had spas on Cejuru Prime. She'd have to ask Wulf.

Every single bit of her skin was polished and smooth as a baby's butt. She smelled like the rarest of white orchids and musk; the scent evoked sex waiting to happen. Every muscle in her body had been kneaded, pummeled and then soothed until she was limp with relaxation. The feeling was almost as good as having sex—almost, but not quite. Sex with Wulf was still the best relaxation technique she'd ever encountered. Sighing at the thought of her sexy warrior, she ran her fingers through her hair. It lay in sexy, bouncy waves around her shoulders.

Wulf would want to eat her up. She couldn't wait.

Garbed in a fluffy white spa robe, she sipped the too-sweet fruity drink the quiet assistant had provided as she waited her turn for a manicure and a pedicure. After which, her transformation from an Alliance Military officer to the soon-to-be-feted mate of a Prime warrior at the inaugural ball at the Cejuru Prime Embassy would be complete.

Yawning, she set the glass down, splashing some of the liquid out and over her hand. Damn, she was clumsy. Not enough sleep and too little food. It was true you couldn't live on love. She giggled.

Giggled? She never giggled.

Her vision blurred and the minuscule private waiting area spun around her. She gripped the arms of the chair. The small room had suddenly become smaller and somehow menacing.

No, the sense of peril wasn't in the room; it was outside, in the main spa.

Strong emotions rode the air like a boat on storm-tossed waves. Fear. Shock. Despair. Then nothing. It was as if all the emotions of the spa personnel had suddenly shut down, leaving a cold, empty hole in the atmosphere.

A sick feeling settled in the pit of her stomach as dizziness now swept over her in waves.

Her weakened senses attempted to seek out the threat. Fighting to remain conscious, she searched the dead space that was now the spa with all her senses wide open. A new emotion rode the atmosphere. The aura was weak at first, undulating on the eddies and whirls of the air, then it grew stronger. The mental feel—the taste on the air currents was hate. Rabid, unceasing hatred for her. And it was coming closer.

"Shit, shit, shit..."

She attempted to stand and fell back into the chair. She clasped her head in her shaky hands as the room whirled around her, making her stomach roil. Drugged. She had to have been drugged. She needed to get as much of the poison out of her system as possible. Leaning over the side of the chair, she stuck her finger down her throat. She gagged as the acidic contents of her stomach emptied themselves onto the floor.

Weakly, she leaned back in the chair and gasped for breath. She was so weak. Too weak. Maybe she'd managed to get the majority of whatever they'd drugged her with out of her stomach. Whatever the substance had been, it was potent. She already had a debilitating amount in her system.

Pinching her naked thigh, she could barely feel it. Her fingers felt as if they were phantom limbs.

"Dammit, widespread neuropathy," she muttered out loud, slurring the words into more syllables than required.

Aphasia also. Not good. Her brain needed a stimulant. And fast.

Recalling her training, she knew she had little time. She had to combat the drug using her body's own hormonal defenses. Cortisol and adrenaline. She needed to get mad—not an issue since she was furious—and move.

Flight or fight. She chose to fight and prayed her body's defenses could meet the battle to come. And it would come. She already sensed the menace stalking her, coming ever closer to this room. Her mind's eye envisioned a hulking black shape, an amorphous mass of dark energy, searching the spa, room by room. It ... he ... wanted her dead.

Struggling to stand, she staggered to the wall, knocking over the chair. The resulting noise sounded like an explosion in the all-too-quiet spa. He had to have heard the noise.

Maybe someone else would hear and come to help her. She searched with all her senses again and still found nothing but her stalker's rage. She leaned against the wall, her forehead relishing the cool against her sweaty skin. There was no one else out there. He killed the entire staff—just to get to her.

She was on her own. She needed a weapon. She needed a defensible position outside of this box of a room. Most of all, she needed to stay on her feet and to walk the drug's effects off before the bastard found her.

Hell, she'd be lucky to be conscious when the son-of-a-frigging-bitch found her.

She did have one other option.

God, he'd go ballistic.

Damning the fact that she was naked under the robe and that her personal communicator and off-duty weapon were secured in a locker at the other end of the spa, she communicated to the only person who might be able to get her help.

"Wulf?"

No answer.

"Wulf?"

Still no answer. Why didn't he answer? It wasn't as if he were out in the galaxy somewhere. Or, had the rebels gotten to him and his brothers somehow?

She swore under her breath in three languages. She staggered along the wall, her goal the doorway to the inner hall. She wanted to get to a space with more exits and more places to hide. This small room was a trap.

As she inched her way along, she sought Wulf's mental touch again.

"Wulf, I need help."

Again no answer. Nothing. She couldn't find him. He wouldn't be closed off; he never was. And, since the space walk on the *Galanti,* she'd kept her side wide open. She'd come to revel in the closeness they shared and now that she couldn't find him, she didn't like it. Fine time for her to realize how Wulf had felt when she was closed to him. She'd share her revelation, if she lived long enough.

So, where in Balcon's Balls was he?

Out in the middle of the damn Tooh Sea, fishing for a predator fish a person couldn't even eat. Damn men! Or, maybe dead at the hands of a rebel sniper? No. He wasn't dead; she'd know in her soul if he were.

Maybe she was too weak, not projecting enough?

"Wulf! I need you!" The energy expended sending the mental scream for help blinded her for a millisecond.

"Damn, that hurt," she muttered, rubbing her forehead as her sight returned.

Then something touched her mind. A sizzle then a pop sounded loudly in her already aching head. Warmth flowed through her and her mind seemed to clear, shoving away the pain and the waves of hatred flowing from the assassin coming ever closer to her.

"Wulf?"

"Lubha? What is it? You are weak."

"Someone drugged me."

Too tired to form mental conversation, she sent him images.

Mel knew he'd gotten the message when adrenaline resulting from his rage spiked through her. She took four steps this time without the need to use the wall to hold herself up. The room stopped spinning enough that her nausea settled down.

"We're almost to port. We'll dock soon. Can you defend your position?"

His mental voice was calm, commanding, but underneath his rage and fears for her burned bright red. His mental touch was everywhere at once, giving her his strength and examining her situation through her senses.

"Yes..."

"Don't sugarcoat it for me, lubha. I sense the evil approaching. Get out of that room now. The locker rooms or the gym would be better for defense."

"I'm trying..."

"What's wrong? What are you not showing me?"

"I am showing you everything. It's the drug they used—it has slowed me down. I'm near the door ... but I can hear him now. Not just feel him. He's too close. I can't get out without him seeing me."

Wulf's roar of frustrated rage caused her heart to pump faster.

"Huw has contacted Maren and the Embassy Guard. And the Alliance Military. Barricade the door and stay alive."

"Well, that was the plan."

"Like I wouldn't have thought of that myself," she muttered under her breath.

Her warrior was absolutely unstable when she was in danger. And, for the most part, she understood it. She'd feel the same way about him being in danger, drugged with no weapons and no back up. Come to think of it, she felt the same way when rabid, man-stealing hussies eyed Wulf as if he were the flavor of the month.

"*Focus,* lubha. *And no other woman interests me. Just you. So your duty is to stay alive!*"

"*Yes, sir. Captain Wulf, sir.*"

His low, throaty growl, the snarly-angry one, not the yummy-we're-having-sex one, came across their mind link. She smiled. Damn, she loved that snarly growl.

Energized by Wulf's presence in her mind, her heart pumped faster. Her body responded, producing the stress hormones which had ensured humanoid survival in the Milky Way for eons. She felt stronger, not her usual one hundred percent, but enough to defend until help arrived.

Weapon. She needed a weapon. She searched the room. There was only the chaise, a small table and the chair she knocked over, and the glass that had held the drugged drink. She thought fondly of her powerful little sidearm in the locker just meters away. It might as well have been light-years for all the good it could do her.

Mental note, never go anywhere completely unarmed. She'd strap a knife to each leg the next time she got spa treatments and the attendants would just have to deal.

Her narrowed gaze returned to the stemmed glass. It was made out of heavy crystal. Here was her weapon—or it would be with a little modification.

She shuffled to the table. Okay, her legs weren't totally working as well as she would've liked. But she could feel her feet and her hands, so the debilitating neuropathy was receding.

Picking up the glass, she dumped the rest of the contents on the floor, then broke the solid crystal goblet against the ledge of the tiny mullioned window. Now she had a weapon. She thrust the sharp, jagged end of the stem between her first and second fingers, palming the base.

She wavered on suddenly unsteady feet. No, she would not faint. That was girly. She was an Alliance military officer and there was no fainting before a battle—or after if she could help it. And then she had better be three pints low on blood or something.

"I'm with you, lubha. *Use my strength. We're on land, and on our way."*

Okay, so she wasn't one hundred percent. An Alliance Military officer was two hundred percent better trained than most, so she should be able to hold her own until some sort of help arrived. Maybe she should inform the enemy of that fact, it might scare him off. She choked back a laugh.

The enemy was only a room or two away. His emotions sickened her with their chaotic litany of hate and prejudice. His malevolent energy reminded her of the Prime traitors on the *Galanti.* This was not just her enemy; this was an enemy of the Prime people and their future. A fanatic, and all her training had taught her that zealots were the worst enemy to face. They cared nothing for the sanctity of life—theirs or anyone else's.

Taking a position behind the door, she waited.

Wulf was a silent, strong presence in her mind. His connection helped her regulate her breathing as he pushed her body to mimic his and produce the hormones needed in her fight to survive. The battle-mate connection was the main reason the Prime had succeeded as a race for so long; it would be a shame to lose the genetics that had evolved over eons because of a lack of female mates for Prime warriors.

The fanatical bastard coming to kill her was a brainwashed idiot, too stupid to live. She would be happy to send him on his way.

The footsteps that had only been a mere echo in her head now sounded loudly. It wouldn't be much longer.

Pumped for action, she smiled, a wicked twist to her lips. "You're messing with the wrong Prime *gemate,* asshole." She gloried in the pure, undiluted and invigorating rage filling her mind and body.

"*Confirming only one on auditory senses, Wulf. Only one.*"

"*Go for the kill. No messing around. You are not up to your usual strength. Whatever they gave you was strong. Do not hesitate. Go for the kill.*"

"*I never mess around.*" She sent him a mental snort. "*And don't worry so much, gemat. No one will take me from you.*"

"*I'm not worried, gemate. I just don't like it when you get bruised. I was so counting on our late-night date.*"

Mel smiled. As was she. Nothing and no one, especially not the crazy bastard coming for her, would keep her from her first ball—and the celebratory sex later.

The threatening footsteps stopped outside the door.

Silence. Absolute silence settled over the spa once more. It was as if she and the man breathing his hatred outside the door to her hiding place were the only two living beings in the galaxy.

The absolute quiet ruled for long seconds and then into minutes.

The drug fought with her body's adrenal glands for supremacy. Wulf's mind-body connection wouldn't allow her body to succumb. He poured his increasing rage across their connection. He was practically feral now, his low, unceasing growls—the raging ones which made her head hurt and her skin itch—reverberated in her head, forcing her body into survival readiness when her brain only wanted to shut down.

"*He's testing to see if the drug has knocked you out. Stay alert, Melina. That's an order!*"

"*I know what he's doing. I won't let him win.*"

She'd lost the feeling to her feet once again. Damn, the drug was potent. Good news was she could still feel her fingers and the makeshift weapon she held. Her hands were steady and her head was in the game. She wanted to move, to stamp her feet, but couldn't allow herself to do so. He'd hear and she'd lose her advantage. He thought she was unconscious, helpless. He'd have an unpleasant surprise.

Finally, the door slid open.

A large, booted foot stepped into the room. The body belonging to it followed slowly. Long legs gave her an estimate of where she should aim her attack. She was going for the most blood loss she could manage. The carotid would be a nice target and meet Wulf's requirement of going for the kill.

She held her breath as he stepped fully into the room. His head turned away from her position, his gaze fixed where he'd thought she'd be.

Stupid amateur fanatic. Never enter a room without scanning. Not military-trained, then. Another advantage on her side.

As he entered, she thrust the sharp point of the crystal stem at his neck. She'd read him correctly as humanoid. So the carotid was where it should be. He was definitely the right coloring and size for a Prime male, but softer. Not a warrior. Another advantage for her.

Her movement attracted his attention and he turned to grab her. She automatically adjusted and kept her forward motion. Her weapon connected with the target; she dragged the sharp crystal across his artery. Blood spurted, hitting her and covering a wide arcing area. Definitely arterial spray.

She'd hit it perfectly, but he kept coming.

Why in the hell didn't he drop?

Stumbling, she managed to get around him into the hallway. He grabbed the left sleeve of her robe and hung on. She swiped the point of the crystal across the back of his hand. He roared in pain and threw a lucky punch hitting her in the jaw.

She fell back against the wall opposite the doorway of the room she'd just left. Still spraying blood, but with a lesser force, he dropped to the floor. Her would-be assassin now attempted to hold in the blood surging from his body. The blood pulsed out of the jagged wound more slowly now as his heart shut down.

If she could've caught her breath, found her voice, she would've told him that it was a lost cause. Nothing short of immediate emergency surgery and lots of units of blood could save him now.

His furious gaze focused on her as the life bled out of him. His mouth contorted into snarl, but no sounds ever made it past his lips. He slumped to the floor. Dead.

With a moaning sigh, Mel slid to the floor, landing on her butt and leaning against the wall. She focused her bleary gaze on his now sightless one. She'd won; he'd lost.

The sound of thudding footsteps and Wulf's much-beloved roar sounded in her ears as she finally allowed the drug do what it was designed for and put her to sleep.

On the way from the Tooh seaport to the spa

"CAN'T THIS VEHICLE GO ANY faster?" Wulf rasped, as they raced from the marina to the resort spa.

He'd monitored Melina's physical and mental status ever since her telepathic cry for help. She was weaker now than before. Even the battle-mate connection wouldn't be able to keep her conscious much longer.

And the danger was real and imminent. He read through their link that the assassin was close to finding her hiding place.

His body grew cold at the evil he sensed. His mate had downplayed the danger to herself with her usual courage. But it was there.

"Something has to be done about the rebels," he said. "We can no longer discount their movement. They have money and inside connections. They'll not stop until they kill us and anyone who supports the policy to reach out to other humanoid races."

"Maren understands this, Wulf," Huw said from the rear seat. "Father and the Council will be made to understand. A report from you and Mel will help, since you've had to battle the fanatics personally. With your battle-mate connection fully formed, you have touched their minds. This will hold much sway with the Council."

"And serve to endanger my mate even more. They will stop at nothing to kill the only known battle-mate."

His brothers' grim expressions proved the truth of his conclusions. Melina would be the prime target of the fanatical rebels. Never mind that she was of the pure blood they professed to desire; she was also the symbol of the alliance with the rest of the galaxy.

"Dammit, drive faster, Iolyn."

"Hold on, Wulf," Iolyn said. "We're almost there. We'll beat Maren and the Alliance Military unit by minutes."

"She doesn't *have* minutes." Wulf stiffened. "He's attacking now!" He roared with frustrated anger and pounded his fist against the dashboard of the ground transport.

"What's happening?" Huw shouted, his hand grasping Wulf's shoulder.

"Melina has stabbed him in the carotid with a wine glass stem," rasped out Wulf. "He's pursuing—Damn, he hit her ... he's weakening, falling, bleeding out." Exhaling loudly, he relaxed under Huw's grasping fingers, his shoulders slumping as the tension seeped out of his body. "He's dead. The immediate danger has passed. My brave *gemate* has once again shown what a warrior she is."

His body trembled with relief and the aftermath of the overwhelming fear. He vowed that never again would this be allowed to happen. He'd never let her out of his sight again.

"*Ansu bhau*," he swore. "I should've been with her."

Huw sighed and patted his brother's shoulder. "Mel wouldn't like it if you hovered."

"Tough," he growled. "She can learn to live with it."

"Mel?" Iolyn urged. "How is she?"

"The drug has taken effect. She wasn't successful in purging all of it from her system." Wulf shook off his own post-adrenaline let down. "She's unconscious. But fine."

Iolyn pulled the vehicle into the drive of the building holding the spa. Sirens from the military police could be heard in the distance.

Wulf was out of the vehicle before it had rocked to a stop. Huw and Iolyn were on his heels as he shoved into the building, roaring Melina's name even though he knew she was unconscious. He unerringly found his way to where she'd fallen, following the mental map she'd provided of the spa.

She lay in a heap on the cold, white marble floor, her robe gaped to display an overly large amount of creamy white skin spattered with the enemy's blood.

"Avert your eyes, brothers," he snarled. He knelt by her side and pulled the lapels of the robe over her cleavage, then closed the garment about her legs.

With gentle fingers he examined the bruise on her face. She looked so small and delicate. The fact that she had once again defeated a male larger and stronger than she amazed and humbled him.

"But, dammit she shouldn't have to," muttered Wulf under his breath.

The sound of men entering the spa echoed down the hallway. "Handle the police," he ordered his brothers. "Send a medic as soon as one arrives. I'm taking Melina someplace more comfortable."

Without waiting for their response, he dead-lifted Melina into his arms then stood up. Cradling her against his chest, he strode away from the bloody scene. He entered a large dimly lit room, then placed her on a massage table, carefully arranging her body so she'd be comfortable. After covering her with several fleecy blankets he found on a shelf, he pulled a chair to sit next to her.

He drew her right hand from under the covers and held it between his, chafing away the cold, rubbing away the imprint of the base of the glass that she'd held so tightly. He'd ask for the piece of crystal. He wanted to keep it; it had saved her life. No, *she* had saved her life, with her improvisation. Her coolness under pressure. Her training. Her reaching out to him for support—as any battle-mate would do.

She was his little warrior—and she meant more than the universe to him.

Huw was correct: Melina wouldn't want him to hover, to surround her with too many safeguards. But it was so tempting, especially when set against the knowledge he could not survive without her. He kissed the hand he held, rubbing it against his cheek.

"I love you, Melina mine," he whispered, choking back unaccustomed tears. His woman scared the living daylights out of him, she was too courageous.

Maren rushed into the room, his concern for his niece broadcasting loudly in the area. "How is she?"

"Unconscious," Wulf murmured. "I sense the drug was an anesthetic of some sort. She's breathing normally. Her body has already gotten rid of most of it. This is just the aftermath."

Wulf turned angry eyes toward the older man. "Who was the *apayebo*?"

Maren sighed. His ghost pale face looked every single one of his sixty standard years. "It was another one of Darga Caradoc's sons, Uly."

"Uly? Wasn't he a history professor?" Wulf's brow creased with shock and disbelief.

"Yes." Maren pulled up another chair and joined Wulf's vigil by Melina's side. "At the university."

Wulf shook his head sadly. "Why?"

Maren shrugged. "Who knows how the rebels recruit the fanatics? The fact your father's family line has produced several of the rebels, albeit not in the direct bloodline, is disturbing."

"Melina thinks there is more to this rebellion than just the spouting of the pure blood philosophy. What do you think?"

"I think your mate is probably correct in her conclusion," Maren said. "Especially when they can recruit a pragmatic academic like Uly who knows that Prime blood has commingled with every humanoid species in the galaxy for eons, and that the last two centuries plus of isolationism was out of character for our people."

Wulf had learned, as all Prime youngsters had, that the DNA of the Caradoc family, or of any Prime family line, would show intermingling with Terran, Volusian and a few other humanoid bloodlines going back a few millennia. There was not a habitable planet in the Milky Way which hadn't been explored by their Prime ancestors. Many of those explorers had brought back mixed-blood humanoid children—or left them on the planets they had visited to add the Prime DNA into the planet's particular bloodlines.

No Prime was a pure blood; it was a convenient fiction the purists used to promote nationalism.

"So, what are they after?" mused Wulf as he absently massaged Melina's palm with his thumb.

"Power, most likely," a soft, tired voice whispered. "Although those first two traitors I met—Prolow and Ullyn— really seemed to believe in the pure blood nonsense. Stupid dupes."

"*Gemate lubha!*" breathed Wulf, as he bent over and kissed her. "You scared me, little one."

"Sorry," she tried to smile, "I didn't plan this, you know."

"I know, *lubha*. I know." He kissed her once again. "I'm so sorry you've been drawn into this mess with the rebels."

"Not your fault." She yawned. "Uncle Tor, we'll need to keep a close eye on the guests tonight. When I appear, alive and well, we might be able to read the emotions of any other rebels in attendance. Then we can have them followed and start rooting out their contacts."

"We're not going tonight!" Wulf announced in a don't-mess-with-me tone in his voice. "It is too dangerous."

"We're going." She glared at him. "You'll be by my side—and we, as a team, will be strong. Not too many know about our abilities at this point, Wulf. We need to take advantage where we can."

"She's right, Wulf," Maren said. "I don't like it any better than you. But if we could start to trace connections, we have a better chance of figuring out who is behind this mess."

Wulf glared at both of them, then shook his head. "I don't like it—and if there were any other way ... well, there isn't." He let out an angry snort. "We need to get a handle on this sooner, rather than later. I want to be able to go about without worrying that my mate is a target for a terrorist group and their hirelings."

Melina turned her hand within his and pulled it to her cheek, cradling it. "I'll stay by your, Maren's, or your brothers' sides the whole evening. I promise."

She pulled his hand to her mouth and licked the inside of his wrist. The warm moisture made him shudder, reminding him of how her mouth had felt upon his body, of how she completed him. He'd protect her in spite of herself. He couldn't lose the joy, the sense of belonging she gave him.

She whispered throatily, "Besides, you did want to see me in that dress and the other stuff you bought me, didn't you?"

"It is my greatest wish," he whispered as he leaned over to kiss her once more.

That and keeping you alive.

CHAPTER SEVENTEEN

Later that evening
The ballroom of the Cejuru Prime Embassy on Tooh 2

"Whatever possessed me to pick out that dress?" Wulf hissed into Melina's ear. "Every man in the room is devouring you with his eyes. You're practically naked."

His mate smiled, her eyes gleaming with mischief. "I told you so, but no, you had to have this dress," she waved a hand down the front of the ivory silk dress that hugged her body like a second skin, "and no other. I, on the other hand, wanted a nice black sheath, with a back and a front—and proper underwear."

"I should've insisted on seeing under the cloak before we left the suite." He glared at an over-eager Volusian who had found the nerve to approach them. The man's pale blue gaze fixed on Melina's breasts, or more likely her nipples showing through the thin pale fabric. "It looked so different on the computer screen."

"Well, I—"

"I know," he growled, "you told me so." He placed his arm around her waist and pulled her into his side as if he could hide her from the eyes of every man in the room. He smelled their envy. He hated them all, including his horn dog brothers. "Are you even wearing underclothes?"

Snuggling against him, she snorted back a laugh. "Yes, if you can call the tissue-thin, transparent teddy you bought me underwear."

He placed his lips near her ear. "I plan to take that little nothing off—with my teeth—later." He nibbled at her lobe. She shivered in response. He smiled. She was so sensitive to his every touch.

"It's always *later* with you, Wulf," she whispered back, taking a nip of his chin. "I like more immediate action."

"I'd be very happy to leave now and take care of my *gemate*'s needs."

"You just want to leave so no man tries to ask me to dance again." She pinched his waist. "The last man is probably still running, looking over his shoulder."

Wulf snorted back a laugh. "He did look like a scared plains hopper, didn't he?"

She mock-glared at him, her eyes betraying her amusement. "Wulf, I swear the man wet himself when you growled at him."

He threw back his head and shouted with laughter.

The noise in the room stopped as everyone turned and stared at him.

He looked down at Melina. "Why is everyone looking at me now?"

"You don't laugh out loud very often," she explained, stroking his jaw. "Plus, the Prime as a whole have the reputation of being humorless."

"And are we?" he asked, his shoulders tensing. His hand rubbed small soothing circles on her bare back. Well, at least the motion soothed him.

"No, I think you just have a different sense of humor than most," she replied. "I like it anyway."

His shoulders relaxed. He hadn't realized that her answer would mean so much to him. *Diew* knew his sense of humor had resurrected itself since he'd met her.

Huw and Iolyn approached them.

"Have I mentioned how much I like that dress, sister?" Huw's eyes roamed over her from head to toe and back again.

"Ten times, brother," Wulf snarled. "And for also the tenth time—How would you like me to rearrange your face?"

"Damn, Wulf," Huw said, his mouth open in false shock, "I thought you were in a good mood. I haven't heard you laugh so hard since you put hot powder in Iolyn's swim briefs when we were children."

"I'd be in a better mood if my brothers would do their job and protect my *gemate* from all the men in this room while I speak to Maren," Wulf responded. "After that, Melina and I will be leaving. After all, we are still on our honeymoon and only have twenty-four more standard hours before we depart for the journey to Cejuru Prime where I'll have to share her with the extended family and the whole damn planet!"

"We'll protect her," Iolyn promised. "But we want combat pay. The men in this room really would like to get close to our sister. And she tells me it's all your fault since you picked out the dress against her advice."

"Just shut up, brother," Wulf growled. "Stay with her. I won't be long."

"So, brothers," Mel said as Wulf walked away, "do you think I'll ever get to wear a, um, revealing gown again in this lifetime?"

"No!" Both brothers shouted, laughing.

Again, people turned to observe two Prime males laughing so heartily. Pretty soon she would have the reputation of being a regular stand-up comic if she kept making all the Prime men around her laugh so hard.

"He learned his lesson on that issue for sure." Huw's his eyes brimmed with laughter. "Now, if we can get him to lighten up on overprotecting you, we'll have won a major victory."

"Yeah, he wasn't doing at all well earlier today," Iolyn said as he moved in closer to cut off a Prime male approaching Mel, one of the many enlisted officers and academy students pulled in to help with serving drinks and finger foods. "Huw, do you know the guy heading for us?"

"No." Huw moved to protect Mel's other side.

Mel looked at the man. As with most of the Prime males here, he was tall, dark, golden-eyed—and craggily handsome. He was also very intent on getting to her. He was so intent that he ignored the presence of her two large brother-kin. That was unusual. Because of their family prestige and military rank, this lowly soldier should have been leery about making such an aggressive approach.

Separating out the many emotions in the room, Mel focused on the man approaching them.

"Uh, guys," Mel whispered, her gaze never leaving the unknown man. "Are you armed?"

"No," Huw whispered. "The embassy guards are the only ones armed. Maren wanted to lower the chances of someone bringing in a sidearm and shooting one of us."

"*This* guy is armed." Another wave of angry emotion had her looking over her shoulder. "So is the guy coming on us from behind?"

Slowly turning her head so as not to telegraph her knowledge of the imminent danger to the two predators, she scanned the room. "We're too exposed. Let's move toward the wall on the northern side of the ballroom. I want something solid and friendly behind my back."

Moving slowly, as if they were taking a stroll around the room, the three of them angled their way to the wall. When they were nearly to their goal, Mel contacted Wulf.

"Wulf? We have a problem. Get the guard in here."

Wulf's angry bellow could be heard throughout the embassy. Mel swore it vibrated the thick stone walls which now guarded their rear.

The two men approaching them started, then grimaced and moved with even more purpose. Their weapons were drawn and aimed at Iolyn, who'd blocked her body from the two with his own, and at Huw.

"You called Wulf?" Iolyn constantly changed the angle of his body so that none of her was exposed to danger.

"Yep."

With Iolyn providing an obstruction for the enemy's line of sight, she moved her left hand down to the slit in her dress and slid out one of the serrated battle-knives she'd strapped there. She slipped it around Iolyn's body, nudging it into his hand. She slid her other hand down the other leg and removed the other knife, keeping it.

"Sorry, Huw," she whispered. "I only brought two knives."

"How'd you manage that?" Huw asked as their backs hugged the wall.

"The guards didn't search me because Wulf glared at them."

Both the brothers shook with silent laughter.

Mel touched Iolyn's back. "Iolyn, when I signal, you go for the one on the left. Huw, you just get out of the way and back me up with the one on the right," she hissed. "Go for the kill."

"Mel—" Huw began, but Mel knew he was going to insist on taking the knife and defending her. She wouldn't let him. She was tired of these idiots attacking her, and she needed to let off some steam.

"Forget it, Huw," she snarled. "The other one is *mine*."

It showed how much trust Huw had in her ability that he didn't argue the point. Instead, he just nodded.

"Now!" she hissed.

She shoved Huw out of the way. Iolyn leapt forward at the same time.

Mel didn't even give her target a chance to shoot. As she dove to the right side with Huw, she threw the knife. It struck him straight through an eye socket. She rolled, then scrambled to the dying man and grabbed his gun, tossing it to Huw. She pulled her knife from the dead man's skull, stood and turned to help Iolyn.

She need not have bothered. Iolyn's throw had been as accurate as hers.

"Melina!" Wulf's shout reverberated in the deathly silent room.

"I'm fine, my *gemat!*" she shouted back.

The room erupted with hushed, excited whispers.

"Did you see her? She is a warrior fit for a Prime male."

"I heard that she is a battle-mate."

"A battle-mate? Those are just legends," another scoffed.

"No longer. She is a battle-mate."

Wulf reached her in several long strides, taking the bloody knife from her hand, he tossed it to Huw.

"You didn't leave one for me, *gemate*," he said as he glanced at the fallen men.

"You were busy, darling. I'll save one for you the next time," she said, breezily.

Wulf pulled her into his arms and hugged her, his face buried in the hair which had tumbled out of its intricate braid during her diving tumble for the assassin's gun.

"I love you, battle-mate."

Mel wiped her hand down the side of her dress, mostly transferring the blood onto her bare thigh. The tissue thin dress had slit open almost all the way to her waist during the short fight. She grasped her mate's face with two steady hands and kissed him.

Pulling away, she whispered against his lips, "I love you, too. I'm feeling a breeze; can I have your jacket?"

Wulf pulled away, glaring at any man in the immediate vicinity whose eyes were anywhere below Mel's neck.

She imagined she was putting on quite a show—the teddy she wore under the dress was transparent. They probably thought she was naked under the dress.

Wulf's gaze swept over her and grimaced. "Damn dress," he muttered. He stripped off his jacket and put it on her. It hung to her knees.

"Thanks, darling." She patted his cheek. He smiled at her and winked.

"Who are they, Maren?" Wulf asked her uncle.

"Two cadets from the Prime military academy," Maren replied. "We had pressed some of the students into catering duty for this function."

"I thought the embassy guard vetted all the help for the event," Huw said. "How did they get weapons in here?"

"I don't know," Maren said, anger coloring every word. "But we'll find out."

Iolyn and Huw flanked Wulf and Mel.

Every eye in the room was on them. Then as if someone had given a silent signal, all the Prime in the room knelt and bowed their heads.

"What are they doing?" whispered Mel.

"They are honoring you," Wulf said. "As a returning Lost One and a battle-mate, you're the symbol of hope for the future of our planet. You're also the first good thing to come out of the pact with the Alliance."

Maren added, "The synchronicity of these two events defies probability. They see you as a miracle. News will spread back to Cejuru Prime. The Council will use you, your actions here and since we reunited with you, as proof for the majority of our people that the alliance is a good thing."

"And the rebels?" she asked. "What will they do, do you think?"

"The fanatics will remain as crazy as ever," Huw concluded.

"And the faction behind the rebel movement will still have its own agenda," Wulf added.

Mel sighed. "Well, no one said winning the war would be easy."

"As always, we take each battle as it comes, *lubha*. However, I would like to be on the offensive side in the future. I'm damn tired of reacting to threats."

"I completely agree with that point." Mel leaned into Wulf's strength and warmth. All of a sudden she was tired and only wanted to crawl into a warm, soft bed with the man holding her so gently, so protectively.

"You are weary, *lubha*," Wulf whispered against her ear, nuzzling her. "Let's go back to the room and lock out the galaxy for the next twenty-four standard hours. Reality will come soon enough once we head out for the home planet."

"Doesn't it always," Mel said. "Life is not a children's tale, and I'm not a legend come to life. I'm afraid that reality is going to be all too with us for some time to come."

"You may not be a legend, but you are my deepest fantasy come to life." Wulf kissed her hair. "And I plan on keeping you alive."

CHAPTER EIGHTEEN

One Standard Month later, orbiting Cejuru Prime

Mel sat back and observed the interactions among selected members of her Gold Squadron's crew and the Prime soldiers who were to trade places with them. The meeting took place in the Commander's Board room on the Prime military space station that circled Cejuru Prime once every eighteen standard hours. The trip from Tooh 10 space dock had been less eventful than the current meetings. In fact, no one, Antarean, mercenaries or otherwise, had tried to kill her or Wulf since the night of the embassy party.

But she wouldn't guarantee that blood might not be shed in this room.

"*Lubha,* should we referee?" Wulf's low rumbling voice contained a tinge of amusement. "I'd hate to see the agreement between our military organizations fail before it fully commenced."

Mel followed his gaze to the most contentious of the pairings in the room.

Galanti's Science Officer, Commander Ard, was in the middle of talking down to his Terran counterpart, Commander

Nadia Petrovich from the *Leonidas.* Talking down was in the figurative sense since Nadia at six-foot-two-inches tall nearly saw eye-to-eye with the large Prime male, who may have had two inches on her. The heat of Nadia's anger projected clear across the room. Lucky for them all Nadia could control her temper.

Nadia would be an excellent fit for the *Galanti.* All of the women Mel had chosen for the formerly all-Prime male ships were like Nadia—smart, strong, self-confident, and totally in control while on duty. Women who could hold their own in a male-dominated military. The Prime would crush any other kind.

"No need to intervene. Nadia will be fine," Mel replied and would have added a word on Ard when some movement in her periphery interrupted her train of thought.

Huw had left his position against the outer perimeter of the room and moved toward Ard and Nadia. His actions reminded her of a raptor swooping to capture its prey.

"Oooh, boy," muttered Mel.

"What?" Wulf asked, his eyes scanning the room for the cause of her concern.

Huw thrust his body between the dueling science officers and was now in Ard's face. Both men were yelling. The exact words of their confrontation were lost in the chaos of the large room and the multiple conversations.

"Your brother just ran interference for Nadia," whispered Mel. "Not smart. She'll hand him his ass for that. Nadia doesn't need—or ask—for help in dealing with peers."

They watched the scene play out—as now did a majority of the teams in the room.

Nadia moved around Huw and got in his face. His hands went up, warding off her jabbing finger. Ard, his lips quirked with amusement, had already figured out the attractive Terran and backed away. By allowing her to handle the angry Huw, Ard displayed his respect for her abilities. A strong message had been sent to every other Prime soldier in the room who would serve alongside her on the *Galanti*. Smart man, that Ard.

Wulf murmured, "Nadia and Ard were just testing each other's limits, yes?"

"Yes," replied Mel. "That transition will work well."

When Nadia turned to continue her conversation with Ard, Huw turned on his heel and stalked off to the side of the room where Iolyn leaned against the wall, calmly observing his brother's humiliation.

"Huw will be smarting for a while. The Iceberg has given another man his congé." Mel chuckled.

"Ice Berg?" Wulf asked, his breath brushing the hair by her ear.

"That's what my crew calls her," Mel explained. "She has a very low tolerance for male shenanigans, as she calls them. Huw playing the gentleman mediator would fall under that classification."

"She does not socialize with the crew?" Wulf frowned. "That would not be good for morale."

"Oh, she's fine while on the ship. She is cordial and respectful of her peers and would die for them," Mel hurried to clarify. "Outside of the ship? No one has ever seen her with a male."

"I trust your judgment, *gemate*," Wulf said, a slightly skeptical tone to his words.

"She's the best science officer I've ever seen—she'll do fine on a ship with a mostly male crew. She'll gain their respect quickly. She has already impressed Ard."

"Then she is very much like you," he whispered. "And you handled me well enough."

"Well, there was added incentive," she teased as she rubbed her cheek against his shoulder.

The small confrontation among Ard, Nadia and Huw seemed to have been the signal to move things ahead. The other teams had their heads together, working in concert rather than at cross-purposes.

"The tension in the room is lessening—well, except for Huw," Wulf laughed, "he looks as if he would like to carry your Nadia off and teach her who's boss."

"I wouldn't if I were him," Mel retorted. "Her last would-be manhandler sported his injuries for quite a while."

The man had also been court-martialed and, after a lengthy stay in the prison ward of the military hospital, sent to the Alliance's prison world for convictions on battery and attempted rape. Mel had confined her crew to the ship or the man would have been lynched—that was how angry they had been over Nadia's treatment.

Wulf frowned. "She was okay? How bad was it?"

Mel shook her head. "It was bad. Nadia took months to heal."

"All the women will be fine on Prime ships, *lubha*," Wulf said. "Prime soldiers do not beat up on women."

"I know." She stroked Wulf's hand, which had fisted on her thigh under the cover of the table. "I have no concerns about that. And all my female soldiers can handle themselves. After all, it was *attempted* rape." She smiled grimly. "Nadia beat the shit out of the bastard and then called the military police."

The sound level in the room decreased measurably as the teams of two finished introducing themselves to one another.

Mel stood up. All activity in the room ceased and all attention turned to her and Wulf at the head of the large oval titanium table.

"You've had a chance to get acquainted. In front of each of you are your formal orders. These just reiterate what you've been briefed on individually by either Captain Wulf or myself."

Mel paused and swept the room with a glance. Every crew member was attentive. The mood in the room was equal parts anticipation and trepidation. Each and every one of them understood the historical significance of this merger of militaries. The Prime had never, in their millennia of existence, allied themselves with any other planet or conference of planets. The non-allied planets of the Milky Way would watch this partnership with close scrutiny.

She continued, "You'll have the opportunity while Gold Squadron is in space dock to visit your new assignments in the company of your exchange counterpart. We expect all exchange partners to thoroughly indoctrinate each other in the idiosyncrasies of their jobs."

"Let us know if you have issues or questions," Wulf added. "Captain Melina and I will be on station for another standard day before heading dirtside. Even then, we'll be in constant contact with Captain Nowicki, who will be officer in charge while we are gone. We will return frequently for briefings and training sessions."

"When will Gold go back out on patrols?" Huw asked, all remnants of his former anger gone from his voice and facial expression. But Mel sensed something boiling beneath the surface. Some emotion she had a hard time pinning down.

"Once Captain Melina and I are sure the merged crews are working together in an optimal fashion," Wulf said. "We anticipate this process will take less than two standard weeks. While Gold completes the personnel merger and the training period, Blue Squadron will cover the outer Perseus spiral, backed up by the all-Prime military ships."

"Is Cejuru Prime going to maintain an all-Prime military presence in this part of the galaxy?" A Prime soldier unknown to Mel asked the question.

"Wulf?" She turned toward him. "Do you want to answer that?"

"Sure. The Prime military units which do not merge into the Gold Squadron will maintain planet order and be used to patrol within the confines of the Cejuru solar system. We expect that to be approximately ten full units."

"What will be our patrol duties when fully merged?" Iolyn asked.

"Gold Squadron, and if needed, any other available Alliance squadron, will patrol the no-man's land between the central portion of the Cygnus-Orion and Perseus spirals, the populated areas of the Perseus spiral minus Cejuru solar system, and the dark space immediately beyond the Milky Way toward Andromeda," Mel answered, then added, "The Alliance considers the Antarean threat grave to the peace of the Milky Way."

A grunt of Prime male approval filled the room her detailing of their new duties.

"As you can tell by Gold's duties, the Alliance takes our future existence as crucial to the defense of the Milky Way from the hostiles in the Andromeda border-space."

Wulf paused, his gaze swept the room. "The Alliance and the Prime Council also understood that Prime soldiers are needed to patrol Prime territory. No native population wants foreign soldiers camped out in their territory, telling them what to do. Any Alliance region that wishes to maintain a local military presence may do so under the treaties signed upon joining the Alliance."

Mel picked up the thread of Wulf's thoughts. "Over time, other Prime military units could be merged into one of the battle squadrons besides Gold if the Prime Council and Military feel that it would benefit them. Any Prime soldier who wishes can ask to be transferred to any Alliance military unit anywhere in the Milky Way."

"For now, Gold will be the test case of the new pact. So do us proud," Wulf said as he stood up. "You are dismissed."

Wulf pulled Mel into his side. "Shall we follow the troops to the bar? Or retreat to our quarters for some private time?" His hand stroked down her back and settled just above the curve of her butt. "It's your call, *lubha*," he whispered in a low husky voice against her ear.

Mel shivered. Wulf's thoughts were positively decadent.

But she shook her head. "Huw and Iolyn need to talk to us. Let's head to the officer's lounge and let them vent."

"Damn, my brothers' timing is awful." Wulf glared at the two culprits, still leaning against the outer wall of the room, obviously waiting for her and Wulf to join them.

"Just wait until they find a mate, I'll be sure to bother them when they want to be alone with their women."

"Hey, we need to eat sometime," she purred. "A big man like you has to keep up his strength."

"I see the logic." Wulf slid his hand down over her rear, cupping it firmly as he nudged her toward the exit. "Later we will take care of this." He patted her bottom.

"Later," she said. "Count on it."

Wulf eyed his brothers as he and Melina approached them.

Brushing a kiss across the top of her head, he grunted. "You are correct—as always. They are concerned. I've sadly neglected to allay my brothers' fears about their place in our new crew."

"Exactly," murmured Melina.

"Huw. Iolyn." Wulf greeted his brothers, his arm around Melina's waist. "Would you like to join us for a drink and some dinner in the Officer's Lounge?"

"That was what we were going to suggest," Huw said as his eyes narrowed. "Are you reading us?"

"Yes," Wulf said. "Melina and I are becoming more adept at picking out emotional purpose. It's not quite reading minds, but if we know the persons well enough we can usually figure out what the issues are."

Huw started at that information, eyeing them warily. Wulf wondered what was wrong with his younger brother. He was awfully jumpy. Huw had always been the most placid of the three of them, but right now he was a roiling cauldron ready to explode.

"Huw—" Wulf began to ask his brother what bothered him when Melina's sharp elbow jabbed him in the ribs.

"Not now, Wulf."

"—lead the way," he finished saying.

"What's wrong with Huw?"

"Nadia is wrong. I think. Well, maybe. Just don't ask. Let him tell us when he is ready."

The four of them followed the last of the exchange partners out of the room. Taking the lift to the top of the space dock's central core, they followed some of the officers from the meeting into the officers' lounge. The enlisted crew had their own lounge/recreation area two decks below the officer's.

As with all Prime military facilities, the room was designed for efficiency, functionality, and ease of keeping it clean. The metal walls were silver-gray, the floors carpeted in a dark gray synthetic. The only color in the room came from the red-wood bar and the bottles of colorful liquors and wines behind it.

Unlike most Prime military facilities, some small effort had been made to create a comfortable space for officers to unwind and socialize when off-duty. To that end, pleasant music played in the background, the lighting was subdued, and comfortable black leather-upholstered booths lined the perimeter of the large room providing an illusion of privacy.

The four took a booth near the bar. The android bartender immediately zoomed over to take drink orders.

Iolyn, Melina, and Wulf gave the server their orders. Huw looked past the droid, glaring at something on the other side of the room.

Wulf followed his brother's icy yellow gaze. "Give the droid your drink order, Huw. And stop staring holes into Ard and Commander Petrovich."

"Valerian whiskey. Make it a double. Neat." Huw turned toward Wulf. "Does that icy bitch have to be on the *Galanti*?"

Wulf turned his head toward his *gemate*. "*Lubha,* would you like to answer our brother?"

"Gladly." Melina turned toward Huw. "Yes."

Iolyn laughed as Huw muttered "*ansu bhau*" under his breath. "Guess you'll have to learn to keep it all business around Nadia."

"Shut up, Iolyn. And since when do you call her Nadia?" Huw huffed.

"Since she asked me to," his brother replied.

"Dammit, she told me to address her as Commander Petrovich," Huw almost whined.

"Was that before or after you tried to interfere in her conversation with Ard?" Melina asked.

"After," mumbled Huw. "I was just trying to mediate. Ard was treating her like shit."

"Nadia is more than capable of handling any man on the *Galanti*," Melina assured him. "Try treating her as an equal."

The look of horror on Huw's face caused Wulf to roar with laughter. Once he gained control, he said, "Seems I recall you telling me to treat Melina as an equal a time or two. You need to practice what you preach, brother."

"Shut up, brother." Huw growled. "No one likes a know-it-all."

Iolyn and Melina laughed at Wulf's angry scowl and Huw's petulant frown.

"Okay, boys," Melina said. "We're here to explain that both of your roles will not change on the *Galanti*. Huw, you will still be chief engineer, and Iolyn, you will still be the chief IT engineer. Wulf and I feel better knowing you have our backs."

Wulf added, "Eventually, you will both captain your own ships—if you wish. You are on the same promotion track in the Alliance Military as you would have been in the Prime."

"Can we choose to remain in the Cejuru System in the Prime Military, if we wish?" Iolyn asked.

"Of course, Iolyn," Melina replied. "We would love for you to stay in the Gold Squadron, but the choice will be yours when the time comes."

The two brothers' tension levels lowered immeasurably after Wulf and Melina's pronouncement. Although, Wulf noted, Huw still sent dagger-like glares toward the booth that Ard and Nadia shared with Captain Nowicki and Commander A'Tem, the chief engineer on the *Leonidas*.

After their drinks were served, Wulf's table ordered their meals.

With a companionable silence settling over the table as they enjoyed their pre-dinner drinks, Wulf hated to broach the topic that concerned him the most. It was the two-ton elephant at the table and could not be ignored.

"We need to root out the leaders of the rebels and put an end to their attempts to kill us and sabotage the pact with the Alliance," Wulf said. "Melina and I want to go on the offense."

"And we need to do it soon," Melina added. "Too much time has been invested in negotiating the agreement between the Prime and the Alliance to allow some malcontents to destroy it."

"Why soon?" Huw asked.

"Calls have been made to Galactic Alliance genetic research labs to send some of their scientists to Cejuru Prime to work alongside Prime researchers. The goal is to determine why the Prime women who are left can no longer carry babies to term," Melina said.

"That's important research," Iolyn agreed. "But the fanatics have concentrated their attacks on us, not the research into the infertility of our women. The purists have just as much to gain by that research as anybody. I don't see them disrupting it."

"If that was all the research entailed, you would be correct," Wulf said. "But the research goes beyond Prime women's infertility and inability to carry to term. The teams will also be looking at the genetic drift issues among the humanoid species."

"Meaning?" Huw asked, his gaze drifting toward Nadia.

Melina was correct. His brother was attracted to the Terran Nadia. But there was a lot of conflict and confusion in his brother's emotions concerning the attraction.

"Let him bring the topic to you, Wulf. Huw is torn about this lust he has for Nadia."

"I hate to see him so upset."

"We'll keep an eye on the situation. Don't worry. My gut tells me she is attracted to him also. She is glancing over here as much as he is over there."

Wulf sought out the table with Nadia. Melina was correct. The attractive blonde's gaze returned again and again to their table. He smiled. His *gemate* read people far better than he ever had—and he was doing better since he bonded with her.

"You do realize, Huw, that there could be problems with non-Prime women conceiving with Prime males?" Melina said. "The research is important. The Prime will not survive without such successful matings."

Huw stared at his hands before glancing at the Nadia as she laughed at something Nowicki said. "I understand that."

"As does the majority of the Prime population," Wulf said. "Both governing councils are concerned that whoever is behind the fanatics would attack these scientists. We can't afford to allow terrorists and their backers to halt the research needed into hominid branch differences that need to be overcome in order for non-Prime females to bear Prime males' children."

"So, will the Alliance send the military to protect these researchers?" Huw asked.

"Yes. In fact, one of our first missions will be to escort the top Alliance geneticist, Dr. Brianna Martin, to the labs on Cejuru Prime," Melina said. "She is an expert on genetic drift and was the one who isolated the gene that kept Volusians from interbreeding with Terrans. Her gene-splicing technique solved the issue."

"Once the scientists are on Cejuru, our part of the job will be done," Wulf said. "The Prime military and planet law enforcement will protect them."

"But if we can stop the power and money behind the fanatics now," Melina said, "we could be a long way to solving the whole purist problem and eliminating the main danger to the scientists."

"So, how will we take the battle to the terrorists?" Huw took a sip of his whiskey and tore his gaze away from the foursome across the room.

"We're going to show ourselves on Cejuru Prime," Wulf said. "Make ourselves targets—lure them to attack, then allow some of them to escape our net to lead us back to their leaders."

Iolyn fisted his hand around his drink. "What if we go to all this trouble and just find a bunch of crazy people?"

"That won't happen," Melina assured him.

"The theory is to cut off the primary funders and planners. Without organized leadership, the fanatics will become toothless." Wulf pulled Melina closer against his side. His voice was grim. "There is more than Prime nationalism and pride in pure bloodlines behind these attacks. Someone with a lot of cunning and intelligence has another agenda. And our line of the family is the target—someone in our family is funding and directing the attacks."

"You still suspect someone in the family," Huw said, his brow raised. "Why now? Why incite the fanatics now? There has always been some crazy purist faction skulking around the edges of Prime politics."

"Because before I found my *gemate,* the power would've died with me. Melina's existence means there will be a next generation of Prime leaders in our line," Wulf said, a muscle clenching in his jaw as he refused to let go of the anger bubbling under his calm facade.

It was hard to keep the anger at bay. The day Melina was found to be his bond mate was the day she came under an ever-present, ever-increasing danger.

He took a breath to calm himself and continued, "While we are no longer hailed as Kings and Princes, we have a great amount of power and the wealth that goes with it. But the lesser Caradocs, what Melina calls the shirt-tail relatives, don't. Someone amongst those relatives wants us dead and out of power. After all most of the attacks so far, with the true crazies like Solar and Prolow being the exception, have been—"

"—assorted cousins like Donte, Regin, and Uly," finished Iolyn, a grim expression on his face.

"*Ansu bhau*," Huw muttered, then gulped his liquor down in one swallow. "Does Father know?"

"He reached the same conclusions we just presented," Wulf said. "Mother and Father plan to have all the Caradocs to a reception at the house the day after tomorrow. Melina and I will leave for the family residence later tonight, arriving under the cover of darkness. I want Melina to get the lay of the land before we engage the enemy."

"We'll come with you," Huw said.

Iolyn nodded. "You'll need us to cover your backs."

"We—all four of us—will cover each other's backs," Melina said.

"That's my little warrior." Wulf pulled her into his side and kissed her cheek. She shivered. But he knew it was not from excitement or anticipation of later lovemaking, but apprehension of the battle to come. He shared her fears, but he didn't plan on losing. He had too much to live for.

CHAPTER NINETEEN

Next morning, Caradoc family home, Cejuru Prime

Mel stood on the balcony off Wulf's and her apartment in the Caradoc primary residence, gazing at the ethereal scenery surrounding the ancestral property. The late night arrival had not allowed her a view of her new home planet before now.

Located twenty kilometers outside of the capital city, the ancestral home was built into the summit of a high mountain, in a range made up of many more high peaks which seemed to go on forever. Lush greenery covered the sides of the peaks, and waterfalls gushed everywhere she looked. The waterfalls flowed into a river that eventually meandered through the mountain valleys and into the capital city where it divided the city into two before flowing to the world ocean that covered half the planet.

Just as on Earth, the Prime species evolved from creatures that had crawled from the ocean.

Besides having an abundance of life-giving water, the planet was extremely temperate, being in the middle of the habitable zone in the Cejuru system. With no tilt to its axis, only the poles froze. Adding to the ideal conditions was the planet's heated core; even when night settled over the part of the planet rotated away from the sun, the air and water temperatures remained mild.

Later, Mel decided she would dress and visit the expansive gardens that stepped down the mountainside of the Caradoc property. She loved flowers, but had never had the opportunity to have a garden. She would ask Wulf's mother to teach her so that she could establish some gardens on the property Wulf owned and where he planned to build them a home for when they were dirtside.

Wulf. A smile crossed her lips at the thought of her *gemat*. A delicate shiver slid down her spine as she recalled his lovemaking on their first night on the planet. As always, the sex had been spectacular. Wulf had taken her to the peak again and again. But somehow, here on this planet, their union had transcended the mere physical and taken them to a place where their minds and souls had become one.

When she'd asked him why their lovemaking seemed more profound than before, he'd replied, "The souls of all the bonded pairs who have gone before have given their approval to our bonding. Their combined spiritual energy permeates the planet and amplifies the true bond."

For the first time in her life, she believed there might be something more beyond the mortal world. The thought gave her peace. Wulf and she were bonded now and forever—she would never be alone again.

Mel turned her head slightly and looked over her shoulder through the glass doors leading to their bedroom. A naked Wulf lay sprawled across the huge bed that seemed to take up about a third of the bedroom. His large muscled frame looked scrumptious, delineated as it was by the sunlight filtering into the room.

She grinned as she turned to head back inside. Wake-up sex sounded good. She found herself quite hungry all of a sudden.

In the periphery of her vision a light flashed. She didn't know what warned her first, the light or the sense of hatred flowing from beyond the house grounds. Whichever it was, she dove to the tiled terrace floor. Milliseconds later a laser blast blew out the glass in the door where her head would've been.

"Melina!" Wulf's angry roar came to her from the bedroom.

"I'm all right!" she yelled back. "Stay there. I'll come to you."

She belly-crawled along the stone floor then opened the unbroken door and shimmied across the threshold into the relative safety of the bedroom. Wulf was there; he pulled her away from the opening and behind the safety of the thick stone walls.

Urgent hands stroked every inch of her body searching for any laser wounds.

"I'm fine. Not hit at all," she reassured him.

Two more laser blasts shattered a mirror across the room from the opening to the terrace and then strafed the bed, setting the bedding on fire.

"You're bleeding, Melina *lubha*," he rasped as a gentle finger swept over her forehead. He traced a path down her face then onto her body, from cut to cut. His angrier-than-hell-gonna-kill-someone growl, the one which set her nerves on edge, increased with each cut visited.

"Probably from the glass door." She grabbed his hand, stopping its bloody game of connect the dots. She brought it to her lips, kissing it. "Sssh, *gemat*. I'm fine. The laser never touched me."

She paused, then grinned. "Guess the bad guys know we're home, huh?"

Wulf glared. "It's not funny. You could've been killed!"

At least he stopped growling. Her headache was thankful for the respite.

"Well, I wasn't." She shuddered and he pulled her closer as if he could absorb her into his body to protect her. "Guess this means no walking through the gardens with your mother later." And, dammit, she wanted to walk through the gardens. Had been looking forward to it. "This is getting ridiculous. I refuse to let these bastards imprison me in your home."

"We'll get them, *luhba*," he whispered against her temple. "You'll get to see the gardens if I have to have an air cordon put around the property."

Seconds passed and there was no more laser fire. Still they stayed on the floor, holding onto each other.

A loud pounding on the door to the hall had her starting within Wulf's arms.

"It's father and my brothers." He ran a soothing hand down her back.

"I know." She pushed out of his arms. "Get dressed. I'll let them in. I have a good idea of the trajectory of the shot. I can show them where the shots originated."

"They've seen me naked before, *lubha*." He smiled.

"Not in my presence they haven't." She swatted him on his so-fine, naked butt. Damn, she'd had plans for that ass. There was always later. "Get some pants on, at the very least."

"Only for you, *gemate lubha*." He leaned down and kissed her lips before strolling toward the walk-in closet. "*And it was your plans for my so-fine-naked ass that awakened me right before the shots hit.*"

"*We'll make time for loving—later.*"

"*It's always later with you, gemate.*"

"Smart ass!" she muttered as she walked to open the main door into their suite of rooms.

Iolyn, Huw, and Wulf's father stood in the hall, dressed in casual attire and bearing weapons. Behind them was a small squad of armed soldiers.

Wulf's father looked her over from head to foot then came back to her head. "You are bleeding, daughter. Huw, get the medic from the guard station."

Huw ran to the stairs leading to the first floor. Concern bled off of him in waves. She must really look bad.

"You are bleeding from at least two dozen places, lubha. *Of course Huw would be concerned."*

Ignoring Wulf's voice in her head, she addressed his father. "I'm fine, Ilar. I managed to hit the ground right before they fired." She gestured at the cuts. "These are from the broken door. It was closed when the shot hit."

Wulf's father gestured to the soldiers. "Two of you go and check the balcony. The rest of you check the grounds. I want to know where the shot came from. Also, secure the area around the house just in case the sniper fire was a ploy to test our security."

The soldiers turned to do as their leader bid after one awe-struck glance at her.

Mel frowned and hissed at the pain. The cut on her forehead was deeper than she'd thought. "Why did they look at me like that?" Mel asked Iolyn. "All I did was duck."

Iolyn smiled. "Sister mine, you don't know how unusual you are. The closest shooting position has to be on the next mountain peak over ten kilos away. The fact you somehow saw or sensed the shooter from that distance is a miracle."

"Iolyn, I saw a flash of light from the corner of my eye," she said. "Anyone could have done that."

"No, my dearest daughter," Ilar said with a smile, "not anyone. What you saw was the shot, and you simultaneously sensed the shooter's emotion and reacted to save yourself. All that had to happen in a split second. You should be dead—but you aren't. Thus, their awe."

"She is lucky to be alive." Wulf surrounded her with his arms, pulling her back against his warm, naked chest.

At least he had pants on. She took a deep breath and almost sighed at the relief his scent and touch provided. Much better than any pain medication.

"I sensed the shooter's hatred at the same instant she did. I was up and running for her as she threw herself to the ground." Wulf gulped and shuddered against her. "I would've been too late to save her. A millisecond later and she would've taken a full blast to the head."

No one said anything for a few seconds. The sound of more guards entering the room broke the silent tableaux.

"Premier, sir." One of the original responding soldiers came to stand in front of them. "The shot had to have come from your honorable sister's home. What are your orders?"

Ilar shook his head. "From Beria's house? I don't believe it."

Mel turned to the soldier. "Lieutenant, why don't I show you exactly where I saw the flash? I am sure Premier Caradoc would want us to be doubly sure."

"Yes, ma'am." The lieutenant saluted and gestured for Wulf and her to precede him to the balcony.

Wulf placed her at his side with his arm around her waist and walked with her outside.

Once there, she used the sight on the lieutenant's laser rifle to find the spot where she'd seen the assassin's laser flash.

"There, about ten kilos away and about one third of the way up the mountain." Mel pointed the position out to the guard who nodded. Wulf's arm tightened on her waist. His angry growl came back to set her nerves on edge once more; his irate rumbling also confirmed that it was the house of his aunt.

"*Wulf, please. Your growling makes me want to kill something.*"

"*I do want to kill someone. Specifically, the person who tried to murder you.*" The growling got louder and harsher. Everyone on the balcony tensed as if waiting for the inevitable explosion.

"Well, you can't—right now. So knock it off."

He ceased the subvocalization, then massaged her waist as he leaned over and whispered against her ear, "Sorry."

"Amazing. You are communicating by telepathy," Ilar said, his eyes glowing with some strong emotion. "You are true battle-mates. I didn't quite believe it when my old friend Tor told me. This family is truly blessed, my daughter."

Blushing, Mel inclined her head. "Thank you, Ilar."

To redirect the conversation away from her and her battle-mate status, which never ceased to embarrass her, she cleared her throat and turned to the guard. "Is that where you projected the shot's origination?" She pointed to the spot once more.

"Yes, Captain Melina." The guard's face was sober. "That is the home of Beria Caradoc-Nabann, the sister to your esteemed father by marriage and the aunt of your *gemat*."

"Well, hell," whispered Mel. She turned worried eyes toward Wulf, then Iolyn and finally to her new father-in-law. "That's not good. We suspected a family member, but not someone so close in blood."

"We'll discuss this later, *gemate lubha*," whispered Wulf. "I want your wounds treated first and you to get a bolus for the pain. And, don't deny that you are in pain, my love. I feel it."

Mel nodded. "Can we get something to eat, do you think? My head hurts, but I suspect it is more from hunger than pain."

Wulf hugged her tightly. Kissing the top of her head, he spoke over it to his brother and father. "We'll get Melina's cuts seen to and then get dressed and meet you in the family breakfast room."

Ilar came over to them and kissed Mel's cheek. "I'm sorry your homecoming has been filled with this strife. It is a sad welcome home for you."

She smiled at Ilar. "We'll get through this—as a family."

"Definitely as a family," Ilar agreed, a smile on his face. He turned to leave, several of the soldiers following him.

Iolyn patted Mel's shoulder before he turned to leave also.

"Iolyn?" Wulf called. His brother halted, a quizzical look on his face. "Get Tor Maren. He also needs to be in on this family meeting."

Iolyn nodded, then shut the door behind him.

"Come, *lubha*. Let's get you cleaned up so the medic can tend the wounds more easily."

Mel nodded. "Maybe we can take a shower together? Conserve some water? Multi-tasking is always good, right?"

Wulf's lips attempted to curve into a smile, but failed. "Whatever you wish, my love. I don't want to miss a single second with you. Life is ... too short. I could've—"

"—but you didn't lose me. I'm fine. Right here in your arms," she reassured him, kissing his *gemat* marking, stroking it with her tongue until it glowed. "Let's celebrate life—and save some water at the same time."

"Yes, let's." He took her lips with so much passion that Mel felt as if she burned from the inside out. Her *gemate* marking pulsed in time with his heartbeat. Wulf's love for her and hers for him was worth fighting for. No one would take this from her. No one.

Pulling her lips from his, she twisted from his arms and pulled him along to the bathroom and the giant shower. For now they'd reaffirm their bond—later would be soon enough to make plans to eradicate the threat to their future.

———

THE SUNNY BREAKFAST ROOM—WHILE IT looked peaceful and a delightful place to begin the day—now held a grim council of war. Wulf's father sat at the head of the table. His wife Lorinda, a statuesque brunette with peridot-colored eyes sat next to him; her beautiful face was a calm mask, but the energy pouring off her told a more turbulent story. Lorinda was coldly furious. And she wasn't the only one throwing off angry vibes at the table. Ilar, Huw, Iolyn and her Uncle Tor were also ready to explode.

"Good morning, everyone," Mel said as Wulf led her to a seat next to his mother.

Lorinda turned and examined her carefully. "Are you okay, child?"

Mel smiled at her mother-in-law. "I'm fine. Just some flying glass."

Lorinda frowned and glanced up at her son. "Wulf?"

"She's fine, Mother." Wulf sat in the chair next to Mel. "If she weren't, she'd be upstairs, resting, with me standing guard."

Mel turned her head and glared at her mate. "You and what army?" She pinched his thigh under the table. Turning back to the table at large, she asked, "So, what's happened since the sniper attack?"

"My sister's houseman stated that we must be mistaken. No sniper fire had come from Beria's home," Ilar said in a monotone. "If there had been such activity, he would've reported the same to the Home Guard."

"The Home Guard?" Mel asked, looking at Wulf.

"Similar to your policemen on Earth," he replied. "Each city on Cejuru Prime has a Home Guard to police the local citizenry."

"Got it." She looked around the table. "With all the negative energy in the room, I'm guessing none of you believe Aunt Beria's servant's story."

Her Uncle Tor spat out a particularly vile swear word in Prime casting aspersions on Beria's origins.

"Tor Maren!" Lorinda said, ice dripping from every syllable. "Such language does not belong at the table in my house. I understand your anger. Your niece, my son's precious bond mate, could have been killed. I share this anger, but only low minds resort to profanities."

"Remind me to clean my language up around your mother."

Wulf's chuckle trickled through their mind link. *"She swears also. She just likes to pull Maren's chain. They practically grew up together. Their mothers were related by marriage."*

"Lorinda, my apologies," Tor said, the gracious diplomat side of him coming to the fore. "But I will probably say a lot worse before this damnable mess is complete."

"Mother, you might as well take a blanket apology from all of us," Huw said. "This is one of those times when profanity is going to fly."

Wulf's mother nodded once. "I understand—but there are ladies present, and gentlemen should be aware."

Huw snorted back a laugh.

"Is something funny, son?" His mother looked down her very aristocratic nose at her youngest son.

"Mel swears like a soldier, mother," he said. "And she is very much a lady—and present."

"Watch it, Huw," Wulf snarled. "Or my lady will kick your butt around the gym later this afternoon."

"Well, maybe not today," Ilar broke in with a chuckle that lightened his serious mien, "but I would like to see that—later. Tor and my sons have told me how well you fight, Melina."

Mel shot him a grin.

"Why not today, father?" Iolyn asked.

Ilar swept the table with a grim look. "After my call to Beria and Luka's home about this morning's attempt to kill Melina, I got a call from Beria inviting all of us to a party this afternoon to welcome Wulf's *gemate* to the family."

"How convenient," muttered Mel. "They are pushing the first meeting on us. Are we going?"

"Father!" Wulf shouted. "It's too risky. We do not control the environment. I will not expose—"

Mel placed her fingers over Wulf's lips. "I think we interrupted the council of war when we came down to breakfast. Your father and my uncle have a plan—and that is why your mother is so upset."

"Exactly, daughter." Ilar smiled at her. "See, Lorinda? She can read the emotional energy in the room. I know that she and Wulf communicate mind-to-mind. The legends weren't all fable and fantasy, but Beria and Luka won't know that detail. This is an advantage for our side."

"She can still be killed, husband," snapped Lorinda.

Mel let out a small sigh. She was really getting tired of reminding people that she was a soldier long before she was Wulf's mate.

"Lorinda ... uh, Mother..." Wulf's mother beamed at her use of the more familiar address "...I'm a soldier. Who better to walk into an obvious trap? This Beria and her husband can't be aware we suspect them. Why would they? They expect to be believed about the sniper—and in point of fact, anyone could have sneaked onto their property and shot at us."

"Melina, *lubha*, you are forgetting one thing," Wulf interrupted. "Ensign Regin Twitter, one of the men who tried to attack you, is the husband of Beria and Luka's daughter Mara. They have to know we've arrested Regin for treason and attempted murder. I'm not sure the welcome mat is being unrolled in good faith."

"Oh ... didn't Regin say his wife had nothing to do with this?" Mel asked, her forehead wrinkling as she tried to recall everything Regin had said and done.

"Yeah, he did," Iolyn confirmed. "He was emphatic about it—but that doesn't mean Aunt Beria isn't in it up to her fat neck."

"Iolyn!" Ilar said in a harsh tone. "It has yet to be proved that my sister is guilty of anything other than being mated to that pompous ass Luka. And if I recall, neither Beria nor Luka approved of Mara's early bonding to Regin."

Ilar turned to Mel. "Regin was always in trouble as a youth. I think my sister and her husband wished he'd gotten killed before he bonded fully with their daughter. *Diew* knows she would've been better off. Regin is and always has been a loser—and just the sort who would take up a cause such as the purist rebels are espousing."

"Early bonding?" Mel asked. "Like my bonding with Wulf?"

"No. More traditional—and much later. He got her pregnant when Mara was thirteen standard years," muttered Wulf under his breath. "We usually like to wait to bond-mark until the female is eighteen standard years."

"Mara and Regin are *gemat-gemate*, yes?" Mel asked, puzzled that Mara's parents could disapprove of the genetic bonding all Prime couples seemed to be subjected to, although she could understand about a teen pregnancy being frowned upon.

"Yes, *lubha*," Wulf said, "but some parents still do not approve of the bond mate. Just because biology selects out the couple, does not mean the couple will fully bond. Luka and Beria would rather have their daughter die single and a virgin than be bonded badly. This is another reason why we need to enlarge the bonding pool and seek the most compatible females from the other humanoid races in the galaxy."

Mel glanced around the table. Each and every person there nodded solemnly at what Wulf had just revealed.

"Okay ... and we are telling me this now?" She turned and glared at Wulf. "Why are we fully bonded then? I was not a happy camper in the beginning, remember?"

"Because you are an adult as am I, and not a juvenile delinquent such as Regin nor a mere teenager such as Mara when the bond was completed." Wulf leaned over and whispered against her lips. "And you loved me from the moment you met me, if you would only admit it to yourself. Just as you love me now. Our bond is true and strong. Regin and Mara's was not perfect."

"Okay. Fine. You made your point," she said.

Wulf's look of satisfaction at her admission flared through his eyes right before he kissed her lips. As he pulled away to sit back in his seat, she grabbed his face and pulled him back for one more deep kiss. When she pulled away, he winked.

She grinned at him, then turned back to the others who had silently and happily observed the exchange. "So? We're going to the party, right, Father?"

"Yes, Daughter," Ilar said, a huge grin on his face. "We are definitely going to the party, and we will take all precautions."

"I'm taking my weapons," she said. "No compromising on that issue."

"Agreed," Ilar said. "And Huw and Iolyn as family members may take a date. I suggest some female members of the Gold Squadron might be appropriate. Of course, they will be fully armed also."

"I concur, Father," Mel said. She eyed her brothers by marriage and smiled, a wicked little twist of her lips which had the two frowning at her. "I have the perfect female crew members in mind. Nadia Petrovich, the *Galanti* science officer—" she threw a narrow-eyed glare at Huw's groan "—and Dr. Lia Morgan, the medical officer on the *Leonidas*. They are both strong and well-trained—and are used to my command."

"Can they get to the surface within the next two hours, Daughter?" Ilar asked.

"Not a problem. How are we to dress for this soiree?"

"It's a poolside party," Lorinda said. "Swimsuits with cover-ups are the usual."

"We aren't swimming, Mother," Wulf said. "No way to hide the weapons. I want the women to have at least a knife and sidearm with them."

"Then a pants outfit or a long dress would do, wouldn't you say, Mother?" Mel asked.

"Either would be fine." Lorinda's face was still a calm mask, but underneath her anger and fear upset Mel.

"*Wulf? Your mother is scared to death with anger on top of it. Will she be able to handle confrontation?*"

"*My mother raised three sons. She can handle anything. I'll make sure Father knows she is extra-emotional, though.*"

"Wulf. Melina. Are you two talking to each other?" Lorinda touched Mel's arm, her fingers shaky and cold.

"Yes, Mother." Mel covered Wulf's mother's hand with her own warmer one. "I am concerned about you. This will be very difficult for you, I think."

Lorinda smiled, a smile of such warmth that Mel could not believe that the same woman was about to explode from within. "You're reading my nerves, yes?" Mel nodded. "I can handle Beria and Luka and anything they dish out. I've hated the woman for years, but I would swear she doesn't know it. I won't reveal anything—well, I won't unless Beria is caught out in her lies. Then I just might hit the bitch."

"Lorinda! Language!" Tor said, a grin breaking out on his face. "There are ladies and gentlemen present."

"Stuff it, Tor." Lorinda followed her sentence up by throwing her napkin at the man and hitting him in the middle of his face.

The table erupted into laughter. After which, they settled down and planned how to make Beria and Luka betray their part in the rebellion.

CHAPTER TWENTY

Later that day, Beria Caradoc-Nabann's Home

Mel held onto Wulf's arm as they entered the home of his Aunt Beria and her husband Luka Nabann. The house was more of a showplace than a home. The large entryway was twice the size of the one at Wulf's family home and was decorated with so much gold trim and carved pillars and molding that Mel wondered just who Beria and Luka were trying to convince of their importance and wealth—those who visited or themselves?

Wulf leaned over and whispered against her ear. "Tacky and overdone, right?"

She grinned and nodded, saying nothing since their hosts were approaching.

Wulf patted her hand as she squeezed his arm. "They don't bite," he whispered, taking the opportunity to nuzzle her neck. At the narrowed glance from his aunt, Wulf added, "Well, at least, not much."

Mel choked off the laugh threatening to burst from her throat.

Beria Caradoc-Nabann was the female version of her brother Ilar. Tall, dark-haired, golden-eyed, and regal-looking.

On Ilar it looked good; on Beria, it looked hard—and cold. Luka Nabann was shorter than his wife, with prematurely gray hair and eyes the color of rotten acorn squash. His thin lips were pursed so tightly Mel was surprised the skin on his face did not crack.

"Welcome to our home," Beria said with all the warmth of an iceberg.

And like an iceberg, Mel was sure the dangerous aspects of Beria's personality were mostly hidden beneath the sharp and frozen exterior she presented to the world. The woman hated them all, to a man and woman. Even though she didn't know who Nadia and Lia were, Beria's frigid glare cut through them like a cold laser.

As for Luka, he radiated no emotions; either he was a total sociopath—or being married to Beria had long ago killed them all.

Mel was pretty darn sure she knew who was the dominant in this sick twosome.

"Beria," Ilar leaned forward and air-kissed his sister's pale cheek. "You look fabulous, as always."

And she did, if one liked mannequins with every hair and article of clothing perfectly situated. Beria gave new meaning to the term control freak.

"Are you reading what I'm reading, lubha?"

"Yes. She hates our guts and would kill us in an instant if she felt she could get away with it."

Mel turned into Wulf's large body and leaned her head against his chest, keeping her eyes on Beria and Luka as they were introduced to the others first. *"Why haven't you ever read her hatred for your family before? It is so strong."*

"Our bond makes it easier. Father and Mother still have no clue. Huw and Iolyn are getting it somewhat because they are reading us—and that is mainly because they know our body language."

Ilar turned to Wulf and Mel and waved them forward.

"And here is Wulf's lovely *gemate*. She is Tor Maren's niece, Captain Melina Dmitros-Caradoc."

Ilar used her Terran family's surname in honor of them finding and raising her. All Prime females took their father's surname with them to their bonding and added it to their *gemat's*.

Beria inclined her head, her demeanor haughty and distant. Luka checked her out from head to toe, then zeroed in on her chest. So, Luka was a breast man? The bastard had the audacity to lick his lips as he leered at her. He reminded her of a reptile tasting the air before striking its prey.

She knew she should've worn something less low cut, but Wulf had picked the outfit and she'd worn it to please him.

Luka's lascivious glances had Wulf stiffening at her side. His low, angry rumble reverberated through his body to hers, raising the hairs on the back of her neck. She nudged him. *"Stop that. That's the growl that makes my teeth hurt."*

"If Luka continues to stare at your breasts, I'll punch him in the face. I've always hated his nose. It's too pointy. Looks like a desert weasel."

"More of a pseudo-lizard. The tongue, I mean. I think you are correct about the nose, definitely a desert weasel."

Wulf's mental laughter had her smiling, and his anger left as swiftly as it had arisen.

"You are so right, my love. He does have the look of an Erian or an Antarean, doesn't he? A perfect match for my cold-blooded bitch of an aunt."

"So, this is Wulf's *gemate*." Beria's narrowed glance swept over her as if she were some lowly servant. Her gaze however skipped over Mel's cleavage and stopped at her hips. "Let's see the marking. I don't believe it. The Lost Ones are gone from us forever." Wulf's aunt glared at him. "Why would you try to foist some Terran female off on our people? Is keeping power in your line so important that you would sink to such base depths?"

"The motive, Wulf? It's just as I—Wulf? Stop the growling. Now you have the rest of the males in your family doing it." Mel rubbed a hand over her forehead in an attempt to assuage the throbbing pain the Caradoc males' growling caused.

The four males' angry vocalizations were so strong that the windows in the entryway vibrated and two jars sitting on decorative pillars fell to the floor with a crash. Even Beria's husband had an expression of shock on his face at his wife's words.

"Stop with the macho-growling-crap, dammit." Mel stepped forward and turned to glare at the Caradoc men. "You are making my bones ache."

Lorinda, Nadia and Lia smiled at Mel. She shot them a grin before she turned and skewered Beria who'd backed away from her brother and nephews. Obviously, they'd never turned the Prime-males'-growl-of-death on her before. She bet Luka had been so emasculated after his marriage to Beria that he'd never subjected his dominant wife to a showing of Prime alpha-male protectiveness, either.

"Aunt Beria," Mel said, a mocking smile on her lips. "I'm not sure why you'd call my *gemat* a liar—but I don't like it. And unlike most women of your acquaintance, I do not need a man to protect or defend me or to defend those who belong to me. Wulf belongs to me. Don't insult him again."

Beria's mouth open and shut like a fish gasping for air. Before she could say something, Mel continued, "Since you don't believe I am a *gemate*, I'm willing, for the sake of peace in the family, to show you."

"No, Melina, you do not—" Wulf said as he stepped closer to her side.

She held her hand up, cutting him off. "Yes, I believe that I *do* need to show her. As do you, my love." Mel turned to Wulf and unbuttoned his shirt and laid it open to demonstrate his marking. "Don't move, darling."

She brushed a kiss across the *gemat* symbol and it glowed in response to her touch. Luka gasped and cast a scared glance at his wife. Interesting response.

Mel kept her eyes on her hosts as she carefully peeled down the lounging pants that coordinated with her top, exposing her *gemate* symbol. It glowed and swirled in response to the stimulation of Wulf's. He traced a gentle finger across the marking. Both markings' colors grew in intensity.

Wulf pulled her to him, placing a gentle kiss on her forehead. "My *gemate lubha*."

Mel nuzzled his bare chest. "My darling *gemat*." She shuddered and wished they could leave so they could hide in their suite of rooms and finish what her show-and-tell act had started.

"Satisfied, sister?" Ilar's tones could have frozen helium3, if the feat were possible. "Please note, the markings are identical in all respects—color, design, size and responsiveness. Note also, it only took a mere brushing of the markings to stimulate the bonding response."

"A full and complete bonding," muttered Luka. "I've never seen one so strong." His nervous gaze sought his wife's, but Beria merely glared at Wulf and Mel as if they were the root of all her problems in the world. And maybe they were.

Visibly collecting herself, Beria swallowed. Her face rearranged itself into the calm, cool facade of a consummate hostess. "I am sorry. I can see I was wrong. Welcome to the family, Melina. Welcome home to Cejuru Prime." Her lips formed a mocking facsimile of a smile. "Best wishes to you, my nephew, on your bonding. May your union be blessed with many sons."

And if that sentiment didn't get stuck in the old bat's craw nothing would.

Wulf inclined his head. "Thank you, Aunt." He gathered Mel even closer, his hand stroking her back. "*Lubha,* do you wish to remain after being so insulted by my father's sister?"

The tension in the entry hall came from Beria. She didn't want them to leave.

"Wulf? Why did she insult us when she wants us to stay?"

"Not sure."

"There is a trap. I can sense it. She has a sort of sick excitement underlying her other emotions."

"I hate you risking yourself this way, lubha.*"*

"Maybe it is you who is at risk, gemat?*"*

Wulf's growl tickled her mind. *"That's the growl I love. It makes me hot."*

"Just wait until I get you alone in our bed."

"It's always later with you, Wulf" His male snort vibrated down her spine.

"We can stay, Wulf," Mel finally answered after the waves of anxiety coming off Beria had made an impression even on Ilar and Lorinda, who both frowned at their hostess with distaste.

"It is understandable that my discovery seems improbable. I'm sure your Aunt won't be the only person to question my turning up at this time in the Prime's history."

Beria heaved a sigh of relief and inclined her head. "You are too kind, Melina." She gestured behind her to some doors leading to an outdoor room. "Please, we have finger foods and drinks on the terrace. And there are swim outfits in the pool house if you wish to take a dip. Please make yourselves at home. Dinner will be ready in about an hour."

Ilar, with Lorinda by his side, led the way to the veranda. Huw and Nadia and Iolyn and Lia followed them. Mel, with her hand on Wulf's arm, brought up the rear.

Wulf leaned down and spoke in a low, harsh tone, "You are not to go anywhere without someone with you. If my dear aunt has planned something, I'd rather she single me out. Also, do not eat or drink anything until Beria or Luka taste it first."

"If you didn't want to stay and play this out, then why didn't you say so!" she hissed back.

Wulf stopped and turned her into his arms, then leaned down for a quick kiss. Anyone looking would think he was following through on the stimulation of their markings. As his lips took hers, he rasped, "It hit me that I could lose you."

As his tongue thrust deeply into her mouth, she answered on their mind-link. "*You won't lose me. And I won't lose you. We'll play this out and trap them if they try something. Our crews surround this property. No one will leave here without someone following.*"

Wulf stroked her back, taking gentle nibbles of her lips. "*You're correct, Melina love. But something could always go wrong. Humor me. Stay with one of us and don't eat or drink unless we can show the food is safe.*"

"*Fine.*" She stroked his chest, then his tightly clenched jaw. "*I promise.*"

He pulled away and smiled at her, stroking a gentle finger along her cheek. "I love you, Melina."

"Ditto, Wulf." She hugged him one last time before joining his brothers and their dates.

———

Since no one trusted the food, most of Ilar's party stuck with bottled Prime beer chilled in a large tub of ice. If Beria and Luka thought their actions strange, they didn't say or do anything to confirm it.

"I think we need to leave before dinner is served," Mel said. "It would look really obvious if none of us touched our food. We can't all be on diets or not hungry." Her stomach chose that moment to growl. "It's the meatball thingies. The smell is making me hungry."

Huw chuckled and tucked Nadia's hand even more tightly against his body. She hissed and glared at him, but said nothing. "Aunt Beria is putting off vibes even I can read."

"She's guilty as sin," Lorinda said, casting her sister-in-law a killing glare. "The longer I'm around you and Wulf, the more I can read the emotions in the room."

"Mother, I'm pretty sure Mel and Wulf are amplifiers for strong emotions," Iolyn said, keeping his tones low so Beria and Luka could not overhear their discussion. "I'd read about the phenomena in books on the battle-mate connection, but because we haven't had such a couple in several centuries it could never be proven before now."

Lorinda smiled and nodded. "I, too, have read the same theories."

"So, when do you think they'll make their move?" Ilar asked as he pulled Lorinda into his side as if to protect her from his sister's evil thoughts.

Wulf shrugged, his eyes never leaving his aunt and her husband as they gave directions to their house servants. "It could be today—or it could be later on the way home. Or, they could be planning something for the party you and Mother have planned. Although that venue would be harder for them to control."

"Or it could be even later, after we let our guard down," Mel added. "Let's push the envelope."

She turned to Nadia and Lia, who both had stuck like glue to Wulf's brothers. "Nadia, would you like to repair with me to the ladies' room?" She smiled at the men and Lorinda. "We'll keep up the stereotypes of women going to the bathroom together. Lia and Lorinda can follow in, oh, say a couple of minutes to report on any suspicious movements and to check on us."

Nadia smiled. "I love action. Don't get to see much of it as a science officer. It'll be like the old days when we trained together, Mel."

"What if they *don't* plan on kidnapping?" hissed Huw. "What if they just shoot you both?"

Wulf growled. "Yeah."

"I'm not easy to kill. I think I've proven this many times since you've met me. Plus, Nadia has my back."

She reached for Nadia's arm. "Besides, they want to make you suffer a while, Wulf. They'll taunt you with my capture. If Beria and Luke are fronting for the rebels, they'll use me as a means of negotiating for concessions on the purity issue."

"But that isn't what Beria really wants," muttered Wulf. "Dammit, she practically admitted her real agenda in the hall earlier. The succession in power is what she is more concerned about."

"But it'll be the dupes she has convinced of her purist agenda who will be doing the dirty work," Mel said in a low voice. "They'll want concessions. And they're expendable, if they are captured. Beria and Luka care nothing for the pawns they're using."

Wulf grunted and nodded. "I agree. But if you're hurt— one little hair—I will strangle my aunt with my own hands."

"I'll help," Ilar said, his face couched in grim lines.

Mel waved their concerns away. "Even if they do manage to whisk us away, we have all sorts of backup plans in place. After all, we knew this could be a trap," she added before she walked away with Nadia by her side.

They approached Beria. "Aunt, Nadia and I need to use the ladies' facilities. Could you direct us, please?"

Beria smiled, well, if you could call a slight curving of pruny, thin lips a smile. "Yes, of course. It is the third door on the right after you reach the top of the stairs."

"Thank you." Mel followed Nadia.

She felt the eyes of Beria boring into her back the whole way up the stairs. The emotions coming off the woman were many. Gloating. Satisfaction. Anticipation. Fear. With hate and sick envy underlying them all. *Yes*. The trap would be sprung in the ladies' room.

"Wulf? Did you get all that?"

"Got it. Be careful."

"Hey, careful is my middle name—just ask my crew."

Wulf's snort made her smile.

Mel was eager to move forward. This would be the first step in stopping the rebels and their destructive movement against the future of the Prime people. With Beria and Luka out of the picture, the rebels would have no money to hire costly mercenaries to do their dirty work and no power at the highest levels of Prime government to distort the truth with council members teetering on the edge of the subject.

"Be ready, Nadia," Mel warned. "Beria is way too happy and excited about us going to the bathroom."

Nadia leaned over as they counted doors. "What do you think? Someone waiting in the room to attack us?" Her science officer reached for the weapon under the back of her flowing top.

"No."

Mel paused outside of door number three. "The room is empty." She swept the hallway with her senses. "They're in one of the other rooms."

Mel opened the door slightly. "Maybe the plan is to come in after we enter."

Nadia nodded. "Go. I'll cover you. And I'll lock the door behind us. That should slow them down if they try to enter later."

They walked into the room. It was a bedroom with doors onto the terrace that circled the house. The bathroom was off to the side, the door open and a light on the vanity to welcome guests into the room.

She looked at Nadia and shrugged, then signaled that she'd check out the closet while Nadia checked the rest of the room. After locking the door into the hall, Nadia went to the doors leading to the terrace and locked them, after looking around outside.

Mel left the closet, then looked over at Nadia who shook her head. She gestured that she would check out the bathroom.

Nadia shooed her on and indicated she'd remain in the room on guard.

"Wulf. No one in this room. We locked all the accesses. I sensed tension from some of the other rooms on this floor, but am not sure how they mean to get to us. I'm betting on cameras in the room at the very least. So now they know we're being cautious. Hopefully, they chalk up our checking out the room to our being Alliance soldiers and being in a strange place."

"I don't like this. Hurry up and get back down here. I'm sending Lia and Lorinda up."

"Okay."

Mel glanced around the bathroom. Since her excuse had been made up, she really didn't need to use the facilities—so she didn't. Just as she was about to leave the bathroom, a thud from the other room caused her to draw her laser pistol from the holster at the back of her waist.

"Wulf. It's going down."

"Nadia?"

Mel sidled into the room. Her friend lay on the floor unconscious. There was no sign of her attacker anywhere that she could see.

Moving into the room, her gun in a two-handed grip, Mel turned in a circle, looking for the origin of the shot or hit which had taken out an Alliance-trained soldier. As she turned, the room began to swim around her. Too late she realized what had happened.

"Gas. Wulf..."

"Ansu bhau. They used gas. Nadia and Melina are down," Wulf snarled. "Iolyn, make sure the men are ready to follow anyone leaving this property."

His angry gaze swept the room and didn't see either his aunt or Luka. "Father, get some of our men in here to find and secure Beria and Luka." His father nodded, then he spoke softly into the com unit he removed from his pocket.

Wulf found Huw at his elbow. "Let's go. We need to stop Lia and Lorinda before they, too, are captured."

"What about Nadia and Mel?" Huw asked.

"We'll join the surveillance teams once they check in with their report on who left the building."

Huw nodded, although he sensed his brother wanted to do something more proactive. Wulf felt the same. But the plan had been to lure the rebels into making a move. Since the plan had worked, they had to play it out to the end and hope their suppositions were correct as to the fate of Melina and Nadia in the scenario.

Just as he and Huw turned to leave the room, Lia, followed by his mother, ran into the room. Lia was disheveled. His mother had blood on her face.

Wulf and his father roared at the same time.

"Lorinda, my love." His father pulled his wife into his arms. "What happened?"

Wulf's mother just shook her head and then laid it on his father's chest and cried.

Lia explained between gasps for breath. "Four large, heavily armed men ... dressed in black with hoods over their heads. As we reached the top of the stairs, they kicked in the door to the room where Nadia and Mel were. They carried them off." Lia's eyes were filled with anguish as she turned them up to Wulf. "We tried to stop them, but failed." She swayed a bit, but managed to stay standing.

"Iolyn, help Lia," Wulf ordered.

Iolyn came to Lia, his arms outstretched as if to pick her up. She waved him off. "I'm fine. I need to see to Lorinda's cut. One of the assholes hit her with a cudgel of some sort."

Beria and Luka entered the room at that point and approached them, false concern on their faces.

Wulf strode to meet his aunt. When he reached her, he picked her up by her clothing and shook her. "Where are they taking them?"

"What? You can't think I had anything to do with this outrage?"

Her look of shock was not very well done. He saw the gleam of satisfaction in her muddy yellow eyes, sensed the gratification of a job well-done in her emotions.

"Aunt, we know you planned this. Trust me, we *KNOW*." He shook her once more. "If anything happens to my *gemate*. I'll kill you with my own hands."

"You don't know anything. I'm a victim as much as you or your mate." She shrugged his hands off her and backed away. "That this outrage should occur in my home. It is unthinkable."

Wulf's father left his wife in Lia's hands and came to stand beside Wulf. "Beria, we know. All the evidence from the attacks of the *Galanti,* targeting Wulf and Melina led to someone in the immediate family. Shots were fired just today from your terrace. And Wulf and Melina confirmed your guilt once they entered this house and read it in your emotions."

Luka choked, then coughed in the background. "They can't do that. Only warriors in battle can sense the strongest emotions—and even then they aren't accurate."

"Not true." Wulf glared at his uncle and aunt. "Since my bonding with Melina, I have her abilities added to mine. We are battle-mates. We read your guilt as soon as we entered the room. *You* are the instigators of the purist rebellion."

"Your purpose is leadership change," Wulf's father stated, his eyes sad. "You always hated that I was the eldest male, didn't you, sister?"

"I should have been born a man. I would have been the better leader." Beria sneered as she drew herself up to her full height. "You'll never find your mate or her friend, Wulf. I told them to kill the bitches as soon as they were away from the house." She laughed. "The nice thing about fanatics—once they are pointed at an objective, they never stop."

Luka attacked as soon as she finished speaking. "You stupid bitch." He slapped her across the face. "They had nothing. Why did you confess?"

Wulf's father pulled the irate man away from Beria.

"Stop trying to act the man for a change," sneered Beria. "I confessed since a battle-mate oath is absolute proof. Even I can see they are fully bonded—and that damn Maren family carried the battle-mate gene."

She shrugged as she sat on the closest chair. "Plus, the rebels are out of my control. Have been for a long time. Eliminating me will not stop them."

"Who leads them, Beria?" Ilar asked.

"I don't know. We always used small fish as go betweens. It could be anybody."

She laughed, a crazy, high-pitched cackle. "Who would've thought when we started this all that Wulf would find a bond-mate—and have her be a battle-mate on top of that?"

Her laughter grew more and more shrill until she fell off the chair to the ground, her body shaking with the hysteria which had overtaken her, white froth coming from her mouth.

"Take her away." Wulf instructed a Council security officer summoned by his father. "Lock her up in our guardhouse until we can take her in front of the Council."

The man nodded and grabbed Beria's arm and pulled her up, then marched her out of the room.

Ilar shoved Luka into another officer's hands. "Put him in a separate room. I wouldn't trust him not to strangle her." His father turned toward him. "Son? Can you touch Melina's mind?"

Wulf shook his head. "She is unconscious and unaware of what is going on. Once she awakens. I'll know it." Wulf turned to his brothers. "What are the surveillance teams reporting?"

"We have two teams following the vehicle taking Nadia and Melina from this house." Huw's voice was riddled with tension. Wulf knew his brother worried for more than just Melina. Huw cared about the Terran Nadia more than he'd admit. "More are joining them. They will stay far enough back so as not to spook the captors. We also have air and satellite support."

"Good." Wulf pointed to two Gold Squad soldiers who had just entered the room. "Take care of Dr. Morgan and my mother."

The men nodded. He strode toward the door.

"Let's join the chase. I don't want Melina and Nadia being held any longer than necessary. If the captors follow Beria's orders, they'll kill our women when they stop. We need to be ready to move on them."

Huw, Iolyn and his father followed Wulf out of the house. No one said a word. They all knew what they had to do.

CHAPTER TWENTY-ONE

Mel lay on something cold and hard. Every muscle in her body protested. The dull pain of incipient bruises told her someone had handled her body as if it were a bag of grain. She kept her eyes closed, faking continued unconsciousness. She was not alone.

In the background a sudden slapping noise, that of a hand against skin, followed by a male grunt. Angry, guttural male voices spoke somewhere near her. The men spoke in colloquial Prime, but she was able to follow the gist of the conversation.

"Stupid. The leader said not to harm the females." Obviously, the one who delivered the slap.

A second male voice responded, "The blonde bitch tried to bite me." Nadia was alive. That was good. "Should I just let her get away with it?"

The slapper snarled. "Are you telling me you cannot subdue one small Terran female without kicking her in the ribs and then attempting rape?"

"She is not as weak as you would suppose," the slappee said. "She broke my skin. I could catch some rare Terran bacteria. You know they are just a step above filthy animals."

The slappee would pay for that remark, Mel vowed.

"Stupid fool." A pause. "Get up. I didn't hurt you. Don't come into this room again. The leader will be by later to determine what to do with the women."

Another slap and then a thud. A wisp of air told her the slappee had fallen to the ground near her. What an idiot. If these were the type of fanatics they were up against, it shouldn't take too long to root them all out of their hiding places and squash them like the low-intelligence-invertebrates they resembled.

She kept her breathing slow and even. Had the slappee hurt Nadia badly? She couldn't chance looking until both idiots were out of the room.

A scuffling noise as the one who'd been knocked to the ground got to his feet. His harsh breathing indicated the slapper had hurt him. Good.

"I thought we were going to ransom them," the slappee said between gasping breaths. Definitely a beta-slug playing at being alpha.

"You aren't paid to think," sneered the slapper, the alpha-slug in this twosome. "Now leave. We have things to do."

Two sets of feet thudded on the ground. The slight whoosh of a door opening then closing, sounded loudly in the otherwise quiet room. A set of tones indicated some sort of electronic lock had been engaged.

Peering between her lashes, without moving her head, Mel checked out the immediate vicinity. She saw no one. Opening up her psi senses, she sensed the two men walking away. No one was in the room other than herself—and Nadia. The sound of the other woman's low moan had Mel struggling to her feet. A wave of dizziness assaulted her, a side effect of whatever they had gassed them with. Taking several deep breaths and closing her eyes, she reoriented herself. She was no use to Nadia—or herself—if she succumbed to the effects of the drug.

Shivering, she opened her eyes and realized she was so cold because she was naked.

"Just peachy," she muttered.

Mel glanced around and found Nadia on the floor near a stone bench of some sort. She was also naked.

Her friend's eyes were open, but her gaze was vague. She was also in pain, probably from the large gash on her forehead. She was still bleeding. Nadia's body was covered with as many bruises and abrasions as her own.

Yep, the slugs would pay.

"Nadia," she moved to the other woman and knelt by her side, "how severe are your injuries?"

"*Dermo.* Shit. My pride hurts more than anything," she hissed as she struggled to sit up.

Mel grabbed an elbow and helped her friend to sitting position, leaning her against the stone bench. There was bedding of some sort on the bench, but it was so filthy Mel didn't want to chance Nadia getting a nasty infection from it. Her friend was better sitting on the dusty, stone floor.

Looking around, she noted the room reminded her a lot of the Prime fortifications she had seen visiting her parents' digs—and more recently on Obam IV. This could be a good thing for the good guys.

"So, you bit the beta-slug?" Mel asked as she gently probed around Nadia's head wound.

"Beta-slug." Nadia snorted. "A slimy little worm. Works for me." She moaned when Mel found the knot on the back of her head. "The creep was poking at your mark-thing, hitting it with a metal baton of some sort. So, I lunged at him and bit his arm. He hit me on the forehead with the baton, knocking me down. I must've hit the back of my head on the stone bench as I fell. I was conscious enough to know that the piece of slimy shit tried to rape me—that's when the other slug came in and started spouting Prime at him."

"Yeah, old beta-slug is in deep shit for sure. We're not to be touched until after the head honcho gets here." Mel checked Nadia's limbs for breaks. "I heard that he kicked you?"

"Maybe ... I was out of it by then," Nadia replied as she moved limbs and stretched her torso. She winced several times. "Nothing broken, but I bet I'll have some dandy bruises. Sort of like yours." Nadia captured her gaze. "Wulf will kill them—won't he?"

A glimmer of laughter poked through the haze of pain which had turned Nadia's eyes a dark, dusty blue. Her friend was fine—hurt—but ready to fight when needed.

Mel chuckled. "Two or three times if that were possible. And Huw might have something to say about your treatment also."

"Why?" Nadia waved her hand as if to erase the question. "Never mind. We have more important things to do."

"Yeah, like get out of here before the big leader comes." Mel stood up and stretched out her back and moved all her limbs. "Looks good to go. Although my *gemate* marking is throbbing and not in a good way, if you catch my drift."

She smoothed tentative fingers over the symbol which pulsed, the colors glowing a sickly peach, green and yellow. "I sure hope Wulf isn't feeling this or he'll single-handedly try to storm this place to get to me."

Nadia got up. Her face filled with disgust. "*Dermo.* Shit. Do you think they ever clean this place?" She used the tip of one finger to check out the bedding on the stone bench. "Are these ancient Prime artifacts, do you suppose?"

Mel laughed. "They've probably been here since the last Prime used this place," she looked around, "during, um ... the Berean Wars."

"You know where we are?" Nadia looked around the room. "Why the Berean War era and not something later?"

"Some prisoner scrawled on the wall. His name, rank and the date." Mel walked to the doorway and pressed on a design in the wall. A small touch pad appeared. "Just as I thought, this is a Prime underground military facility. A lot like the ones I helped excavate as a child and on my vacations from the military."

"Like the ones discovered in Siberia on Earth?" Nadia looked around with far more interest than she'd previously displayed. Her gaze was sharper now, more that of the keen-eyed starship science officer she was than the bruised and confused woman of before.

"Yes. This is an ancient site. Let's hope they didn't change the Prime universal access codes during the Berean Wars." Mel leaned her head against the door. "I don't hear the slug-boys—or anyone else for that matter. Find something to use as a weapon. We're breaking out of this place."

Nadia examined the edges of their prison as Mel tried the access codes most commonly used by the ancient Prime. A trilling beep-beep-beep indicated the lock was disengaged.

Mel grinned. "Gotcha!"

"Here." Nadia thrust a heavy metal rod at her. "I found these under a pile of rocks. I'd take the rocks, but they are really heavy and awkwardly shaped."

Mel laughed softly. "Double-gotcha. These are machete-like weapons used by the ancients. The Prime called them battle-blades and they are very similar to what the Alliance adapted from the Volusian military. Great for skewering Antareans and Erians."

"A weapon designed for pseudo-reptiles? Should work on slimy slugs."

Mel grinned and nodded.

Nadia looked at the black metal in her hands. "How does it work? I don't see any switches."

"Stand back." Mel held the rod in front of her. Using her thumb she manipulated a portion of the base. A sharp, serrated two-edge blade shot from the rod.

"Whoa!" Nadia held hers out and fumbled around the base. After a few seconds, she smiled. "Aha." An identical blade shot out. "How do you lock them in place?"

"They're locked automatically. We won't worry about sheathing them," Mel said. "I expect we'll be putting them to good use." She switched her blade to her non-dominant hand, and then pressed the opening mechanism on the door. It slid open with a barely perceptible *whoosh*.

"So," Nadia said after she followed Mel into the dimly lit underground corridor. "Which way?"

Mel looked in the direction the slugs had gone. "We go the opposite way of where our captors went—" she peered at the wall in front of her and smiled, "—and then up. We'll follow the upper path out of the facility."

She moved to the handholds carved into the corridor's stone walls and began to climb, the serrated battle-blade clutched in her left hand as she used her right to pull herself up. "If I'm correct, we'll be able to exit through a back way and out onto the mountainside."

"What about Wulf and our men?" Nadia followed her up the wall. "Won't they be at the front, trying to figure a way in?"

"I'll let Wulf know we are getting out of the way so they can hit the facility in a full-out assault."

Mel slipped over the cleverly hidden curtain wall and sat down. Nadia followed and sat beside her. Her friend was paler than normal. "How's your head?"

"Aches. A little dizzy at times." Nadia turned glittering blue eyes on her. "I've had and survived worse. I'm good to go."

Mel nodded. "Good. 'Cause we'll be holding the rear guard until backup arrives. We really need some kind of powered weapon. But if we have to, we'll stab any slugs trying to slither out the back door."

"How will you let Wulf know we're free?" Nadia asked, a frown on her lips. "They took our weapons and com units when they took our clothing."

"Telepathy." Mel looked at her friend. "I thought you would've heard that rumor already."

"I had."

Mel sensed Huw had told her.

Nadia turned to crawl the way Mel wanted them to go. "I just didn't believe him."

Bingo.

"Believe it." Mel followed Nadia. "Follow the series of red dots at your eye level. That's the way to an exit. Keep alert while I contact Wulf. I should be able to sense someone on this upper corridor even as I communicate with him, but can't guarantee it."

"Don't worry, Mel," Nadia murmured. "I have some empathic ability. I'll sense anyone ahead of us, wanting to do us ill."

Mel was surprised to hear Nadia had psi ability; it wasn't in her service record. Although it wasn't unusual for some Terrans to have such abilities, they tended to classify them as gut instincts left over from primitive man. It would be interesting to see how Nadia and Huw worked together.

Because whether the two of them admitted it or not—they were attracted to one another. Yes, both were in the insult and denial stage of their relationship. Both were alphas—just as she and Wulf were. Lots of explosive chemistry and independent stubbornness. Should be interesting to watch them feel their way to one another.

Mel opened up her mind, lowering the protective shield she'd raised upon waking in pain. She hadn't wanted her *gemat* to attack until she and Nadia were out.

"*Wulf?*"

"*Melina? Are you okay? Why were you closed to me?* Ansu bhau, *woman. You must stay open. I thought we had dealt with this issue. I thought you were seriously hurt ... I could only reach your dream self. Dammit, Melina!*"

"I was unconscious until about ten minutes ago and then I had to assess the situation. No use giving you an incomplete sitrep."

"No excuses, Melina. I'm serious, lubha; *if you don't stay open in situations such as this I will spank your so-fine butt until you can't sit for a month."*

"Rain check? We need to let you know what's going on."

Wulf's grumbly growl echoed in her head. Her womb clenched at her man's passionate rage. He'd been terrified for her. An ass-warming was the least she owed him. She grinned and sent him a mental image of one of his deepest fantasies. The growl rumbled louder and she swore she had a mini-climax.

"Lubha, that is so bad." His relieved laughter tickled her consciousness. *"Where are you? We're outside of what looks to be an older Prime underground fortification. Father seems to remember it being used for training after the Berean Wars."*

"He's correct. I'm taking Nadia out the back way. We'll let you know when we're outside the mountain so that you can attack at will."

She touched Nadia's ankle and hand-signaled a halt. They'd reached the exit. Nadia nodded and started examining the wall.

"We're at the exit door. We only have Prime battle-blades, kindly left in our little locked room, to defend the back entrance. Send us some backup once I give you the outside location. Okay?"

"Got it. I'll send Huw and Iolyn."

"Oh and besides weapons, send us something to wear—"

Wulf cut in. *"You're naked!"* His gentle touch traveled over her body. *"The bastards bruised your marking?"* The growl traveling along their connection was like a buzz saw on speed.

"Wulf, Stop—my head!" She grasped her head, fell onto the floor and curled into a fetal position. She dry-heaved until she thought she'd choke. The growling stopped as quickly as

it had started. Gentle invisible fingers stroked her head in apology.

"I'll be coming up there with Huw. Don't engage the enemy. Just give me directions, lubha. *I'll be there soon."*

Nadia placed her arm around Mel's shoulder and brushed some hair from her face. "What happened? You looked as if you had a convulsion or a fit."

Mel peered at her friend. The lovely Russian's cornflower blue eyes were dark with worry. "Wulf has two growls. The sexy-I'm-so-pissed-off-at-you-I-want-to-fuck-you-blind growl and the really-pissed-off-I'll-kill-you growl. The first makes me hot—the second one, although aimed at the enemy, hurts me. I just got a dose of both."

She neglected to mention the assorted growls he made while making love to her—some things were just plain private.

Nadia shook her head. "*Dermo.* I'm in trouble then. Huw does the same, although I suspect I don't feel them as strongly as you."

The Russian straightened from her crouch and pulled Mel up with her. "Let's go. I found the same mechanism you used in the room. I opened the outside door and reconnoitered. We are alone up here."

"For now." She allowed Nadia to help her through the exit.

The sky was overcast. She shivered. "We need cover until Huw and Wulf get here."

"Huw? He's coming?" Nadia blushed, a full-body blush that made her head wound look even more bloody. "We're naked."

"Can't be helped. We need clothing and weapons—and backup. Once the enemy realizes we're gone or that they're trapped—they'll use the back way just as we did." Mel captured Nadia's eye. "As for Huw, no matter what may or may not be going on between you two—Huw is a gentleman and an officer. He will not goad you about this."

"That's not what I'm worried about." Nadia settled behind a rock with a good view of the entrance and a good defensive position. "I'm afraid he'll go off half-cocked and get himself killed trying to avenge us."

Nadia had said "us," but Mel intuited that her friend had meant just "me."

"Yeah," Mel chuckled, "he could do that. He's very similar to his brother. I'm not sure how their mother survived all that alpha-male testosterone all these years. The woman deserves a medal."

Nadia smiled weakly at her obvious attempt to lighten the mood.

Mel joined her, crouching down, her arm with the weapon lying lightly across her knees. "Good choice of rock, Nadia."

Looking around, she sensed Wulf's current location.

"Wulf, we are half way up the mountain in a direct line of sight from your current position. I see a path beginning in an outcropping of rocks to your left about twenty degrees."

She also sent him an image of what the exit looked like and the position of Nadia's and her rock.

"Got it. Hold on, love. We're coming."

"Father, Huw and I will join Nadia and Melina on the mountain." Wulf pointed toward the spot Melina had described. "The women are safe, but have minimal weapons and are watching the only back way out of the underground fortifications."

"They are unhurt?" His father's concern for the women was evident in his dark gold eyes.

"Yes." Wulf shook his head, swiping shaky fingers through his hair. "No. I think Melina is downplaying their injuries. I sensed her pain—and her concern for Nadia."

"Nadia is injured?" Huw stiffened and cast an agonized glance at the mountainside. "Let's go. I don't like them up there alone—and undefended."

"They got themselves away from their captors, brother," Iolyn said. "I'm sure they are in a defensible position and have armed themselves."

"They have," Wulf said, "but they're naked—and their weapons are ancient battle-blades they found in the old fortification." Both Iolyn and Huw snarled something which would never be translated. "Which is why Huw and I will go get them. Do not attack until you hear my battle cry."

"Go quickly, my sons," his father urged. "I'll direct the attack at your signal." His father glanced around at the approximately twenty crewmen called in from Gold Squadron. "I know your and Melina's crew will fight superbly."

One sharp jerk of his head was the only acknowledgment he gave his father as he turned and led Huw toward the path that would lead them to the women.

"Wulf," Huw murmured "What did Melina tell you?"

"Nothing. Absolutely nothing. Which is why we're heading up to play defense rather than attacking and killing the *apayebote* who took our women."

"Your woman," Huw corrected. "Nadia is nothing to me but a fellow officer and crew member."

"Congratulations. You said that with a straight face, brother," snorted Wulf. "Who are you fooling? You've got the hots for Nadia Petrovich and have since you first met her."

"She is Terran, brother," Huw said. "I'm holding out for a Prime bond mate such as yours."

Wulf grunted. "And what if you never find one? Are you willing to be alone forever?"

When his brother didn't answer, he chanced a sidelong glance. Huw's face was creased in worry lines. His expression grim—and sad. No, his brother wouldn't be happy alone. Of the three of them, Huw had always been the most light-hearted, the most family-oriented.

"*Lubha? Are you okay? We have started toward you.*"

"*We're fine. Cold. Thirsty. Sore. But we'll do. Why are you sad?*"

"*Huw is denying his attraction to Nadia. Says he wants a Prime mate and will do without if he doesn't find one.*"

"Well, we'll see. Once he sees her ... well, we'll see."

"You were talking with Melina," Huw stated. "Are they okay?"

"Yes. We'll see them soon—around the next curve."

Both of them sped up. Senses wide open, Wulf searched for any unseen enemy lurking in the rocks along the well-trod path. Huw's head was up, his gaze scanning. His brother caught his glance, and Wulf shook his head. Nothing out there but the women.

Increasing their speed, they rounded the corner.

Melina stood and protected Nadia, who leaned against a rock. Their science officer was pale and bleeding sluggishly from a head wound. Both women sported multiple bruises and cuts.

All of this Wulf took in one glance. He moved toward Melina, who moved toward him. Huw, swearing under his breath, raced to Nadia.

"Melina." Wulf pulled her into his arms. His lips covered her face with gentle, loving kisses as he pressed her gently into his strength and warmth, his face against her hair.

"*Diew*, life with you is never boring."

"Never. I'll never leave you." She stroked his back.

"Promise."

"I promise."

Reluctantly he released her. Sweeping a comprehensive glance over her nakedness, he categorized her injuries, then pulled his tunic over his head. He let out a ragged breath, throttling back his anger. "You are not just bruised, little one."

"Nadia is the one who is hurt. A few bruises aren't going to stop me," she said in a huff as she took the shirt he offered and pulled it over her head. "There. Now if I fight I don't have to worry about my ass hanging out in the wind."

She threw Wulf a jaunty grin. "You can order the attack now, my *gemat*. I can feel the men's eagerness to kick ass all the way up here."

Wulf laughed. He let out a loud, guttural roar that echoed off the surrounding mountains. Several Prime battle cries answered his. The sound of laser fire soon followed.

Wulf gestured to the defensive position the women had found. "Shall we? I expect some rats shall leave the scene via the back door."

"Slugs—and they slither," Melina said as she allowed him to put his arm around her to lead her back to Nadia and Huw.

"What?" Wulf asked.

"Nadia and I decided they were slugs," Melina explained. "Slimy, cold-blooded and with no spines."

"I'd like to cut off the *apayebo's* balls that would treat women such as he did you," Huw spat. His shirt now covered Nadia, and the Russian woman's head lay on Huw's thigh, her eyes closed.

"Is Nadia okay, brother?" Wulf asked.

Melina nudged him in his side. His gaze captured hers and she winked.

"Huw is not all that indifferent, now is he?"

"I agree. But it will not be an easy battle. I am assuming Nadia is in denial also?"

"Some. Wulf, she's empathic. She can differentiate between the growls."

"Ahhh. It will be interesting to watch, eh?"

Melina grinned and nodded. Her smile left her face as her head jerked up. Her nostrils flared as if she smelled something bad.

Wulf sniffed the air, tuning into her senses. At first, he found nothing, then he smelled it too. The sharp acidic smell of sweat brought on by sphincter-weakening fear. The slugs were close to the fortification exit.

"Huw! Arm Nadia and take your positions. The battle is coming to us," Wulf ordered as he pulled Melina to another outcropping. He shoved a laser pistol into her hands, then took his place at her side. "Shoot to kill, my love. I want these *apayebote* dead."

"What about questioning them?" Melina aimed the pistol at the door to the fortification. "The leader is neither Beria nor Luka. It is someone else."

"That's right, *lubha*." Wulf aimed his laser rifle. "My bitch of an aunt admitted she had lost control of the purists she used to further her own agenda. She didn't even care that she'd started something that might destroy our world."

"Bitch is right," snarled Melina. "Did you strangle her?"

Wulf laughed harshly. "No, but I promised to if you were hurt."

"They're coming," Melina replied. "Huw. Nadia. Be alert."

"Nadia is unconscious, Mel," Huw muttered. "Point out the *apayebo* who did this. I want to slice him up into little pieces and then grind them under my heel."

"Just shoot. If he isn't in this bunch," Melina replied with a snarl of her own, "I'll take you to him personally. He tried to rape Nadia after she stopped him from beating on my *gemate* marking."

"Huw, I will help you kill this offal," Wulf said, his tones colder than the Alliance's prison planet in winter.

Huw nodded. "I get first dibs, though."

"Agreed." Wulf growled, then said, "Sorry, *lubha*. I forgot your head hurts."

Melina kissed his bare arm. "Growl all you want. Our combined adrenaline rush has made me forget all about it."

At that point the door opened and five Prime males ran out of the mountainside.

Wulf took out the first man. Melina got the second. Huw got the third. With three down, the other two were outnumbered. They dropped their weapons and raised their hands.

"I'll jam the door mechanism from this side, trapping any others," Melina offered.

Wulf sent her an angry glance. "Why didn't you do that before?"

"I wanted to see how familiar they were with the facility," she said. "Also, it reveals something about the enemy."

"What's that?" Wulf spat the words.

"They aren't well-trained." Melina pulled up the key pad and entered a lock-down code. "The ones we've gone against in the past had some military background. I wanted to see what the dirtside rebels were made of. No militarily trained soldiers would've poured out the back that way. They would've had defenses inside, lured our men in and, picked them off one-by-one."

"Such as you did on Obam IV?" Wulf smiled. "Okay, I see your point. And your conclusion?"

"The rebels we dealt with on the *Galanti* were recruited by Beria and Luka from family members for their own ends. I think you'll find the first two rebels, Prolow and Ullyn, were distant family members of Luka's who had purist leanings."

"Beria and Luka," spat one of the two rebels still standing. "Opportunistic, selfish aristocrats the both of them. They were not truly of the cause."

"That's the beta-slug, talking. Alpha-slug is dead over there," Melina said. "Beta was the one who assaulted both Nadia and me."

Huw roared and dropped the other man whom he'd tied up with the man's own clothing. He lunged at beta-slug and knocked him to the ground. The man stayed down, cowering at Huw's feet. "Get up, you coward. Let's see how you fight against a man instead of helpless, naked women."

Wulf grabbed Huw by the shoulder. "Wait, brother. This can be done later. We need to get Nadia to a doctor."

Huw grimaced, then nodded. He did manage to aim one good kick at the beta's ribs. Wulf smiled at the groan of pain. Yeah, he'd make sure both Huw and he had a chance to talk with the rotten coward. Maybe the slug—as Melina called him—would die while trying to escape.

"Wulf," Melina said, a warning note in her voice. "He must go in front of the judiciary—and then the Alliance Military tribunal. He kidnapped two Alliance officers."

"Sister," Huw protested. "Can't we just rough him up a bit?"

"That doesn't bother me, Huw." Melina eyed Wulf. "But my mate wants to kill him."

"So do I," Huw said. He looked at Wulf. "If *I* can't kill him, *you* can't."

"Fine." Wulf nudged Melina. "Go to Nadia. Keep an eye on the other prisoner. I sense a team of our crew coming up to help. Huw and I will go further up the path and teach this man a lesson—leaving him to live to stand trial." Barely.

His *gemate* pursed her lips, but nodded and walked to Nadia and sat down, her pistol aimed at the rebel lying on the ground, trussed up like a game bird waiting for the spit.

Wulf grabbed one arm of the beta-slug and Huw, the other, then they dragged the rebel along the path.

Smiling grimly, Wulf said, "Huw, I'll give you three standard minutes to teach this turd a lesson. Then I'll take one minute. After that, he can look forward to rotting on one of the Alliance's frozen prison planets for the rest of his life, serving as a fuck toy to the other prisoners."

"Sounds good to me," Huw muttered. "There is not one portion of Nadia's body which isn't bruised. Her forehead was split open and she has a knot on the back of her head. The man deserves eternal butt-fucking for that alone."

"He beat on Melina's marking. Eternal butt-fucking is almost too good for him." Wulf stopped and dropped the arm he held. "But I promised Melina we would let him live. So be it. Avenge your woman, brother."

"She's not mine," Huw retorted, then proceeded to beat the shit out of the man who'd harmed Melina and Nadia.

Wulf shook his head and muttered, "You protest too much."

The future would be very interesting indeed.

EPILOGUE

Later that evening, Caradoc family residence

Wulf entered his suite of rooms. Passing through the sitting area, he entered the dimly lit bedroom.

Melina sat up in bed, wearing one of the sheer night garments he had bought for her. Her bruises showed faintly through the pale green silk. He rubbed his chest, his *gemat* marking aching in sympathy for the abuse the rebel slug had perpetrated upon hers.

"How are you feeling, *lubha*?" He stripped his clothing off as he approached the bed.

She pulled the covers aside. He crawled in and pulled her against his side.

"I'm sore." She turned to him and placed a kiss on his shoulder. "But I need you to love me. To make me feel better." She smiled saucily, a twinkle in her glorious green eyes. "I think you need to kiss every single bruise."

"I can do that." He stroked a finger across the swell of her breasts, exposed by the deeply cut bodice. She shivered in response.

"Wulf?" Her gaze turned quizzical. She cupped his chin

338

with one hand, pulling his face to hers. "I sense something bad has happened. What is it?"

"Father and I went to interrogate Beria and Luka further about their involvement with the purists." He paused and sighed heavily. "They were both dead."

Melina gasped. "How? Who?"

"They were poisoned. Probably in their evening meal. As for who, isn't it obvious?"

"The purists."

"Yes. Probably payback for the loss of so many of their men."

Melina laid her head against his shoulder and idly stroked his thigh with a finger. "So, the leader of the purists is able to adapt and plan."

"Looks like it," Wulf said, as he began to remove the delicate confection she wore. "I still think you are correct in surmising that the rebels have very little military training—which gives us an advantage. But the leader—"

"The leader has inside connections at the highest level and the ability to kill political prisoners in a maximum security cell," Melina concluded.

"Yes," Wulf whispered against her hair. "Such a man could prove to be a formidable foe."

"Let's worry about it—later," she whispered against his lips.

Wulf smiled and bit her lower lip so very gently. "It is always later with you, *lubha*."

"For some things, my love," she replied, "but not for this." She stroked his glowing *gemat* marking. "I always love you now."

THE END

PREVIEW OF PRIME CHRONICLES: BOOK 2
PRIME SELECTION

Commander Nadia Petrovich, Science Officer of the Alliance *Starship Galanti*, has a problem—which has nothing to do with science. Her problem is Commander Huw Caradoc, the *Galanti's* Chief Engineer. She and the stubborn Prime male have a growing connection he refuses to acknowledge—a bond that could drive him mad.

They are connected psychically and the bond grows stronger every day. If Nadia didn't know it was impossible, she would suspect they were mating in the Prime tradition—a biological imperative that locates and marks a Prime's optimum mate. But she isn't Prime, as Huw tells her and anybody who'll listen.

Nadia's emotional anguish couldn't have come at a worse time. The Prime and Galactic Alliance merger is finally under way, and the all-male Prime crews are learning how to work with female Alliance crew members. The Antareans threaten the outer arms of the Milky Way, and Prime rebels wreak havoc on the Prime home planet and elsewhere.

Despite the conflict surrounding them, Nadia and Huw will not be able to avoid their fate or their growing love. Prime selection will make the decision for them whether the timing is right or not.

AN EXCERPT FROM

PRIME SELECTION

Sunrise, Cejuru Tarn

Galactic Alliance Commander Nadia Petrovich, recently appointed science officer of the *Starship Galanti,* scanned the flat plain upon which the Prime Military had built their fortifications. She hunted for movement, for anything out of place, to clue her into the enemy's position.

The "enemy" in this instance was the Prime Elite squadron that had been selected to challenge the battle-readiness of Gold Squadron and its newly merged Prime and Alliance soldiers. The real reason for the joint exercise was to test whether Prime soldiers could work effectively with the female soldiers of Gold, which was why Nadia was in charge of this particular session and her equal-in-rank Prime counterpart, Commander Aeron Ard, was not.

Nadia took in a deep breath of the thin, cool morning air, appreciating the fact Tarn had enough oxygen in its atmosphere that they could do away with head-to-toe survival gear. Then something in the air made her stiffen. She looked around and saw nothing to cause the uncomfortable feeling.

Her skin prickled and the fine hairs on the nape of her neck stood on end. Her pulse increased as adrenaline flooded her bloodstream. Her body's fight-or-flight response had kicked in big time—but over what?

Something wasn't right on Tarn. This feeling of impending danger had been there in one way or another since her Gold Squad team had been dropped off on the planetoid two standard hours earlier. She'd written the feeling off as nerves for the upcoming training session, but now, with her scouting partner alongside, it forced its way to the forefront of her mind.

For the second time in as many minutes, she swept her gaze over the flat, dry land toward the octagon-shaped compound built of the gray limestone found on the planet. It was built for optimal defense with three of its sides abutting the foothills of Tarn's main mountain range and the other five facing the stark, flat plains of what was once an ancient sea. The compound's perimeter was fully lit, but the military facility inside looked abandoned. Her empathic senses told her that was a lie.

The buildings teemed with the emotional auras of sentient beings—a chaotic cloud of emotions that created the anxiety she felt.

But where were the perimeter guards? Where were the Prime scouts who should have been scouring the land and gaining intel on her team for the war games? Was this part of the Prime squad's plan?

For over the last standard half hour, she and her scouting partner, Commander Joen Dakkin, Communications Officer for the *Galanti*, had made their way from the mountain cave system where their team had secured a base of operations. They'd seen no one. Something was very wrong, and her heart rate elevated another notch or two.

"It's been too easy," she muttered. "Do they think we're stupid? That we'll just waltz in because it looks abandoned?"

"If it makes you feel any better, Aeron agrees. It's wrong. All wrong. Has been since we landed without anyone attempting to score points on us." Joen's voice was flat, emotionless.

Nadia glanced at him and instinctively used her empathic ability to test his mood. He was boiling mad under the calm demeanor, a volcano ready to erupt at a moment's notice.

"Shit. I knew something wasn't right." Mentally, she kicked her own ass for not going with her gut. "Our landing wasn't challenged. When we secured the cave system as our headquarters, Aeron seemed happy, but as we set up base operations he grew more and more concerned. I should've confronted him then."

She'd treated Aeron with titty fingers since she'd been given command of the op. She hadn't wanted to challenge him overly much, since that might damage his stupid Prime male machismo. All the Alliance female soldiers had been tiptoeing around the Prime males—and the Prime males, around the women. It had been like watching a nature video of skittish she-cats and a bunch of alpha-cats scenting each other out, testing each other's limits.

Both races still had a long way to go before they understood the other. But then, this training session and others like it had been arranged for that very reason.

Lesson learned—next time her gut told her to challenge the big Prime male, she would.

Since Aeron wasn't here, she only had the Prime male next to her to obtain the information she needed. Her sense of dread was increasing exponentially now—something bad was coming down. "What do you think is going on?"

Joen scowled and shook his head. "Not sure. But something's awry. Our empathic feelings are connected to our fellow Prime during battle situations—and that would include the Prime stationed here. Aeron and I sensed nothing on landing. No excitement or anticipation of the war games to be played out. We should've sensed *something*."

And wasn't that odd? She sensed all sorts of emotions, so many she had a hard time singling out any other than Joen's. But unlike the Prime, Nadia's empathic abilities worked with all sentient beings—and there were sentient beings out there. She just didn't see them—yet.

Joen stared at the empty plain. The only thing visible out there was scrubby foliage and dust devils as the heat of the early morning sun met the chilled air of the night. He turned to look at her. His eyes glowed with the intense emotions roiling within him. "Aeron chalked the lack of emotional readings, other than our own Prime team members, up to the fact no other Prime were nearby when we landed and set up base camp."

He scowled and rubbed a hand over his dark, close-cut hair. "But that read wrong also. Any Prime soldier worthy of the name would have, at the very least, established perimeter alarms on the cave system we chose and had spotters in the mountains."

The caves had turned out to be a storage area for excess supplies and munitions for the military facility and would've been a coup for any invading force.

"Plus, why didn't our opponents challenge our predawn landing?" Joen frowned. "They knew we were coming sooner or later. Prime are always vigilant."

"We're on the same page. I had the same thoughts and feelings." Nadia clenched her jaw. "And there are other intelligent beings on this planetoid—and the emotions I'm picking up aren't particularly friendly. Call me overcautious, but we need to send our scouting teams back to base, regroup, and figure this out. It smells like a clusterfuck in the making."

"That's not overly cautious. It's a very wise call." Joen's golden eyes darkened with his concern. "You'll find Aeron has arrived at the same conclusions."

Nadia didn't particularly care if Aeron had or not. This was her op, her responsibility. If something bad happened, it was on her. There were too many science, engineering, and medical personnel and officers on this particular operation, crew members who normally didn't get exposed to battle situations. This training was supposed to be not only a test of the newly merged crews, but also a refresher training for skills some hadn't used since basic training. She refused to risk her people. The situation was feeling more and more explosive.

Nadia switched her com unit to team-wide communications. "All team members are ordered back to base. Code Foxtrot-Uniform-Bravo-Alpha-Romeo. Proceed with caution. Commander Nadia out."

If it wasn't FUBAR yet, it soon would be. Her gut was doing backflips at the increasing sense of danger.

"Ard, here. Logistics officer is in total agreement." Aeron sounded grim. "My teams are securing base camp. Suggest switching to alternate Com Code Tango-Tango-Two-Four."

"Agreed. All team members switch to Com Code Tango-Tango-Two-Four." Nadia sighed with relief. Aeron was thinking along the same line—regroup and defense. Maybe, between the two of them, they could figure out what was wrong.

"Let's pull back, Joen."

Nadia rose to a crouch behind the boulder where they'd taken shelter. They'd gotten as close to the Prime facility as they could and were about thirty meters away from a side entrance to one of the buildings that did not back up to the foothills. She hadn't been overly concerned about being seen since their uniform jackets and pants changed colors to blend with the desert and mountainous landscapes surrounding the military facility. Even the laser target sensor vests, which registered the low impulse laser fire for war gaming, had the same ability to merge into the background.

Between their camo and the large rocks scattered on the flat land from some past tectonic activity, she and Joen should be able to retreat as easily as they'd infiltrated. Once they made it into the foothills and the thick forests that grew there and up onto the mountains, they would be home free.

Empathic senses blaring and movement on their right had Nadia tackling Joen to the ground as a stream of laser fire streaked across where his torso had been. If Joen had been hit, it would have registered on his vest as a kill shot.

Instead, the stream hit her arm, and she hissed in pain. The searing burn of a fully powered laser blast shot up and down her dominant arm. Her eyes watered as she inhaled the smell of her burnt flesh and jacket sleeve. Her nerve endings screamed. She called upon every iota of her warrior forebears' strength to stay alert and aware and not succumb to the bowel-burning pain.

One hundred Gold Squad members relied on her command decisions, and no laser burn would stop her. Only death could do that—and she didn't intend to meet death today.

"Live fire! Live fire! Code Red. Code Red," she screamed into her com unit as she shoved Joen behind a boulder.

While she listened for chatter in response to her call, she pulled her laser sidearm. Thank God, her hand still worked. The laser hadn't cut any major nerves, just all the little painful ones. She rearmed her laser for live fire.

Nadia glanced at Joen who'd rolled out from under her once they were behind cover. He was dirty, but uninjured, and was arming his laser for live fire also.

"Nadia…" Joen's voice was a low snarl. It reverberated over her skin like a swarm of stinging insects.

His aura glowered in her mind's eye. The heat of his anger danced and burned its way along the edges of her empathic senses as if seeking a connection, warrior to warrior. *And isn't that strange?* The energy flowed from his body in churning waves. *So, this is what a Prime male's battle rage, his* batel rabia, *felt like.* The man could power a transport shuttle on the energy coming off his body.

"Nadia…" Joen touched her hand.

She flinched and pulled her hand away. His touch had disrupted her ongoing sensory scan of him, of their surroundings. She focused on his grim face.

"We have no intrateam communications," he said. "I can't raise any of our squad. We have no off-planet communications either."

"Fuck!" she muttered, testing the air around them for any hint of a further attack. "Can you fix the problem?" As Joen opened his mouth to answer, Nadia motioned for quiet.

The shooter approached their hiding place. He was very close. His eagerness for the kill was palpable; it tasted like day-old meat and copper.

She pointed one finger in the direction from which the would-be killer approached … no, wait … there were two of the fuckers. She added another finger. At this point, she could care less who the shooters were; they'd used live, full-stream laser fire and had attempted to kill Joen. They were the enemy. They needed to be eliminated.

Joen nodded, raised his weapon, and indicated with an angling of his head that he'd go right.

Nadia mouthed, "Go" and went left as Joen dove right; they let loose killing streams at the same time. She nailed her target in the torso and knocked him on his back. Joen's man was down also.

Joen checked on the two assassins. He turned and sliced his hand across his neck. Both were dead. He hurried to join her as she headed away from the Prime installation.

"Prime?" she asked in a low, noncarrying tone as they used boulders and dips in the land to hide their retreat.

From her quick glance, neither man had the look of a Prime male—who were almost uniformly tall, very muscular, dark-haired, and bronze-skinned with golden or amber eyes—even though they wore the Prime uniform. Some really bad juju was going on. She and her officers would try to make sense of it later—once all her people were safe and their base camp secure.

Nadia only hoped her order to return to base camp had been received. But in case it hadn't, she headed south to where another scouting team would've set up for surveillance of the military facility. She wouldn't head back to base until she was sure all her scouts were heading in and weren't under attack. As she and Joen moved swiftly, she listened for the high whine of laser fire.

"Not Prime," Joen finally answered. A sense of urgency poured off his aura.

She glanced at him from the corner of her eye. His normally bronze skin was more of a pale gold. He was scared—almost sick with it. "What's wrong?" She looked around searching for the enemy and saw and felt nothing. They were alone for the time being.

"Lia is out with one of the scouting teams." Joen's voice held more than concern for a fellow officer; it held gut-wrenching anguish. "She's a doctor, a healer. She shouldn't be here."

"Lia's a trained Alliance soldier. This is exactly where she should be. Give her some credit." Nadia would question what was going on between Lia and Joen later. "Stay alert, soldier. We have to get *all* our people to safety."

Joen's lips firmed and his color returned—but underneath, his emotions stirred and reflected rage and determination.

Laser fire sounded ahead of them. They increased their speed. As they sprinted from the cover of one set of rocks to the next, Nadia shoved away the pain of her wound and her worry. This was war—and her soldiers needed her.

Prime Selection *is currently available as an e-book at Liquid Silver Books, Amazon, B&N, iBooks and other on-line retailers. And will be available in print at Amazon in early 2015.*

Interested in finding out about other books by Monette Michaels? Follow her at FaceBook or visit her website.

www.facebook.com/authormonettemichaels
www.monettemichaels.com

ABOUT THE AUTHOR

Monette Michaels is the pen name for a multi-published author of suspense/thrillers. She's been married to the love of her life for far longer than she cares to remember. IIer home is in Central Indiana.

www.ingramcontent.com/pod-product-compliance
Lightning Source LLC
Chambersburg PA
CBHW070158260626
47160CB00002B/380